Pregnant by a regal rogue…

The Princes' Brides

Three passionate, intense romances from a
classic Mills & Boon author!

In July 2010 Mills & Boon bring you four
classic collections, each featuring three favourite
romances by our bestselling authors

THE PRINCES' BRIDES
by Sandra Marton
The Italian Prince's Pregnant Bride
The Greek Prince's Chosen Wife
The Spanish Prince's Virgin Bride

TYCOON'S CHOICE
Kept by the Tycoon by Lee Wilkinson
Taken by the Tycoon by Kathryn Ross
The Tycoon's Proposal by Leigh Michaels

THE MILLIONAIRE'S CLUB:
JACOB, LOGAN & MARC
Black-Tie Seduction by Cindy Gerard
Less-Than-Innocent Invitation by Shirley Rogers
Strictly Confidential Attraction by Brenda Jackson

SAYING 'YES!' TO THE BOSS
Having Her Boss's Baby by Susan Mallery
Business or Pleasure? by Julie Hogan
Business Affairs by Shirley Rogers

The Princes'
Brides

SANDRA MARTON

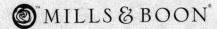

First published in Great Britain 2010
Harlequin Mills & Boon Limited,
Eton House, 18-24 Paradise Road, Richmond, Surrey TW9 1SR

THE PRINCES' BRIDES © by Harlequin Enterprises II B.V./S.à.r.l 2010

The Italian Prince's Pregnant Bride, The Greek Prince's Chosen Wife and
The Spanish Prince's Virgin Bride were first published in Great Britain by
Harlequin Mills & Boon Limited in separate, single volumes.

The Italian Prince's Pregnant Bride © Sandra Myles 2007
The Greek Prince's Chosen Wife © Sandra Myles 2007
The Spanish Prince's Virgin Bride © Sandra Myles 2007

ISBN: 978 0 263 88106 6

05-0710

Printed and bound in Spain
by Litografia Rosés S.A., Barcelona

Sandra Marton wrote her first novel while she was still in primary school. Her doting parents told her she'd be a writer some day and Sandra believed them. In secondary school and college she wrote dark poetry nobody but her boyfriend understood – though, looking back, she suspects he was just being kind. As a wife and mother she wrote murky short stories in what little spare time she could manage, but not even her boyfriend-turned-husband could pretend to understand those. Sandra tried her hand at other things, among them teaching and serving on the Board of Education in her home town, but the dream of becoming a writer was always in her heart.

At last Sandra realised she wanted to write books about what all women hope to find: love with that one special man, love that's rich with fire and passion, love that lasts for ever. She wrote a novel, her very first, and sold it to Mills & Boon® Modern™ romance. Since then she's written more than sixty books, all of them featuring sexy, gorgeous, larger-than-life heroes. A four-time RITA® award finalist, she's also received five *Romantic Times* magazine awards and has been honoured with RT's Career Achievement Award for Series Romance. Sandra lives with her very own sexy, gorgeous, larger-than-life hero in a sun-filled house on a quiet country lane in the north-eastern United States.

**Don't miss Sandra Marton's exciting new novel,
Falco: The Dark Guardian, available in August 2010
from Mills & Boon® Modern™.**

THE ITALIAN PRINCE'S PREGNANT BRIDE

BY
SANDRA MARTON

CHAPTER ONE

SHE came hurrying along the sidewalk, enveloped from head to toe in black suede, stiletto-heeled boots clicking sharply, her head bent against the rain-driven wind, and barreled into Nicolo just as he stepped from the taxi.

The doorman moved forward but Nicolo had already dropped his briefcase and caught her by the shoulders.

"Easy," he said pleasantly.

Her hood fell back as she looked up at him. Nicolo, always appreciative of beauty, smiled.

She was beautiful, with elegant bones, a mouth that looked soft and inviting, and eyes the deep blue of spring violets, all that framed by a mass of honey-colored loose curls.

If someone had to run you down, this was surely the woman an intelligent man would choose.

"Are you all right?"

She pulled out of his grasp. "I'm fine."

"My fault entirely," he said graciously. "I should have watched where I was—"

"Yes," the woman said, "you should have."

He blinked. She was looking at him with total disdain. His smile faded. Though he was Roman, he'd spent a good part of his life in Manhattan. He understood that civility was not an art here but it was *she* who'd run into *him*.

"I beg your pardon, *signorina,* but—"

"But then," she said coldly, "I suppose people like you think you own the street."

Nicolo lifted his hands from her shoulders with exaggerated care.

"Look, I don't know what your problem is, but—"

"You," she said crisply, "are my problem."

What was this? A Mona Lisa with the temperament of a hellcat. Innate old-world gallantry warred with new-world attitude.

Attitude won.

"You know," he said brusquely, "I apologized to you when there was no need, and you speak to me as if I were scum. You could use some manners."

"Just because I'm a woman—"

"Is that what you are?" His smile was as cold as his words. "Let's see about that, shall we?" Temper soaring, logic shot to hell, Nicolo pulled the blonde to her toes and kissed her.

It lasted less than a second. Just a quick brush of his mouth over hers. Then he let go of her, had the satisfaction of seeing those violet eyes widen in astonishment…

And caught the rich, sweet taste of her on his lips.

Sweet heaven. Had he gone *un po' pazzo?*

He had to be. Only a crazy man would haul a mean-tempered woman into his arms on Fifth Avenue.

"You," she said, "you—you—"

Oh, but it had been worth it. Look at her now, sputtering like a steam engine, that icy demeanor completely shattered.

She jerked free of his hands. Her arm rose. She was going to slap him; he could read it in those amazing eyes, eyes that flashed lethal bolts of lightning. He probably deserved it—but he'd be damned if he'd let her do it.

He bent his head toward hers. "Hit me," he said softly, "and I promise, I'll make your world come crashing down around your ears."

Her lips formed a phrase he would not have imagined women knew. Not the women in his world, at any rate, but then none of them would have accused a man of something clearly their fault.

Why be modest? The truth was, not a woman he'd ever met would have blamed him even if he were at fault.

The hellcat glared at him. He returned the look. Then she swept past him, honey-blond mane glittering with raindrops, black suede coat billowing after her like a sail.

He watched her go until she was lost in the umbrella-shrouded crowd hurrying through the chilly March rain.

Then he took a deep breath and turned his back to her.

His eyes met the doorman's. Nothing. Not the slightest acknowledgment that anything the least bit unusual had happened but then, this was New York. New Yorkers had long ago learned it was wisest not to know anything.

And a damned good thing for him.

Kissing her had been bad enough. Challenging her to call the police…

Nicolo shuddered.

How stupid could a man be? He could have ended up with his face spread across Page Six. Not exactly the publicity one wanted before a meeting with the ninety-year-old head of an investment firm that prided itself on decorum and confidentiality.

The rain was coming down harder.

The doorman already had his suitcase. Nicolo picked up his briefcase and walked into the hotel.

His suite was on the forty-third floor, which gave him an excellent view of the park and the skyline beyond it.

When he started looking for a permanent place to live in the city, he'd want a view like this.

Nicolo tossed his raincoat on a chair. If all went well, he'd contact a Realtor after Monday's meeting.

If? There was no "if" about it. The word wasn't in his lexicon. He never went after something without making damned sure he knew when, where and how to get it. That approach was a key to his success.

He toed off his shoes, stripped away his clothes and headed for the shower.

He was fully prepared for Monday's meeting and his long-anticipated buyout of Stafford-Coleridge-Black.

His financial empire was huge, with offices in London, Paris, Singapore, and, of course, Rome.

It was time for Barbieri International to move into the New York market. For that, he wanted something that would be the crown jewel of his corporation.

In the rarefied echelon of private banking, that could only be Stafford-Coleridge-Black, whose client list read like a Who's Who of American wealth and power.

Only one thing stood in the way: SCB's chairman, James Black.

"I have no idea what you'd think to discuss with me," the old man had said when he'd finally agreed to take Nicolo's phone call.

"I've heard rumors," Nicolo had answered carefully, "that you are considering a change."

"You mean," Black had said bluntly, "you've heard that I'm going to die soon. Well, I assure you, sir, I am not."

"What I have heard," Nicolo had said, "is that a man of your good judgment believes in planning ahead."

Black had made a sound that might have been a laugh.

"Touché, Signore Barbieri. But I assure you, any changes I might make would be of no interest to you. We are family owned and have been for more than two hundred years. The bank has been passed from one generation to another." A brief, barely perceptible pause. "But I wouldn't expect you to understand the importance of that."

Nicolo had thought how good it was that they were not face-to-face. Even so, he had to work hard to control his temper. Black was an old man but he was in full command of his faculties. What he'd said had to be a deliberate, if thinly veiled, insult.

This high up the ladder, the international financial community was like an exclusive club. People knew things about each other and what Black knew was that Nicolo's wealth and stature, despite his title, had not come from legacy and inheritance but had been solely self-created.

As far as the James Blacks of this world were concerned, that was not a desirable image.

Probably not desirable as far as Fifth Avenue honey-blondes were concerned, either, Nicolo mused, and wondered where in hell that thought had come from?

What mattered, all that mattered this weekend, was his business with Black. It had mattered enough during that phone call to keep his tone neutral when he responded to the flinty old bastard's gibe.

"On the contrary," Nicolo had said. "I *do* understand. Completely. I believe in maintaining tradition." He'd paused, weighing each word. "I also believe you would do your institution a disservice if you refuse to hear what I have to say."

He'd gambled that Black would bite. Not that it was all that much of a gamble, considering what Nicolo knew.

SCB had, indeed, always been family-owned and operated. The problem was that the old man was facing his ninetieth birthday and his sole heir was a grandchild still in school.

Still in school…and a girl.

Nicolo was sure that "tradition," to James Black, meant handing the reins of the company to an heir, not an heiress. Black had never made a secret of his feelings about women in business.

And that was probably the one thing the two men could agree on, Nicolo mused as he stepped from the shower. It was what he would build his argument on, Monday morning.

Women were too emotional. They were unpredictable and undisciplined. They did well as assistants, even, on occasion, as heads of departments, but as ultimate decision-makers?

Not until science figured out a way women could overcome the dizzying up-and-down ride of their hormones.

It wasn't their fault—it was simply a fact of life.

And that, Nicolo thought as he dressed in gray flannel trousers, a black cashmere turtleneck and mocs, was his ace in the hole.

Nicolo was the only investor who could afford the indulgence of buying SCB privately. That meant that Black had nowhere to turn except to him, unless he wanted to sell his venerable institution to one of the giant conglomerates hungering for it, then live long enough to see it disappear within the corporate maw.

He was the old man's salvation and they both knew it. The moment of truth had come last week when Black's secretary phoned and said her employer would agree to a brief meeting solely as a courtesy.

"Of course," Nicolo had said calmly but when he hung up, he'd pumped his fist in victory.

The meeting meant only one thing: the old man had admitted defeat and would sell to him. Oh, he'd undoubtedly make him dance through a couple of hoops first, but how bad could that be?

Nicolo slipped on a leather bomber jacket and shut the door to his suite behind him.

He wouldn't dance, but he'd move his feet in time to the music. Do just enough to placate the old bastard.

Then Stafford-Coleridge-Black would be his.

Not bad for a boy who'd grown up in not-so-genteel poverty, Nicolo thought, and pressed the button for the elevator.

The rain had stopped, though the skies were gray and soggy.

The doorman flagged a cab.

"Sixty-third off Lexington," Nicolo told the driver.

He was meeting friends at the Eastside Club. The three of them had agreed, via e-mail yesterday, on the benefits of a quick workout, especially since both Nicolo and Damian had just flown in.

Private planes or not, a man felt his muscles tighten after a seemingly interminable international flight.

Then they'd go somewhere quiet for dinner and catch up on old times. He was looking forward to that. He, Damian and Lucas had known each other forever. For thirteen years, ever since they'd met at a pub just off the Yale campus, three eighteen-year-old kids from three different parts of the world, all of them wondering how in hell they'd survive in this strange country.

Survive? They'd flourished. And formed a tight friendship. They saw each other less frequently now, thanks to their individual business interests, but they were still best pals.

And still single, which was exactly how they all wanted it. In fact, they always began the evening with the same toast.

"Life," Lucas would say solemnly, "is short."

"And marriage," Damian would add even more solemnly, "is forever."

The last part of the toast was left to Nicolo.

"And freedom," he'd say dramatically, "freedom, gentlemen, is everything!"

He was smiling as his cab pulled up in front of the Eastside Club. It was housed in what had once been a block of nineteenth-century brownstones that had been gutted, completely made over and combined into one structure.

A very exclusive health club.

The Eastside didn't advertise. No plaque or sign identified it to passersby. Membership was by invitation only, reserved for those who valued privacy and could afford the steep fees that guaranteed it.

For all that, the club was completely lacking in pretension. There were no trendy exercise gadgets, no bouncy music, and the only part of the gym with a mirrored wall was the free-weight area so that you could check your reflection to see if you were lifting properly.

What there were, in addition to the weights, were punching bags, a pool and a banked indoor track.

Best of all, the Eastside was for men only.

Women were a distraction. Besides, Nicolo thought as he inserted his key card in the front door lock, it was a relief to get away from them for a while.

He had enough women to deal with in his life. Too many, he sometimes thought, when ending a relationship led to tears. He was, he'd heard whispered, "an excellent catch." He scoffed at that but to himself, he admitted it was probably true.

Why not be honest?

"Good evening, Mr. Barbieri. Nice to see you again, sir."

"Jack," Nicolo said amiably. He signed in and headed for the locker room.

He had money. A private jet. Cars. He owned a ski lodge in Aspen, an oceanfront estate on Mustique, a *pied-a-terre* in Paris and, of course, there was the *palazzo* in Rome, the one that had supposedly come to the Barbieri family through Julius Caesar.

That was what his great-grandmother had always claimed.

Nicolo thought it more likely it had come to them through a thief in Caesar's time, but he'd never contradicted her. He'd loved the old woman as he'd never loved anyone else. He'd always been grateful he'd made his first million and restored the ancient but decrepit *Palazzo di Barbieri* before she'd died.

Her pleasure had brought joy to his heart.

He'd liked making her happy. In fact, he liked making most women happy.

It was only when their demands became unreasonable, when they began to talk of The Future, of The Importance of Settling Down—and he could almost actually feel the physical weight they put into the phrase when it tumbled from their lips—that Nicolo knew that Making Them Happy wasn't as important as Not Making a Commitment.

No way. Not him. Not yet.

For an evening? Of course. A week? Yes. Even a month. Two months. Hell, he wasn't the kind of man to jump from bed to bed….

What would the woman in the black suede coat be like in bed? A honey-maned tigress? Or an ice queen?

Not that he gave a damn. It was simply a matter of intellectual curiosity.

He liked women who enjoyed their femininity. Enjoyed being appreciated by a man.

Nicolo hung his things in his locker.

It didn't take a psychiatrist to figure out that the tigress was not such a woman. Although, in the bed of the right man, perhaps she could be.

The mane of hair. The delicate oval face. The amazing eyes, that tender mouth. And, yes, he'd felt its tenderness even in that brush of his lips against hers…

Fantastico.

Hell. He was giving himself a hard-on over a woman who'd insulted him, who he would never see again. He didn't want to think about her or any woman. Not this weekend. No distractions. No sex. Like an athlete, he believed in abstinence before going *mano a mano*.

He needed to focus on Monday's meeting.

Nicolo pulled on gray cotton running shorts, a sleeveless, ancient Yale sweatshirt and a pair of Nikes.

A hard, sweaty workout was just what he needed.

The gym was almost empty. Well, it was Saturday night. Only one other guy was in the vast room, pounding around the track with the lonely intensity of the dedicated runner.

Damian.

Nicolo grinned, trotted over and fell in alongside him.

"Any slower," he said, picking up the pace, "we'd be walking. You getting too old to run fast?"

Damian, who at thirty-one was exactly the same age as Nicolo, shot him a deadpan look.

"I'll call the paramedics when you collapse."

"Big talk."

"A hundred bucks says I can beat you."

"Twenty times around?"

"Forty," Nicolo said, and shot away.

Moments later, they finished in a dead heat and turned to each other, breathing hard and grinning from ear to ear.

"How's Rome?" Damian said.

"How's Athens?"

The men's grins widened and they clasped each other in a bear hug.

"Man," Damian said, "you're a sweaty bastard."

"You're not exactly an ad for *GQ*."

"How was your flight?"

Nicolo took a couple of towels from a stand beside the track and tossed one to Damian.

"Fine. Some weather just before we landed, but nothing much. Yours?"

"The same," Damian said, wiping his face. "I really like this little Learjet I bought."

"Little," Nicolo said, laughing.

"Well, it's still not as big as yours."

"Mine's always going to be bigger than yours, Aristedes."

"You wish."

It was an old line of banter and made them grin again.

"So," Nicolo said, "where's Lucas?"

"We're meeting him in—" Damian looked at his watch. "In two hours."

"You guys picked a restaurant?"

"Well, more or less."

Nicolo raised an eyebrow. "Meaning?"

"Meaning," Damian said, "our old friend bought himself a club. Downtown. *The* club of the minute, he says."

"Meaning, crowded. Noisy. Lots of music, lots of booze, lots of spectacular-looking women out for a good time…"

"Sounds terrible," Damian said solemnly.

Nicolo smiled as he draped his towel around his shoulders. "Yeah, I know. But I have an important meeting Monday morning."

"Well, so do I."

"Very important."

Damian looked at him. "So?"

"So," Nicolo said, after a moment, "I'm hoping to finalize a deal. With James Black."

"Whoa. That *is* important. So, tonight we celebrate in advance, at Lucas's place."

"Well, I want to stay focused. Get to bed at a decent hour tonight and tomorrow night. No liquor. No distractions—"

"*Thee Mou!* Don't tell me! No sex?"

Nicolo shrugged. "No sex."

"Sex is not a distraction. It's exercise. Good for the heart."

"It's bad for the concentration."

"That's BS."

"We believed it when we played soccer, remember? And we won."

"We won," Damian said dryly, "because the competition was lousy."

"I'm serious."

"So am I. Giving up sex is against the laws of nature."

"Idiot," Nicolo said fondly. The men walked to the free weights area and made their selections. "It's just a matter of discipline."

"Unless, of course, there was such an instant attraction you couldn't walk away." Damian grunted as he lifted a pair of twenty-pound weights. "And how often is that about to happen?"

"Never," Nicolo answered—and, unbidden, the image of the blonde with the hot eyes and the cold attitude flashed before his eyes.

He had been reaching for the twenty-pound weights, too. Instead he lifted a pair of heavier ones and worked with them until his mind was a pain-filled blank.

* * *

Farther downtown, in a part of Manhattan that was either about to be discovered or still a slum, depending on a buyer's point of view, Aimee Stafford Coleridge Black slammed her apartment door behind her, tossed her black suede coat at a chair and kicked off her matching boots.

The coat slid off the chair. The boots bounced off the wall. Aimee didn't give a damn.

Amazing, how a day that began so filled with promise could end so badly.

Aimee marched into the kitchen, filled the kettle with water, put it on to boil and changed her mind. The last thing she needed was a caffeine buzz.

She was buzzing enough without it, thanks to her grandfather.

Why had he summoned her to his office, if not to make the announcement she'd been anticipating?

"I shall retire next May," he'd told her almost a year ago, "when I reach ninety, at which time I shall place Stafford-Coleridge-Black in the charge of the person who will guide it through its next fifty years. A person who will, of course, carry on the Stafford-Coleridge-Black lineage."

Lineage. As important to James as breathing but that was fine because she, Aimee, was the only person with both the necessary lineage and the proper education to assume command.

She had a bachelor's degree in finance. A master's degree in business. She'd spent her summers since high school interning at SCB.

She knew more about the bank than anyone, maybe even including Grandfather, who still believed in a world devoid of computers and e-mail.

Aimee marched into the bedroom and methodically stripped off the gray wool suit and white silk blouse she'd deemed appropriate for the meeting with Grandfather this afternoon. She'd wanted to look businesslike, even though she knew damned well you could do as much business in jeans as you could in Armani.

She'd even worked up a little speech of assurance about how she wouldn't change a thing, though she'd mentally crossed her fingers because there were things that definitely needed changing.

She'd presented herself at his office precisely at four. James was a stickler for promptness. She'd kissed his papery cheek, sat down as directed, folded her hands...

And listened as he told her he had not yet reached a decision as to who would replace him.

Be calm, she'd told herself. And she had been, or at least she'd managed to seem calm as she asked him what decision there was to make.

"You already said it would be me, Grandfather."

"I said it would be someone capable," James said briskly. "Someone of my lineage."

"Well—"

The look on his face had frozen her with horror. "You don't mean...Bradley?"

Bradley. Her cousin. Or her something. Who understood the complexities of second cousins twice removed, or whatever the hell he was? Bradley had been wimping around the bank for years, interning the same as she had, except he'd never done a day's work, never done anything except try to grope her in the stockroom.

"Not Bradley," she'd finally breathed.

"Bradley has a degree in economics."

Yes. From a college that probably also gave degrees in basket-weaving.

"He's well-spoken."

He was, once he had three or four straight vodkas in him.

"And," her grandfather had said, saving the best for last, "he is a man."

A man. Meaning, nature's royalty. A prince, whereas she was a lesser creature because she was female.

Grandfather had risen to his feet, indicating that she was no longer welcome in the royal presence.

"Be here Monday morning, Aimee. Ten o'clock sharp. I'll announce my decision then."

Dismissed, just like that.

Sent out the door, down the wheezing old elevator, into the street where she'd walked blindly, no idea where in hell she was or where she was going, which was why she hadn't seen the man and he'd almost knocked her down.

That despicable, horrible man who'd insisted it was she who'd walked into him. Who'd accused her of not being a woman when, damn him, it was the very fact that she *was* a woman that was going to deny her the one thing she wanted in life.

What a fool she'd been. What an idiot. She'd turned down two wonderful job offers because she'd believed— she'd been stupid enough to believe—

She'd been anguishing over that when the man charged into her.

As if she were invisible, which she undoubtedly was because she was female. Oh, the arrogance of men. Of him. The way he'd clasped her shoulders and looked down at her from the lofty heights of his lofty maleness.

"Easy," he'd said, and smiled, and that—the smile, the slight foreign huskiness to the word, the broad shoulders, the ink-black hair, the midnight-blue eyes and the face that was the male equivalent of what had launched a thousand ships, *that* was supposed to make up for his rudeness?

Aimee had told him what she thought of him.

Men didn't like honesty. She'd learned that a long time ago. And this one, this—this bad-mannered stranger, had decided she needed a lesson, that she needed a graphic reminder of her place in the universe...

He'd kissed her.

Kissed her! Put his mouth on hers, the arrogant, miserable son of a bitch....

His firm mouth. His soft mouth. His mouth that was, any woman could tell, made for long, deep kisses...

God, she was in bad shape. Anger, adrenaline, whatever you called it, was pumping through her veins. She was completely stressed out.

A man would know what to do to ease such stress.

He'd go to a gym and sweat it out. Actually that would work for her, too, but her gym, a gym for women, was closed. Hey, it was Saturday. Date night for the fairer sex, right?

"Such crap," Aimee said.

She could almost feel the steam coming out of her ears.

Or a man would call up his buddies, meet them someplace crowded and noisy and guzzle beer. That's what men under pressure did, didn't they? Go out, drink, talk about stupid things, pick up women?

Sex was the great relaxer. Everybody said so. Okay, not her because she'd had sex and it had been far from memorable but according to everything she'd read, sex could lower your stress levels every time.

Aimee snorted.

Imagine if a woman did that. Called a friend, went someplace loud to drink and looked for a guy to pick up. Went to bed with him, no strings, no ridiculous exchange of names and phone numbers. Just bed.

Just sex.

Of course, some women did. They went looking for sex.

Sex with a stranger. A stranger with dark hair. Blue eyes. A square jaw, straight nose, firm mouth. And that little accent…

The phone rang. Let it. Her voice mail could take the call.

Hi, her recorded voice said briskly. *You've reached 555-6145. Please leave a message after the tone.*

"Aimee, it's Jen."

The last person she wanted to talk to! Jen had taken a job with Fox and Curtrain after Aimee pointed her toward it.

"I'm not going to take it," she'd said, "so why shouldn't you?"

Why, indeed?

"Aimee, look, I know this isn't your thing but a new club opened right near me and it's supposed to draw a hot crowd. And it's Laura's birthday, remember her, from the second floor in our dorm? She's in town and a bunch of us are getting together to, you know, check out the club…" There was giggling in the background and Aimee rolled her eyes. "Okay, Laura's right. To check out the guys, see if they're as hunky as everybody says."

"Jen?" Aimee said, picking up the phone.

"Oh, you're there! Listen, I don't know what you're doing tonight, but—"

"I'm not doing anything. I've had—it's been one of those days, you know?"

"All the more reason to go with us. Have a drink, listen to some hot music—"

"Get picked up by some hot guy," a female voice in the background said, to another round of giggles.

"That's the last thing I need," Aimee said. "I mean, is that all I'm good for? To go to a club where the music's so loud I won't be able to think? To let a guy pick me up, buy me a drink—"

"Yeah. I know. It's a meat market out there—but sometimes, well, sometimes that can be fun. You know. No BS. Just an evening of fun and games."

"It's bad enough men think that's what we're all about. That we're useless except in the kitchen or the bedroom. We don't have to play into their stupid fantasy."

Silence. Then Jen cleared her throat. "Okay," she said carefully, "so just forget that I—"

"Not that I couldn't be some jerk's idea of a centerfold playmate, if I wanted."

"Uh, Aimee, look, I have to run, so—"

"I could go to this club with you. Dance, drink, let some guy pick me up for a night of mind-blowing sex!"

The telephone line hummed with silence again. Then Jen spoke.

"So, uh, are you saying you want to go with us?"

Aimee took a deep, deep breath. "You're damned right I am," she said.

Twenty minutes later, dressed in a red silk dress she'd bought on sale and never had a reason to wear, ditto for a pair of strappy gold sandals, Aimee took a last look in the mirror, gave her image a quick salute, then headed out the door.

CHAPTER TWO

LUCAS'S CLUB was everything Damian had promised.

Like most hot Manhattan nightspots, it was in a neighborhood that had once been grungy and commercial and now was grungy and upscale. Streets that had once been relegated to the nitty-gritty of daily life now came alive after dark. Warehouses had given way to expensive, exclusive clubs.

Lucas's place was located in a dark brick building with shuttered windows. There was no sign to indicate that what had once been a factory was now Le Club Hot.

No sign. No published telephone number. You either knew the club existed or you didn't, which went a long way toward sorting out the clientele, Nicolo thought wryly as he opened a heavy, brass-hinged door and stepped, with Damian, into what might have been the small lobby of an upscale hotel.

The behemoth who greeted them was not someone you'd ever find behind a reception desk. They gave him their names, he checked a list, then smiled.

He pressed a button, and the wall ahead of them slid back.

"Wow," Damian said softly.

Nicolo had to agree. "Wow" summed it up.

The first thing you noticed was the noise. Music, heavy on bass, went straight into your blood.

Then you realized that the room you'd walked into was huge.

The designer had carefully left the exposed overhead pipes and old brick walls but everything else—the lighting, the endless Lucite bar, the elevated dance floor and the music—was dazzlingly modern.

"You could play American football in here," Damian murmured. "Especially since the place comes equipped with so many cheerleaders."

He grinned, and Nicolo grinned back at him. It was true. The room was filled with people, more than half of them women. Young. Stunning. Sexy. Faces recognizable from European and American magazine covers and movies.

What an idiot he'd been, letting what happened this afternoon get him worked up. Damian had it right. This was what he needed. Lights. Music.

Women.

This was the way to relax.

"Barbieri! Aristedes!"

Lucas was making his way through the crowd toward them. The men exchanged handshakes and then Lucas rolled his eyes and grabbed them both in a bear hug.

"Ugly as always," he said, raising his voice over the pulsating beat of the music, "but not to worry. I've told a bunch of lies about you both and made you sound so interesting that people are willing to meet you, despite your looks."

The three of them grinned. Then Lucas pointed toward a suspended, transparent staircase.

"My table's up there," he shouted. "On the mezzanine. It's quieter…and the view is *óptimo!*"

He was right. The table overlooked the dance floor and the sound level dropped from deafening to ear-shattering.

And the view was, indeed, excellent.

"What scenery," Damian said.

He meant, of course, the women. Nicolo nodded in agreement. He'd already acknowledged that the scenery was spectacular. All those lithe, gyrating bodies. The lovely faces…

Was there a woman on the dance floor with eyes the color of violets? With hair the honey-gold of a tigress?

"Nicolo? Which do you prefer?"

Nicolo blinked. Lucas and Damian were looking at him, along with a girl in gold hot pants and a skimpy black tank top.

"To drink," Lucas said, with a little laugh. "Whiskey? Champagne? The club special? It's a Mojito. You know, rum, lime juice—"

"Whiskey," Nicolo said, and told himself to stop being a fool and start having a good time.

But that was a problem.

It turned out you couldn't have a good time just by telling yourself to have one. You had to relax before you had fun, and now that the woman with the violet eyes had pushed her way into his head, he knew damned well "fun" wasn't going to happen.

No matter how much he tried.

He ate. He drank. He listened while Lucas and Damian caught up on old times. The three of them hadn't seen each other in months; there was a lot to talk about and he forced himself to join in the conversation.

After a while, his thoughts drifted. To the woman. To how he'd dealt with her. The more he thought, the angrier he became.

At her.

At himself.

What kind of man let a woman make a fool of him?

"Nicolo?"

Another blink, this time at Damian, who was watching him through slightly narrowed eyes.

"You okay?"

"Yes. Sure. I told you, it's—it's this meeting Monday, and—"

Lucas snorted. "My friend, you're as transparent as glass. What's on your mind is a woman."

No. It wasn't true. Well, yes. There was a woman on his mind but not in the way Lucas meant.

There were no women in his life to think about.

He'd ended an affair a month ago, and *grazie a Dio* that he had. The lady in question had been like so many others, beautiful and accommodating at first, then simply beautiful and boring.

But then, that was in the nature of things—or was it? Somehow, he couldn't envision the blonde with the violet eyes ever being accommodating or boring.

She would always be a challenge.

Any other woman, given the situation, would have accepted the apology he'd offered. Hell, any other woman would have done more than that.

He was always lucky with women. They liked him and he liked them. So, any other woman would have smiled and said it was nice of him to say it was his fault but, really, it was hers.

And he'd have understood her smile, returned one of his own and said, well, perhaps they might have a drink while they decided who owed whom an apology....

Nicolo brought his bourbon on the rocks to his lips and took a long drink.

Damn it, the woman was haunting him and for a reason that was insulting.

Such insolence! Why had he tolerated it? Such audacity! And he'd let her get away with it.

His eyes narrowed.

What she'd needed was a real lesson in how a woman should behave. Not that pale excuse of a kiss but something she would have remembered, something that would have shaken her loose of that cold disdain.

He should have dragged her against his body. Taken her mouth, parted her lips with his and filled her with his taste. Let her understand that she was female and he was male and despite the ridiculous conventions of this misbegotten century, what that meant was that he held supremacy when it came to things such as this.

But he had done none of those things. And now, for all he knew, somewhere in this vast city she was laughing at him. At how easily she'd cut him down to size.

Laughing, perhaps, with her lover.

A woman with a face like a madonna's would surely have a lover.

Would he be a man she could command? Yes. Of course. And what a pity that was because what the lady needed was a lover whose touch would make her tremble. Whose kisses would melt her icy hauteur. Who would make love to her until she begged for mercy…

"Barbieri!"

Nicolo forced the darkness away, looked at the expressions on his friends' faces—and realized that he had held his glass so tightly it had shattered.

Whiskey puddled on the table.

"Merda," he growled, and dabbed furiously at the spreading pond of golden liquid with a napkin.

"Never mind that. Did you cut yourself?"

Had he? Nicolo checked.

"No. Not a scratch." He forced a laugh and held out his hand. "See? Relax, Reyes. There won't be a lawsuit."

But Lucas wasn't buying into the poor attempt at humor.

"*Amigo,* I'm not the one who needs to relax. You're wound tighter than a spring."

Nicolo thought about denying it but what was the point? These men knew him too well.

"You're right. I am, and I'm sorry I'm spoiling your evening." He pushed back his chair. "The truth is, I can't keep my mind on things tonight, so I'm going to head back to my hotel. I told you, that meeting—"

"We've known you too long to fall for that. Tough negotiations don't stress you, Barbieri. You live for them." Laughing, Damian nudged Lucas in the ribs with his elbow. "It's a woman. Admit it."

Nicolo gave a deliberately careless shrug. Maybe if he made light of it…

"Okay," he said, "it is. But I'll get over it."

"Of course you will." Lucas leaned closer. "And I know the quickest way to do it. It's like drinking, Nicolo. Remember, back in college? The hair of the dog cure after too much partying? You wake with a hangover, you get rid of it by taking a drink. Well, you have a woman on the brain, you cure that by—"

"Lucas," a soft voice purred, "darling Lucas, here you are! We've been looking everywhere."

Five women had materialized beside the table. All stunning. All smiling as if they'd found the lost treasure of the Amazons.

"The hair of the dog, my man," Damian whispered, and Nicolo thought, *Why not?*

Chairs were dragged over. Introductions were made. Champagne corks popped. After a few minutes, one of the women—her name was Vicki—turned to Nicolo.

"Lucas tells me you're a royal"

Nicolo looked over her shoulder. Lucas grinned and winked.

"Lucas is a comedian," he said.

"I'm famous, too." She giggled. "Well, not yet but someday. Maybe you've seen me? I've been in—"

A list of plays. Or TV shows. Or something. He didn't know, didn't care, and stole a surreptitious glance at his watch. When could he get out of here without insulting the lady or putting a damper on the party?

Not that she wasn't beautiful. And friendly. She smiled a lot. Put her hand on his arm. Asked him the questions a man likes to be asked.

It was an old game, one he'd played often. The outcome was always understood. And pleasant.

Amazingly pleasant.

He felt his blood tingle. Damian was right. Lucas, too. This was what he needed. A willing, beautiful woman. A game with a predictable ending. A night's pleasure.

Wasn't it bad enough the woman with the violet eyes had made a fool of him once? Was he going to let her do it again by keeping him from what waited for him now?

Nicolo pushed back his chair. Took Vicki's hand.

"Dance with me."

He led her down the steps to the dance floor. Salsa music blasted the air, its insistent beat almost as sexual as the moves of Vicki's ripe body lightly brushing his.

Yes. This was good. This was what he needed…

But it wasn't. It was the wrong body, teasing his. The wrong face, lifted to his and smiling. The wrong eyes, filled with heat and desire.

Basta, he thought in disgust, and he put his arms around the woman and brought her tightly against him as the music segued into something slow and sexy.

She settled close against him as if she'd been waiting for the invitation. Her hair tickled his nose. It was stiff and smelled of hairspray.

Those honeyed curls this afternoon had been soft and fragrant with rain.

"It's terribly noisy here," Vicki said, her breath warm against his ear.

Why don't we find a quieter place? That was the next line. His, or in these days of supposed equality, it could be—

"Why don't we find a quieter place?" she whispered.

Nicolo cleared his throat.

"You know," he said, "I think that's—I think it's—" *An excellent idea.* "I think I'll have to take a rain check on that," he heard himself say.

She looked as surprised as he felt but, damn it, he didn't want this woman.

No substitutes, he thought as the music began to pound again, and the need, the desire he'd been suppressing all these hours ignited and threatened to consume him.

He knew what he wanted. What he needed. And there had to be a way, had to be something he could do to—

Nicolo caught his breath. He stopped dancing, let the other dancers and the music swirl around him.

There she was!

Honey-colored curls. Violet eyes. The woman who was driving him insane. No black suede coat. No hood. No boots. Instead she wore a clinging scrap of crimson silk that barely covered her body. Gold sandals, all straps and sky-high, needle-sharp heels. She was dancing, if you wanted to call it that. Moving in a man's arms. Breasts swaying. Hips rotating. Head up, eyes locked to the man's face, mouth turned up in a smile…

A smile she had denied him.

"Nicolo?"

Vicki, whatever her name was, said his name. Said something more and put her hand on his chest. He brushed it aside. Stepped away. Abandoned her in the middle of the crowded dance floor.

The part of his brain that was of this century knew all that. Knew, too, that his response to the events of the afternoon might not be entirely rational.

But the part that was as old, as savagely male, as time whispered, *This is what I want. And I'm going to have it.*

And Nicolo heard nothing else.

The music had turned wild; the throbbing pulse matched the insistent thump of his blood, the beat of his heart….

The fury eating inside him.

Fate, always capricious, had decided to favor him tonight. The woman who'd made a fool of him was here.

Now, he could even the score.

He shouldered his way through the crowd, eyes locked to his quarry. She was oblivious to him. Good, he thought grimly. He wanted to reach her before she had time to think.

But halfway there, she suddenly stopped dancing. Her partner said something; she didn't answer. Instead she moved out of his arms and stood like a doe at the edge of a clearing, sensing the presence of a hungry predator.

Later, Nicolo would wonder if it weren't the whole world that had gone still and waited, waited, waited.

A minute, an eternity, swept by. Then the blonde raised her head and looked directly at him.

He let a tight smile curve his mouth. Whatever beat its wings within him must have been in that smile, because the color drained from her face.

She took a step back.

He thought, again, of the doe.

Run, he thought.

And, just as if she'd read his mind, the woman with the violet eyes swung away from him and fled.

Nicolo didn't hesitate. He went after her.

CHAPTER THREE

YOU COULDN'T end up in the same place with the same man twice in one day. Not in a town the size of New York.

At first, when she saw him, Aimee told herself it had to be some other tall, dark-haired guy. There were tons of dark-haired, good-looking men in the city.

A second glance and that hope vanished. It was the overbearing, supermacho jerk who'd kissed her. It had to be. The truth was, nobody else would be as…

All right. No other man could possibly be as easy on the eyes. He was despicable—but he was gorgeous.

The last few minutes, she'd felt… What? A premonition? She didn't believe in any of that stuff, but how else to explain that tingle at her nape? That feeling that eyes were following her as she danced with Tom or Tim or, dear God, she couldn't even remember the name of the guy who'd bought her a drink, then led her onto the dance floor.

He was nice enough. Good-looking enough. And he was working hard at making an impression.

And he wasn't the stranger from this afternoon.

No way would Tom, or whoever he was, grab a woman and kiss her, look at her through icy deep-blue eyes in a way that would make the memory of him lodge itself in her brain.

She hated men like the Neanderthal, no matter how hot-looking a Neanderthal he might be.

So, yes, it was good that the guy dancing with her wasn't like that... Wasn't it?

Of course it was.

He'd been coming on to her like crazy. And she'd tried her best to respond. Smiled. Laughed. Gone onto the dance floor and did her best to lose herself in the music, working off her frustrations to its insistent beat the way she'd have worked them off in the gym.

And then, suddenly, she'd felt a tingle, as if someone was watching her.

Well, of course, someone was watching her! People danced, other people watched.

Aimee had danced harder, throwing herself into the music with abandon, and the guy with her kept saying things like, "Wow, you're good, baby," and "That's it, babe, way to go," as if he were cheering her on.

Objectifying her, she'd thought with detached clarity—except, wasn't that part of the deal tonight?

She'd come here to have fun, she'd thought grimly. To pick up a man. She was going to have a good time.

Except, she wasn't.

She despised places like this. Not the club itself: it was, she had to admit, spectacular. It was what went with the place. The noise. The lights. The crowd. The desperate pickup lines.

And this was not the time to turn into an anthropologist studying the natives.

So she'd agreed when Jen said it was absolutely fantastic, laughed at what she assumed were jokes, let a nice-looking guy buy her a margarita, tell her she was the most beautiful woman in the place and lead her to the dance floor.

And tried not to cringe each time Ted or Tim or Tom called her "baby."

And worked really, really hard at pretending she was having fun when the truth was, she didn't belong here, didn't want to be here, certainly didn't want to go home with Ted-Tom-Tim or anybody else for a night of meaningless sex.

She'd never treated sex casually. Never had a one-night stand. Never, not once.

Why on earth had she thought she'd want to now?

Because, a sly voice inside her had whispered, *you thought it just might make you forget the stranger. The one with the hard, beautiful face and the body that was all muscle.*

The one who kissed you as if he had the right, as if he could kiss you, do anything to you that he wanted.

That you *wanted.*

And that was when Aimee felt the tingling, looked around... And saw him. The stranger from this afternoon. Watching her with what could only be fury in his eyes.

He was angry? At *her?* That was crazy. *She* was the one who was angry. And "angry" wasn't the word. She'd been the one harassed by him. By his attitude. His arrogance. His unwanted kiss.

His eyes met hers. Everything faded. The insistent throb of the music, the people around her, everything.

Aimee stopped dancing.

It was all she could do not to run.

The look in his eyes terrified her...but the slow heat spreading through her veins terrified her even more.

She took a long, deep breath. Or tried to. For some reason, she couldn't seem to get any air into her lungs.

Suddenly the rage in his expression changed. Something else glittered in his dark blue eyes. Something male that she despised.

The innate male determination to dominate.

To dominate, in bed and out.

With breathtaking swiftness, she felt a rush of heat sweep through her. Her nipples tightened; a honeyed warmth spread low in her belly.

No, she thought frantically, no! She'd never want someone like him to put his hands on her. His mouth on her. To take her, hard and fast, again and again until she collapsed in his arms....

He started toward her, heedless of the people in his way, everything about him focused, with hot intensity, on her.

And she turned and ran.

She went through the crowd blindly, banging into people, ignoring their indignant protests. Her heart was racing.

God, oh God, oh God!

He was the hunter. She was his prey. A sob rose in her throat and, just in time, she spotted the flashing neon sign that marked one of the club's unisex bathrooms.

Jen had dragged her into it earlier.

"Doesn't look like a bathroom at all," Jen had bubbled.

Right now, it looked like a sanctuary.

Aimee pulled open the door. Slammed it after her. Started to turn the lock...

Bang!

The door flew open and the man burst into the room. She shrieked and fell back, reached behind her to the vanity. Wrapped her hand around a heavy bottle of something. Hand lotion. Body oil. Who gave a damn what it was? It was a weapon.

That was what counted.

"Don't," she said.

Her voice shook. Was that the reason for the little smile that began at the corner of his mouth?

"Get out of here! Do you hear me? Go away or I'll scream."

He laughed. She couldn't blame him. There wasn't a chance in the world anyone would hear her. You wouldn't hear a siren above the music. It was muted here, but it still filled the room like the beat of a giant heart.

She raised the bottle over her head. "One step," she panted, "just one, and I'll smash you with this!"

He laughed. "You already tried that, remember?"

"I'm not kidding! You—you unlock that door and get the hell out of here or so help me—"

He started toward her. She let fly with the bottle but he dodged and it shattered against the wall.

"Listen to me." Her voice trembled; she hated herself for it but she knew damned well there was nothing she could do to prevent it. "This is a terrible mistake. You won't—you won't get away with—"

"At first," he said, his tone almost conversational, "I thought, 'Well, that is just the way she deals with men.'"

She'd noticed his accent this afternoon. You couldn't miss that husky, sexy quality to his voice. It seemed more obvious now, his pronunciation more careful.

"I told myself it was not important."

Aimee swallowed. "Look, what happened this afternoon—"

"Still," he said, in that same easy way, as if he were explaining the day's news to a friend, "still, I admit, it bothered me. That a woman should be so impolite. So downright rude. But I put it out of my head."

"I didn't do anything! It was—it was just something that happened."

"Just something that happened." He nodded. "Yes, that's an excellent way to put it. In fact, that is exactly the conclusion I reached."

He was inches away from her now, so close that she had to tilt her head up to see his eyes. Even in her heels, he was much taller than she. And, God, much bigger.

"But then I saw you, here."

"You mean, you followed me here!"

"You give yourself too much importance, *cara*. Do you really think I have nothing better to do than to spend my time following you?" A little muscle was ticking in his cheek. "I came here with friends. To enjoy the evening." He paused. "And, it would seem, so did you."

"Yes. And—and my date will be looking for—"

"Your date didn't move a finger to prevent you from abandoning him. Or to keep me from going after you." He paused, and she saw his eyes darken. "I noticed that you treated your gentleman friend differently than you treated me."

"I don't know what you mean."

"*Cara*. Please, don't try my patience. You laughed with him. Smiled when he spoke to you."

"Of course. I mean, I know him—"

"Really? What's his name?"

"Ted," Aimee said quickly.

"No. It is not."

It had been a gamble, but a good one. Nicolo watched as the woman worried her bottom lip. He'd guessed right. She had no idea who she'd been dancing with. She'd picked the man up.

For many of its patrons, that was the purpose of a place like this.

Her business, of course.

That was what he'd told himself, when he first saw her with the man.

But he'd watched as she smiled. Flirted. Shook her hips, her breasts. Practiced the fine art of seduction.

For another man.

Not for him.

Not for him, he'd thought, and suddenly he'd known that confronting her, kissing her, would not be enough.

He wanted her.

It didn't make sense but it didn't have to. His body, his blood, knew what he needed.

And what he needed was this beautiful, condescending stranger dancing with him...

Dancing in his bed.

Slowly he reached out, laced one finger under the thin strap of her red dress and tugged. She stumbled toward him, arms raised, hands balled into fists.

He caught her wrists in one hand.

"Don't struggle," he said in a low voice. "It will only make things worse."

"Please." Her voice trembled. "Please, don't do this."

"I told you this afternoon, you lack manners, *cara.*"

"Let me go! Damn you—"

"The next time 'something happens,' as you called it, between you and a man, you will know how to respond."

"If you're after an apology..."

"And if I were, would you finally offer one?"

She was terrified; he could see it in her face, feel it in the trembling of her body. Her gaze locked on his, and he felt a rush of disappointment.

She was desperate, desperate enough so she was, in fact, going to apologize. And then, as a civilized man, he'd have to let her go...

Wrong.

Her chin lifted; terrified or not, her eyes blazed with defiance.

"Only a barbarian would think that taking a woman by force is the way to get even for damage to his ego."

"Is that what you think? That I'm going to rape you?" The muscle flickered in his jaw again; he cupped her face with his free hand and held it steady. "You know better." His voice was low and husky. "I saw the way you looked at me a few minutes ago."

Color stained her cheeks. "I don't know what you—"

"Yes," he said, "you damned well do."

His head lowered to hers, and he kissed her.

His mouth was hard. Hungry. Hot against hers. Aimee jerked against the restraint of his hand, tried to twist her face away but he wouldn't permit it.

Instead he brought her closer, crushing her tightly against him so that she could feel the strength of him, the power....

The thrust of his straining erection.

A whimper rose in her throat.

"Stop," she said, against his mouth, but he went on kissing her, his fingers sliding into her hair, twisting the curls around his hand, backing her against the wall so that now she was pressed against him from breast to groin.

"Kiss me back," he said in a thick whisper.

No, she told herself frantically. She wouldn't. She wouldn't. She wouldn't...

Aimee gave a strangled cry, rose to him and opened her mouth against his.

He groaned. Let go of her wrists and threw his arm around her hips, lifting her against him. His tongue teased her lips, slipped between them and she tasted his hunger, his need, his rampant masculinity.

"Say it," he growled against her mouth. "Tell me what you want. What you've wanted ever since this afternoon."

Blind to logic, to reason, blind to anything but the feel of him, the scent of him, Aimee gave up lying.

"You," she whispered. "Only you. All day. All evening. I couldn't think of anything else, couldn't get you out of my head—"

He cupped her face in his hands. Kissed her, deeply. Thrust his leg between hers and she moaned at the feel of it against the tender flesh between her thighs.

She moved against him. Moved again, but it wasn't enough, wasn't enough...

She moaned.

The sound damned near sent Nicolo over the edge.

The taste of her was exquisite. She was strawberries and cream, spring rain and summer sun. She was everything a man could imagine a woman might be, if only in a dream.

He lifted her from the floor. Her arms rose; she wound them around his neck.

"Yes," he said, and he grasped her slender thighs and brought them around his hips.

He thought of taking her to his hotel. To her apartment. To a place where he could undress her, touch her, watch her eyes as he entered her.

But not now.

Now, he needed this. Needed her. Needed to bury himself in her, needed it more than his next breath.

Locked in a dance as old as time, mouths fused in mutual hunger, Nicolo carried Aimee to the marble vanity. Sat her on its edge. Fumbled between them. Unzipped. Freed himself. Put his hand between her thighs, groaning as he felt the wet heat of her against his fingers, and tore aside the scrap of silk that kept her from him.

"Look at me," he commanded.

She did, fixing those incredible violet eyes on his face.

"Yes," she said, and he thrust forward, sank into her, felt her close around him.

She cried out instantly; he felt the pulse of her muscles

as she came and then he exploded within her, came in a rush of almost unbearable ecstasy.

She trembled.

Then she gave a little sob and dropped her head on his shoulder.

Nicolo put his arms around her. Stroked her silken hair. Whispered to her, his native language soft on his tongue while he tried to figure out what in hell had just happened.

This was not the first time he'd had quick, hot sex. It was not the first time he'd had sex in the hidden heart of a public place.

Both could be exciting.

The truth was, sex was always exciting. But this, what had just happened... He'd never experienced anything like it.

He didn't even know this woman's name.

He hadn't used a condom.

Madre del dio, was he losing his mind?

And then she sighed. Her breath tickled his throat. She lifted her head and looked at him, her eyes filled with uncertainty, her mouth gently swollen from his kisses, and Nicolo forgot everything but the soft, sweet feel of her mouth, her arms, her thighs.

"I don't—I don't know what happened." Her voice was shaky, her face white except for two spots of color high on her cheeks. "I never—God, I never—"

"No. Nor have I."

She started to speak again and he knew what she would say, that this was wrong, that he had to let her go.

He knew of only one way to keep her from saying those words.

He kissed her.

Gently at first but then—then, the fierce wave of desire swept over him. And over her. He felt her swift intake of breath, the whispered plea against his lips, and suddenly he was deep inside her again, rocking against her, swallowing her cries, coming when she came and knowing that it still wasn't enough, that he needed more....

Someone pounded on the locked door.

The woman in his arms blanched.

"It's all right," he whispered, but she shook her head.

"No. Someone's outside. They'll see—"

He brushed his lips over hers. Then he set her on her feet and did what needed to be done to make himself presentable. She did the same, but he saw that her hands were shaking.

"*Cara.* Don't be—"

"Hey, you gonna be in there all night?"

Nicolo looked down into the face of the woman he'd just made love to. "It's time we introduced ourselves," he said softly. "My name is—"

She put her palm over his mouth. "No. No names. This was—it was only a dream."

He caught her hand, pressed his lips to it, then closed her fingers over the kiss.

"A dream. *Si.* And there is no need for the dream to end so soon."

"No. I can't. I—"

"We can," he said fiercely. "We can do anything, if this is a dream."

She shook her head but he drew her into his arms and kissed her, telling her without words how it could be between them, how it would be when they had all the time and privacy they needed.

Her lips softened. Clung to his. She sighed, and he cupped her face with his hands.

"Come with me," he whispered.

She shook her head again; he kissed her again.

"Is there another man?"

"No," she said quickly. "But—"

"We're adults, *cara*. Both of us are free. Come with me. Be with me tonight."

He kissed her and the world spun around them. Then he lifted his head and looked down into her eyes.

"Yes," she said softly.

Nicolo felt his heart soar. He encircled her waist with his arm, drew her against him, led her to the door and unlocked it.

A man was waiting outside.

"It's about time. I mean, how long did you…" His gaze fell on Aimee and he raised his eyebrows. "Oh. I get it. Hey, no problem. I had a babe like this with me, I'd—"

"Watch your mouth," Nicolo said, his voice cold and flat.

The man's face went pale. He stepped out of their way. And Aimee thought, *What am I doing?*

She'd just had sex with a stranger. A stranger she knew nothing about, except that he could be hard and cold and terrifying….

Her nameless lover drew her close. "Don't think," he said, as if he'd read her mind. "Not tonight."

She looked up at him, into those blue eyes that could go from winter ice to summer sun. Remembered the feel of his hands on her. The feel of him in her, and let the last vestige of sanity slip away.

There was a taxi at the curb. It took them uptown, to a hotel on the park.

He had a suite. It was huge. Luxurious.

Was money a good character reference? she thought, and would have laughed but he was taking her into his arms, slipping the straps of her dress from her shoulders. Cupping her breasts, tasting them, ohgod,ohgod,ohgod…

The hours after that were a blur of excitement. Of whispers and sighs and explorations. Aimee lost herself in a sea of sensation....

And shot awake in the gray hours before dawn, suddenly aware that she was wrapped in the embrace of a man she didn't know.

A hot tide of shame engulfed her.

Trembling, she disentangled herself from the possessive curve of his arm. Dressed in the dark, slipped from the sumptuous suite and sneaked down the service staircase because the thought of facing the elevator operator made her feel ill.

Moments later, Nicolo came awake and reached for his lover.

The bed, the sitting room, the bathroom were empty.

He cursed, pulled on trousers and shirt, hurried out into the corridor, but she was gone. He rang for the elevator. No, the operator said, he hadn't taken anyone down to the lobby.

He went to the reception desk, demanded to know if the clerk had seen a woman with honey-blond hair and violet eyes. The answer there was the same.

She had vanished.

As the sun rose over the city, Nicolo paced his rooms while he tried to figure out how in hell he would find a nameless woman in a city of eight million people.

The one certainty was that he would find her.

Nicolo Barbieri did not believe in defeat.

By Sunday evening, Nicolo had learned an ugly lesson.

A man didn't have to believe in defeat to be subjected to it.

You couldn't find a woman without a name, not even if you slipped hundred-dollar bills to the club's bouncer and all its bartenders.

They all said the same thing. Lots of women came through the doors on a Saturday night. So what if one had hair the color of honey and eyes the color of violets? That didn't mean much to them.

All right, Nicolo told himself coldly.

It didn't meant much to him, either.

A woman had let him pick her up and take her to bed. She'd probably done the same thing dozens of times before. So what if he never saw her again? All that bothered him was that she'd slipped from his arms without a word.

It didn't, *she* didn't, mean a thing.

He told himself that as he showered Monday morning. Told himself, too, all that mattered was what had brought him to New York. The meeting at SCB with James Black. The acquisition of the old man's kingdom. Nothing was as important as—

The phone rang.

Nicolo flung open the shower door and grabbed for the receiver.

The woman. It had to be.

But it wasn't. It was Black's secretary, calling to cancel the meeting. Black was indisposed. The secretary would be in touch when he was available again.

Nicolo said all the right things. Then he hung up the phone and stared blindly at the mirror over the vanity.

Was it true? Or had Black simply decided not to see him? The old man had a reputation. He liked to treat people like marionettes.

The woman with the violet eyes was the same. She seduced a man, gave him a few hours' taste of what it was like to possess her and then she slipped away.

Nicolo's hands knotted into fists.

Black would pay by selling him SCB. As for the

woman… She would pay, too. Somehow, he would find her and teach her what it meant to walk out on him.

He was as certain of that as he was of his next breath.

CHAPTER FOUR

SUMMER had finally arrived.

No more chilly wind and soaking rain. Instead the city was wrapped in soft breezes and warm sunshine.

The weather was so spectacular that even New Yorkers smiled at each other.

Aimee didn't notice.

Memories of what she'd done, that she'd gone to bed with a stranger, haunted her, intruded when she least expected.

Walking down the street, she'd turn a corner and see a tall, broad-shouldered man with dark hair and her heart would skip a beat.

Or she'd be in bed, asleep, and suddenly he'd materialize in her dreams.

She'd see his beautiful, hard face. His powerful body. And he'd touch her, kiss her, do things to her no one had ever done, make her feel things she'd never felt....

Until one night in a stranger's arms.

She tried not to think about that because it seemed so wrong. Still, in her sleep, she'd moan at his touch and awake, shaken and breathless, her skin hot, her body aching for his possession even though her conscious mind knew she despised him, despised herself....

No. It was not turning out to be a good summer, she

thought as she stepped from the shower on a balmy June morning. The man. The ugliness of what she'd done.

Then, that same weekend, her grandfather's stroke.

Her mouth tightened.

Good old Bradley had rushed to the rescue. By the time she reached the hospital, her cousin was there with two of his SCB cronies. He had a piece of paper in his hand, James's signature scrawled across it.

Something that he and his pals swore was James's signature, anyway.

"Uncle has made me his surrogate until he recovers," he'd told her with ill-concealed triumph.

Aimee tossed aside her bath towel and went to the closet.

She should have fought him. Hired an attorney. But she'd felt such despair that Sunday, such self-loathing, that fighting Bradley was the last thing she'd wanted to do.

Bradley settled into James's office and immediately began making decisions that left her reeling, but there was nothing she could do. He was in charge until Grandfather recovered. She'd thought of going directly to James, but she had no way of knowing what condition he was in. He was in seclusion at his home, surrounded by doctors, nurses and therapists, and supposedly had left strict orders that he did not want to see visitors.

Hands tied, Aimee had only been able to wait. And wonder.

Yesterday, the waiting had ended.

James's secretary—Bradley's secretary, now—had phoned and told her she was expected at Stafford-Coleridge-Black promptly at ten this morning.

"I'm sorry, Miss Black," the woman said crisply when Aimee started to ask questions. "I can't tell you anything except to assure you that you'll have all the answers tomorrow."

As if she needed them, Aimee thought bitterly. She knew exactly what would happen this morning. Her cousin, seated behind James's imposing desk, would flash his oily smile and tell her he was in charge, permanently.

She'd fight him, of course, just on principle. But she'd lose. Bradley had that document and witnesses. She had nothing—certainly not the money for a protracted court battle.

Lately she didn't even have the energy.

She was tired all the time. Exhausted, really. Plagued by bouts of nausea.

Stress, she'd told herself. Over her grandfather because, despite everything, he was her blood and she loved him. Over what would become of Stafford-Coleridge-Black, because she loved it, too.

And stress over that night. What she'd done. That she'd let a stranger seduce her—

Except, he hadn't. She'd gone to him willingly. Eagerly. Making love with him was the most exciting thing she'd ever done. Sex had never been like that before. Sex would never be like that again, especially since she couldn't imagine being with another man….

Aimee blinked.

She had more important things on her mind this morning.

Yesterday, she'd finally gone to her doctor for a check-up. He'd listened to her litany of complaints, examined her, had his nurse take blood and urine samples and told her he'd have lab reports in a few days.

"Not to worry, Ms. Black," he'd said briskly. "I suspect whatever ails you is simple to deal with."

Vitamins, she'd thought. More rest.

Fewer dreams.

Still, it was hard not to worry until the lab results were in and now, on top of everything else, she had this meeting Bradley had orchestrated, undoubtedly so he could crow with triumph as he told he'd taken permanent control of the reins.

When she was dressed—cotton summer suit, low heels, light makeup—Aimee looked in the mirror. The woman looking back at her was the woman she really was. Intelligent. Educated. Competent.

She bore no resemblance to the woman in the bathroom mirror that night at the club…

No. She would not let those memories take over this morning.

Bradley was about to knife her in the back, but she'd be damned if she'd let him see her bleed.

She would show absolutely no emotion today, no matter what happened.

That was the plan, and it would have worked…except for what she found waiting for her in the Stafford-Coleridge-Black boardroom.

Grandfather, not Bradley, sat ramrod-straight in his usual chair at one end of the long mahogany conference table.

The stranger she'd gone to bed with was seated at the other.

Nicolo was not in a good mood.

He was in New York for the first time since the episode three months before and he'd found the night had tainted his feelings about the city.

Unfortunate.

He'd always enjoyed spending time in Manhattan. Now, he couldn't wait to see the last of it. And, he thought, with a not-so-discreet glance at his Tag Heuer watch as he sat waiting for the meeting in James Black's office to begin, he would be doing that soon.

Just this one last session with Black and the deal he and the old man had worked on the past two weeks, via a volley of faxes and phone calls, would be completed.

Yesterday, when they'd met face-to-face, Black told him there was just one last point to agree upon.

"Just one," he'd repeated, his voice quavering because of the stroke that had, it was said, almost killed him.

"And that is?" Nicolo had replied.

Black had wagged a bony finger. "Nothing a smart man won't be willing to accede to, Prince Barbieri, I assure you."

Nicolo had almost reminded him that he didn't use his title, but he'd decided to play along. Black obviously liked the idea that Nicolo was royalty. Why do anything to spoil the finalization of the deal?

Not that he was concerned over this last point, especially since he was sure he knew what it was. They'd agreed on a price. On a takeover date. What could be left to discuss?

Only Black's repeated concern that the company his ancestors had founded not lose its identity among Nicolo's holdings.

The old man, he was sure, was going to want some sort of guarantee, and Nicolo had come up with one.

He would keep the bank's name, Stafford-Coleridge-Black, intact.

In fact, he'd almost said so yesterday in hopes of avoiding this morning's meeting, but he suspected that giving in without at least a small battle would only make Black ask for something more.

So he'd agreed to today's meeting, which had meant spending another night in the city.

Another night plagued by memories of how he'd let a woman make a fool of him.

Dio, how ridiculous he was! He'd had a night of sex—the best sex of his life, and that was saying a great deal. A night of fantastic sex, with no morning-after to deal with. No female batting her lashes over coffee, telling him how wonderful he was, asking when she would see him again.

Ask half a dozen men what was wrong with that scenario and they'd laugh and say there wasn't a thing wrong with it.

Mind-blowing sex. No names. No commitment. A man's fantasy.

Then why was it driving him insane, that she'd left his bed while he slept? Why should it bother him?

He still winced when he recalled how he'd gone searching for her in the hall. Made a fool of himself with the elevator operator, the night clerk. Taken a cab to that damned club and demanded answers.

Embarrassing? A little…

Hell. A lot.

A woman should not be the one who walked out of a relationship. Even if that "relationship" only lasted a few hours. Yes, he knew all about the Age of Equality but a woman had never walked out on him, not under any circumstances.

This one had, and he didn't like it.

That was why she was in his head, even now. Even when he was about to complete a deal he'd worked on, dreamed of, for years. Instead of concentrating on it, he was thinking about a woman who—

"Prince Barbieri?"

Who should consider herself fortunate he'd had no way to locate her because if he had—

"Prince Barbieri. Sir? If you please—"

"*Si,*" Nicolo said, and cleared his throat. "Are you ready to begin? I was, ah, I was just reading through my notes, and—"

And, he looked up.

The world tilted.

The woman with the violet eyes was standing in the doorway staring at him just as he was staring at her, as if one of them was an apparition.

He saw the color drain from her face. Saw her mouth drop open. Saw the swift rise and fall of her breasts beneath the jacket of a demure blue suit.

"Demure" was the word for her, all right. Whoever she was, whatever she was doing here, today she was playing the part of a virgin.

A muscle knotted in Nicolo's jaw.

He shoved back his chair. Rose to his feet, his eyes never leaving her. She took a quick step back. Her lips formed a silent plea.

No!

He forgot everything. The boardroom. The old man. The deal he'd worked so long to finalize.

"Yes," he said grimly. "Oh, most definitely yes, *cara!*"

She shook her head. Stumbled back another step…

"Do you two know each other?" Black asked.

Nicolo swung his head toward the old man. "What?"

"I said, have you met my granddaughter before, Your Highness?"

Nicolo, a man who had glibly talked his way into the presence of captains of industry and heads of nations during his determined rise to the top, opened his mouth, then shut it again.

Black's granddaughter? This—this creature who would sleep with a stranger and then disappear into the night was his granddaughter?

Yes. Of course. A spoiled rich brat, accustomed to playing a seductive nymph by night and a sweet virgin by day. He'd seen lots of women like this. The rich seemed to specialize in breeding them.

"Grandfather." Her voice shook but Nicolo had to give her credit for recovering fast. "I—I didn't realize you were busy. I'll come back later. This afternoon. Or tomorrow. Or—"

"Prince Barbieri? Please, sit down. You, too, Aimee. This meeting very much concerns you."

Her stricken gaze swept from the old man to Nicolo.

Nicolo narrowed his eyes. What the hell was going on here? The temptation to tell Black he would not talk business in front of the woman was strong, but he suspected Black would not back down. He wanted her here, but why?

Nicolo had no choice but to learn why.

"What a pleasant surprise," he said, his tone silken, "Miss… Is it Miss Black?"

She nodded. "That's—that's correct."

"Ah. In that case, please, join us."

The look she gave him told him she'd regained her composure.

"My grandfather's already asked me to stay. I don't need your invitation."

"Aimee!"

"No. That's all right, Signore Black." Nicolo drew his lips back in a cold smile. "Your granddaughter is right. These are your offices, not mine."

"But not for long," the old man said.

Aimee looked at him. "What does that mean?"

"Sit down, Aimee, and you'll find out."

Nicolo pulled out the chair beside his. "An excellent suggestion, Miss Black." His voice hardened. "Sit down."

He saw her throat move as she swallowed. Then she raised her chin, ignored him and took the seat to the right of her grandfather. Nicolo sat down, too, and Black cleared his throat.

"Well," he said briskly, "you haven't answered my question. Do you know each other?"

"We—we might have met before," Aimee said.

"Have we?" Nicolo flashed another icy smile. "Perhaps your memory is better than mine. After all, if we'd met, we'd know each other's names, wouldn't we?"

Color painted crimson patches on her cheeks but when she spoke, her tone was cool.

"I really don't see that it matters." She turned to her grandfather. "Who is this man? And why is he here?"

Black folded his gnarled hands on the highly polished wood before him.

"Aimee, this is Nicolo Barbieri. Prince Nicolo Barbieri, of Rome."

Her expression showed how little impressed she was by his title.

"I suppose you expected to find Bradley." Black glanced at Nicolo. "My nephew and Aimee's cousin."

Aimee didn't answer. She was stunned by the presence of the stranger she'd slept with. Why was he here? And what was he going to say about that night?

"Aren't you curious as to why Bradley isn't present, Aimee?"

A good question. Bradley would never miss the chance to see her reaction as control of SCB was placed permanently in his hands.

Aimee sat up straight. Finding this—this man here had driven logical thought out of her head and she could not let that happen, not if there was the slightest chance of talking sense to her grandfather.

"I am curious," she said. "Knowing Bradley, I'd assume he'd want to be here to gloat."

James chuckled. "As you can see," he told Nicolo, "my granddaughter believes in being frank." He turned his attention to Aimee. "But Bradley has nothing to gloat about. I am, as you can see, in control of things again and after examining the records of the past three months, I can see that I was wrong to put Bradley in charge."

Aimee put her hands in her lap and clenched them into fists.

"I'm glad you realize that, Grandfather."

James nodded. "It's the reason you're here today."

"Excuse me," Nicolo said with barely concealed impatience, "but I would like to be let in on what is happening here, Signore Black. What has this woman—"

"My granddaughter. My own flesh and blood."

"What has she to do with our agreement?"

"What agreement?" Aimee said, looking from her grandfather to Nicolo.

"Aimee believes she should take over as head of Stafford-Coleridge-Black, Prince Barbieri."

Nicolo's mouth twitched. A woman, *this* woman, in charge of a private bank worth billions? He would have laughed, but the old man's expression was serious.

At least now he understood why Aimee Black was in the room. Her grandfather wanted her present for the announcement of his decision to sell the bank to Nicolo. Was it because he thought she'd take the news better than hearing it another way? Was it because Black thought, as he did, that her hope to head SCB was laughable?

Nicolo didn't give a damn.

For weeks, he'd imagined all the ways in which he could get even with this woman but what was about to happen was better than anything he'd considered. Her shock when she learned that he, of all people, was going to get what she so obviously—so foolishly—wanted, was more than he could have hoped for.

Sometimes, he thought, sitting back in his chair, sometimes, a man got very, very lucky.

"My granddaughter worked here summers for many years."

"How nice," Nicolo purred.

"She studied finance, economics and business."

Nicolo tried to look impressed. Amazing, what they taught rich girls in boarding school these days.

"She knows how I felt about keeping SCB in the family."

Nicolo nodded. "Unfortunately," he said politely, "fate did not cooperate."

"No. Not until now."

Nicolo frowned. Even a prince could smell a rat when it got close enough. "I'm afraid I don't understand, Signore Black."

James looked at Aimee. "How badly do you want to keep Stafford-Coleridge-Black in our family?" he said softly.

Aimee's heart began to race. "You know the answer to that, Grandfather."

"Now, just a moment, Black." Nicolo sat forward, his eyes narrowed and fixed on the old man's face. "We have a deal."

"What deal?" Aimee said.

"We have a tentative agreement, Prince Barbieri. Subject, as you know, to the outcome of this meeting."

"I do not like being hustled," Nicolo said sharply.

"Hustled?"

"Hustled. Played for a fool. Pushed for more money."

"This is not about money, Your Highness."

"*Dio,* will you stop calling me that? Call me by my last name. My first name. Just stop with the nonsense." Nicolo slapped his hand on the table. "Damn it, just tell me what you want."

James took a long breath.

"I want this institution to be in the hands of someone

with experience. Someone with a record of achievement that I can trust."

"That someone is me," Nicolo said coldly, "and we both know it."

"I also want it to be the legacy I leave to future generations of Blacks. Call it pride, call it what you will, Barbieri, but I don't wish to see two hundred years disappear."

"I understand." Nicolo took a breath, too. For a couple of minutes, he'd thought the old man was trying to tell him the sale was off. Impossible, of course. Black was not a sentimentalist. He would never leave the bank in the hands of an irresponsible female. "And that is why I'm sure what I say next will please you, *signore.* I've decided to retain the name of the bank. It will be known as Stafford-Coleridge-Black, just as it has for generations."

Aimee snorted. Nicolo shot her a warning look.

"Do you find this amusing, *signorina?*"

"I find it arrogant, *signore.* Can you actually believe my grandfather is naïve enough to think you've decided to keep a name that's worth its weight in gold in financial circles as an act of kindness?"

Nicolo gave her a long, cold look. Then he turned to James.

"With all due respect," he said, in a tone that made it clear the words were a polite lie, "I will not continue this meeting with your granddaughter present."

"With all due respect," Aimee snapped, "*you* are the outsider here, Prince Barbieri."

"You know nothing about this."

"I know everything about it."

Nicolo's mouth thinned. "What you know," he said slowly, "has nothing to do with boardrooms or corporations or responsibility. The only person here who does not know that is your grandfather."

Aimee sprang to her feet. "You—you no good, insolent son of a—"

"Stop it!" James's voice was sharp. "Aimee. You are to show the prince respect."

"Respect? If you knew—if you only knew what this man is really like. If you knew the truth about him—"

"Tell him," Nicolo said softly. "Go on, Miss Black. Why not explain things to your grandfather?"

Aimee stared at him, eyes glittering with angry tears, lips pouting with suppressed rage, breasts rising and falling with each breath.

It made him remember how she had looked that night, in his arms.

In his bed.

With a swiftness that stunned him, he felt his body harden.

"Why is he here?" she said, her voice rising. "I demand to know the reason!"

James Black looked from his granddaughter to the one man he was certain could guide the company he loved through the twenty-first century. Bradley couldn't do it. Aimee had tried to make him see that, and she'd been right. In the short time the boy had been at the helm, the company had lost clients and come close to taking dangerous changes of direction.

That left only one other Black to head the bank.

Aimee.

In the endless weeks of his recuperation, James had finally reviewed the proposals she'd made and he'd ignored. They were, he'd been forced to admit, good.

Excellent, actually.

And Aimee was of his blood.

But she was also a woman. A young woman. Even if he managed to convince himself that her sex was not a drawback, her inexperience was.

How could he entrust her with the responsibility handed down by generations of Staffords, Coleridges and Blacks?

He'd put thoughts of Aimee aside. Concentrated on Nicolo Barbieri. The man had the intelligence, the courage, the experience to move SCB forward.

If only he carried the right blood, James had thought...

And the solution had come to him.

Barbieri was young. Thirty, thirty-two. Something like that. Aimee was in her midtwenties.

Once upon a time, nations had forged bonds through marriage. So had powerful institutions. Men and women had been joined in matrimony so they could produce children who carried the proud ancestry of both.

"Grandfather, I want an answer. Why is Nicolo Barbieri here?"

Black looked at the Italian prince, then at his headstrong American granddaughter.

"He is here," he said calmly, "to make you his wife."

CHAPTER FIVE

FOR A MOMENT, no one spoke. No one moved. Even the dust motes hovered in the silence.

Then Aimee collapsed into her chair and made a choked sound. Was she laughing? One glance at her and Nicolo knew she wasn't. She looked the way he felt, as if an elephant had suddenly appeared in their midst.

"A bad joke, Grandfather. Now tell me the real reason."

"That is the real reason." James was unsmiling as he met her eyes. "You have some good ideas, Aimee, but you're too inexperienced to run SCB."

"I'm fully capable of running SCB. And in the event I needed advice, I'd turn to you."

"If I could rely on lasting long enough to do that," her grandfather said bluntly, "I wouldn't be handing my company to someone else."

"I'm not someone else. I'm your granddaughter!"

"You need guidance, Aimee." The old man paused. "And you need a husband. A woman's function is to marry and bear children."

Fascinated, not yet believing what was happening, Nicolo sat back and became a silent observer.

"You're a century behind the times, Grandfather."

"So it would seem. Which is why I'm willing to see

you as second-in-command to a man capable of running my company."

"Second-in-command?" Aimee's voice rose. "Do you actually think I'd agree to such an arrangement?"

"Stafford-Coleridge-Black needs strong, proven leadership. It also needs, as you have pointed out many times, new blood. His Highness can provide both those things." Black fixed her with an autocratic eye. "He can also provide our bank with a new generation of leaders."

A flush rose in her cheeks. "You speak as if—as if I'm a broodmare!"

"I speak sense, child," Black said, somewhat more gently. "You know I do. This is the perfect solution to everything."

A muscle knotted in Nicolo's jaw as silence fell over the room again. The offhand comment about providing the bank with a new generation was, perhaps, the most infuriating of all the infuriating things the old man had said.

If he took Aimee Black to bed, breeding a future generation of bankers would not be the reason.

What about the night you spent with her, Nicolo? A man who doesn't use a condom is a man flirting with fatherhood.

A knot formed in his belly. He'd never done such a foolhardy thing before, forgotten protection in the rush to take a woman, but then, he'd never done anything as crazy as making love to a stranger, either.

He looked at Aimee.

Nothing to worry about, he thought coldly. A woman who slept with a nameless man would be using protection of her own. She looked innocent now, in that demure outfit, tears glittering in her eyes, but it was all an act.

An act, he thought, and felt anger overtake surprise. What a pair they were, the old man and his granddaughter.

Did they really take him for such an easy mark?

Perhaps it was time to remind them of who he was.

"Excuse me," he said, his voice dangerously soft, "but perhaps I might say a word… Or would that spoil this rather amusing little scene?"

"Your Highness." James Black cleared his throat. "Maybe I should have mentioned this to you during an earlier meeting, but—"

"Indeed, *signore.* Maybe you should have."

"I considered it, but—"

"But, you were afraid I'd laugh in your face."

"I admit, I thought it possible you might see my idea as…unpalatable."

The woman gave a soft moan, as if she'd only just remembered his presence. Nicely timed, Nicolo thought, and decided the game had gone on long enough.

"There is more than that possibility," he said coldly, as he pushed back his chair. "There is that certainty."

"Your Highness—"

"Yes," Nicolo said through clenched teeth, "that is who I am. I am Prince Nicolo Antonius Barbieri, of a lineage much older and far more honorable than yours, and you would do well to remember it."

Had he really said that? *Dio,* he had. And his speech was going from lightly accented to the way it had been when he'd first come to this country to attend university, thirteen years ago.

It was a measure of his rage, and rage was not a good thing. A man could only succeed when his emotions were under control.

Nicolo stood and wrapped his hands tightly around the top rung of his chair.

"You were right, Signore Black. I would have brought this bank the leadership it needs. And, someday, I will surely produce the sons who will succeed me." He flashed a look at Aimee, whose cheeks were crimson.

Good, he thought with savage pleasure. It was a joy to see her humiliated.

"But I will do that with a woman of my choosing, who brings pride to my name and not dishonor."

Aimee's chair fell back as she scrambled to her feet and rounded the table to face him, head high, lips drawn back in a snarl.

"You—you no good, dissolute son of a bitch!"

"*I* am dissolute?" Nicolo let go of the chair and pounded his fist on the table. So much for self-control. "No, Miss Black. I hardly think it's *I* who should bear that label."

"You think, because you're a man, you can keep to a different level of morality? Let me tell you something, Prince Whoever You Are—"

"Do not think to lecture *me* about morals, Miss Black. Not unless you want me to tell your grandfather about the night we spent together." He paused, and his mouth twisted. "Or does he already know the salient details?"

All the color drained from her face. "What?"

"Your grandfather gives as good a performance as you. Not quite as enjoyable as the one you gave this spring, but still more than acceptable."

James looked from one of them to the other. "I'm afraid I don't understand."

"Of course you understand." Nicolo gathered his papers together and stuffed them into his briefcase. "I am Italian. My people go back to the time of Caesar. My bloodlines flow with conspiracy."

"What conspiracy?" Black sputtered.

"Which of you planned this?" A smile slashed across his face. "No matter. It comes to the same thing—though

I admit, I choose to believe the added touch of seduction was the lady's idea."

"Don't," Aimee said, reaching out her hand. "I beg you. Don't say anymore."

"She and I would meet, seemingly by accident. I would find her coldness enticing."

"Aimee? What is he talking about?"

"Then the sex. Incredible sex, but then, nothing less would do. And the coup de grâce. The disappearing act and the hope that I'd want more of what I had that night, enough so that when I learned the identity of my seductress, this little melodrama could be played for its full impact." He looked at Aimee. "That was a nice touch, by the way, that 'I'd never marry this man' routine. My compliments. If I hadn't known better, I'd have believed it."

Her eyes, the color of pansies in the rain, pleaded with him to stop.

For one brief moment, he remembered how terrified she'd been when he followed her into the bathroom at Lucas's club. How worried that someone would see them.

And he remembered what he had not permitted himself to remember until now, the way she'd trembled when he took her to his bed, the way she'd looked up at him when he made love to her, really made love to her, kissing her slowly, savoring her taste, taking all the time in the world to caress her and stroke her and, at last, enter her, how her face, her whispers, her caresses had told him that what she was feeling, what he was making her feel, was new and incredible and had never happened to her before.

Liar, Nicolo thought, and anger became rage so fierce it slammed into him like a fist.

"Wasted effort," he said roughly. "You understand, Black? I'm not interested in you or your bank or your slut of a granddaughter."

Aimee whipped her hand through the air and slammed it against his jaw. Nicolo grabbed her wrist and put enough pressure on it to make her yelp.

"Don't," he said, his voice soft with malice. "Do you hear me? Don't do anything you will regret."

"I couldn't regret anything more than being with you that horrid night!"

She was shaking now, her eyes glistening with hatred for him. That was fine. Let her hate him. God knew, he hated her and the despicable old man who sat watching them.

James Black was sick, all right, but it had nothing to do with his stroke. His sickness was moral depravity.

The old man loved his damnable bank more than his granddaughter, who he'd sent to seduce him.

The night had been a travesty of passion. All of it. The deep kisses. The sighs. The way she'd framed his face with her hands and brought his mouth to hers while her dark-gold hair spread in abandon over his pillow.

Cursing, Nicolo reached for her now, dragged her to her toes and crushed her mouth beneath his. She cried out and it only made him more furious, hearing the cry, remembering how differently she had cried out in his arms that night.

The old man said something in a sharp voice. Nicolo ignored him. He went on kissing Aimee Black until her cry became a moan, until her mouth softened and clung to his.

Then he flung her from him, grabbed his briefcase and strode from the room.

Amazing, what an hour in a quiet place could do for a man's disposition.

An hour—and three bourbons, straight up.

Nicolo looked at the half inch of amber liquid that remained in his glass, sighed and pushed it away.

He was much calmer. Still furious at the Blacks and the ugly game he'd been dragged into, but at least he had regained his equilibrium.

What he needed now was coffee, perhaps a bite to eat. Then he'd go to his hotel, phone his pilot, have him ready the Learjet.

A few hours, and he'd be home.

Goodbye, New York. Goodbye, James Black. Goodbye, acquisition of Stafford-Coleridge-Black.

He could live without all of them. The city, the crazy old man, the bank.

There were other private banks in the United States, maybe not quite as suitable for his purposes, but they would do. He still had the short-list from which he'd ultimately chosen SCB. As soon as he returned to Rome, he'd tell his people to begin researching them in depth all over again.

It wasn't as if he'd fixated on this one financial institution....

As if he'd fixated on this one beautiful woman.

A lying, scheming, bitch of an immoral woman.

And, damn it, he didn't know why what had happened should have made him react with such rage.

The bartender caught his eye. Did he want another drink? Nicolo shook his head, then mouthed the word, *coffee.* The guy nodded.

He'd been around long enough to know that the days of the old robber barons were not over. Scandals in the world of high finance erupted as frequently as squalls over the Mediterranean. Seemingly intelligent men did amazingly stupid things to advance their own interests.

James Black was no different.

Neither was his granddaughter, who had been willing to sleep with a stranger to whet his appetite for a dynastic merger.

"Your coffee, sir."

Nicolo looked up. *"Grazie."*

"Will there be anything else?"

"Si." What was with all this Italian? When in Rome… or, in this case, New York… "Yes," he said. "A sandwich."

"What kind would you like?"

"Anything. Roast beef is fine." He smiled. "Something to keep the bourbon company, *si?"*

More Italian, he thought as the bartender moved off. A clear sign he was still distressed, though surely not anywhere near as much as before. The whiskey, now some much-needed logic, were working their magic.

The simple fact was that Black was a man who would do whatever was necessary to get what he wanted.

So would his granddaughter.

Nicolo drank some coffee.

And, really, how different did that make her from some other women he'd known? Women who dressed in a way meant to gain a man's interest. Who went to bed with a man and performed whatever tricks they imagined might win them points. Who lied to a man's face, promised love and devotion forever, all in hopes of landing a suitable husband.

Of all the women he'd known, Aimee Black was the last woman in the world he would ever consider marrying. Her morals were lacking and it wasn't because she'd slept with him that night.

It was because she'd done it as part of an act.

Nicolo took another mouthful of coffee.

Maybe his ego demanded it. Maybe his male pride required it. Whatever the reason, he'd wanted to believe that the woman with the violet eyes had felt the same uncontrollable hunger he had felt. That she could no more have kept from making love with him than she could have stopped breathing.

That what had happened that night was the most exciting memory of her life, and that they had created that memory with equal passion and desire.

He could see her now, that night in his bed. Eyes dark with pleasure. Skin fragrant with her need...

"Your sandwich, sir."

Nicolo blinked. Had he ordered a sandwich?

"Would you like anything else? More coffee?"

Nicolo pushed the plate aside, rose to his feet and dropped a hundred-dollar bill on the table.

"No," he said brusquely, and added what he hoped was a polite smile and a hurried, *"Grazie."*

It wasn't the bartender's fault that what he wanted, what he damned well would not be denied, could not be found in this bar.

Aimee sat slumped on the sofa in her apartment, face buried in her hands.

Her anger was gone, replaced by a terrible emptiness in her heart.

"Let me explain," Grandfather had said.

Explain what? That he'd been willing to sell her to a foreigner to get what he wanted for his precious bank?

She'd fled his office, ignored his voice calling after her, stumbled into a taxi and gone home.

She'd never harbored any illusions about her grandfather's feelings for her. His lack of feelings, she amended, with a bitter smile. She'd accepted it.

What other choice did she have?

He'd taken her in after she'd lost her parents. He'd

raised her, or maybe it was more accurate to say he'd paid a series of nannies and housekeepers to raise her. He'd sent her to the best schools; he'd seen to it she had tennis and skiing and riding lessons, all the things his fortune could buy.

But he'd never really loved her.

What he loved was his bank and the dead Staffords, Coleridges and Blacks who'd founded it. Everything else, including her, was secondary.

Even so, she'd never dreamed him capable of such a cold-blooded scheme. That he'd want to marry her off to a stranger....

Except, Nicolo Barbieri—Prince Barbieri—was not a stranger. He was the man she'd made love with endless times in a few short hours.

How could she have done that? Climaxed in his arms when she hadn't even known his name?

Nausea roiled in her belly. Aimee clamped her hand to her mouth, raced to the bathroom and reached it just in time. A couple of moments later, pale and shaken, she flushed the commode and sank down on the closed seat.

God, she felt awful. She was tired of throwing up, tired of just plain feeling tired.

This time, at least she had a reason for feeling so rotten. Who wouldn't, after today?

That son of a bitch. Prince Barbieri. Prince of Darkness, was more like it. To call her a—a—

She couldn't even think the word.

How could he believe she'd deliberately seduced him? Offered herself as bait for her grandfather's vile proposition?

She'd slept with Nicolo Barbieri because—because she'd been upset. Anxious. Stressed.

Aimee groaned and put her face in her hands again.

She'd slept with him because she'd wanted to. Because he was the most exciting man she'd ever seen and because she'd fantasized about him all that afternoon.

That was why she'd refused to exchange names.

To make what had happened real would have meant despising herself for what she'd let him do....

And ever since that night, she'd wanted him to do it all again.

No wonder he'd looked at her with such loathing today. She loathed herself. But to believe she'd deliberately—

The ringing of the phone made her jump.

She didn't want to talk to anybody. Especially her grandfather and that was probably him calling. He was furious at her. She'd walked out of his office without a word, ignored his demand that she come back.

Let the answering machine deal with him. She wasn't going to.

Another ring. Then the machine picked up.

Hi. You've reached 555-6145. Please leave a message after the tone.

"Ms. Black, this is Dr. Glassman's office. Your test results are in. Please call our office between the hours of eight and—"

She ran for the phone, snatched it up. "I'm here! I mean, this is Ms. Black."

"Ms. Black? Please hold for the doctor."

Aimee held, imagining the worst. Why not, on a day like this? A brain tumor. A rare blood malady. Or—her breath caught at how stupid she was not to have thought of it sooner.

Or an illness of the kind people got these days, from having unprotected sex.

No. Not that.

Whatever else he was, she could not imagine the Prince of Darkness having that kind of disease.

"Ms. Black? Dr. Glassman here…"

Aimee listened. And listened. Then she put down the phone and stared blankly at the wall.

She'd thought right.

Nicolo Barbieri hadn't give her a disease.

He'd given her a baby.

She sat motionless for hours, wrapped in her robe, oblivious to the passage of time.

What to do? What to do?

She was single. Unemployed. Living on temporary jobs because she refused to let her grandfather support her.

No money, no prospects, this small apartment in a not-very-good neighborhood….

This time, it wasn't the phone that beat shrilly against the silence, it was the doorbell.

Aimee ignored it. Whoever it was would go away. The UPS man with a package, the super to drill a peephole in the door, something she'd been requesting for months.

The bell rang again. And again. Whoever was out there was persistent.

Aimee sighed, rose to her feet and went to the door. She undid the locks. The chain. Cracked the door an inch….

And felt the blood drain from her head.

"No," she said. "No—"

"Yes," Nicolo growled, and just as he had that fateful night, he put his shoulder to the door and forced it open.

CHAPTER SIX

THEY SAID TIME defused anger.

The hell it did.

In the thirty or forty minutes Nicolo had spent looking up Aimee Black in the telephone directory, then taking a taxi all the way downtown, through the tangled snarl of midmorning traffic, his anger didn't cool one bit.

If anything, it changed to something so hot and fierce he could damned near feel it inside him.

It was bad enough she'd been part of the ugly scam her grandfather had designed. If the actual seduction wasn't part of it, at least the come-on was.

What was worse was that she'd kept lying to him, not only that night but again this morning.

She had intended to entice him. He was certain of that. Now, she'd lied about what she'd felt in his arms. She hadn't intended to get caught up in her own game, but she had.

He was certain of it.

He knew women. The little things they did when they wanted to boost a man's ego. The things they did when their passion was real.

What Aimee felt had been real.

The throaty little moans. The soft cries. The lift of her

hips to his. Real. All of it. So real, he knew he'd never forget anything they had done together.

And he was damned well going to force her to admit it. She might have come on to him deliberately but after the first few minutes in his arms, everything had changed.

Aimee had followed where he led, all the way to ecstasy.

Dio, just thinking about it was making him hard, and if that wasn't ridiculous, he didn't know what was. He was a man who had his pick of women and even the occasional ones who started by pretending his touch drove them crazy soon forgot to pretend.

There were half a dozen women waiting for his return to Rome. One phone call, he'd have whichever of them he wanted ready to welcome him into her bed.

But he would be less a man if he didn't end this in a way that made it clear who was the victor, not just by walking out on the deal James Black had engineered but by forcing the old man's accomplice-in-crime to admit that what she'd felt in his arms had been real.

It was the penalty she'd pay for her duplicity.

Nobody lied to Nicolo Barbieri and got away with it, especially not a woman who had haunted his days and nights for three entire months.

The cab pulled up in front of a tired-looking, five-story tenement. James Black's granddaughter, Saturday night's party girl, lived here?

Maybe he had the address wrong.

There was only one way to find out.

Nicolo handed the cabbie a bill and told him to wait. Then he climbed the grimy steps to the front door. An unlocked front door.

Not a good idea in a neighborhood like this, but how Aimee lived was not his problem.

The door opened on a small vestibule, thick with the

faint but unmistakable odor of beer and other, less palatable things. The only signs of life were the mailboxes set into a stained gray wall.

Nicolo scanned the nameplates. A. Black lived in apartment 5C.

The door that opened into the house itself had no lock, either. None that was usable, anyway. Ahead, a dimly lit staircase with time-worn treads rose into the gloom.

Nicolo started up.

By the time he reached the fifth floor and apartment 5C, he was almost hoping he'd come to the wrong place. This was the kind of building that epitomized the things people tried to avoid when they lived in Manhattan.

So what? he told himself again. How Black's granddaughter lived was her affair.

He hesitated. Had coming here actually been a good idea? What would he gain by forcing her to admit she'd enjoyed what they'd done together? Was his ego that fragile, that it needed affirmation from a woman like this?

Before he could change his mind, Nicolo pressed the bell button.

Nobody answered.

He rang again. And then again. Okay. He'd come here, she wasn't home. That is, she wasn't home if he even had the correct address, which he doubted...

The door swung open. Not far, just a couple of inches, but enough for him to see the woman who'd opened it.

Aimee.

She stared at him. Her eyes widened. "No," she whispered, "no…"

What would come next was in those wide eyes. Besides, they had done this dance before.

She started to slam the door but Nicolo was too quick. She cried out and fell back as he put his shoulder to the door and forced it open. A second later, he was inside a tiny foyer.

Aimee was pressed against the wall, looking up at him with fear in her eyes.

He felt a tightening in his gut.

She hadn't been afraid of him that night... But this wasn't that night. It was good that she was afraid. Hell, it was what he wanted. When he was done with her...

"No," she said again, her voice high and thin.

Her eyes rolled up. She collapsed as if she were a marionette and someone had cut her strings.

Nicolo caught her before she crumpled to the floor. It was an automatic move but he knew damned well the faint was simply another outstanding performance....

Merda. His heart skipped a beat. It was not an act. She was limp in his arms.

He looked around frantically, saw a small sofa and carried her to it. "Ms. Black. Aimee. Can you hear me?"

Stupido! Of course she couldn't hear him. She was unconscious. What did you do for an unconscious woman?

Cold compresses. And spirits of—of what? Ammonia? Who in hell had spirits of ammonia lying around in this day and age?

A doorway opened onto a kitchen. Nicolo hurried inside, grabbed a towel from the sink, stuffed it with ice cubes from the fridge's freezer tray and ran back into the living room.

Aimee lay as he'd left her, small and unmoving, her pulse beat visible in her slender throat.

"Aimee," he said softly.

She didn't respond. Nicolo knelt beside her. Slipped his arm around her shoulders and lifted her to him.

"Aimee," he said again, and gently placed the ice pack against her forehead.

After a moment, she groaned.

"That's it, *cara*. Come on. Look at me. Open your eyes and look at me."

Her lashes fluttered but her lids stayed down. Nicolo drew her closer. Held her against him, eased her silky curls from the back of her neck and ran the ice pack lightly over the nape.

She moaned softly, her breath warm against his throat.

He closed his eyes.

He had forgotten what it was like to hold her. The delicacy of her bones. The floral scent of her hair. The un-blemished softness of her skin.

His arms tightened around her. "Aimee," he whispered.

Suddenly he held a wildcat in his arms. She pulled back, curled her hands into fists and pounded them against his shoulders.

"Get away from me!"

"Aimee! Stop it!"

"What are you doing here?" Her voice shook. "Get out. Do you hear me? Get out!"

Nicolo grabbed her wrists in one hand. "Damn it, you fainted! Would you rather I'd left you lying on the floor?"

"I'd rather never see your face again!"

His mouth thinned. He let go of her and rose to his feet.

"My sentiments, exactly, Ms. Black. Where is your telephone?"

"What do you want with the telephone?"

"I'm going to phone for an ambulance. Then it will be my pleasure to walk out that door and not look back."

"No!" Aimee sat up quickly. Too quickly; the room seemed to give a sickening lurch and the all-too-familiar nausea sent a rush of bile up her throat. "I don't—I don't need an—"

"*Dio,* look at you! You're white as a ghost."

"I am fine," she said carefully, as she rose to her feet.

The room tilted again. She took a deep breath, then slowly let it out. "Thank you for your help, Prince Barbieri. Now, get the hell out of my apartment."

"Not until I know you're all right."

"Why would you give a damn?"

"Why? Well, let's see. I rang the bell. You opened the door, saw me and did an excellent imitation of a Victorian swoon." His smile was lupine and all teeth. "I'm sure you'll forgive me if I tell you I can envision a scenario in which you end up accusing me of somehow causing that swoon."

He meant it as an insult, she knew, but Aimee could only think how close to the truth he'd come.

"I just thanked you for your help, didn't I?"

"You're a superb liar," Nicolo said coldly. "Or did you think I'd forget that?"

"We've been all through this."

"Yes. We have. And you lied." His eyes narrowed as they met hers. "You told your grandfather I seduced you when we both know that what happened in that club, and in my hotel room, was by mutual consent."

Aimee stared up at him. His face might have been the stone face of a Roman emperor, his eyes unseeing and unfeeling. It was impossible to imagine she'd slept with this man.

He was, indeed, a stranger.

"Is that why you came here? To hear me admit that I— that I let you seduce me?"

"That you let me seduce you?" Nicolo folded his arms and gave a hollow laugh. "Such clever phrasing."

Aimee's legs were like rubber. She'd never fainted before but she thought she might damned well do it again if she had to keep up a conversation with this arrogant ass who was in a snit because he believed she'd come on to him deliberately.

She could only imagine how he'd react if he knew she carried a baby.

His baby.

A choked laugh caught in her throat. Prince Nicolo Barbieri's child. He wouldn't believe it. Well, who could blame him? She could hardly believe it, either.

She couldn't be pregnant. She took the pill. She'd been taking it for a couple of years now, not to prevent getting pregnant. Why would she, considering that the last time she'd been intimate with a man before she'd slept with Nicolo Barbieri was her senior year at college?

She took it to regulate her period, but what had happened to its primary function as a contraceptive?

Accidents happen. She could almost hear the tut-tutting voice of her boarding school's sex-ed teacher. *Remember, ladies, accidents happen.*

Her legs buckled.

"Dio!" Nicolo grabbed her shoulders as she collapsed on the sofa. "That's it. You need a doctor."

"I need you to go away." Aimee struggled up against the pillows as he took his cell phone from his pocket. "What are you doing?"

"Calling for an ambulance."

"No! I don't want an ambulance. Damn you, will you just—"

"Then tell me your physician's number."

Her physician's number. The man who'd made her pregnant wanted to call the doctor who'd just told her about that pregnancy. Wild laughter rose in her throat.

"You find this amusing?"

"No. Not amusing. Just—just…"

Aimee shook her head. The only thing she wanted was to bury her face in her hands and weep. That meant getting Nicolo Barbieri out of her apartment and out of her life.

Time to ditch her stupid pride.

"You came here to hear me admit that—that what happened between us was as much my idea as yours." She paused, touched the tip of her tongue to her dry lips. "All right. I admit it. I'm equally responsible for what happened." She shuddered and drew the lapels of her robe together. "I behaved irresponsibly. But not like—like what you called me. There was no plan. No orchestration. There was just—there was just you, and me, and some kind of insanity…."

Her voice faded away but she had said enough. Nicolo had what he'd come for: her admission that she'd wanted him as much as he'd wanted her.

The rest didn't matter. He knew that now.

He no longer gave a damn whose idea the meeting had been, hers or the old man. What mattered was that once he'd kissed her, once he'd touched her, she had belonged to him.

"Please. Go away now. I—I'm tired. I want to lie down."

His brow furrowed. She was more than tired. She looked… What? Ill? Frightened?

Terrified.

Of him? That was what he'd wanted, wasn't it? That she be afraid of him? And yet—and yet, suddenly, he wanted something more. Something just out of reach….

"Aimee." Nicolo squatted beside her and took her hands in his. Her fingers were ice-cold. "*Cara.* You need a doctor."

"No." She shook her head; the lustrous honey curls shifted like strands of heavy silk around her pale face. "I don't. Really. I'm fine."

Plainly, something was wrong. She needed help. He wanted to grab her and shake some sense into her.

Or take her in his arms and kiss her. Tell her she had

nothing to fear, not from him. Not from anything, as long as he was here to protect her....

Dio, was he losing his mind?

Nicolo shot to his feet. "Tea," he said briskly.

She looked up at him as if he'd lost his sanity. Perhaps he had but she wouldn't let him call a doctor and he'd damned if he'd leave her when she looked like a ghost.

"Tea cures everything, or so my great-grandmother used to say."

Aimee didn't know whether to laugh or cry. He was human after all. He had to be, if he'd had a great-grand-mother.

She stood up. He reached out a steadying hand but she ignored it.

"Thank you for the suggestion," she said politely. "I'll make myself a cup of tea as soon as you— What?"

"I will make the tea."

He would make the tea. Aimee bit back another wave of what she knew was hysterical laughter.

This arrogant prince, this stranger who'd fathered the collection of cells in her womb, would make the tea.

That's all they were, at this point, weren't they? Just cells?

"You will drink some tea, and then I will leave." He smiled. "Agreed?"

His mood had changed. He'd gone from threatening to charming, and she knew the reason. It was because he'd gotten his way. He'd wrung a humiliating admission from her.

Oh, but his smile was devastating.

Maybe the realization showed in her face, because he moved closer and looked at her through eyes gone as dark as the sea.

"Aimee." His hands framed her face. "I'm sorry if I frightened you."

"You don't have to explain."

He shook his head, lay a finger lightly over her mouth.

"I was angry. At you. At your grandfather." He took a breath. "At myself, for wanting you so badly that night."

"Please—"

"I never wanted a woman as I wanted you." His voice roughened. "I think I might have died if you had turned me away."

What did a woman say to such an admission? That she'd have died, too, if he hadn't made love to her? That he'd made her feel things she'd never imagined? That she'd never forget that night in his arms?

All true—and now she carried his baby. For one moment, she'd forgotten that.

Aimee took a quick step back.

"The kettle's on the stove. The tea's in the cupboard over the sink. I'll—I'll just—I'll just go and wash my face…."

"Damn it, we have to talk about that night! You can't keep pretending it didn't happen."

Aimee shook her head, turned and fled. Just as she had that night, Nicolo thought, and thought, too, of what had happened when he caught her.

It would be the same now. All he had to was go after her….

"Damn it!"

He swung away, marched into the kitchen and grabbed the kettle. She had fainted. She was ill. What kind of animal was he to think of sex now?

Besides, he wasn't interested in getting involved with Aimee Black. As beautiful as she was, as much as he might want to make love to her, he'd never fully trust her.

No matter what she claimed, he would always see James Black's hand in all that had—

The telephone rang.

Nicolo glanced toward the bathroom. The door was still closed; he could hear the sound of water running.

The phone rang again. Should he take the call? No. Surely she had voice mail….

Click.

Hi. You've reached 555-6145. Please leave a message after the tone.

A short metallic ring. Then a voice.

Hi, Ms. Black, this is Sarah from Dr. Glassman's office.

Nicolo put down the kettle. He knew he shouldn't listen to a private message but what was he supposed to do? Put his hands over his ears? Besides, this was from a physician.

Now, perhaps, he'd know why Aimee had fainted.

…vitamins. And iron. I meant to tell you that when we spoke earlier. Also, the doctor thought you might want a recommendation for an OB-GYN…

An OB-GYN? What in hell was that?

…absolutely fine, but it's always a good idea to start with an obstetrician early in your pregnancy and, of course, you're already in your third month….

The floor tilted under Nicolo's feet. *Pregnant?* Three months pregnant? What did it mean? What in hell did it mean that a woman he'd had sex with three months ago was—

Aimee flew past him and slapped the machine to silence. Her face had gone from white to red.

"Get out," she said. Her voice trembled as she pointed her finger at the door. "Damn it, Barbieri, do you hear me? Get out! Get out! Get—"

And with cold, relentless clarity, Nicolo knew. He knew exactly what it meant.

He had put a child in Aimee Black's belly.

CHAPTER SEVEN

AIMEE TRIED to tell herself this was all a bad dream.

Any second, she'd wake up, safe and in bed.

No phone messages from a receptionist who didn't understand the meaning of privacy. No Nicolo Barbieri staring at her like a man who'd just seen his life flash before his eyes.

Most of all, God, most of all, no baby growing inside her belly.

But it wasn't a dream.

Everything that was happening was hideously real, from the red light blinking with impersonal determination on her answering machine to the man standing in her tiny kitchen, dwarfing it with his size.

With his fury.

As if he had anything to be furious about.

It was she who was pregnant, she who would agonize over the life-changing decisions ahead, she who would pay the price for one night's madness.

Male and female. Yin and yang. Poets made the balance sound romantic but it wasn't. Men led. Women followed. That was what the world expected, and what too many women accepted.

She'd always known that. She'd watched her father treat

her mother like an amusing, if sometimes trying, possession.

Her grandfather had done his best to deal with her the same way but she hadn't permitted it. She'd *never* permitted it....

Until the night she fell into the arms of this stranger who stood watching her through accusing eyes.

At least she had herself under better control now. She took a steadying breath—there was no point in letting him see how upset she was—and looked straight back at him.

"Goodbye, Prince Barbieri."

It was like speaking to a statue. "Explain yourself," he growled.

Explain herself? The cold demand chased away whatever remained of her nerves.

She didn't need to explain herself to anyone.

"It's a small apartment," she said evenly. "Do you really need me to explain how to get to the front door?"

Her attempt at sarcasm backfired. The look on his face grew even colder.

"That call."

"That *private* call, you mean."

That, too, got her nowhere. "You are pregnant," he said flatly.

Aimee said nothing. Nicolo took a step toward her.

"Answer me!"

"You didn't ask a question."

His eyes narrowed. "I warn you, this is not a time for games." He jerked his head toward the telephone. "That message. Does it mean you are with child?"

Such an old-fashioned phrase. Another time, she might have found it charming. Now, she found it a measure of how much Nicolo Barbieri belonged in a world that was as far from her own as Earth was from the moon.

"That message was for me. I have no intention of discussing it with—"

He was on her before she could finish the sentence, his hands hard on her elbows as he lifted her to her toes.

"You are three months pregnant!" His grasp on her tightened. "Three months ago, you slept with me."

"I told you, I am not going to discuss this!"

"You will discuss whatever I wish, when it concerns me." He lowered his head until his eyes were on the same level as hers. "How many other men were you with three months ago?"

Oh, how she hated him! And yet, he had every right to think that way about her. She'd gone into his bed with no more planning than the slut he'd called her. With less planning, she thought, or she wouldn't be pregnant!

"I asked you a question."

"And I told you to get out." Aimee's voice trembled; she hated herself for the show of weakness. "You have no right—"

"You will answer me! How many others were there?"

She wrenched free of his hands. "A hundred. A thousand. Ten thousand! Are you satisfied?!"

The expression on his face was terrifying. She didn't care. Let him think whatever he liked. Let him think anything, so long as he went away and left her alone.

"I assume," he said, his voice clipped, "that is an exaggeration. Still, all things considered, do you actually know who the father is?"

She'd asked for the insult by her behavior that night and by her answer a moment ago. Still, it took all her control not to launch herself at him and claw out his eyes.

"Whoever it is, it isn't your problem."

"That is not an answer."

"It's the only one you're going to—"

He caught her again, pulled her roughly into his arms and kissed her savagely.

"Does that shake your memory, Aimee? Does it remind you that I have every right to demand answers—or have you forgotten I spent half the night spending myself inside you three months ago?"

Her face flamed. "I hate you," she said, struggling against his iron grip. "You're a bully. You're disgusting. You're—"

He kissed her again, harder than before, his lips, his teeth, his hands all a harsh reminder of his power.

"I am all that and more. Now answer the question. Who fathered the child you carry? Was it me?"

Her mind raced. All she had to do was say no. That would be the end of it.

And yet, how could she?

She didn't care about lying to Nicolo. But lying to the tiny life within her…

There was something terrible in that.

She knew thinking that way was crazy but everything that had happened today was crazy. Why not this, too?

Besides, the truth wouldn't change anything. This was her responsibility. She wasn't naïve; she knew how these things went. In school and then here in the city, she'd known women who'd been in the same fix. Things always ended the same way. The men denied being responsible. Or, if confronted by irrefutable proof, made some kind of settlement to avoid a nasty legal action and then went on with their lives.

The women ended up making decisions that would affect them forever. Abortion. Adoption. Single-motherhood. Choose the one you hoped would be best for you, for your baby, then live with it.

This would be no different. Considering that Nicolo

hadn't already run out the door, his solution to the problem was surely going to be money.

Not that she gave a damn.

She was not weak. She could handle this on her own, and to hell with Nicolo Barbieri.

The sooner he understood that, the better.

"Is this baby mine?" he demanded.

Aimee looked up in defiance. "You're goddamned right it is."

Except for the almost-painful tightening of his hands on her flesh, he showed no emotion.

"You are certain?"

An ugly question, but she didn't flinch. "Absolutely."

"There was no one else who could have—"

"No."

"Because, I promise you, Aimee, I will demand blood tests."

"What you'd want is a DNA test," she said coldly. "They're a much more reliable proof of paternity, according to a law class I took in college." She smiled thinly. "But bothering with the test would be a waste of time."

His lips drew back from his teeth in what might have been an attempt at a smile.

"That decision will be mine. It will not be yours."

His accent was growing more and more pronounced. She'd already figured out that was a sure sign he was having trouble controlling his temper.

Too bad.

She had a temper, too. And there was a limit to how many insults a woman, even an imprudent one, had to take.

"Believe me, Prince Barbieri. I've only done a few foolish things in my life." Aimee jerked free of his hands. "And going to bed with you rates as number one."

His face darkened. "Insulting me at a time like this is not wise."

"Then don't insult me by calling me a liar! You asked the question. I answered it. Unfortunately you don't like the answer, but that doesn't change that fact that it was you who made me pregnant."

"I *made* you pregnant." His words were filled with soft malice. "Such an interesting way to phrase what happened that night, *cara.*"

She felt the heat rise in her cheeks. "What happened was that I'd had too much to drink."

"I don't recall you having anything to drink."

His assessment was closer to the mark than hers. She'd had one drink. Actually, a couple of sips of one drink, but she wasn't going to be sidetracked into a discussion of why she'd had sex with him when she didn't understand it herself.

"The point is, you impregnated me."

"Now you describe a laboratory experiment." He moved toward her slowly, gaze locked to hers, and though she hated herself for it, she took a step back. "But that was not what happened in that bathroom or in my bed."

"There is no reason to have this conversation."

"Ah, but there is." He was a breath away now, his eyes glittering with heat as her shoulders hit the wall. "I think you need reminding of what we did that night."

"I have all the reminding I need."

"*Si.* So it would seem. My child in your womb." His gaze flattened. "Was this part of the great plan?"

Aimee blinked. "What?"

"Such an innocent face, *cara.*" His mouth twisted with derision. "And such a devious scheme. The clever meeting on the street. The coincidental meeting at the club. The seduction." He cupped her face, raised it to his until the midnight-blue of his eyes filled her vision. "And now, this. An heir to your grandfather's kingdom. A child of my blood from the womb of a Stafford-Coleridge-Black descendant." His gaze darkened. "Such an amazing set of coincidences."

"You are," Aimee whispered shakily, "an evil man."

"I am a logical man. One who assumed you were using protection."

"I was. It failed."

"How convenient it failed when failure was most necessary."

Her eyes filled with angry tears. "I despise you!"

"That really breaks my heart, *cara*."

"When I think that—that I let you touch me—"

"You *let* me touch you?" Nicolo gave a sharp bark of laughter. "You begged me to touch you. I remember every word. Every whisper."

"I must have been out of my mind."

Aimee's face was white with exhaustion. Clearly this was taking its toll and, just for a second, Nicolo's anger lessened.

She was pregnant. And she had been so ill just a short while ago….

So what? he thought coldly.

She had brought it all on herself. Did she really expect him to believe her birth control protection had failed? A woman like her… Surely she would know all about such things.

And what about you?

The thought whispered its way from the depths of his conscience. He had to admit, it was a fair question.

He had taken Aimee without a condom. And he always used a condom, even if a woman said it wasn't necessary.

Perhaps he was old-fashioned but protection was a

man's responsibility, especially in today's sometimes ugly world.

So, what had become of his sense of responsibility that night?

It had flown out the window along with the ability to think with his brain instead of his body.

He'd wanted Aimee more than he'd ever wanted a woman in his life. *Dio,* he was getting hard, just remembering.

Nicolo cursed, spun away from her and paced across her kitchen. He ran his hands through his hair and told himself he was crazy.

His entire world had been upended and he was thinking about what it had been like to make love to a woman who was a stranger to him in every way that mattered.

What he had to think about was not that. It was what he should do next.

Should he contact his attorney? Demand to speak with her physician? What were his financial responsibilities, now and in the future?

Whenever an acquaintance married and had a child, he'd think, yes, I suppose I shall have a son, too, sometime in the future. Perhaps because his father had hardly ever been around when he was growing up, being a parent had never seemed anything more than a vague idea.

Now, it was fast becoming reality, assuming a lab test said Aimee Black was telling the truth. Assuming she wanted to remain pregnant.

Nicolo's jaw tightened.

That would, of course, be her decision.

But it was a great deal to take in all at once. A child. His child. In the womb of a woman who had stirred him so that he'd forgotten everything he'd ever known about self-control.

To hell with that. Angry at Aimee, angry at himself, he swung toward her again.

"I assume you've made plans."

"They don't concern you."

"What are those plans?"

"I just said—"

"Whatever you do, you will need proper care."

"Didn't you hear me? What I do is not your concern."

"The message from your doctor. I gather he found you well."

"*She* found me well," Aimee said, with a lift of her chin.

Could a man laugh at such a moment? Nicolo found that at least he could smile.

"I stand corrected. And this—this OP?"

"OB-GYN. And we're not going to have this conversation."

"This is a specialist?"

"Damn it, Barbieri—"

"I see I am no longer that magnificent creature, the prince," he said dryly.

"You are an intruder. And I want you to out of my home immediately."

"What is this OB-GYN?"

"An obstetrician. Must I phone the police to get rid of you?"

"And tell them what, *cara?* That it annoys you to discuss your pregnancy with the man responsible for it?" He flashed a thin smile. "I suspect the officers who respond to your call would enjoy something to lighten their day."

"Nicolo." Her voice was weary. "Why are you doing this?"

He strode to her and cupped her elbows. "I am doing it," he said sharply, "because you claim my child lies in your belly."

"You asked for the truth. Don't blame me if…" Aimee gasped and tried to catch his hands. "What are you doing?"

"Opening your robe," he said calmly, as he undid the sash. "I want to see this pregnancy of yours."

"I told you, it's not…" Her breath caught as he spread the lapels of her robe wide. "Damn you, Nicolo—"

"It is my right," he said coldly.

It was. Wasn't it? The right of a man to see the body of a woman who claimed she carried his baby?

Dio, he had almost forgotten how beautiful she was.

The night they met, she'd worn something wickedly sexy under that incredible crimson dress. A black bra. A black thong. Both silky and small enough to hold in the palm of his hand.

Now, she wore sensible white cotton. A bra and panties. And it didn't matter. She had the kind of body that didn't need black silk to make it sexy.

Was it too soon to see the changes his child would bring? Her belly was still flat. Her breasts…were they already a little fuller?

"Nicolo." Her voice was husky. "Nicolo…"

"I'm just curious, *cara.*" His voice was husky, too. And rough. As rough as the sudden pounding of his heart. He reached out, placed his hand over her belly again. "Still flat," he said, as if it didn't matter that he could feel the heat of her skin through the plain white cotton panties.

"Nicolo."

He looked up, his eyes dark as they met hers. She was trembling; her lips were slightly parted and he remembered how they had parted for him that night. How greedily he had tasted her mouth. Her ineffable sweetness.

"What of your breasts?" he said in a low voice. Eyes locked to hers, he cupped one delicate mound of flesh. She gave a little moan; her eyes went from violet to black. "Have they changed yet?"

He felt her nipple engorge behind the cotton of her bra. She moaned again as he moved his thumb across the swollen tip and he knew he could have her. Take her again and again, until he'd rid himself of this need to possess her....

Dio, perhaps he *had* lost his mind! Quickly he stepped back.

"So," he said briskly, as if nothing had happened, "we must discuss what to do next. What is right."

Aimee pulled her robe together. She was shaken; he could see it, but he could see that she wasn't going to admit it.

"What is right," she said, "is for you to get out of my life."

"I intend to as soon as we settle this."

"It's settled. This is my problem and I'll decide what's right."

Nicolo nodded, but was that correct? Was the choice solely hers? What did a man do at a time like this? He'd never had to make the decision but he knew the obvious answers.

The trouble was that the obvious answers didn't apply when you were the man involved in actually making the decision.

And what a hell of a decision this was.

He had made Aimee Black pregnant. Forget the nonsense about other men. He had always trusted his gut instinct in business; he trusted it now. He would own up to his responsibility, financially.

That was his decision.

What she did after that was hers.

Nicolo reached into his pocket, took out his checkbook and a gold pen.

"I don't want your money!"

He looked up. Aimee was watching him, her eyes almost feverish in her pale face.

"You said you will do whatever is right. And so shall I." He uncapped the pen. "Five hundred thousand. Will that be—"

"Five hundred thousand dollars?"

His eyebrows rose. "Is it not enough?"

Aimee flew at him and slapped the checkbook and pen from his hand. "Get out," she growled. "Get out, get out, get—"

"Damn it," Nicolo snarled, grabbing her wrists before she could slug him, "are you insane?"

"Do you think your money can change what's happened? That it can buy back my dignity?" Tears of anger rose in her eyes to glitter like jewels on her lashes. "I don't want your money, Nicolo. I don't want anything from you except your promise that I'll never see your face again!"

Her tears fell on his hand like the rain that had fallen on them both the day they'd met.

He suspected he would never forget that meeting, or Aimee.

Her defiance. Her passion. Her determination.

An inadvertent smile lifted the corner of his mouth. If ever a man wanted sons—even daughters—Aimee would be the woman to bear them. Such fire. Such courage…

His breath caught.

Suddenly he knew what was right. How had it taken him this long to see it?

He let go of Aimee's hands. Then he picked up his checkbook, retrieved his pen, put them both back in his pocket. A roll of paper towels hung over the kitchen sink. He tore off half a dozen sheets and held them out to her.

She shoved them away.

"I just said, I don't want anything from you!"

"Perhaps you'll make an exception," he said calmly, "considering that your nose is running."

She flushed, grabbed the towels, put them to her nose and gave a long, noisy blow.

"Much better."

"Good. I wouldn't want to offend Your Highness's delicate sensibilities."

Her voice was shaky but he could see her self-control returning. He had the feeling she was going to need it.

"I know you're being sarcastic, *cara,* but—"

"Such perception!"

"—but, sarcasm aside, it's inappropriate to address me by my title."

Aimee burst out laughing. "Now you're going to give me lessons in court etiquette? God almighty, what a horrible human being you—"

"I do not believe in such formality," he said, cursing himself for a fool because he knew damned well a man couldn't sound more formal than he did right now. He paused, took a breath and got on with it. "Particularly from the woman who is about to become my wife."

CHAPTER EIGHT

MARRY HIM?

Marry Nicolo Barbieri.

The man who had seduced her. And he had, no matter what he claimed. He'd started it all. Followed her into that bathroom. Locked the door. Lifted her onto the marble vanity. Torn aside her panties.

Thrust deep into her…and even now, despite everything, just thinking of what it had been like made her body quicken.

What was the matter with her, that she should still feel desire for him? She couldn't blame him for making her pregnant—she hadn't been thinking any more clearly than he that night—but there was no escaping that he'd made love to her….

And then called her a slut because he believed she'd been part of some ugly scheme of her grandfather's.

Why wouldn't he think that? Nicolo was every bit as ruthless and driven as the coldhearted old man who'd raised her.

James was willing to sell her for the good of his kingdom. Nicolo was willing to buy her for the same reason. He'd probably been willing to do it from the instant her grandfather suggested it.

All that indignation this morning, the fiery show of contempt for her and her grandfather, had been a lie to placate his own ego. He'd needed to justify a devil's bargain and she and her answering machine had handed it to him, all prettily gift-wrapped and tied with a great big bow.

She was pregnant with his baby. What better way to agree to marrying her than by making it seem a gallant gesture?

Except, she knew the truth.

The Prince of All He Surveyed was about as gallant as a fifteen-century monarch weighing the benefits of a royal marriage—except for one enormous difference.

No matter what he thought, she wasn't governed by the rules of James Black's kingdom. She was not a princess. She didn't have to marry a tyrant she didn't know, didn't love, didn't even like.

"Well, *cara?* Has my proposal swept you off your feet, or shall I take your silence as wholehearted agreement?"

Aimee looked up. Nicolo's words were sarcastic but his eyes were cool and watchful. He had to know she wasn't going to agree—or maybe he didn't. He was just arrogant enough, imperious enough, to assume his proposal—and wasn't that an amazing thing to call it—was everything a woman in her situation could want.

She almost laughed. He was in for one hell of a surprise!

Learning she was pregnant, having to make all the tough choices that came next without anyone to help her, was the most terrifying thing that had ever happened.

Only one thing could possibly be more frightening: marriage to a man like the Evil Prince.

Aimee tossed her head, as if none of this was worth discussion.

"I have lots to say," she said evenly. "But for both our

sakes, I'll stay with thanks but no thanks and, oh, by the way, don't let the door hit you in the butt on your way out."

Good, she thought. Not original, but concise. She'd have liked it better if he showed some reaction but he didn't. No look of surprise. Not even anger. All he did was smile and, God, she hated that smile, the all-knowing insolence of it.

"Perhaps 'proposal' is the wrong word," he said smoothly.

"At least we can agree on that. 'Decree' is the word that came to my mind." Aimee smiled, too, and lifted her chin. "There's only one problem. You may be a prince but I'm not one of your subjects. Your ridiculous pronouncements don't mean a thing to me."

"So much for my attempt at being gallant."

She'd been right. And what was that tiny twinge of regret all about? She knew she was a pawn in a game played between Nicolo and her grandfather.

Now, *he* knew that she knew it.

Dark Knight takes pawn. Checkmate.

"That's unfortunate, Aimee." Another of those quick, infuriating smiles lifted one corner of his mouth. "The easiest path to a goal is generally the preferable one."

"And the easiest path to the door is right behind you. Goodbye, Nicolo. I hope I never have the misfortune of seeing you again."

Still no reaction. Damn it, she wanted one! Didn't the man know when he was being insulted?

Apparently not.

Instead of heading for the door, he picked up the things he'd dropped and took a little black notebook from his pocket, flipped it open, found the page he wanted and frowned.

"Wednesday," he said briskly. His frown deepened.

"No. On second thought…" Another glance, a nod, and then he scrawled something with the pen. "I must be in Rome by Wednesday but I am free tomorrow." The pen and notebook went back into his pocket; he folded his arms and looked at her, his expression unreadable. "Will ten in the morning be suitable?"

"I have no idea what you're talking about."

"For our marriage, *cara*. What else have we been discussing?"

Aimee laughed. That, finally, got a reaction. Oh, if looks could kill…

"You find this amusing?"

"Actually I find it incredible. I'm sure people trip over their feet in an effort to please you but here's a news flash, Prince." Her laughter faded; her face became as stony as his. "I am not marrying you."

"You are pregnant."

"I am pregnant. *I* am pregnant," she repeated, pounding her fist between her breasts for emphasis. "And *I* am perfectly capable of handling the situation myself."

"What happened is my responsibility."

"A little while ago you were busy saying it was mine."

"I was wrong." He drew himself up. "I am the man and such things are a man's duty."

Another time, the ridiculous speech might have made her roll her eyes. Not now. He meant it. Or wanted to think he meant it. Or wanted *her* to think he meant it.

Anything, to get his hands on her grandfather's bank and extend the scope and power of the Barbieri empire.

"How nice," she said softly. "And how amazing, that you should turn into this—this ethical creature instead of the son of a bitch we both know you—"

A cry broke from her throat as he clasped her shoulders. "Call me whatever you like. Hate me as much as pleases you. It changes nothing. I live by a set of rules that necessitate I accept responsibility for my actions." His grasp on her eased. "Perhaps it took me a while to accept that but what I learned just now took me by surprise."

"Have you ever counted how many times you use the words 'I' and 'me' and 'my'? Try it sometime. You might be surprised. Oh, and here's another thing that might surprise you." She pulled free of his hands. "Did you think I wouldn't notice that marrying me will drop Stafford-Coleridge-Black right into your hands?"

"An undeniable fact, I agree."

"Then, let me be more direct." Aimee's eyes were hot with warning. "I will not marry you under any—"

Nicolo cursed, grabbed her, hauled her into his arms and captured her mouth with his. It was sudden; she had no time to think, no time to do anything except let it happen….

No time to keep her lips from parting hungrily under the pressure of his.

When he drew back, she stood motionless, heart racing, body tingling, while he watched her through narrowed eyes.

"There is an American expression," he said softly. "Win-win. Do you know it, *cara?* It is the perfect way to describe what I have in mind."

"I know what you have in mind. And I don't want any part of it."

"Your grandfather wants an heir. I want SCB."

"And you'd marry me to get it."

"James says you are an intelligent woman. Can't you see beyond your pride?"

Did he think that was why she wouldn't agree? Because of her pride? Did he think that if he'd wanted her—*her,* not an expansion of his empire—she'd have agreed to this outrageous marriage?

"You're right," she said, her voice shaking, "I do have too much pride to marry someone like you."

His eyes went cold. "This discussion is over."

"You said that before. And I agree. It's over. So are your pathetic attempts to convince me to marry you."

"I was going to tell you that I would be willing to let you try your hand at helping me run SCB, once it is mine." His mouth thinned. "Now, I would not even allow you to play at being in charge of the mail room."

"What a coldhearted bastard you are."

"No," he said calmly, "not at all. For all intents and purposes, I had no father. I would wish better for my child."

"Such a noble sentiment! Too bad I know that this is all about SCB. Well, I don't give a damn for SCB! And nothing you say or do can make me change my mind."

Nicolo smiled thinly. "I wonder if you'll feel that way when I tell your grandfather that you carry my child, that I have offered to marry you and that you have refused."

"Do it," she said recklessly. "I hate you. I hate him—"

"You may hate me, *cara,* but you don't hate that old man. If you did, you wouldn't have been so hurt by the things he said this morning." His gaze hardened. "Your grandfather hasn't much longer to live," he said bluntly. "Would you have him die knowing you denied him the things only you can give him?"

Aimee knotted her hands. "Is there anything you won't do to get your own way?"

"Win-win, *cara,*" he said softly. "A peaceful close to your grandfather's long life. Legitimacy for our child." He drew her against him, his arousal swift and obvious against the V of her thighs. "And a bonus," he said, his voice low and rough. "Or must I remind you what it was like when we made love?"

"It was sex, not love. And if you really think I'd ever let you touch me again—"

Nicolo laughed, gathered her against him and kissed her.

She struggled. Fought. But his kiss was deep and all-consuming and in a heartbeat, she was kissing him back.

It was the same as the night they'd met.

The fire. The hunger. The heavy race of her heart. The only way she could keep from falling was to clutch his jacket, rise on her toes, cling to him and cling to him until he let go of her.

It took a moment to catch her breath. By then, he had strolled to the door.

"Ten o'clock," he said over his shoulder. "And be prompt. I don't have time to waste."

"You—you—"

Blindly she snatched a glass from the counter and flung it. It shattered against the wall an inch from his head but he didn't turn around. If he had—if he had, he thought grimly as he yanked the door open and went into the hall, God only knew what he'd have done.

There was a limit to how much of a woman's anger a man had to take.

Halfway down the stairs, he took out his cell phone and called his attorney.

"This is Nicolo Barbieri. I wish to be married tomorrow," he said brusquely, aware and not giving a damn that this was exactly the kind of arrogance Aimee had accused him of. "The woman's name is Aimee Stafford Coleridge Black." He listened for a moment, then made an impatient sound. "Rules and regulations are your concern, *signore,* not mine. Find a way around them, make the necessary arrangements and send a report, the paperwork, whatever is necessary, to me at my hotel. No, not as soon as you can. Tonight."

Nicolo snapped his phone shut and stepped into the street. It was raining again. *Dio,* what was with this combination? Rain, and Aimee Black. It was as if the skies were trying to tell him something. He had no coat, no umbrella and from what he could see, there wasn't a subway station in the vicinity. No bus stops, either, and as always when it rained in Manhattan, the taxis seemed to have vanished.

He was at least forty blocks from his hotel.

He began walking. The exercise would do him good. Maybe he could work off some of his anger.

Aimee wasn't the only one who was furious.

He was, too.

At her. At himself. At how easily she could make him lose his grip on logic and self-control, the very qualities that had helped him build what she so disparagingly referred to as his kingdom.

He knew men who lived on the largesse of those impressed by a useless title.

Not Nicolo.

He had worked hard for all he had, though Aimee made it clear she didn't think so. She didn't like him. Didn't respect him.

Why in hell was he going to marry her?

To gain Stafford-Coleridge-Black? Ridiculous. He wanted it, yes, but not enough to tie himself to a woman he didn't love.

To give her unborn child a name? He wasn't even sure the child was his. How had he forgotten that?

And even if it was, he didn't need to marry Aimee to accept the responsibilities of paternity. He could even make it a point to be part of the child's life.

Well, as much as he could.

If he'd been calmer, he'd have seen all this right away. But Aimee had forced a confrontation. Her anger had fueled his and he'd let her wrest control of the situation from him.

She was good at that.

The only time he'd been in command was the night he'd made love to her. She had been his. Moaning at his touch. Sighing at his kisses. Trembling under his caresses.

Nicolo cursed.

It had been nothing more than sex, as she'd so coldly pointed out. It was just that the passage of time had made it seem more exciting than it had actually been.

And even if it had been extraordinary, why would he want to tie himself to her? To any woman, but especially to this one, who had the disposition of a tigress?

That was fine in bed but out of it a man wanted a sweet-tempered, obedient woman. He knew dozens like that, every one beautiful and sexy and a thousand times easier to handle.

Which brought him back to reality and the knowledge that he couldn't come up with a single, rational reason to go through with this wedding, and what a hell of a relief that was.

Nicolo slowed his steps. The rain had stopped. The sun was out. Taxis prowled the streets again. He hailed one, got inside and told the driver the name of his hotel.

He would go to Aimee's apartment at ten tomorrow morning because he had said that was what he would do, but when he arrived, he'd tell her he'd changed his mind, that he didn't want to marry her.

He'd tell her the rest, too, that he would support the child—and her, of course—and, in general, do the right thing.

Problem solved.

Nicolo folded his arms, sat back and smiled. He was soaked to the skin but he was happy.

* * *

Hours later, the bellman delivered a thin manila envelope from Nicolo's attorney.

A note inside assured him that all he had to do in the morning was take the attached documents and his prospective bride to a building in lower Manhattan, ask for a particular judge and he and the lady in question would be married within the hour.

That there was no longer a prospective bride was beside the point. The papers were simply a reminder of how foolish he'd almost been, and he shoved them aside.

He went to bed at eleven. At midnight, he got up and paced the confines of the suite. When he lay down again more than an hour later, he fell into troubled sleep. His dreams were murky and unpleasant, involving a small boy wandering the somber halls of Stafford-Coleridge-Black in search of something nameless and elusive. Each time the child was on the verge of finding it, Nicolo woke up.

At dawn, he gave up, phoned down for coffee, rye toast and the *Times* and the *Wall Street Journal*. Showered, shaved and dressed in chinos and a navy shirt with the sleeves rolled up, he sat by the sitting room window to have his breakfast and read the papers.

The coffee was fine. The toast was dry. So was the writing in both the *Times* and the *Journal*. Why else would he be unable to focus on any of the articles?

Nicolo tossed them aside and checked his watch for what had to be the tenth time since he'd awakened. Seven-thirty. Too early to show up at Aimee's door and tell her she could forget about marrying him.

He could imagine how happy that would make her. She might even smile, something he hadn't seen her do since the night he'd taken her to bed.

He was happy, too. If he was feeling grim, it was only because he wanted to get the damned thing over with.

Seven forty-five.

Seven fifty.

Seven fifty-seven.

"*Merda*," Nicolo snarled, and shot from his chair.

He could arrive at Aimee's any time he wanted. There was no right time to deliver good news. Besides, she didn't have to be ready. She wasn't going anywhere.

Traffic was heavy and it was almost eight-thirty when he climbed the steps to Aimee's building. Yesterday's rain hadn't done much to clean the grungy stoop.

The first thing he'd do would be to buy her a condo in a decent neighborhood.

This was not a fit place to raise her child.

He paused outside her apartment, then rang the bell. He rang it again. She might be in the shower, getting ready for his arrival. Or, knowing Aimee, *not* getting ready.

It almost made him smile.

Whatever else she was, she was brave. He'd never known a woman to stand up to him before. He knew damned well yesterday's argument wasn't over. The second she opened the door and saw him, she'd lift her chin in that way she had and tell him what he could do with his marriage proposal.

He'd let her rant for a few seconds and then he'd say, *There is no proposal*, cara. *I have decided I would sooner live with a scorpion than with you.*

The door opened.

Everything he'd anticipated was wrong.

Aimee didn't lift her chin. She didn't rant. And, even though he'd shown up more than an hour early, he could see that she had been waiting for him.

She wore a simple yellow sundress and white sandals

with little heels. Her hair was pulled into a ponytail, her face was bare of makeup and her eyes were suspiciously bright as if she'd been crying.

She looked painfully young, heartbreakingly vulnerable—and incredibly beautiful.

For one wild moment, Nicolo imagined taking her in his arms, telling her she had nothing to be afraid of. That he would be good to her, that he would take care of her...

He frowned, then cleared his throat.

"Aimee. I have come to tell you—"

"What? More threats?" Her chin rose now, just as he'd expected. "Let me save you the trouble." She took a shaky breath. "I thought it through." She gave an unsteady laugh. "Actually, it's all I thought about since you left yesterday. And—and you're right, Nicolo. I have no choice but to marry you."

He stared at her in disbelief. *Say something,* he told himself, *tell her you've changed your mind!*

"You were right. About my grandfather. I want to hate him but I can't. He raised me. He gave me all the things he believed I needed and if I needed more, his love, his respect..."

Aimee stopped the rush of words. Why bare her soul? She was going to marry Nicolo Barbieri. That was enough.

"He's old," she continued, her voice low. "And growing frail. I don't want to look back after he's gone and know I denied him the only things he ever asked of me, the bank in your hands, and—" color rose in her cheeks "—and your child."

Nicolo said nothing. After a few seconds, Aimee cleared her throat. "So, I'll marry you."

"But?" His smile was thin. "Don't look so surprised, *cara.* One would have to be deaf not to have heard that unspoken word."

"This marriage—it will be in name only. A legal convenience that will end on my grandfather's death."

Aimee waited, trying to read Nicolo's expression, but it told her nothing.

"No sex," he finally said, his voice silken.

She nodded. "None."

"And tell me, *cara*. What am I to do when I want sex?"

The seemingly subservient woman of the last few moments disappeared. Aimee's eyes flashed with her old defiance.

"You'll do whatever you must but you'll be discreet about it."

Nicolo burst out laughing. She felt her hands ball. How she wanted to slap that laugh from his face!

"Let me be sure I understand this. I marry you. I give you my name. My title. And at some point in the future, we divorce and I end up with alimony payments and child support. In return for all this, you will not complain when I keep a mistress. Is that right?"

He didn't wait for an answer. Instead he swept her into his arms and drew her against him.

"Here is how it will be," he growled. "You will be my wife. You will be available to me whenever I wish. Night. Day. Anywhere, anytime. If I also want a mistress, I will have one."

"I won't marry you under those conditions!"

"*Si.* You will. And if there is a divorce, it will be because I have wearied of you." She tried to wrench free; his hold on her tightened. "And before you say, 'no, Nicolo, I won't marry you under those conditions,' consider this." He leaned toward her, eyes glittering. "I can take this child from you the day it's born. Do not shake your head! I am Prince Nicolo Antonius Barbieri. No court would deny me the right to my own flesh and blood. Is that clear?"

"You no good, evil, vicious bastard," she hissed, "you son of a—"

Nicolo captured her mouth with his, kissed her again and again until she trembled in his arms.

Then he picked up the small suitcase near her feet and jerked his head toward the door.

CHAPTER NINE

SOME WOMEN dreamed about their weddings.

Would the day be sunny? What kind of gown? Would it be sweet and romantic, like something Scarlett would have worn in *Gone with the Wind*, or would it be sexy and sophisticated? And then there was all the rest. The setting. The attendants. The guests. The flowers.

Aimee was glad she'd never wasted time on such silly dreams, otherwise—otherwise what was happening now might make her weep. A high-ceilinged room in a tired municipal building. A judge who'd seemed surprised to see them until his secretary whispered something in his ear. A pair of witnesses plucked from the clerical staff.

And Nicolo, her stern-faced groom, standing beside her.

Oh, yes. It was a damned good thing she'd been too busy studying to think about weddings.

Marriage had only been a distant possibility. Friends had married; Aimee had smiled and said all the right things but mostly she'd thought, *Not me, not yet, maybe not ever.*

She had things to do, a life to live, and if she ever did marry, it would be someone the exact opposite of her grandfather.

Yet today she was marrying a man who made her grandfather look like a saint, a stranger taking her as his wife as if they'd been sent back to a time when men and women married for reasons of—

"Miss?"

—for reasons of title and expediency that had nothing to do with love or romance or—

"Miss?"

Aimee blinked. The judge smiled in apology.

"Your name again, miss? I'm terribly sorry but—"

"No," Aimee replied, "that's all right, Your Honor. I understand."

She did. She understood it all. The impersonal setting, the equally impersonal words. Why would he remember her name?

The only surprise came when it was time for Nicolo to put a ring on her finger.

The cold stranger who'd made it clear this would be a marriage on his terms, who'd undoubtedly browbeaten some poor soul at City Hall into issuing a marriage license in less than twenty-four hours, had neglected to buy a wedding ring.

Admitting his error made him blush. It was lovely to see, she thought with dour satisfaction.

"I don't need a ring," she said coolly. Coolly enough so even the two bored witnesses looked at her.

"My wife needs a ring," Nicolo said grimly, tugging one she'd never before noticed from his finger. "We will use this," he said, his accent thick enough to trip over.

The ring was obviously old, its slightly raised crest almost worn away, and it was so big that Aimee had to clench her fist to keep it from falling off.

That was fine.

Clenching her fist helped keep her from screaming, "Stop!"

But there was no going back. In the dark hours of the

night, agreeing to this marriage had seemed the only thing she could do. For her grandfather and, yes, for her baby. Her unborn child was entitled to be free of the stain of illegitimacy.

The arrangement could work, she'd told herself as she sat by the window, staring blindly out at the neighboring brick tenement that was her entire view. Her child would get his father's name. Nicolo would get the bank. She would get the satisfaction of giving her grandfather the one thing not even his vast fortune could buy.

It would all be very civilized…and how could she have been stupid enough to believe that? If only she'd kept her mouth shut. Telling Nicolo she'd marry him but she wouldn't sleep with him had been like waving a bone at a caged and hungry wolf.

It only made him want what he couldn't have.

She shouldn't have said anything. After all, he couldn't force her to sleep with him. Nicolo Barbieri was a tyrant, but he wasn't a savage.

Was he?

God oh God, what was she doing?

What had she been thinking?

Aimee swung toward Nicolo, oblivious to the judge, the witnesses, the ceremony.

"Nicolo," she said urgently, "wait…"

"…husband and wife," the judge said, and offered an election-year smile. "Congratulations, Prince Barbieri. Oh, and Princess Barbieri, of course. Sir, you may kiss your bride."

Nicolo looked at her. His eyes told her he knew exactly what she'd been about to say; the proof came when he bent his head and put his mouth to her ear.

To the onlookers, it probably looked as if he was whispering something tender but it was hardly that.

"Too late, *cara*," he murmured, the words a steel fist in a velvet glove.

Then he shook the judge's hand, thanked the witnesses and drew Aimee's arm through his.

"Time for the newlyweds to be alone," he said, with a little smile.

The judge and the witnesses laughed politely.

Aimee trembled.

He'd told the taxi driver to wait by circling the block; the cab appeared just as they came down the courthouse steps.

Nicolo opened the door, motioned Aimee inside and climbed in next to her.

"Kennedy," he said. "The General Aviation facility."

Aimee stared at him as the cab pulled into midmorning traffic. "What?"

"The airport. The area where corporate jets are—"

"I know what Kennedy is," she said impatiently. "But why are we going there?"

Nicolo raised a dark eyebrow. "Where did you think we would go, *cara?*" His smile was silken. "Are you in such a rush to be alone with me that you hoped we'd go to my hotel?"

No way was she going to let him draw her into that kind of conversation! Aimee folded her hands in her lap.

"I asked you a question. Do you think you could give me a straight answer?"

His smile faded. "We're going home."

Home? She stared at him blankly. They hadn't discussed where they'd live but then, they hadn't discussed much of anything.

"Did you think we would live in New York?"

That was precisely what she'd thought.

"My home is in Italy," he said brusquely. "In Rome. My

house is there, my corporate headquarters... Don't look so stricken, *cara*. New York isn't the center of the world."

It was the center of *her* world. Didn't he see that?

"But—but—"

"If you're concerned about not packing enough clothes, you can shop tomorrow."

Did he think this was about clothes? She would have laughed, except laughter was too close to tears.

"I'm not concerned about that."

"If it's because we haven't told your grandfather, don't be. I'll call him from the plane."

"Nicolo." Aimee swallowed dryly. She had to find the right way to say this without sounding as if she was begging. "I've lived here all my life."

"And I," he said coolly, "have lived in Rome."

"Yes, I know that, but—"

"You are my wife."

His voice had turned hard; even the cabbie, sensing something, reached back and closed the privacy partition.

"But surely—"

"If you wish, I will consider the purchase of a flat in New York." Why tell her he'd decided on that when he first became interested in buying SCB? "But my primary residence—our primary residence—will be *Roma*."

"But—but—"

"Stop sounding like a motorboat," Nicolo said impatiently. "You are my wife. You will behave as such, and you cannot do that from a distance of thirty-five hundred miles."

Aimee felt the blood drain from her head. "Nicolo. Please—"

"This discussion is at an end."

Nicolo folded his arms and turned his face to the window.

"What discussion?" Aimee said bitterly. "You don't discuss things, you make pronouncements."

He gave her one final, unyielding look. "Get used to it," he said.

After that, there was silence.

Hell.

Nicolo glowered as he stared blindly out the window.

He was certainly doing his best to prove Aimee right and be just what she had called him. A no-good bastard. A son of a bitch. He was sure she'd have used other names, far more colorful ones, if only she'd known them.

But what did she expect?

First she told him how much she hated him. Then she told him she'd marry him. Then she said he was never to touch her.

He was the one with a title but his wife had been a princess long before she'd met him. A Park Avenue princess, accustomed to giving orders and getting her own way.

And he had married her.

He must have been out of his mind! How in hell had he let it happen?

He'd come to his senses last night, realized he didn't have to marry this woman. He didn't need her grandfather's bank. He hadn't needed a child, either, but since one was on the way, he'd finally figured out that he could do the right thing for it without marrying its mother....

It.

Not much of a way to think about one's *bambino* but then, he didn't know the sex. Damn it, he didn't even know if it *was* his child.

What in hell had happened to him, to make him do something so impetuous as marrying Aimee? Just because she said the baby was his....

Why believe her? Anything was possible with a woman who screwed like a bunny and wouldn't even exchange names.

Except, he knew he was the father. Knew it in his bones, and to hell with how ridiculous that sounded. He knew it, that was all, and because he hadn't been fast enough on his feet this morning, now he was stuck with the consequences.

He glanced at Aimee, sitting stiff and silent in the corner of the taxi, as far from him as she could get.

I feel the same way about you, he wanted to tell her. *I'm no happier about what we just did than you are. I don't want to look at you, talk to you, touch you...*

A lie.

He wanted to touch her, all right. Take her in his arms and kiss her until her lips were warm and softly swollen. Tear that demure-looking sundress off her body, bare her breasts to his eyes and mouth.

Bare her belly to his caress.

Her belly. Her womb. His child.

His child. That was why he'd married her. Of course it was. Why else would a man tie himself to a beautiful, hard-headed, ill-tempered woman he didn't know?

Nicolo glanced at Aimee again.

Why else, indeed?

He had phoned his pilot before the ceremony; when they reached the airport, the plane stood ready for departure.

He took Aimee's hand as they stepped out of the terminal. She didn't fight him. He almost wished she would. That might be better than letting her hand lie limply in his.

The pilot was already on board. The copilot and the cabin attendant were waiting on the tarmac, both of them smiling.

Nicolo had told them of his marriage.

"*Congratulazioni, Principe, Principessa,*" the attendant said.

"Best of luck to you both," the copilot chimed in.

"Thank you," Nicolo replied.

Aimee said nothing.

Nicolo gritted his teeth. When they were alone in the cabin, he swung her toward him.

"I expect you to treat my people with courtesy!"

"What would you know of courtesy?" she said.

Their eyes met, hers daring him to ask her what she meant, but he knew better.

"Take a seat," he growled.

"Aren't you going to tell me what seat?"

Nicolo gritted his teeth again. At this rate, he would be toothless in a week.

"Do not test me, *cara.* I don't like it."

She smiled brightly, then sank into the first seat on the portside.

"Put the seat-back up."

She did.

"Close your safety belt."

She closed it.

"Damn it to hell, are you a robot?"

Aimee widened her eyes. "Isn't that what you want?"

He cursed, bent down and caught her chin in his hand. "I told you not to test me," he said with controlled rage in his voice. "Stop it now, or you will regret what happens next."

She jerked away from him. "I regret everything that's happened already. Why should I fear what happens next?"

Nicolo glared at her. He wanted to slap her. To kiss her. To throw her over his shoulder and carry her to the small bedroom in the rear of the cabin….

Was this what having a wife reduced a man to?

He looked at the seat next to hers. "I already do," he said coldly, and walked to the last seat on the starboard side and buckled himself in.

Moments later, they were skyborne.

Once they'd reached cruising altitude, Nicolo used the plane's satellite phone to call James Black.

At first, the old man didn't believe him.

"Married? Impossible," he scoffed. "There are laws. No one can get married so quickly."

"Aimee and I are married," Nicolo said coldly. And then, because he couldn't contain the words, "I expected you to be delighted by the information, *signore*. After all, it was part of your plan."

"An excellent plan, Your Highness, as I'm sure you now agree."

"There is more."

"Of course. The papers, transferring ownership of the bank to you. I'll start the procedure tomorrow."

Nicolo ran a hand through his hair. Amazing. He'd just told Black his granddaughter was married and all the old man could think about was his damnable bank.

"As I said, Signore Black, there is more."

"More?"

Suddenly Nicolo didn't want Black to know about Aimee's pregnancy. The baby was a private matter, not another thing over which the old man could gloat. Let him think the acquisition of the bank was the reason for the marriage.

"*Mi dispiace, signore.* A, um, a detail I just thought of but we can let the lawyers handle it."

"Then, I'll get my people to work immediately. Where shall they send the documents? To your attorney? Your office? It shouldn't take more than a week. Two, at the most. Are you at the hotel you were at before?"

"I have left the city, Signore Black. I—that is, we—are en route to my home in Rome."

"Excellent. I'll give instructions to forward the documents to you there. Goodbye, Your Highness."

Click. End of conversation. Nicolo was holding a dead phone.

Black hadn't inquired after Aimee. He hadn't asked to speak to her.

Nicolo put the phone aside. As far as her grandfather was concerned, Aimee was a gambit in an intricate business maneuver.

At least the old man would not be able to use her anymore.

He looked at the front of the plane. At Aimee, at his wife, who sat so rigidly in her seat. What was she thinking? In less than two days, her world had turned upside down.

Her grandfather had all but told her that her only value was as a lure. She'd learned she was pregnant. She had been coerced into marriage.

And yet, she remained proud. Strong. Defiant.

Nicolo imagined going to her. Taking her in his arms. Telling her that everything would be all right, that she could trust him to take care of her, that he—that he—

That he what?

He had used her, too. He'd wanted the bank and now he had it.

Nicolo put back his seat, shut his eyes and did his damnedest not to think.

An hour out of New York, the attendant, a pleasant young woman who'd been with him for several years, appeared with a bottle of Dom Pérignon and a pair of flutes.

"I hope you don't mind, sir," she began, "but we all thought…" She fell silent, her eyebrows reaching for the sky as she took in the seating arrangements.

"Thank you," Nicolo said quickly, "but my wife is exhausted and I didn't want to disturb her. Perhaps we'll have the champagne later."

"Of course, sir."

He smiled. Or hoped the way he curved his lips at least resembled a smile. Had he actually just explained himself to an employee? He didn't explain himself to anyone, ever.

"If we change our minds," he said, still straining to sound polite, "I'll ring."

The attendant knew a dismissal when she heard one. "Yes, sir," she said, and started back toward the cockpit.

Aimee stopped her.

"Wait," he heard her say.

The attendant leaned over the seat, listened, then smiled.

"That's very kind of you, *Principessa. Grazie.*"

Nicolo waited a few minutes after the attendant left. Then he walked up the aisle and took the seat next to Aimee's. Her face was turned to the window.

"Are you awake?"

The truth was he didn't give a damn one way or the other. He was tired of her silence, her coldness, of the way she'd made him look foolish during the ceremony and again now.

It was time he made things clear.

She was his wife. She would treat him with respect at all times.

"Did you really think I could sleep?"

"Your behavior continues to be unacceptable."

She looked at him then and the despair he saw in her eyes was like a knife to the heart.

That pain, knowing that she held him solely responsible for it, made him even more angry.

"Perhaps you didn't hear me," she said, as politely as she might speak to a servant. "I apologized."

"Perhaps you whispered your apology," he said coldly, "because I didn't hear it."

"I meant that I apologized to Barbara. The cabin attendant. It was sweet of her to bring champagne and I wanted her to know I hadn't meant to be rude. You were right. There's no reason for me to be discourteous to those who work for you."

He could almost hear the part she left unsaid, that there was every reason to be discourteous to him.

In the name of all the saints!

All right. He had to calm himself. Not take every word, every intonation, as a personal affront. She was his wife; they had to find a way to make the best of things.

He would offer a conciliatory gesture.

"Well, that was generous of you." He hesitated. "Would you like to join me for dinner?"

She turned her face to the window. "I'm not hungry."

"It's another three hours until—"

"I said, I'm not hungry."

So much for conciliatory gestures. And that tone of voice! When had she begun using it? Did she know what an insult it was, to be spoken to that way?

She had surely grown up with servants and after watching how she'd just dealt with Barbara, he'd damned well bet she'd never treated an employee or a servant as she was treating him.

If he'd whisked her away from a life of deprivation, she might behave differently....

What an ugly thing to think!

Still, she might at least show some interest in him. In her new life. In where he was taking her.

He didn't know why that should matter, but it did.

"I live in Rome," he said, after the silence became too much. "In the oldest part of the city. The *palazzo's* been in my family for centuries, but it wasn't in very good repair until I—"

"I don't care."

Nicolo didn't think. He reacted. Grabbed her, hauled her out of her seat and onto his lap. She started to scream and he captured her mouth with his, thrust his tongue between her lips, slipped his hands under her skirt.

She bit him. Beat at his shoulders with her fists. It didn't stop him. Nothing would. He had taken enough.

Her panties tore in half and she cried out, the sound muffled by his kiss.

"Such a lady you are now, *cara*," he said against her mouth. "Such an elegant, bloodless gentlewoman with everyone except me."

"Nicolo. If you do this—"

"You'll what? Scream? Go ahead. You'll only embarrass yourself. I am Nicolo Barbieri. The sooner you learn what that means, the better."

He kissed her again and again, his hand moving against her flesh under her yellow skirt, cupping her, touching her, hating himself for what he was doing, hating her for what she had reduced him to, wanting what had happened between them that first night, that magical night, to happen again….

But not like this.

His kiss softened.

The stroke of his fingers became tender. He whispered Aimee's name between gentle kisses and all at once, she sighed against his mouth.

Her arms went around his neck.

Her lips parted beneath his.

And the petals of the sweetly feminine bud between her thighs began to bloom, the dew of it sweet and welcome against his palm.

Nicolo groaned. Shifted Aimee so that she was straddling him. Reached for his zipper...

And realized that even as she kissed him, his wife was weeping. Weeping as if her heart might break.

Nicolo went still. Then he groaned, though not with desire, and folded her into his arms.

"Don't cry," he murmured. "Please, *il mio amante,* don't cry."

He whispered to her, soft English words giving way to softer ones in Italian as he rocked her gently against his heart and stroked her honey-colored curls back from her face.

Gradually Aimee's sobs faded. She sighed deeply; he felt her breathing slow.

And knew she was asleep. Asleep, in his arms.

Nicolo sat without moving, his heart filled with a sweet, soaring emotion. Tenderness, he thought in surprise.

Tenderness.

Time slipped by. Finally, carefully, he depressed the button that reclined the leather seat. He lay back, drew Aimee even closer until she was lying in his arms, her body softly pressed against his, this woman fate had brought into his life.

This wife he hadn't wanted. This wife he didn't want...

She sighed, curved her arm around his neck. He felt the warmth of her breath, the warmth of her.

Something shifted inside him.

Nicolo closed his eyes and buried his face in Aimee's hair. He held her that way until he knew they were on their approach to Rome.

Then, carefully, he eased his arms from around his

sleeping wife, rose and went back to his seat in the rear of the cabin.

It was a lot safer than staying where he was.

CHAPTER TEN

SOMEONE was gently shaking Aimee's shoulder. She came awake slowly, lips curved in a hesitant smile.

"Nicolo?" she whispered.

"No, *Principessa. Scusi.*" The attendant smiled in apology. "The prince is in the rear of the cabin. Shall I get him for you?"

"No!" Flustered, Aimee sat up and ran her hands through her sleep-tangled curls. "That won't be necessary."

"I'm sorry to disturb you, but we'll be on the ground in a few minutes. Safety regulations require you to fasten your seat belt and return your seat to an upright position."

"Of course. Thank you."

The flight attendant nodded and made her way to the cockpit. Alone again, Aimee checked her watch. Had she really slept for most of the flight? It was too long a time; it had left her feeling groggy.

She always reacted that way to transatlantic flights. Groggy. Disoriented...

Had she dreamed of being in Nicolo's arms? Dreamed he'd begun to make love to her?

She had responded. God, yes, she'd responded....

And started to weep, knowing it was wrong. Wrong to want him, to need him, to yearn for his possession.

"Shh," he'd murmured, going from passion to tenderness in a heartbeat, holding her close, rocking her in his arms, promising that she had nothing to fear, that he would always take care of her...

It had to have been a dream.

If Nicolo had tried to make love to her, she wouldn't have let him. And he'd never have been satisfied with simply holding her in his arms. He hadn't married her for that.

He'd married her for the bank. For the child in her womb.

For sex.

The plane gave a gentle lurch as the wheels touched the runway. Aimee undid her seat belt. By the time she rose to her feet, Nicolo was at her side. His hand closed around her elbow.

"Thank you," she said politely, "but I'm perfectly capable of managing on my own."

"Are you always this gracious, *cara,* or is it something you reserve for me?"

Aimee jerked away from him and walked to the door. The pilot and copilot smiled and touched their hats.

"Buona notte, Principessa."

Principessa. That was who she was now. Was the title supposed to make up for the loss of her independence?

She forced a smile, wished them a good evening, too, and went down the steps to the tarmac.

It was night. She'd known it would be; still, the sense of disorientation swept over her again. She must have swayed. Stumbled. Something, because Nicolo gave an impatient snort and put his arm around her waist.

"I said—"

"I know what you said." He drew her close and led her toward a black Mercedes that waited a few yards away, a uniformed driver standing rigidly beside it. At their approach, he snapped his heels together, saluted and opened the rear door.

Apparently the sight of his employer half carrying a woman through the night was not unusual.

"*Sede benvenuta, Principe.*"

"*Grazie,* Giorgio. Aimee, this is my driver. Giorgio, this is *mia moglie.* My wife."

Giorgio touched his cap again. "*Principessa,*" he said, but he didn't so much as blink.

Why would he? Nicolo wasn't just his boss, he was of royal blood. In America, especially in Manhattan, royals were just another species of celebrity. The gossip columns gushed over their doings but real people, New York people, hardly took notice.

This was not New York.

This was Rome. Nicolo's turf. It meant something here, to be known as a prince.

Aimee shuddered. In that single moment, she finally understood what had happened to her.

She'd left more than her old life behind. She'd left who she was—and who she might have been.

Her husband was everything she'd fought against all her life, and she was all but helpless to fight his demands... though he'd learn soon enough that she'd damned well die trying.

And for all of that, she still melted when he touched her.

Aimee's heart began to race. She wasn't ready for this! No one could be. So many changes, so many pages torn out and discarded from the life she'd planned for herself...

She began to tremble and despised herself for it but the more she tried to stop, the more she shook. She tried covering it with a flippant remark about the great Prince Barbieri being too important to have bothered with Customs.

Nicolo wasn't buying it.

"Are you ill?"

"I'm fine."

Her teeth, clicking like castanets, spoiled the lie. Nicolo muttered something, put his arms around her and drew her into his lap.

"Don't," she said, but he ignored her, drew her closer until she was encased in his warmth.

She tried to sit up straight, even now that she was in his lap, but it was impossible. For one thing, she felt silly, perched like that.

For another, he wouldn't permit it. His arms tightened around her and he gathered her closer to him.

"Stop being foolish," he said sternly. "I am not about to sit here and listen to your teeth chatter."

Finally she gave up fighting and lay back in his arms. As soon as she did, she knew it was what she wanted to do, despite her protests.

Though it made no sense, being in Nicolo's arms made her feel safe.

They rode in a silence broken only by the soft purr of the car's engine through the dark, winding streets of a sleeping Rome.

After a while, Aimee realized the Mercedes was climbing a hill.

"The Pallatine," Nicolo said, as if he'd read her mind. "My home—our home—is on its crest."

Ahead, a high gate swung slowly open. The car moved through it, then along a straight, narrow road that lay like a ribbon of black velvet. Tall Roman pines on either side blocked out the sky.

Suddenly a building loomed up before them.

"The Palazzo Barbieri," Nicolo said softly. "It has been in our family since the time of Caesar."

The night was too dark, the *palazzo* still too far away to see clearly, but Aimee didn't have to see the details to know the palace would be a hulking, joyless paean to antiquity.

It would swallow her whole.

She shuddered, and Nicolo cupped her face and turned it to his.

"*Cara,*" he said softly, "don't be afraid."

"I'm not," Aimee answered quickly, as if the lie might make it true. "I've never been afraid of anything in my life."

Nicolo looked at her defiant expression and thought it might be true. Or, at least, that she had learned, early, that showing fear could be dangerous.

It was a lesson he understood.

Courage, a show of it, anyway, was the conqueror of demons. It was how he had overcome poverty and, he suspected, how his wife had survived James Black's attempts to control her life and undermine her spirit.

His wife.

This beautiful, brave woman was his wife. Had he taken a moment to tell her he was proud to have made her his *principessa?* To tell her that he knew theirs was a rocky start but he would do his best to make her happy? To tell her—to tell her that he was not sorry he'd made her pregnant, because he wasn't. He wasn't. He—

"*Principe Nicolo. Siamo arrivato.*"

Nicolo blinked. The car had stopped; Giorgio stood beside the open rear door, eyes straight ahead, back rigid, chauffeur's cap square on his head.

How many times had he told the man he didn't want him to show subservience or, even worse, to wear that ridiculous cap?

All right. Time to take a deep breath. This was becoming a habit, letting his anger at himself turn into anger at others.

He stepped from the car, Aimee still in his arms. She struggled; he tightened his grasp.

"Really, Nicolo, I'm all right now."

"Really, Aimee," he said in near-perfect imitation of her tone, "you are not all right. It is late, you are tired and you are with child."

She shot a look at the driver.

"Nicolo!"

"My wife is pregnant, Giorgio," Nicolo said, and started up the wide steps to the door of the *palazzo*.

A quick smile tugged at the driver's lips. Aimee felt her face flame.

"Shh," she hissed.

"Tomorrow, first thing, we shall see an OB-GIN."

"OB-GYN, and must you announce it to the world?"

"I should have thought of it sooner. *Dio,* for all I know, you should not have taken such a long flight."

"For goodness' sakes," she said, glaring at him, "I'm *pregnant,* not—"

Aimee heard a loud gasp. She looked around. The *palazzo* doors had swung open on an enormous entrance hall....

And she had made her announcement to six, God, to seven people, all of them staring at her and beaming.

"Buona notte," Nicolo said pleasantly. "Aimee. This is my staff."

He rattled off names and duties. A housekeeper. Two cooks. Three maids. A gardener. They curtsied, bowed, smiled. Aimee, trapped in Nicolo's arms, wishing the floor would open so she could drop through it, did her best to smile back.

"And this," he told the little assemblage, "is *mia moglie.* My wife."

A gasp. A giggle. A hand quickly clapped over a mouth.

"As she has already told you, she is pregnant with my child."

Aimee started to bury her face in his throat but the sound of his voice stopped her.

Since she'd told him she was pregnant, Nicolo had gone from disbelief to shock to a stern acceptance of responsibility.

Now—now, his words resonated with pride. He sounded like a man who was happy his woman was having his baby.

She tilted her face up to his. For a heartbeat, they looked deep into each other's eyes.

Then the staff of the Barbieri *palazzo* broke into wild applause.

Aimee blushed. Nicolo laughed and dropped a light kiss on her lips. Then he carried her up the stairs.

A sweet moment, she thought in surprise, after a day of darkness...

But it didn't last.

He carried her down the hall, through another pair of massive doors, put her on her feet...

And everything changed

They were in a bedroom. His bedroom. You didn't need a sign on the wall to tell you that.

The room was huge and handsome, assuming your idea of "handsome" involved a marble fireplace big enough for an ox roast flanked by a pair of burnished-by-time leather sofas, a—a *thing* on the wall that was surely a crossbow...

And a bed the size of Aimee's entire apartment back in Manhattan.

Nicolo had already shut the door and tossed his jacket on a chair. *Say something,* she thought, searched frantically for something clever and instead blurted, "This is your room."

He looked at her as if she were a not-terribly-bright five-year-old.

"How clever of you, *cara*."

She needed to be calm. After all, he'd been very civilized just a few minutes ago.

"And where—" She cleared her throat. "And where is mine? I told you—"

"My memory is excellent," he said coolly. His hands were at his belt buckle. "I know what you told me. That we would have—what is it called? A marriage of convenience."

"Yes. And you—" The belt fell open. "Must you do that?"

"Do what?"

"You're—you're undressing…."

He pulled his shirt over his head. Muscles rippled in his forearms and biceps. Don't look, she told herself, but only a fool would have averted her eyes from the wide shoulders, the silky covering of coal-black hair on his broad chest, the washboard abs, the burgeoning male beauty she knew made up the rest of him.

"*Si*. I am undressing. It's what I generally do when it's late and I'm tired." His eyes met hers. "And ready for bed."

Her knees turned to water. Her heartbeat accelerated. *Don't look. Don't answer. Don't let him draw you into this game.*

"Aren't you ready for bed, too, *cara*?" He came toward her, the look on his face more powerful than any aphrodisiac. Slowly he reached out, trailed a lazy finger the length of her throat. "Aimee," he said in a low, husky voice, "come to bed."

She stared at him, hypnotized by his words, his eyes, by the intensity of her own desire because she wanted him, wanted him, wanted him….

"No," she said in a choked whisper and fled past him, into the bathroom, slammed the door and locked it.

"Aimee."

Nicolo's fist pounded against the door. Aimee dragged in a sobbing breath and closed her eyes.

"Aimee. Open this door!"

She shook her head as if he could see her. She would not open it. She would never open it or give herself to him because if she did—if she did, he would have everything. The respect she'd never been able to wrest from her grandfather. The bank that should have been hers. The child he'd put in her belly…

And her.

Most of all, worst of all, he'd have her. Her body, her soul, her passion…

And what would remain of Aimee Black then? Nothing. She would disappear. Everything she'd worked so hard to be, the independent woman she was, would be consumed in the fire of their lovemaking.

But she could survive that.

She could thrive on it.

Oh, she could…if only what Nicolo felt for her was more than desire. If what he felt was—if what he felt was—

"Aimee, damn it!" The door shuddered under another blow. "When will you stop running? When will you admit what you want, what we both want?"

Never, she thought, never!

Another blow against the door. Not his fist this time. His shoulder. And the door swung open and banged against the tiled wall.

Aimee cried out. Jumped back, fists raised. She would fight him to keep him from dominating her.

"Damn you, Nicolo—"

"Perhaps," he said grimly, "but you are my wife. You

will do as I say. And what I say, tonight, is that I'm tired of you pretending you don't want me when we both know damned well you do."

He reached for her. Dragged her into his arms. She swung at him; he caught both her wrists, trapped her hands between them. Took her mouth…

And tasted not her anger but her tears, just as he had on the plane.

Dio, he thought. *Dio,* what was he doing?

"Aimee."

He tried to lift her face to his. She wouldn't let him.

"Aimee. *Mia cara…*"

The sound of her weeping was killing him. Nicolo cursed softly, swept his wife into his arms and held her close, his mouth against her temple.

"Don't cry," he whispered, "Aimee, *il mio tresoro,* I beg you, don't cry."

She was pregnant, ill and exhausted. And all he'd thought about was himself.

Slowly he gathered her to him. Rocked her against him. Pressed light kisses into her hair.

Little by little, her weeping stopped.

"Good girl," he said softly.

Nicolo stepped out of the bathroom and carried her to the bed. He sat down, his back against the silk pillows, his wife in his arms, his cheek pressed to the top of her head.

"Forgive me, *amante,*" he whispered. "You were very brave today and I have repaid that bravery with terror."

Aimee drew in a staggered breath. Nicolo reached to the night table, took a handful of tissues from a box and brought them to her nose.

"Blow," he said softly.

She did. The sound made him smile.

"Such a big sound for such a delicate female," he said.

"I'm not delicate."

He smiled again. Her voice was small but still, she couldn't let his throwaway remark pass without argument. The look of a tigress and the heart of one, as well.

"More tissues?"

Aimee shook her head.

"You sure? I'm getting good at this. Paper towels, tissues…who knows? Someday, I might even work up to a handkerchief."

Did her lips curve in a smile? He wanted to believe they had.

"Aimee." He tilted her face to his. This time, she let him do it. "*Cara,* I am sorry."

Nothing. Well, what had he expected? She hated him.

"It is something I do, this—this thing of making quick decisions, of not asking advice."

Not true. He made decisions that seemed quick but only after he'd done his homework. He didn't ask advice often but when he did, he respected the answers he received.

He was not a man given to impulse, especially in his private life. He'd seen too many men with money and power make spur-of-the-moment choices about women, and end up paying for it for the rest of their lives, financially and emotionally.

To give in to impulse was dangerous. A sure road to disaster. Emotion had no part in decision-making…

Except when it came to Aimee. To wanting her. Needing her. Desiring her, in his arms, his bed, his life…

Nicolo frowned.

Aimee was exhausted, but she wasn't the only one. So was he. Otherwise, he wouldn't be having such strange thoughts.

Carefully he eased her from his arms, onto the bed beside him, then rose to his feet.

"Sleep here tonight," he said carefully. "We can discuss our room arrangements tomorrow. Meanwhile, I'll ring for Anna. She'll help you undress and get to bed."

He looked down at his wife. Her hair was spread across the pillows—*his* pillows—in a wild, honey-soft tangle. Her face was still pale, her eyes glittered from the tears she'd shed, her mouth trembled….

And he knew that he wanted her for more than the child she carried, certainly for more than the bank her grandfather owned. He wanted her for reasons he couldn't understand and that made it all the more important to step back, walk away….

But he didn't.

Instead he took her hands in his.

"Or," he said gruffly, "I can undress you. I can put you to bed and lie with you, *cara*. Not to make love to you but to hold you in my arms as you sleep…and to promise you that I will honor you, care for you, that I will not frighten you again."

He wasn't sure what he expected her to say. Anything from "no" to "are you insane?" would probably have suited… But when she finally answered him, it was in a whisper so soft he had to bend his head to hear it.

"I—I feel safe when you hold me."

He swallowed. "You should, *cara*. After all, I am—I am your husband."

Their eyes met. Aimee smiled. Nicolo smiled back. Then he went to his closet and returned with a pair of burgundy-colored silk pajamas.

"Stand up," he said softly.

Aimee obeyed. Turned her back so he could unzip the yellow dress. Strip it from her. Under it, she wore only a scrap of white lace.

Nicolo swallowed again. Decided that leaving the bit

of lace would probably be the only intelligent thing to do, but why worry about intelligence?

A man who stripped a woman naked, then didn't touch her, had no claim on intelligence.

Carefully he hooked his thumbs in the panties. She gave a little gasp and he acted as if it were important that he was easing them down her hips, her long legs.

"Lift your foot. Now the other," he said and that gave him away. Was that thick, rough voice really his?

He tossed the scrap of lace aside. Rose to his feet. Did his best not to look at his wife but how could he not, when she was so exquisite? He had not seen her naked since the night they'd met but he remembered, oh, yes, he remembered....

Her body had changed. He would not have imagined it possible but it was even more beautiful now that she carried his baby. Her breasts were larger, her nipples darker. And her belly... Was he wrong, or was it just slightly fuller?

By all the saints, he was going to lose his sanity if he didn't cup her breasts, lift them to his lips and kiss them. Kneel before her, put his mouth to her belly, to her feminine delta...

Nicolo dropped the burgundy pajama top on the bed and turned his back. "There," he said briskly. "That's for you. I'll wear the bottoms. Okay?"

He sensed her nod of acquiescence; he was not fool enough to look at her to make sure. As it was, he was doing mental multiplication tables to try to keep from becoming erect.

He had promised all he'd do was hold her in his arms and that was what he would do.

Quickly he took off what remained of his own clothes, stepped into the PJ bottoms and tied them.

"Ready?"

"Ready," Aimee said softly.

A deep, deep breath. Then he swung around. Her sandals stood neatly beside the bed; her panties were on the night table.

She was under the blanket.

God was merciful, after all.

Nicolo forced a smile, lifted the covers and slid in beside her. For a moment, neither of them moved. Then he turned, and she turned, and suddenly she was in his arms.

She smelled of flowers.

Her skin was silky.

Her hair was soft.

Eight times three is twenty-four. Twenty-four times two is forty-eight. Forty-eight times two is ninety-six. Ninety-six times, Dio, *ninety-six times ninety-six is—is—*

Nicolo shut his eyes, gathered Aimee into his embrace. She sighed, her breath a susurration of sweet warmth against his throat.

Please, he thought, please, let her fall asleep quickly. Once she did, he'd get up, read a book. Do some work. Anything but lie here with Aimee in his arms because, of course, he would not sleep. This was too much. She was half-naked, they were completely alone…

He smiled.

And she had not called him a name in easily half an hour. That was a first.

It was a night of firsts. He'd never had a wife before, never even had a woman in this bed until now. He'd never slept with one without making love to her and most of all, most of all, he'd never held a woman against him and felt—and felt—

He drew back a little. Another minute, he'd carefully push back the covers, leave the bed—

"Nicolo?"

His wife's voice was soft as the touch of a feather.

"Yes, *cara?*"

"Did I fall asleep in your arms on the plane, or was it a dream?"

Nicolo brushed his lips lightly over hers. "It was not a dream, *amante.* You slept just like this…and I hated to leave you."

"I'm sorry you did," she whispered.

A second later, she was asleep.

Get up, Nicolo told himself, you damned fool, get out of this bed right now.

Instead he rolled onto his back, taking Aimee with him, her head nestled in the curve of his shoulder, her arm thrown lightly over his chest.

He stared up at the ceiling, at a tiny bit of moonlight caught in the ancient fresco of cherubs and fauns.

"Ninety-six times ninety-six," he whispered into the darkness, "is—is nine thousand two hundred and sixteen."

Then, to his amazement, he closed his eyes and slept.

CHAPTER ELEVEN

SOMETIME JUST before dawn, it began to rain.

The windows were all open; a breeze ruffled the curtains and brought with it the scent of the gardens that surrounded the *palazzo*.

Aimee was warm and safe in Nicolo's arms, her body sprawled half over his, hearts beating in unison.

She was asleep.

He was awake.

Awake, and enduring the sweetest kind of torture. The feel of her against him. The whisper of her breath against his naked shoulder. The gentle weight of her thigh over his.

Nicolo was trapped halfway between the heaven of holding his beautiful wife in his embrace and the hell of knowing he had promised he would not touch her.

It had seemed an easy promise to make.

Aimee was exhausted. She was pregnant. And he had no wish to risk the fragile peace that had sent her into his arms hours before by doing something foolish.

Except—except, he hadn't expected her to drape herself over him like this. To sigh so sweetly each time she shifted against him. He hadn't expected to want to wake her with his kisses, with his caresses, and tell her that somewhere between yesterday and today, he had gone from feeling like a man in a trap to a man who had—who had met his destiny.

A destiny he welcomed.

Nicolo frowned into the darkness.

How could that be? His life was perfect. The pauper prince had made himself one of the world's richest men. He was respected. Admired. He had everything a man could possibly want….

And now, he had more.

A child on the way. And a wife.

Aimee. Bright. Articulate. And exasperating. But *Dio,* what courage she had! Choosing a life she didn't want, a life that was the opposite of the one he knew she'd desired, because it was the right thing to do.

Aimee, who excited him more than any woman he'd known.

Was she his destiny?

Not that he believed in such things. A man was born into the world. Beyond that, the life he lived was his own. You made choices, walked a path you controlled.

Or maybe not.

Was there a force people called fate? Did it wait for the chance to scoop you up and put you on a different path? A path you'd never intended to follow?

Was that what had happened to him?

Two days ago, he'd been Nicolo Barbieri, prince of a royal house of Rome. A man who headed a financial empire. Who answered to no one.

Aimee sighed and burrowed closer.

Now, he was Nicolo Barbieri, husband and soon-to-be father. It was an impressive responsibility, one he surely hadn't planned or wanted….

And yet, it felt right. The baby in Aimee's womb. Aimee in his arms. In his bed.

Aimee, his bride. His wife. His—his—

Nicolo frowned. Carefully he eased his arm from her shoulders, his leg from beneath her thigh. He needed a cup of espresso. Or a walk around the garden. Or maybe he'd turn on his computer, check his e-mail. Yes. That was what he would do. In the confusion of the last few days, he'd damned near lost touch with his office.

He had never done that before.

He sat up, rose from the bed and ran his hands through his hair.

This was not good, this disruption in his life. He had a company to run, people who looked to him for direction. He had to get back on track. He would shower, turn on the computer. His housekeeper would be up soon; over a quick breakfast, he'd talk with her, ask her to explain the functions of his household to Aimee when she came down, arrange for Giorgio to drive her to whatever shops she wished. Oh, and he would contact his physician, ask him to recommend the best OB-GYN in Rome.

No more of this nonsense. Of putting everything aside just because he'd made a woman pregnant and married her—

"Nicolo?"

He swung around. Aimee was sitting up against the pillows. He could see her clearly in the rain-washed light of dawn. Her eyes filled with uncertainty. Her cascade of tousled curls. The outline of her breasts under his pajama top.

This was his wife. His woman. His Aimee.

Everything else flew out of his head. Something swept through him, an emotion so powerful it made his breath catch.

"Yes, *cara*," he said softly. Smiling, he went to the bed and sat down next to her. "I'm sorry. I didn't mean to wake you."

Aimee pushed her hair away from her eyes.

"I didn't mean to sleep so late."

"No, sweetheart, it isn't late at all. The sun's barely up. I just—I just couldn't sleep anymore."

"Jet lag," she said, with a little smile.

"Si," he said, because that was easier than explaining what had driven him from the bed.

And what had now brought him back to it.

"Go back to sleep, *cara.* You need your rest."

"No. No, I'm—I'm—" She went white. "Oh. Oh…"

She shot from the bed so quickly that he had only risen to his feet by the time she slammed the bathroom door after her.

"Go away," she gasped when he flung it open, and then she bent over the commode and retched.

Nicolo's heart turned over. He cupped her shoulders, steadied her until the spasm passed. Then he turned her in his arms, despite her protests.

"I will take you back to bed," he said firmly. "And you will stay there until the doctor arrives."

"I'm not sick. This is just a thing that happens to some women when they're pregnant." She looked up with a shaky smile. "I'll be fine once I wash up. You'll see."

She was right about the vomiting. He knew that much. He also knew that he'd been terrified, seeing her suffer.

"Nicolo. Please. Go away and let me clean up."

Aimee watched him consider the situation and wondered if this was how he looked in his office, so dark, determined and brooding. Finally he nodded curtly, took a new toothbrush from a drawer in the vanity, showed her where the towels were, the comb, the hairbrush….

"Nicolo," Aimee said gently. "I'll find everything on my own. I promise."

She had to swear she would call him if she felt ill, that

she wouldn't lock the door so he could reach her quickly if necessary.

Finally she was alone.

She showered. Washed her hair, brushed her teeth, wrapped herself in a huge towel....

And tried not to think about the man waiting in the next room.

Her husband.

She had slept in his arms all night. Close to him. Warmed by him. Comforted by his presence.

She'd also been awake when he'd awakened this morning.

She'd wanted to tell him that, but she'd been mortified to find herself draped half over him. Besides, what did you say to your husband when you didn't know him?

Good morning didn't seem to cut it.

Especially when what you really wanted to do—what you *really* wanted was not to say a word but to clasp his face, bring his mouth to yours, kiss him and tell him that you'd changed your mind, you didn't want to be his wife in name only....

Aimee shut her eyes. Took a deep breath. Opened the door. With luck, Nicolo would have dressed and gone by now....

He hadn't.

He was standing in the middle of the room, bare-chested, arms folded, eyes almost black as he looked at her.

"Are you better?"

She nodded. "I'm fine."

His gaze swept over her. The towel was big but that gaze made her feel naked.

"We will see a physician today."

"Really, I'm—"

"You're beautiful."

His voice was husky. The sound of it, that look in his eyes, made her heart turn over.

"No. I mean, I haven't dried my hair. And I'm already gaining weight. And—"

"Where is this weight?"

"My breasts. My belly. Not much, but—"

"I want to see."

A heavy silence descended on the room. Aimee's eyes met Nicolo's.

"I want to see the changes my child has made in you," he said softly as he started toward her. He stopped inches away, his hands now at his sides, his eyes hot on hers. "Let me look at you."

"Nicolo." Her tongue felt thick. She swallowed, swallowed again. "I don't think—"

"That's right. Don't think." He reached out, grasped the edge of the towel she clutched to her breasts. "It is a husband's right to see his wife." And before she could muster a shield of anger at that bit of arrogance, he added a single word that left her defenseless. "Please."

Aimee took a deep breath. Then, slowly, she let go of the towel.

For what seemed an eternity, Nicolo stood still. Didn't touch her. Didn't do anything but sweep his eyes over her nakedness.

Then he cupped her breasts. Feathered his thumbs over her nipples. Ran his hand down her ribs and over her belly.

He looked up at her, and what she saw in his face made her heartbeat stumble.

"Aimee," he said thickly, "my wife. My beautiful, amazing wife…"

The next instant, she was in his arms.

He kissed her hungrily and she returned his kiss. Her arms wound around his neck as he carried her to the bed and lay her down among the sheets of softest Egyptian cotton.

He kissed her hair, her temple, her throat. Her soft moans, the way she lifted herself to him, stoked the flames he'd tried so hard to control.

He told himself he would be gentle. She was pregnant. She'd been ill. She needed tenderness, not the fire that burned within him....

And then her lips parted. The tip of her tongue stroked into his mouth—and Nicolo was lost.

He bent to her breasts, sucked the nipples deep into his mouth. Aimee cried out, arched toward him and it was all he could do not to part her thighs and bury himself inside her.

She tasted of honey. Of cream. Of all the delicacies in the universe. He loved the sweetness of her skin, the tang of salt as it began to heat under his caresses.

He loved everything about this. About her. The way she responded to him, without holding anything back.

That first night, their coming together had been wild, almost savage, but now he realized she'd let him be the aggressor.

Now, she was the one, telling him with every motion, every sigh, that she wanted him. Wanted this. Wanted all he could give her and more.

Her hands explored his shoulders. His chest. She kissed his throat, touched her tongue to the hollow where he knew his heart must be racing.

"Nicolo," she whispered, and her fingers brushed the tip of his straining erection.

He let her explore him, loving her touch, her caution, her, yes, her innocence, but when her hand closed around him, he knew it was time to take control of her and of himself.

"No," he said roughly and caught her wrists, pinned them high over her head, held her captive to his lips, his teeth, his kisses until she was sobbing with need.

"Please," she whispered, "please…"

Nicolo tore off his pajama bottoms, kicked them away. Knelt between his wife's thighs and kissed that tender flesh. She cried out, arched to him again and he brushed the back of his hand over the honey-colored curls that guarded her femininity.

Aimee cried out. Bucked under him and he caught her wrists again, this time in one hand, and used the other to touch her.

She was wet.

Fragrant with arousal.

She was sobbing. Pleading. And he—he was going to explode if he didn't take her soon.

Her clitoris was swollen with passion and when he finally let go of her wrists, slipped his hands under her bottom and brought her to his mouth, her taste was exquisite.

Aimee cried out and he moved up her body, spread her thighs wide and she wrapped her legs around his hips.

"Now," he said, and entered her on a long, hard thrust.

Her cry was high and sweet and all he had ever yearned for. He surged forward again and she screamed, flung her head back and came apart in his arms again and again as he held her, as he caught her mouth with his and drank in her sobs.

"Nico," she whispered against his mouth and he shot over the edge, let go of who he was, who he had been, all of it lost in the warm, welcoming body of his wife.

A lifetime later, Nicolo stirred. Aimee was still beneath him and he began to roll away from her, but she put her arms around him and held him close.

"Stay," she whispered.

He wanted to. He would stay like this forever, if he could.

"I'm too heavy for you, *cara mia*."

"I don't care."

She sounded so determined, it made him smile.

"Let's try reversing things." He rolled onto his back and took her with him so that she was sprawled on top of him. "How's that?"

She gave the kind of long sigh that reached straight into his heart.

"It's wonderful."

Oh, it was. More than wonderful, he thought, wrapping his arms even more tightly around her. They lay that way for a few minutes, until his heartbeat and hers had slowed. Then he cupped the back of her head and brought her mouth to his for a tender kiss.

"Are you all right?" he said softly.

Her lips curved against his. "I'm very all right."

Nicolo grinned. "I agree completely, *Principessa*. In fact…" Another kiss, longer than the last. "You are wonderfully all right.

"I liked what you called me," he said, stroking the curls back from her face.

Aimee propped her chin on her hands. "What I called you?"

"*Si*. Nico." He smiled. "No one ever called me Nico before."

"Never?"

"Never. My governesses always referred to me as *Principe*." He chuckled. "Except for one daring Englishwoman who called me Master Nicolo."

"Were there many governesses?"

He nodded. "My parents were always traveling. My

great-grandmother lived with us but she was already very old when I was born, so I was raised by governesses. And whenever my parents came home, they'd find fault with the governess of the moment and fire her."

"They were that awful?"

"Some were better than others but none were 'awful.'"

"Then, why?"

Nicolo sighed. "It took me a while to figure it out but I finally realized it was jealousy. My mother would see my attachment to a governess and that was the kiss of death."

Aimee framed his face between her hands.

"If your mother wanted you to love her, why didn't she stay home and take care of you herself?"

"It was just the way they were, *cara,* she and my father. Their lives were all about self-gratification. No responsibility. No money, either. The *palazzo* was falling down around my ears by the time I inherited it—but that was how they lived, on their titles and the largesse of their friends."

"And now?"

Nicolo lifted his mouth to hers for a kiss. "And now, *amante mia,* it no longer matters. They are both gone. A plane, taking them to a polo match in Palm Springs…"

"Oh, I'm sorry."

"It's all right, sweetheart. To tell the truth, I didn't know them well enough to miss them."

"A child shouldn't grow up that way."

The fervor in her voice made him smile.

"No. I agree." He stroked his hand down her back. "And you, *cara?* How was life with James Black… Or do I not have to ask?"

Aimee sighed. "He took me in when my parents died. I'll always be grateful to him for that. I was very little, you see, and there was no money… My father had married a woman Grandfather didn't find suitable, and…"

"And," Nicolo said, trying to control his sudden anger, "he did his best to make your father pay for it and to hell with how it affected you or your mother."

There was a time Aimee would have defended her grandfather. She'd have said he'd done what he thought was right, but now she'd married a man who had done what he thought was right and it had nothing to do with what he'd wanted for himself but only with what he wanted for others.

For her and their unborn child.

"Yes," she said softly, "he didn't care about anyone but himself. But my parents were happy, Nicolo. They adored each other and they adored me. I loved them so much and then—and then they died and I went to live with Grandfather, and—and—" She gave a sad little laugh that almost broke his heart. "There he was, stuck with the child of a woman he'd never acknowledged. A girl child, at that."

"I'm sure he didn't hide his disappointment," Nicolo said, his voice harsh.

"I wasn't what he wanted. I had no desire to learn to become the perfect wife to his idea of the perfect husband."

"A man he'd choose," Nicolo said, rolling her beneath him. "A captain of industry, with blood as blue as your grandfather's."

Aimee ran her fingers through Nicolo's tousled black curls. "Were you listening to all those conversations?" she said with a little smile.

"A man who could control you, as he had not been able to do."

Her smile faded. How quickly he'd understood. "Yes."

"And who would love Stafford-Coleridge-Black more than he loved you."

Aimee tried to look away. Nicolo wouldn't let her. He

caught her face between his palms and held it steady under his gaze. Her eyes glittered, but she forced a smile.

"And he got what he wanted," she said lightly, "from the blue blood all the way to Stafford-Coleridge-Bl—"

Nicolo silenced her with a deep, passionate kiss.

"I married you," he said fiercely, "not your grandfather's financial empire."

"It's all right. You don't have to try to make it sound as if—as if—"

"I married you because you carry my child. And because you are a strong, beautiful, fascinating woman."

"Please." Her voice trembled. "You don't have to lie."

"No lies, *cara*. Not now, not ever. Do you really think I'd have married you to get my hands on that damned bank?"

Even as he spoke the words, he knew they were true. He had married Aimee because she was going to bear his child, and because—because—

Because what? The answer was tantalizingly close.

For now, all he could come up with was the way to prove to his wife that he wanted her.

"Tomorrow," he said, "I will contact your grandfather. I will tell him that I do not want his bank."

"But you *do* want it! I won't let you do that for me."

"I am doing it for me, *cara*. Because—because I am— I am happy." He saw the smile that lit his bride's face and his heart seemed to expand within his chest. "I am very happy," he said softly, "and it has nothing to do with your grandfather's bank." Nicolo shifted his weight so Aimee could feel what lying against her had done to him. "I'm happy because of this," he whispered. "My child in your womb. And you, *anima mia,* forever in my arms."

"What does that mean? *Anima mia?*"

He smiled. "It means that you are my soul."

Tears glittered on Aimee's lashes. Was it possible to go from despair to joy so quickly?

The answer came a heartbeat later, when Nicolo slid deep inside her. Yes. Oh, yes, it was possible.

"Nico," Aimee whispered, "Nico…"

Then, for a very long time, there was no sound but the gentle patter of the rain and the softness of the lovers' sighs.

CHAPTER TWELVE

"BUON GIORNO, cara mia."

Nicolo's soft voice was the first thing Aimee heard as she awakened. She was lying close to him; he was on his belly, smiling down at her as her eyes fluttered open.

Her heart turned over. What a perfect start to a new day. To a new life.

"Buon giorno, Nicolo," she said softly.

She almost laughed at the look on his face. "You speak Italian?"

"Of course," she said, as if there could be no question about it. *"Buon giorno. Buono notte. Grazie. Per favore.* Oh, and, of course, *espresso, cappuccino,* and, um, *gelato."* She grinned. "See? All the essentials. Good morning. Good evening. Thank you, please, two kinds of coffee and the best ice cream in the world. How's that for speaking the language?"

Nicolo grinned back at her. "Ah. A high school trip to Italy."

"A Miss Benton's Academy trip to Five Famed Cities of Europe, if you please." She touched the tip of her finger to his lips, smiling when he caught it between his teeth and took a mock ferocious bite. "Twelve very proper young women, three even more proper chaperones, five cities, fifteen days." She rolled her eyes. "Truly memorable, but not in the way Miss Benton would have preferred. Evelyn got sick from too much onion soup in Paris, Louise sneaked ouzo into her room in Athens and got snockered—"

"Snockered?"

"The only slang word Miss Benton would have permitted as a descriptive," Aimee said primly, laughter dancing in her eyes.

"And you, *cara?* Did you dine on too much soup? Did you get snickered—"

"Snockered."

"*Si.* Did you get snockered on ouzo?"

"I behaved like the obedient little girl I was." Aimee's smile slipped a notch. "Not that it mattered."

"You mean, your grandfather still paid you no attention," Nicolo said, wrapping her in his arms as he rolled onto his side.

"I mean, obedient or not, I was still the wrong sex for a Black grandchild."

Nicolo wanted to rise from the bed, fly to the States and grab the old man by the collar, hoist him to his toes and tell him what a selfish, stupid, coldhearted SOB he was….

Instead he did the next best thing.

"I think you're the perfect sex," he murmured, and ran his hand slowly down her body.

She smiled, as he'd hoped she would.

"Mmm. Right now, I think so, too."

"So, aside from being a good girl, what were you like when you were a teenager?"

"Shy. Quiet. Skinny as a stick."

He caressed her again. "Seems to me you've grown up since then."

That won him another smile. *"Grazie."*

"Would you like to learn more Italian?"

Aimee wound her arms around his neck. "For instance?"

"Sei molto bella."

"Which means?"

"It means, you are very beautiful." Nicolo's voice grew husky. "Incredibly beautiful, *cara.*"

"Grazie."

"Wrong answer."

Her eyebrows rose. "Thank you is the wrong answer?" He nodded. "Well, what should I have said in response?"

"You should have said, *Baciami,* Nico, *per favore.*"

Her lips curved. She'd caught on to the game.

"Baciami, Nico, *per favore,"* she said softly.

"With pleasure," he whispered, and kissed her.

Another kiss. And another, kisses that grew deeper and longer until Nicolo knew that soon, there'd be no turning back.

He groaned, kissed her one last time and rolled onto his back. Aimee made a sound of protest that went straight to his heart, and he gathered her closely against his side.

"We have things to do this morning."

"More important than this?"

"Nothing is more important than this... Except, perhaps, our ten o'clock appointment with Dr. Scarantino."

She rose up on her elbow. "Who?"

"I spoke with my physician about a doctor for you and the baby."

"Already?"

"I made the call hours ago," he teased, "while you lazed in bed."

"And why was I lazing in bed, do you think?"

Nicolo's eyes darkened. "If I answer that question, we'll miss our appointment with the best OB-GIN in all of *Roma.*"

Aimee brushed a lock of dark hair from her husband's forehead. She smiled, loving the way he mangled the abbreviation.

"After that, we'll stroll along the Via Condotti. Do you like Armani, *cara?* Valentino?" He smiled. "Who are your favorite designers, hmm? Tell me, and we will visit their shops today."

Her favorite designers were whatever was on sale in SoHo. Not taking money from her grandfather had long ago become a way of life.

"Nicolo. I brought a suitcase. I don't need—"

"And," he said, "then a stop at Bulgari for a proper wedding band. One that fits you and will tell the world that you are mine." He paused; his expression grew serious. "I did something else this morning, as well. I sent a fax to your grandfather, informing him that I do not wish to purchase his bank."

"No. I've thought about that. And I can't let you—"

"The choice is mine, *cara*. And I have already made it."

The words were arrogant, masculine…and wonderful. Aimee sighed and lay her head against her husband's shoulder.

"You are enough for me, Aimee. Do you understand?"

Was she enough? She had to believe it. Nicolo had sacrificed ownership of her grandfather's financial empire for her.

"Do you understand?" he said, rolling her onto her back.

"Yes," she said, "yes…"

He kissed her. Kissed her again… And forgot everything but making love to his wife.

A prince and his princess could surely be a few minutes late for an appointment.

* * *

The obstetrician—not an OB-G-Anything but *uno medico l'ostetrico*—was middle-aged, pleasant and, to Aimee's relief, spoke excellent English.

His calm demeanor was just what Nicolo needed.

Somehow, finding himself waiting in the doctor's private office while Aimee was examined had turned him from a man whose wife was having a baby into one whose wife was about to do something no female on the planet had ever done before.

He sprang to his feet when she and the doctor reappeared.

"*Cara*. Are you all right?"

"Yes. Of course. I'm—"

"Doctor? Is my wife well?"

"She is fine, *Principe*."

"The baby, too?"

"The baby, too."

"You are sure?"

The doctor smiled. "I am sure."

"And what must we do to keep things that way?"

"The usual, *Principe*. A healthful diet. Exercise. No caffeine, no cigarettes."

"That's it?"

The doctor spread his arms wide. "*Si*. That is it."

Nicolo cleared his throat, the memories of the night and the morning suddenly vivid.

"And, ah, and what of, ah, what of restrictions on, ah, on her activities?"

Aimee blushed. The doctor hid a grin. "If you refer to sex—"

"*Si*."

"Sex is a perfectly healthy activity."

Nicolo clasped Aimee's hand. "What else should we know?"

"In a few weeks, we will do some tests—we do them

for all pregnant women," the doctor added quickly, when Nicolo paled. "It is, how does one say it? Pro forma. Ultrasound. Blood work. Nothing out of the ordinary."

"You are sure?"

"I am quite sure."

Moments later, on the sidewalk, Aimee stopped and turned to Nicolo.

"I didn't want to embarrass you in front of the doctor," she said quietly, "but—but if you wish, they could do an additional test. For DNA. To prove to you that this baby is—"

Nicolo drew her close and silenced her with a kiss. "There is nothing you need prove to me, *cara*," he murmured. "We have agreed to tell each other only the truth, *si?*"

"*Si*. Yes. But if—"

"No lies," he said softly. "Not between us. Not ever."

He bought her more clothes than she could wear in a lifetime and when she whispered that it was a waste of money because, soon, she wouldn't fit into any of them, he held a quiet conversation with one of the shop assistants, who looked at Aimee and smiled.

"We will take all this," Nicolo said, gesturing to the stacks of trousers and sweaters, dresses and gowns Aimee had tried on.

Then he whisked her back into his car, to an elegant boutique that specialized in fashions for expectant mothers.

"I'll never wear all these things," Aimee said as the new pile of garments grew larger.

"I want you to have them," Nicolo said.

A pronouncement, not a suggestion. That was how her

husband faced the world, with authority and determination.

How he had now faced her grandfather because he wanted her, not Stafford-Coleridge-Black.

It seemed impossible. Nicolo's trips to the States. His meetings with James. He'd wanted the bank that same way, with authority and determination.

Not enough to marry her, of course…

But he *had* married her, because it was, he'd said, the right thing to do, once he knew she carried his heir.

In other words, he'd met James's conditions of sale.

Why insist on turning his back on the deal now?

For her. Only for her, Aimee thought, and something wonderful and just a little bit terrifying stirred in her heart.

At Bulgari, they looked at platinum wedding bands. For men as well as women because, Nicolo said, a husband should wear a ring as well as a wife.

Such a simple statement but it filled Aimee with joy.

Was it really only yesterday she'd stood before a judge, her heart cold as she took vows that bound her to this man?

Her heart was anything but cold now.

"Aimee?"

She looked up. Nicolo was watching her, a little smile on his face.

"What are you thinking, *cara?*" he said softly.

That I was wrong about you, my husband. That you are a kind, generous, wonderful man….

Not even she was foolish enough to bare her soul so quickly.

"I was thinking that—that it's going to be hard to choose rings when they're all so beautiful."

"Then let me simplify things and—"

"Nicolo," she said quickly, "are you sure you don't want the bank?"

He looked at her as if she'd gone crazy. "Didn't you ask me that a little while ago?"

"But—"

"But what? I gave you my answer. There are other banks." His smile tilted. "Besides, this particular bank should only have gone to you."

"It couldn't. My grandfather—"

Nicolo silenced her with a kiss.

"Now," he said softly, leaning his forehead against hers, "as to selecting rings… It's a warm day. You have been on your feet too long."

"I haven't. I sat in the car, sat at those shops, sat here—"

"There's a little café just down the street. Giorgio will drive you there."

"Giorgio will not drive me just down the street!"

"Fine. Then you will walk there, take an umbrella table, order espresso for me and a lemonade for you."

Aimee shook her head. "I think I've just been had!"

Nicolo gave her the kind of grin that made her blush.

"As soon as we get home, *cara*," he whispered, "I promise. For now, wait for me at the café." He paused. "Please."

How could she resist after that? Aimee rose on her toes and pressed a light kiss to her husband's mouth.

The café was crowded but she found a table shaded by a bright yellow Cinzano umbrella, dutifully ordered Nicolo's espresso and her cool drink, and waited.

Moments later, she saw him coming toward her. She began to smile—but the smile turned to astonishment.

"Nicolo! What are you doing?"

A silly question. He had dropped to his knees before

her. That not only got her attention, but it got everyone else's.

He took a small box from his pocket, opened it and revealed a ring that shone with all the fire an exquisitely set ten carat diamond could provide.

"Aimee," he said softly, "I know I should have asked you this question yesterday but the old saying says it is never too late to do the right thing." He took her hand and slipped the ring on her finger. "Will you be my wife?"

Tears filled Aimee's eyes. "Yes," she said, laughing and crying at the same time. "Oh, yes, Nico, yes, yes, yes—"

The café filled with cheers as she flung her arms around his neck and kissed him.

And, just that quickly, she knew the shocking truth.

She was deeply, passionately in love with her husband.

He had bought wedding bands, too, of course.

A wide one set with diamonds for her, a more austere version of the same ring for himself.

Still, even several weeks later, Aimee would catch sight of the solitaire and the wedding band glittering on her left hand and wonder how all this could have happened.

Didn't it take time to fall in love? Didn't you have to get to know a person? His likes, his dislikes. His favorite foods, his favorite movies, all that and more.

She and Nicolo were still learning those things but none of them seemed terribly important.

One look into her husband's eyes in that café and she'd tumbled straight off the edge of the earth.

Or maybe it had happened when they met. Maybe what she'd experienced in Nicolo's arms that first night had been more than mind-blowing sex.

Maybe it had been love, even then.

What did it matter? She loved her husband. He was every-thing she'd wanted without ever knowing she'd wanted it.

There'd been a man, once, when she was in college. He'd talked of a future together. Of how he'd be there for her, sup-portive of her pursuing a career despite being married.

It had all sounded wonderful until it was time to apply to grad school and she told him about her grandfather, about how he thought her attending graduate school was foolish. About how hard she was going to have to work to change his mind about letting a woman inherit SCB.

You mean, you might not inherit the company? he'd said.

That night, he'd dropped her at the apartment she shared with three other women.

I'll call you, he'd told her.

He never did.

He'd been her one lover, until the night she met Nicolo.

Nicolo, who wanted her. Not what she could bring him. Nicolo, who she loved with all her heart.

She wanted to tell him. Wanted to take his face between her hands, look into his eyes and say, *Nico, my husband, I adore you....*

But she couldn't. She was a liberated woman with two degrees, a woman who could hold her own in the toughest business crowd but when it came to love, she couldn't say the words without hearing them first.

Someday soon, Nicolo would say them.

He would tell her he loved her because, surely, he did. His actions, his lovemaking, his sacrifice of her grand-father's bank...

Why would a man do those things, if not for love?

It was only a matter of time before he said the words.

Except—except, as time slipped past, doubt crept in. Nicolo was the same. Kind, tender, generous. Passionate.

So passionate, even as her belly grew more rounded, that there were times she wept with joy as she came in his arms.

But a little voice had started whispering things she didn't want to hear.

Are you sure, Aimee? it would say slyly. *Will he really tell you he loves you? Are you sure he's not just manipulating you the way your grandfather did all those years he let you think you'd take over at the bank?*

James's lie kept you docile.

Maybe this is Nicolo's lie. To tame you. To keep you warming his bed.

The thoughts were ugly. And untrue. Absolutely untrue. Aimee blocked them out…but sometimes, in the darkest part of the night, the voice still whispered to her and when it did, her heart turned cold.

Her birthday was fast approaching.

Nicolo reminded her of it.

"How did you know?" she said, and he gave her a smug grin and said he'd known it from the day they married. "It's on your passport, remember? Tucked away in my safe."

It was, he said, an important birthday.

"Twenty-five," she said, and gave a dramatic sigh. "A quarter of a century."

Nicolo laughed and caught her up in his arms. "I'm serious, *cara*. It is important." His eyes darkened. "I want you to have a very special day. We'll drive north, to Tuscany. I have a house there. It's much smaller than the *palazzo,* very quiet, very private…" He smiled. "I'll take you to my favorite little *trattoria* so you can practice your Italian by ordering all the local dishes."

She smiled back at him. "It sounds wonderful. I can't wait."

"And I can't wait to see your face when I give you your

birthday present. I think—I know—it will make you very happy."

He put her on her feet. Aimee lay her hand over her belly.

"You've already given me the best gift in the world," she said softly.

Nicolo put his hand over hers just as the baby gave its first kick. She knew she'd never forget the incredulous look that came over his face.

"Was that my son?"

"Or your daughter."

He kissed her. And after that, she stopped listening to that sly little voice because, without question, what it said was a lie.

CHAPTER THIRTEEN

AIMEE'S BIRTHDAY fell on a Saturday.

Which was, Nicolo said, perfect for their visit at the house in Tuscany.

"There's an infinity pool and a hot tub, and a terrace that looks out over the valley. No servants, just a housekeeper who comes in only a couple of times a week." He took Aimee in his arms and kissed her. "We'll have all the privacy we could want, *cara,* so I can teach you some new words in my language and, better yet, show you exactly what they mean. How does that sound?"

It sounded wonderful. Almost too wonderful to be true, but then, the last several weeks had all been like that.

The only thing that could be more perfect would be if Nicolo said he loved her. Aimee hoped that might be the special gift he had for her. A sweet declaration of his love.

Then, life would be perfect.

They planned to leave early Friday morning but Nicolo had to go to his office first to sort out a minor emergency.

Aimee walked him out the front door.

"I'll be back in an hour, no more," he said, as he kissed her goodbye.

"Not a minute more," she answered, kissing him back.

He smiled, but then his expression grew serious. "Are you happy here, with me, *cara?*"

She answered by pressing her mouth to his again.

"Sometimes," he said, his arms tightening around her, "sometimes I think it was fate that sent you on a collision course with me in front of that hotel, and sent us to the same club that evening." He took her face in his hands. "And, lately, I think, too, that we should repay fate's kindness to us by making peace with your grandfather."

Aimee sighed. "I know. I've thought about it. He's old. And frail. And I suppose, in his own way, he did what he thought was right."

Nicolo brushed his mouth gently over hers.

"I am glad you feel that way, *cara,* because—because that plays into my birthday gift for you."

"Making peace with James? I don't understand."

"You will," he said, and kissed her again. "I will explain this weekend, I promise."

"Nicolo! That's not fair. At least give me a hint."

"A hint. Hmm." He grinned. "All right." He put his hand on her rounded belly. "Part of your gift is as much a gift for our baby as for you."

"Some hint! I'm more confused than before!"

Nicolo rolled his eyes. "One more hint, woman, and then my lips are sealed. Let's see…" He took her hand, turned it over and touched his finger to a line across her palm. "I see a journey in your future," he said, his tone as solemn as any fortune-teller's. Then he looked up and grinned. "No more questions, *Principessa.* Nicolo the *Magnifico* has finished telling the future for now."

Aimee laughed. "You're a hard man, Nicolo the Magnificent."

"And you are soft, *cara,*" he said huskily, "as soft as silk in my arms."

A long, deep kiss. Then he trotted down the steps, got into his Ferrari and roared away.

She looked after the car until it vanished through the gates. Then she went back into the *palazzo,* out onto the terrace overlooking the rear gardens, smiling as she gazed over the riotous colors of the flowers.

A hint? Nicolo had given it all away. Her "special birthday gift" was a trip to New York and a reconciliation with James.

It was a generous gesture for her husband to make.

Nicolo was a proud man. Her grandfather's attempt to manipulate him had backfired because of that pride. Now, he'd overlook it and make peace for her sake, and for the sake of their child.

"You're a good man, Nico," she whispered softly. "A wonderful man—"

"Signora?"

Aimee turned around. "Yes, Anna?"

"I have finished packing your suitcase."

"Thank you." Ridiculous, really. She was perfectly capable of packing her own things but Nicolo insisted Anna do it. The further she went in her pregnancy, the more convinced he was that she needed to be treated with extra care.

"I put in all the things you asked for. The cotton tops, the linen trousers. But I wonder… Will you and the *Principe* be dining out? Shall I pack some long gowns? An evening purse? Shoes?"

It was an excellent question and only Nicolo knew the answer.

"I don't know," Aimee said with a little laugh. "Thank you for thinking of it. I'll phone my husband and ask."

The nearest telephone was in Nicolo's study. She'd been in the room often, sitting curled in a corner of the sofa, reading, while he did e-mail. Now, for the first time, she went behind her husband's oversize antique desk, sat in his chair, reached for the phone and dialed his office.

Nicolo picked up after a few rings.

"*Cara?* Are you all right?"

"I'm perfectly fine."

"Good. Good. For a moment, I thought—"

"Nico," she said gently, "really, I'm okay. I just wanted to ask if—"

"I'm on the phone with Paris. May I put you on hold for a few minutes?"

She assured him that he could and settled back to wait.

Soft music played over the telephone line and Aimee hummed along, dah-dah-dahing just a little off-key. Still humming, she plucked a pencil from the desk, pulled a scrap of paper toward her, began to draw stick-figure babies and mommies and daddies….

And stopped.

What was that?

A fax. A fax on her grandfather's letterhead, dated two days after she had married Nicolo.

My dear Prince Barbieri. Once again, let me repeat what I told you when you telephoned. I am delighted by the news of your marriage to my granddaughter…

Well, she knew what this would be about. It was James's response to Nicolo telling him he would not be purchasing the bank.

I am equally delighted by your reminder of my commitment to sell you Stafford-Coleridge-Black.

The pencil dropped to the desk from Aimee's suddenly nerveless fingers.

I also wish to assure you that I am moving forward
with the paperwork necessary to proceed with the
sale. It will take a few weeks but I assure you,
Principe, everything will go forward as promised.

Aimee's heart gave a wild lurch.

Nicolo had never told her grandfather he would not
buy SCB? No. It had to be a mistake….

It wasn't.

The proof was just under the fax, contained in a legal
document pages and pages long.

The last page was the one that mattered. It stated that
Barbieri International was now the owner of Stafford-
Coleridge-Black.

Aimee's hand flew to her mouth.

God. Oh dear God! Her husband had lied to her. Lied,
even as he'd held her in his arms and vowed there would
never be any lies between them.

The bank was his. That was why he'd married her after
all. For the bank. And telling her about it was to be her
special birthday present.

He couldn't keep it a secret forever. Mention of the sale
was bound to turn up in magazines and newspapers.
Nicolo had to break the news to her before that happened.

That was the reason he was taking her away.

Her husband would spend the weekend making love to
her. And when she was completely dazzled by all the hours
in his arms, he'd tell her what he'd done. That he'd bought
the bank. He'd make it sound as if he'd just done it, and
that he'd done it solely to reconcile her with her grandfather.

He'd say that he'd done it for her. And that would be
the biggest lie of all.

Everything, *everything* he'd done, was for himself. It had

all been in preparation for this moment. His supposed concern for her. His affection for her. His love for her and, all right, he'd never used the word but she'd begun believing that he loved her, that he wanted her for herself, not for the bank….

"Cara?"

The bank. The horrible bank. The bank that had always been more important than she was, first to James, now to Nicolo—

"Cara? Are you there?"

Aimee's throat was tight. Not with sorrow. With anger. With rage. Bone-deep, hot-blooded rage.

"I'm here, Prince Barbieri," she said in a low voice. "But not for long."

"What? Aimee? Aimee—"

She dropped the phone. Ran up the stairs to the bedroom. To her husband's bedroom, a room she'd willingly shared because she'd believed in him, in the life she'd thought they were building together.

Her suitcase was on the bed.

She upended it, threw open her dressing room doors, yanked clothes from their hangers, clothes she'd brought with her from New York; tossed them into the suitcase and, damn it, she was blinking back tears. Tears, and for what? She was angry, not hurting.

Oh God, not hurting!

A sob broke from her throat. Quickly she forced the suitcase shut, grabbed it and ran from the room.

She was halfway down the stairs when Anna looked up and saw her.

"Principessa!" Anna's voice was filled with horror. *"Principessa.* What are you doing? You cannot carry that by yourself."

"I *am* carrying it," Aimee said. "Just watch me."

"But *Principessa*... Giorgio? Giorgio, *venuto qui!* Quickly, Giorgio!"

Giorgio, looking bewildered, hurried toward Anna from the kitchen wing.

"Giorgio." Aimee took a breath. "Good. I wish to go to the airport."

The man stared at her.

"The airport, Giorgio. I want you to take me there."

He looked at her blankly.

"*L'aeroporto, capite?* Damn it, I know you understand!"

"*Principessa.*" Anna was wringing her hands in distress. "*Per favore,* I cannot let you do this. The *principe*—"

"To hell with the *principe!* Tell Giorgio to take me to the airport or I'll go out the door and start walking."

Anna swallowed audibly. So did Giorgio. Aimee ran down the rest of the stairs and brushed past them.

"*Attesta!*" Giorgio shouted. "I will do it."

A moment later, they were speeding out the gates in the big Mercedes, the *palazzo* a blur on the horizon.

Aimee chose an airline at random.

Giorgio wanted to park the Mercedes so he could carry her suitcase inside but she told him to pull to the curb. Once he did, she got out of the car and ran into the terminal.

Soon, she knew, she'd be out of time.

Nicolo would come after her. It would put a dent in his pride if he let her run away.

Fate was cooperating. There was no one in line at the ticket counter. Yes, there was a flight to New York this morning. Yes, there was an available seat.

Thank goodness, Aimee still had her old credit card... But she didn't have her passport.

"I am sorry, Ms. Black," the clerk said politely, "but I cannot issue a ticket if you have no passport."

"I have one," Aimee said desperately, "but I can't get at it. My husband—"

The clerk's polite mask gave way to a look of empathy.

"I understand, but there's nothing I can do. Are you American? Perhaps if you go to your embassy—"

"They won't help me. My husband is—my husband is—"

"I am her husband," an imperious voice growled.

Aimee spun around. Nicolo stood just behind her, his eyes black with tightly controlled anger.

"I am Principe Nicolo Antonius Barbieri," he said. "And my wife is correct. Her embassy cannot help her." His hand closed, hard, on Aimee's elbow. "No one can help her," he said coldly, "because she belongs to me."

"Let go," Aimee panted. "Let go, Nicolo, or—"

"Or what?" His lips drew back from his teeth. "Do you think making a scene will help you? I promise, it will not. Do you remember how Giorgio clicks his heels and salutes me?" His mouth twisted. "The police will do the same. This is my country, and I am a prince."

Aimee stared at the cold, arrogant stranger who was her husband.

"I hate you," she said in a low voice. "I despise you, Nicolo! Do you know that?"

He grabbed her suitcase, tightened his hold on her elbow and started walking. She had no choice but to follow.

He led her out of the terminal. His Ferrari was at the curb, the big Mercedes just ahead of it.

Giorgio sprang from the car, opened the rear door, took one look at his employer's face and scrambled into his seat behind the wheel.

"Get in."

"I will not get in! I'm leaving. There's nothing you can do to stop—"

Nicolo snarled a word, picked her up and put her in the car. Then he climbed in beside her and banged a fist on the closed privacy partition. The Mercedes leaped away and merged into the traffic exiting the airport.

"Now," he said, turning his hot, furious gaze on Aimee, "tell me what you think you are doing."

"Tell Giorgio to turn this car around." Aimee shot to the edge of her seat and pounded on the partition. "Giorgio? Take me back to the airport."

There was no response. The car kept moving forward.

"I'm leaving you, Nicolo," Aimee said. "Do you hear me? I am leaving you, and there's nothing you can do to stop me."

"I won't have to do a thing." Nicolo folded his arms. "Customs will do it for me. You have no passport."

"I'll get one. I'll phone the American Embassy. They won't give a damn that you call yourself a prince, especially when I tell them that you're really an arrogant, deceitful, lying—"

"Be careful, *cara*. It is not wise to add fuel to a fire that is already burning."

It was hard, being so close to him. Looking into the eyes she'd foolishly let herself believe shone with love for her.

His eyes were cold now. Cold and flat and empty.

Suddenly Aimee felt almost unbearably weary. He was right. He was a prince. A macho male. He held all the cards; she held none. He'd lied to her. Hurt her in the worst possible way but he'd shown her kindness, too.

There had to be a shred of kindness left for her in his heart.

Aimee sank back against the seat.

"Don't do this," she whispered. "Please, Nicolo. Just let me go."

"There was a time you called me Nico."

She looked at him. His voice was low; the anger in his eyes had been replaced by bewilderment... But he was a good actor. She knew that better than anyone.

"A mistake," she said. "Everything was a mistake."

"*Cara.* I do not understand. I left, you were happy. The next thing I know—"

"The next thing you know," she said, trying to sound cold, trying not to give way to tears, "the next thing you know, the game's up."

"What game? What are you talking about?"

"Your game. This game. You and me." She took a deep breath. "It's over. I don't want you anymore."

"Why do you not want me? What happened?"

"I came to my senses, is what happened."

"Meaning?"

"Meaning, I realized what a—a joke this has been. You. Me. This farce of a marriage."

"Is that what our marriage is to you? A joke?"

Another change of tone. There was warning in it now but Aimee was beyond heeding that warning.

"You know it is."

She cried out as he pulled her to him. His lips crushed hers; his kiss was savage and deep but it didn't touch her heart.

He had lost his power to seduce her.

He would never have that power again...except, except, God, she was going to cry.

Going to?

She was crying already, tears burning her eyes as she fought against them and she didn't want to give him the satisfaction of seeing her weep because—because there was nothing to weep about. She didn't love him, she'd never loved him—

"I don't love you," she gasped, tearing her mouth from his.

The words came out before she could stop them. Nicolo raised his eyebrows.

"Strange. How could you not love me when you never claimed to love me?"

"I meant—I meant I didn't love you, even when I thought I did."

"Yet you never said those words to me."

"I said, I *thought* I loved you. But I didn't. It was all sex. You knew that. You used it against me."

"I see. I used sex to make you fall in love with me."

"Yes. No. I didn't fall in love with you. Damn it, you're twisting everything, the way you always do."

"What have I twisted in the past?"

"You know damned well what you twisted. And I'm not going to do this! I'm not going to give you the chance to try to convince me not to leave you because I've made up my mind. I *am* leaving you—and you won't lose a thing, because the bank is already in your pocket!"

Nicolo cocked his head. "Really? The bank is in my pocket?"

Aimee slammed her fist against his chest. "Don't," she cried. "Don't make fun of me. Don't lie! Don't, don't, don't…"

Tears began streaming down her face.

You could only pretend to hate the man who owned your heart for just so long and then the enormity of losing him, of having been a pawn that meant nothing to him, became too painful to bear.

She sagged against his hands.

"Please," she said brokenly, "please, Nicolo, if you have any feeling at all for me, let me go."

"Cara." His arms went around her; he gathered her close despite her struggles and drew her into his lap. "Tell

me what happened. What hurt you. Tell me, so I can make it go away."

"What happened," she said as a shudder racked her body, "is that I discovered the truth."

"No," he said gently, "I don't think that's possible because if you knew the truth, if I had told it to you a long time ago, you would not be weeping in my arms."

"I'm not weeping," Aimee said, her body shaking with her sobs.

"Of course not. You're too strong to cry. Isn't that right, *cara?*" His smile tilted as he took a white linen square from his pocket and handed it to her. "I told you I'd work up to a handkerchief someday."

Aimee wiped her eyes, blew her nose, then balled the hankie in her fist. "Now. What is this truth that has made you want to leave me?"

She lifted her head and met his eyes. "I found the fax."

"What fax?"

"The one from my grandfather, assuring you he'd sell the bank to you."

His face fell. "Ah."

"Yes. Ah, indeed. I found everything. That fax—and the papers that showed the sale had gone through."

"What else did you find?"

His tone was neutral. At least he wasn't going to try to deny the truth.

"Isn't that enough?" Her voice broke. "I'd married you. I'd agreed to live with you, to be your wife. Why did you have to lie? Why did you tell me you weren't going to buy the bank? Why did you make me fall—make me fall—"

"What, *cara?*" Tenderly he brushed her honeyed curls back from her cheeks. "What did I make you do?"

Why hide it now? Her pride lay in tatters; by the end of this, she would have none left to lose. Then she would leave him. She couldn't live this way, loving him and knowing he had never loved her.

And yes, she loved him. Despite everything, she loved him. She would always love him.

"*Cara*," Nicolo said softly, "are you telling me that you love me?"

She didn't answer.

And, for the first time in his life, Nicolo found himself terrified of what a woman's answer might be because if his wife didn't say that she loved him—

If she didn't, he would be lost.

Lost, because he loved her with all his heart. He would always love her. The vows they had taken said it would be until death, but that was wrong.

He would love her until then, and beyond.

Months ago, a woman had run into him on the street and she'd left him in a rage he hadn't been able to understand.

When he saw her again, in a club that same night, his rage had changed to desire so savage it had baffled him.

And, through the twists and turns of destiny, he had married her.

He'd told himself he'd done it for the child they'd created but even then, deep inside, he'd known that he'd done it for a simpler reason.

He loved her.

And that love had grown until it was the most important thing in his life. But he was too much an idiot—all right, too much a coward to admit it.

After all, he had never loved anyone before.

No. That wasn't true. He'd loved his parents, but they had not loved him. He'd loved his *gran-nonna*, but she had died. He'd even loved a couple of his governesses, but they'd disappeared like puffs of smoke.

He would not, could not make himself that vulnerable again.

Instead he'd come up with ways to show what he felt for his wife. The engagement ring. The wedding bands. *Dio,* he had never thought he'd want to wear a ring. Wasn't a ring a more civilized version of shackles?

It turned out it was not. A ring was a way of telling the world he adored his wife.

His problem then had been telling the same thing to his wife. Words had terrified him. Suppose she hadn't felt the same? So he'd come up with what had seemed a clever plan.

He'd tell her grandfather he didn't want to buy the bank.

Good, as far as it went. His Aimee's smile, when he told her what he'd done, had filled him with happiness….

Then, a little while later, he'd thought of something even better. He'd buy the bank, then give it to his wife as a gift.

So clever. So brilliant…

So stupid.

His plan had backfired. And now, his wife wanted to leave him.

No, he thought fiercely, no….

"Aimee." Nicolo took a deep breath. "I asked you a question, *cara.* I asked if you love me."

"Nicolo—"

"But that was wrong. I should have spoken first. I should have said—I should have told you that I adore you, *bellissima mia.* That I cannot imagine living without you." She shook her head, turned it away and he cupped her chin, gently but firmly forced her to look at him. "You are my heart, Aimee. You are my life."

"Nicolo. I *saw* the papers. I saw—"

The Mercedes had stopped a long time ago. Nicolo looked out, saw the broad steps that led into the *palazzo*. Giorgio, clever man, was nowhere in sight but the front door of the *palazzo* stood open.

Nicolo carried his wife from the car, up the steps and into the house. She told him to put her down but he kissed her to silence, carried her into his study and gently set her on her feet, though he wasn't taking any chances.

He kept his arm around her while he rifled through the papers on his desk, found the one he wanted and held it out to her.

"What is that?"

"It is the gift I intended to give you this weekend, the gift I hoped would take the place of the words I was too much a coward to say, that I love you, I need you, that I cannot live without you."

Aimee looked up at him, her eyes still awash in tears.

"Read it," he said gently. "*Per favore,* sweetheart, I beg you. Read it."

Slowly Aimee took the document from him and began to read. Halfway through, she blinked. Looked up and shook her head.

"Nicolo. I don't understand. This says—"

"It says that the damnable bank is yours, *amante.*"

"But it can't be. My grandfather—"

"Sold it to me. And as soon as it was mine, I told my attorneys to change the name of the owner from Barbieri International to Aimee Black Barbieri." His voice softened. "It should always have been yours, *cara.* And now, it is."

"You mean, you bought it just so you—"

"*Si.* It is my gift to you, a gift I give you with all the love in my heart, now and forever. You must believe me. I love you, love you, love you—"

And then Aimee was in his arms, her mouth on his, and the papers transferring SCB from husband to wife were on the floor where they belonged, because nothing was or would ever be as important as the love between Prince Nicolo Antonius Barbieri and his princess….

At least, nothing as important until the birth of a little prince a few months later.

His name was Nicolo James Antonius Barbieri and, yes, he was named for his father and his grandfather because it was amazing how news of his only granddaughter's pregnancy had mellowed a stern, cold old man.

And when little Nicolo—Nickie, to his adoring parents—was two weeks old, he attended the first big event of his life.

The marriage, the real marriage of his mother and father because, his papa said, a beautiful woman deserved a beautiful wedding.

Aimee carried a bouquet of white roses and pink orchids, from the *palazzo's* greenhouse. Her gown was made of cream antique lace and had a flowing train.

Nicolo wore a black dinner suit with a white rosebud in his lapel.

The baby wore white, too, a little silk suit handmade by Anna, who wept when she was asked to be the baby's godmother.

The ceremony was held in the conservatory of the *palazzo,* lit by hundreds of white candles, scented by thousands of white roses while a string quartet played softly in the background.

It was a small wedding, attended only by James Black, a couple of Aimee's friends from her college days and, of course, the groom's two confirmed bachelor pals, a Spaniard named Lucas and a Greek named Damian. They slapped Nicolo's back, kissed his bride, said how happy they were for them both and agreed, in low voices over glasses of excellent *vino,* that marriage was okay for Nicolo but it would never be right for them.

Although, Damian admitted, Nicolo certainly did seem happy.

Just look at how he was smiling. At how he kissed his son good-night when Anna said it was time for her to put the baby to bed. At how he danced with his wife, and how he swept her into his arms midway through the evening, kissed her, then carried her through the conservatory and into the *palazzo.*

"Time for a toast," Lucas said, raising his glass.

Damian looked at him and grinned. They both knew exactly how the old toast was supposed to go, but not tonight.

Not ever again, where Nicolo was concerned.

"To Nicolo," Lucas said.

The men touched glasses.

"And to Aimee," Damian added. "May they live happily ever after."

The guests cheered, and the sound carried through the softness of the night and through the open windows of the second-floor bedroom where Nicolo was just putting his bride on her feet.

"I love you," he whispered against her mouth.

"Ti amo," she said, against his.

Then he drew her down into their bed where they made that vow of love again, this time with their bodies, their souls and their hearts.

THE GREEK PRINCE'S
CHOSEN WIFE

BY
SANDRA MARTON

My special thanks to Nadia-Anastasia Fahmi
for her generous help with Greek idioms.
Any errors are, of course, entirely mine!
Sandra

CHAPTER ONE

DAMIAN was getting out of a taxi the first time he saw her.

He was in a black mood, something he'd grown accustomed to the last three months, a mood so dark he'd stopped noticing anything that even hinted at beauty.

But a man would have to be dead not to notice this woman.

Stunning, was his first thought. What he could see of her, anyway. Black wraparound sunglasses covered much of her face but her mouth was lusciously full with enough sexual promise to make a monk think of quitting the cloister.

Her hair was long. Silky-looking. A dichromatic mix of chestnut and gold that fell over her shoulders in a careless tumble.

And she was tall. Five-nine, five-ten with a model's bearing. A model's way of wearing her clothes, too, so that the expensive butterscotch leather blazer, slim-cut black trousers and high-heeled black boots made her look like she'd stepped straight out of the pages of *Vogue*.

A few short months ago, he'd have done more than

look. He'd have walked up to her, smiled, asked if she, too, were lunching at Portofino's…

But not today.

Not for the foreseeable future, he thought, his mouth thinning.

No matter what she looked like behind those dark glasses, he wasn't interested.

He swung away, handed the taxi driver a couple of bills. A driver behind his cab bleated his horn; Damian shot a look at the car, edged past it, stepped onto the curb…

And saw that the woman had taken off her sunglasses. She was looking straight at him, her gaze focused and steady.

She wasn't stunning.

She was spectacular.

Her face was a perfect oval, her cheekbones sharp as blades, her nose straight and aristocratic. Her eyes were incredible. Wide-set. Deep green. Heavily lashed.

And then there was that mouth. The things that mouth might do…

Hell!

Damian turned hard so quickly he couldn't believe it but then, he'd gone three months without a woman.

It was the longest he'd gone without sex since he'd been introduced to its mysteries the Christmas he was sixteen, when one of his father's many mistresses had seduced him.

The difference was that he'd been a boy then.

He was a man now. A man with cold hatred in his heart and no wish for a woman in his life, not yet, not even one this beautiful, this desirable…

"Hey, dude, this is New York! You think you own the sidewalk?"

Damian swung around, ready and eager for a fight, saw the speaker…and felt his tension drain away.

"Reyes," he said, smiling.

Lucas Reyes smiled in return. "In the flesh."

Damian's smile became a grin. He held out his hand, said, "Oh, what the hell," and pulled his old friend into a bear hug.

"It's good to see you."

"The same here." Lucas pulled back, his smile tilting. "Ready for lunch?"

"Aren't I always ready for a meal at Portofino's?"

"Yeah. Sure. I just—I meant…" Lucas cleared his throat. "You okay?"

"I'm fine."

"You should have called. By the time I read about the, ah, the accident…"

Damian stiffened. "Forget it."

"That was one hell of a thing, man. To lose your fiancée…"

"I said, forget it."

"I didn't know her, but—"

"Lucas. I don't want to talk about it."

"If that's how you want it—"

"It's exactly how I want it," Damian said, with such cold surety that Lucas knew enough to back off.

"Okay," he said, forcing a smile. "In that case… I told Antonio to give us the back booth."

Damian forced a smile of his own. "Fine. Maybe they'll even have *Trippa alla Savoiarda* on the menu today."

Lucas shuddered. "What's the problem, Aristedes? Pasta's not good enough for you?"

"Tripe's delicious," Damian said and just that easily,

they fell into the banter that comes with old friendships.

"Just like old times," Lucas said.

Nothing would ever be like old times again, Damian thought, but he grinned, too, and let it go at that.

The back booth was as comfortable as ever and the tripe was on the menu. Damian didn't order it; he never had. Tripe made him shudder the same as Lucas.

The teasing was just part of their relationship.

Still, after they'd ordered, after his double vodka on the rocks and Lucas's whiskey, straight up, had arrived, he and Lucas both fell silent.

"So," Lucas finally said, "what's new?"

Damian shrugged. "Nothing much. How about you?"

"Oh, you know. I was in Tahiti last week, checking out a property on the beach…"

"A tough life," Damian said, and smiled.

"Yeah, well, somebody has to do it."

More silence. Lucas cleared his throat.

"I saw Nicolo and Aimee over the weekend. At that dinner party. Everyone was sorry you didn't come."

"How are they?" Damian said, deliberately ignoring the comment.

"Great. The baby's great, too."

Silence again. Lucas took a sip of his whiskey.

"Nicolo said he'd tried to call you but—"

"Yes. I got his messages."

"I tried, too. For weeks. I'm glad you finally picked up the phone yesterday."

"Right," Damian said as if he meant it, but he didn't. Ten minutes in and he already regretted taking Lucas's call and agreeing to meet him.

At least mistakes like this one could be remedied, he thought, and glanced at his watch.

"The only thing is," he said, "something's come up. I'm not sure I can stay for lunch. I'll try, but—"

"Bull."

Damian looked up. "What?"

"You heard me, Aristedes. I said, 'bull.' Nothing's come up. You just want a way to get out of what's coming."

"And that would be…?"

"A question."

"Ask it, then."

"Why didn't you tell Nicolo or me when it happened? Why let us hear about it through those damned scandal sheets?"

"That's two questions," Damian said evenly.

"Yeah, well, here's a third. Why didn't you lean on us? There wasn't a damned reason for you to go through all of that alone."

"All of what?"

"Give me a break, Damian. You know all of what. Hell, man, losing the woman you love…"

"You make it sound as if I misplaced her," Damian said, his voice flat and cold.

"You know I didn't mean it that way. It's just that Nicolo and I talked about it and—"

"Is that all you and Barbieri have to keep you busy? Gossip like a pair of old women?"

He saw Lucas's eyes narrow. Why wouldn't they? Damian knew he was tossing Lucas's concern in his teeth but to hell with that. The last thing he wanted was sympathy.

"We care about you," Lucas said quietly. "We just want to help."

Damian gave a mirthless laugh. He saw Lucas blink and he leaned toward him across the table.

"Help me through my sorrow, you mean?"

"Yes, damn it. Why not?"

"The only way you could help me," Damian said, very softly, "would be by bringing Kay back."

"I know. I understand. I—"

"No," he said coldly, "you do not know. You do not understand. I don't want her back to ease my sorrow, Lucas."

"Then, what—"

"I want her back so I can tell her I know exactly what she was. That she was a—"

The men fell silent as the waiter appeared with Damian's second double vodka. He put it down and looked at Lucas, who took less than a second to nod in assent.

"Another whiskey," he said. "Make it a double."

They waited until the drink had been served. Then Lucas leaned forward.

"Look," he said softly, "I know you're bitter. Who wouldn't be? Your fiancée, pregnant. A drunk driver, a narrow road…" He lifted his glass, took a long swallow. "It's got to be rough. I mean, I didn't know Kay, but—"

"That's the second time you said that. And you're right, you didn't know her."

"Well, you fell in love, proposed to her in a hurry. And—"

"Love had nothing to do with it."

Lucas stared at him. "No?"

Damian stared back. Maybe it was the vodka. Maybe it was the way his old friend was looking at him. Maybe it was the sudden, unbidden memory of the woman outside the restaurant, how there'd been a time he'd have wanted her and not despised himself for it.

Who knew the reason? All he was sure of was that he was tired of keeping the truth buried inside.

"I didn't propose. She moved in with me, here in New York."

"Yeah, well—"

"She was pregnant," Damian said flatly. "Then she lost the baby. Or so she said."

"What do you mean?"

"She'd never been pregnant." Damian's jaw tightened. "The baby was a lie."

Lucas's face paled. "Hell, man. She scammed you!"

If there'd been one touch of pity in those words, Damian would have gotten to his feet and walked out. But there wasn't. All he heard in Lucas's voice was shock, indignation and a welcome hint of anger.

Suddenly the muted sounds of voices and laughter, the delicate clink of glasses and cutlery were almost painfully obtrusive. Damian stood, dropped several bills on the table and looked at Lucas.

"I bought a condo. It's just a few blocks from here."

Lucas was on his feet before Damian finished speaking.

"Let's go."

And right then, right there, for the first time since it had all started, Damian began to think he'd be okay.

A couple of hours later, the men sat facing each other in the living room of Damian's fifteen-room duplex. Vodka and whiskey had given way to a pot of strong black coffee.

The view through three surrounding walls of glass was magnificent but neither man paid it any attention. The only view that mattered was the one Damian was providing into the soul of a scheming woman.

"So," Lucas said quietly, "you'd been with her for some time."

Damian nodded. "Whenever I was in New York."

"And then you tried to break things off."

"Yes. She was beautiful. Sexy as hell. But the longer I knew her… I suppose it sounds crazy but it was as if she'd been wearing a mask and now she was letting it slip."

"That's not crazy at all," Lucas said grimly. "There are women out there who'll do anything to land a man with money."

"She began to show a side I hadn't seen before. She cared only for possessions, treated people as if they were dirt. Cabbies, waitresses…" Damian drank some of his coffee. "I wanted out."

"Who wouldn't?"

"I thought about just not calling her anymore, but I knew that would be wrong. Telling her things were over seemed the decent thing to do. So I called, asked her to dinner." His face turned grim and he rose to his feet, walked to one of the glass walls and stared out over the city. "I got one sentence out and she began to cry. And she told me she was pregnant with my baby."

"You believed her?"

Damian swung around and looked at Lucas. "She'd been my mistress for a couple of months, Lucas. You'd have done the same."

Lucas sighed and got to his feet. "You're right." He paused. "So, what did you do?"

"I said I'd support her and the baby. *She* said if I really cared about the baby in her womb, I would ask her to move in with me."

"Dear God, man—"

"Yes. I know. But she was carrying my child. At least, that's what I believed."

Lucas sighed again. "Of course."

"It was a nightmare," Damian said, shuddering. "I guess she thought it was safe to drop the last of her act. She treated my staff like slaves, ran up a six figure charge at Tiffany…" His jaw knotted. "I didn't want anything to do with her."

"No sex?" Lucas asked bluntly.

"None. I couldn't imagine why I'd slept with her in the first place. She thought I'd lost interest because she was pregnant." He grimaced. "She began talking about how different things would be, if she weren't…" Damian started toward the table that held the coffee service. Halfway there, he muttered something in Greek, veered past it and went instead to a teak cabinet on the wall. "What are you drinking?"

"Whatever you're pouring."

The answer brought a semblance of a smile to Damian's lips. He poured healthy amounts of Courvoisier into a pair of crystal brandy snifters and held one out. The men drank. Then Damian spoke again.

"A couple of weeks later, she told me she'd miscarried. I felt—I don't know what I felt. Upset, at the loss of the baby. I mean, by then I'd come to think of it as a baby, you know? Not a collection of cells." He shook his head. "Once I got past that, what I felt, to be honest, was relief. Now we could end the relationship."

"Except, she didn't want to end it."

Damian gave a bitter laugh. "You're smarter than I was. She became hysterical. She said I'd made promises, begged her to spend her life with me."

"But you hadn't."

"Damned right, I hadn't. The only thing that had drawn us together was the baby. Right?"

"Right," Lucas said, although he was starting to realize he didn't have to say anything. The flood gates had opened.

"She seemed to plummet into depression. Stayed in bed all day. Wouldn't eat. Went to her obstetrician—at least she said she'd gone to her obstetrician—and told me he'd advised her to get pregnant again."

"But—"

"Exactly. I didn't want a child, not with her. I wanted out." Damian took another swallow of brandy. "She begged me to reconsider. She'd come into my room in the middle of the night—"

"You had separate rooms?"

A cold light flared in Damian's eyes. "From the start."

"Sure, sure. Sorry. You were saying—"

"She was good at what she did. I have to give her that. Most nights, I turned her away but once…" A muscle knotted in his jaw. "I'm not proud of it."

"Man, don't beat yourself up. If she seduced you—"

"I used a condom. It made her crazy. 'I want your baby,' she said. "And then—"

Damian fell silent. Lucas leaned forward. "And then?"

"And then," Damian said, after a deep breath and a

long exhalation, "then she told me she'd conceived. That her doctor had confirmed it."

"But the condom—"

"It broke, she said, when she—when she took it off me—" He cleared his throat. "Hell, why would I question it? The damned things do break. We all know that."

"So—so she was pregnant again."

"No," Damian said flatly. "She wasn't pregnant. Oh, she went through all the motions. Morning sickness, ice cream and pickles in the middle of the night. But she wasn't pregnant." His voice roughened. "She never had been. Not then, not ever."

"Damian. You can't be sure of—"

"She wanted my name. My money." Damian gave a choked laugh. "Even my title, the 'Prince' thing you and I both know is nothing but outdated crap. She wanted everything." He drew a deep breath, then blew it out. "And she lied about carrying my child to get it."

"When did you find out?"

"When she died," Damian said flatly. He drained his glass and refilled it. "I was in Athens on business. I phoned her every night to see how the pregnancy was going. Later, I found out she'd taken a lover and she'd been with him all the time I was gone."

"Hell," Lucas said softly.

"They were on Long Island. A narrow, twisting road on the Sound along the North Shore. He was driving, both of them high on booze and cocaine. The car went over a guardrail. Neither of them survived." Damian looked up from his glass, his eyes bleak. "You talked about grief before, Lucas. Well, I *did* grieve then, not for her but for my unborn child…until I was going through Kay's papers, tying up loose ends, and found an article she'd clipped from some magazine, all about the symptoms of pregnancy."

"That still doesn't mean—"

"I went to see her doctor. He confirmed it. She had never been pregnant. Not the first time. Not the second. It was all a fraud."

The two friends sat in silence while the sun dipped below the horizon. Finally Lucas cleared his throat.

"I wish I could think of something clever to say."

Damian smiled. "You got me to talk. You can't imagine how much good that's done. I'd been keeping everything bottled inside."

"I have an idea. That club of mine. Remember? I'm meeting there with someone interested in buying me out."

"So soon?"

"You know how it is in New York. Today's hotspot is tomorrow's trash." Lucas glanced at his watch. "Come downtown with me, have a drink while I talk a little business and then we'll go out." He grinned. "Dinner at that place on Spring Street. A pair of bachelors on the town, like the old days."

"Thank you, my friend, but I wouldn't be very good company tonight."

"Of course you would. And we won't be alone for long." Another quick grin. "Before you know it, there'll be a couple of beautiful women hovering over us."

"I've sworn off women for a while."

"I can understand that but—"

"It's what I need to do right now."

"You sure?"

Inexplicably an image of the woman with green eyes

and sun-streaked hair flashed before Damian's eyes. He hadn't wanted to notice her, certainly didn't want to remember her…

"Yes," he said briskly, "I'm positive."

"You know what they say about getting back on the horse that threw you," Lucas said with a little smile.

"I told Nicolo almost the same thing a year ago, the night he met Aimee."

"And?"

"And," Damian said, "it was good advice for him, but not for me. This is different."

Lucas's smile faded. "You're right. Well, let me just call this guy I'm supposed to meet—"

"No, don't do that. I'd like to be alone tonight. Just do a little thinking, start putting this thing behind me."

Lucas cocked his head. "It's no big deal, Damian. I can meet him tomorrow."

"I appreciate it but, honestly, I feel a lot better now that we talked." Damian held out his hand. "Go have your meeting. And, Lucas— Thank you."

"Para nada," Lucas said, smiling. "I'll call you tomorrow, yes? Maybe we can have dinner together."

"I wish I could but I'm flying back to Minos in the morning." Damian gripped Lucas's shoulder. "Take care of yourself, *filos mou.*"

"You do the same." Lucas frowned. Damian looked better than he had a few hours ago but there was still a haunted look in his eyes. "I wish you'd change your mind about tonight. Forget what I said about women. We could go to the gym. Lift some weights. Run the track."

"You really think it would make me feel better to beat you again?"

"You beat me once, a thousand years ago at Yale."

"A triviality."

The men chuckled. Damian slung his arm around Lucas's neck as they walked slowly to the door. "Don't worry about me, Reyes. I'm going to take a long shower, pour myself another brandy and then, thanks to you, I'm going to have the first real night's sleep I've had in months."

The friends shook hands. Then Damian closed the door after Lucas, leaned back against it and let his smile slip away.

He'd told Lucas the truth. He did feel better. For three months, ever since Kay's death, he'd avoided his friends, his acquaintances; he'd dedicated every waking minute to business in hopes he could rid himself of his anger.

What was the point in being angry at a dead woman?

Or in being angry at himself, for having let her scam him?

"No point," Damian muttered as he climbed the stairs to his bedroom. "No point at all."

Kay had made a fool of him. So what? Men survived worse. And if, in the deepest recesses of his soul he somehow mourned the loss of a child that had never existed, a child he'd never known he even wanted, well, that could be dealt with, too.

He was thirty-one years old. Maybe it was time to settle down. Marry. Have a family.

Thee mou, was he insane?

You couldn't marry, have kids without a wife. And there wasn't a way in hell he was going to take a wife anytime soon. What he needed was just the opposite of settling down.

Lucas had it right.

The best cure for what ailed him would be losing himself in a woman. A soft, willing body. An eager mouth. A woman without a hidden agenda, without any plans beyond pleasure…

There it was. That same image again. The green-eyed woman with the sun-streaked hair. Hell, what a chance he'd missed! She'd looked right at him and even then, trapped in a black mood, he'd known what that look meant.

The lady had been interested.

The flat truth was, women generally were.

He'd been interested, too—or he would have been, if he hadn't been so damned busy wallowing in self-pity. Because, hell, that's what this was. Anger, sure, but with a healthy dollop of Poor Me mixed in.

He'd had enough of it to last a lifetime.

He'd call Lucas. Tell him his plans for the night sounded good after all. Dinner, drinks, a couple of beautiful women and so what if they didn't have green eyes, sun-streaked hair…

The doorbell rang.

Damian's brows lifted. A private elevator was the sole access to his apartment. Nobody could enter it without the doorman's approval and that approval had to come straight from Damian himself.

Unless…

He grinned. "Lucas," he said, as he went quickly down the stairs. His friend had reached the lobby, turned around and come right back.

Damian reached the double doors. "Reyes," he said happily as he flung them open, "when did you take up mind-reading? I was just going to call you—"

But it wasn't Lucas in the marble foyer.

It was the woman. The one he'd seen outside Portofino's.

The green-eyed beauty he hadn't been able to get out of his head.

CHAPTER TWO

OH, WHAT a joy to see!

Damian Aristedes's handsome jaw dropped halfway to the ground. Seeing that was the first really good thing that had happened to Ivy in a while.

Obviously his highness wasn't accustomed to having his life disrupted by unwanted surprises.

Damian's unflappable, Kay had said.

Well, okay. She hadn't said it exactly that way. Nobody can get to him, was probably more accurate.

Not true, Ivy thought. Just look at the man now.

"Who are you? What are you doing here?"

She didn't answer. The pleasure of catching him off guard was wearing off. She'd prepared for this moment but the reality was terrifying. Her heart was hammering so hard she was half afraid he could hear it.

"You were outside Portofino's today."

He was gaining control of himself. His voice had taken on authority; his pale gray eyes had narrowed.

"Are you a reporter for one of those damned tabloids? I don't give interviews."

He really didn't know who she was. She'd wondered about that, whether Kay had ever shown him a photo or pointed out her picture in a magazine, but she'd pretty much squelched that possibility at the restaurant, where she'd followed him from his Fifty-Seventh Street office.

He'd looked at her, but only the way most men looked at her. With interest, avarice—the kind of hunger she despised, the kind that said she was a plaything and they wanted a new toy.

Although, when this man had looked at her today, just for a second, surely no more than that, she'd felt— she'd felt—

What?

She'd seemed to lose her equilibrium. She was glad someone had joined him because she knew better than to confront him with another person around.

This discussion had to be private.

As for that loss of equilibrium or whatever it was, it only proved how dangerous Damian Aristedes was.

That he'd been able to mesmerize Kay was easy to understand. Kay had always been a fool for men.

That he'd had an effect on Ivy, even for a heartbeat, only convinced her she'd figured him right.

The prince of all he surveyed was a sleek jungle cat, constantly on the prowl. A beautiful predator. Too bad he had no soul, no heart, no—

"Are you deaf, woman? Who are you? What do you want? And how in hell did you get up here?"

He'd taken a couple of steps forward, just enough to invade her space. No question it was a subtle form of intimidation. It might have worked, too—despite her height, he was big enough so that she had to tilt her head back to meet his eyes—but Ivy was not a stranger to intimidation.

Growing up, she'd been bullied by experts. It could only hurt if you gave in to it.

"Three questions," she said briskly. "Did you want them answered in order, or am I free to pick and choose?"

He moved quickly, grasped her wrist and forced her arm behind her back. It hurt; his grip was strong, his hands hard. She hadn't expected a show of physical strength from a pampered aristocrat but she didn't flinch.

"Take your hand off me."

"It'll take me one second to phone for the police and tell them there's an intruder in my home. Is that what you want?"

"You're the one who won't want the police involved in this, Your Highness."

His gray eyes focused on hers. "Because?"

Now, Ivy thought, and took a steadying breath.

"My name is Ivy."

Nothing. Not even a flicker of interest.

"Ivy Madison," she added, as if that would make the difference.

He didn't even blink. He was either a damned good actor or— A tingle of alarm danced over her skin.

"You are—you are Damian Aristedes?"

He smiled thinly. "A little late to ask but yes, that's who I am."

"Then—then surely, you recognize my name…"

"I do not."

"I'm Kay's sister. Her stepsister."

That got a reaction. His eyes turned cold. He let go of her wrist, or maybe it made more sense to say he dropped it. She half expected him to wipe his hand on his trousers. Instead he stepped back.

"Here to pay a condolence call three months late?"

"I'd have thought you'd have been the one to call me."

He laughed, although the sound he made had no mirth to it.

"Now, why in hell would I do that? For starters, I never knew Kay had a sister." He paused. "That is, if you really are her sister."

"What are you talking about? Certainly I'm her sister. And, of course you know about me."

The woman who claimed to be Kay's sister spoke with authority. Not that Damian believed she really was who she claimed to be.

At the very least she was up to no good. Why approach him this way instead of phoning or e-mailing? What the hell was going on here?

Only one way to find out, Damian thought, and reached for his cell phone, lying on the marble-topped table beside the door.

"What are you doing?"

"Calling your bluff. You won't answer my questions? Fine. You can tell your story to the cops."

"You'd better think twice before you pick up that phone, Mr. Aristedes."

His intruder had started out full of conviction, like a poker player sure of a winning hand, but that had changed. Her voice had gone from strong to shaken; those green eyes—so green he wondered if she were wearing contact lenses—had gone wide.

A scam, he thought coldly. She was trying to set him up for something. The only question was, what?

"Prince," he said, surprising himself with the use of his title. Generally he asked people to call him by his first or last name, not by his honorific, but if it took royal arrogance to shake his intruder's self-control, he'd use it. "It's Prince Damian. And I'll give you one second to start talking. How did you get up here?"

"You mean, how did I bypass the lobby stormtroopers?"

She was trying to regain control. Damned if he'd let it happen. Damian put down the phone, angled toward her and invaded her space again so that she not only stepped back, she stepped into the corner.

No way out, except past him.

"Don't play with me, lady. I want straight answers."

She caught a bit of her lower lip between her teeth, worried it for a second before releasing it and quickly touching the tip of her tongue to the flesh she'd gnawed.

Damian's belly clenched. Lucas had it right. He'd been too long without a woman.

"A delivery boy at the service entrance held the door for me." She smiled thinly. "He was very courteous. Then I used the fire stairs."

"If you're Kay's sister, why didn't you simply ask the doorman to announce you?"

"I waited all this time to hear from you but nothing happened. Telling your doorman I wanted to see you didn't strike me as useful."

"Let me see some ID."

"What?"

"Identification. Something that says you're who you claim to be."

"I don't know why Kay loved you," Ivy said bitterly.

Damian decided it was the better part of valor not to answer that. Instead he watched in silence as she dug through the bag slung over one shoulder, took out a wallet and opened it.

"Here. My driver's license. Satisfied?"

Not satisfied, just more puzzled. The license said she was Ivy Madison, age twenty-seven, with an address in Chelsea. And the photo checked out. It was the woman standing before him. Not even the bored Motor Vehicle clerks and their soulless machines had been able to snap a picture that dimmed her looks.

Damian looked up.

"This doesn't make you Kay's sister."

Without a word, she dug into her purse again, took out a business-card size folder and flipped it open. The photo inside was obviously years old but there was no mistaking the faces of the two women looking at the camera.

"All right. What if you are Kay's sister. Why are you here?"

Ivy stared at him. "You can't be serious!"

He was…and then, with breathtaking speed, things started to fall into place.

The sisters didn't resemble each other, but that didn't mean the apple had fallen far from the tree.

"Let me save you some time," Damian said coolly. "Your sister didn't leave any money."

Those bright green eyes flashed with defiance. "I'm not here for money."

"There's no jewelry, either. No spoils of war. I donated everything I'd given her to charity."

"I don't care about that, either."

"Really?" He folded his arms. "You mean, I haven't ruined your hopes for a big score?"

Her eyes filled with tears.

Indeed, Damian thought grimly, that was exactly what he'd done.

"You—you egotistical, self-aggrandizing, aristocratic pig," she hissed, her voice shaking. "You haven't spoiled anything except for yourself. And believe me, Prince or Mr. or whatever name you want, you'll never, ever know what you missed!"

It was an emotional little speech and he could see she was determined to end it on a high note by shoving past him and striding to the door.

There was every reason to let her go.

If she was willing to give up so easily and disappear from his life as quickly as she'd entered it, who was he to stop her?

Logic told him to move aside.

To hell with logic.

Damian shifted his weight to keep her trapped in the corner. She called him another name, not nearly as creative as the last, put her arms out straight and tried to push him away.

He laughed, caught both her wrists and trapped her hands against the hard wall of his chest. Anger and defiance stained her cheeks with crimson.

"Damn it, let go!"

"Why, sweetheart," he purred, "I don't understand. How come you're so eager to leave when you were so eager to see me?"

She kicked him in the shin with one of her high heeled boots. It hurt, but he'd be damned if he let her know that. Instead he dragged her closer until she was pressed against him.

He told himself it was only to keep her from gouging his shin to the bone.

And that there was no reason, either, for the hot fist of lust that knotted in his groin as he looked down into her flushed face.

Her eyes were wild. Her hair was a torrent of spun gold. Her lips were trembling. Trembling, and full, and delicately parted, and all at once, all at once, Damian understood why she was here.

What a thickheaded idiot he was!

Kay had obviously told Ivy about him. That he had money, a title, an eye for beautiful women.

And now Kay was gone but Ivy—Ivy was very much alive.

Incredibly alive.

His gaze dropped to her mouth again. "What a fool you must think me," he said softly. "Of course I know why you're here."

Her eyes lit. Her mouth curved in a smile. "Thank God," she said shakily. "For a while there, I thought—"

Damian silenced her in midsentence. He thrust his hands into her hair, lifted her face to his and kissed her.

She cried out against his mouth. Slammed her fists against his chest. A nice touch, he thought with a coldness that belied his rising libido. She'd come to audition as her sister's replacement. Well, he'd give her a tryout, all right. Kiss her, show her she had no effect on him and then send her packing.

Except, it wasn't happening that way.

Maybe he really had been without a woman for too long.

Maybe his emotions were out of control.

Sex, desire—neither asks for reason, only satiation and completion. He wanted this. The heat building inside him like a flash-fire in dry brush. The deep, hungry kiss.

The woman struggling for freedom in his arms.

She was pretending. He knew that. It was all part of the act. He nipped at her bottom lip; she gave a little cry and he slid his tongue into her mouth, tasted her sweetness, caught the little sound she made and kissed her again and again until she whimpered, lifted herself to him, flattened her hands against his chest…

Thee mou!

Damian jerked away. The woman stumbled back. Her eyes flew open, the pupils so enormous they'd all but consumed the green of her irises.

What the hell was he doing? She was just like Kay. A siren, luring a man with sex—

Her hand flew through the air and slammed against his jaw.

"You bastard," she said in a hoarse whisper. "You evil, horrible son of a bitch!"

"Don't bother with the theatrics," he snarled. "Or I'll call you some names of my own."

"I don't understand why Kay loved you!"

"Your sister never loved anything that didn't have a price tag on it. Now, go on. Get the hell out before I change my mind and call the police."

"She loved you enough to let you talk her into having this baby!"

Damian had swung away. Now he turned around and faced Ivy Madison.

"What are you talking about?"

"You know damned well what I'm talking about! She lost the first baby and instead of offering her any comfort and compassion, you told her to get out because she couldn't give you an heir."

Could a woman's lies actually leave a man speechless? Damian opened his mouth, then shut it again while he tried to make sense of what Ivy Madison had just said.

"You would have tossed away the woman who loved

you, who adored you, just because she couldn't give you a child. So my sister said she'd give you a baby, no matter what it took, even after the doctors said she couldn't run the risk of pregnancy!"

"Wait a minute. Just wait one damned minute—"

Ivy stared at him, emerald eyes bright against the pallor of her skin.

"You used her love for you to try to get your own way and you didn't care what it did to her, what happened to her—"

Damian was on her in two strides, hands gripping her shoulders, fingers biting into her flesh, lifting her to her toes so that their faces were inches apart.

"Get out," he said in a low, dangerous voice. "Do you hear me? Get out of my home and my life or I'll have you arrested. And if you think you'll walk away after a couple of hours in jail, think again. My attorneys will see to it that you stay in prison for the next hundred years."

It was an empty threat. What could he charge her with besides being a world-class liar? He knew that. What counted was that she didn't.

But it didn't stop her.

"Kay was in love with you."

"I just told you what Kay loved. You have five seconds, Miss Madison. One. Two—"

"She found a way to have your child. You were happy to go along with it but now, you refuse to acknowledge that—"

"Goodbye, Miss Madison."

Damian spun Ivy toward the door. He put his hand in the small of her back, gave her a little push and she stumbled toward the elevator.

"I'm going to call down to the lobby. If the doorman

doesn't see you stepping out of this car in the next couple of minutes, the cops will be waiting."

"You can't do this!"

"Just watch me."

The elevator door opened. Damian curled his fingers around her elbow and quick-marched her inside.

Tears were streaming down her face.

She was as good at crying on demand as Kay had been, he thought dispassionately, though Kay had never quite mastered the art. Her face would get red, her skin blotchy but despite all that, her nose never ran.

Ivy's eyes were cloudy with tears. Her skin was the color of cream. And her nose—damn it, her nose was leaking.

A nice touch of authenticity, Damian told himself as he stepped from the car and the door began to close.

"I was a fool to come here."

Damian grabbed the door. Her words were slurred. Another nice touch, he thought, and offered a wicked smile.

"Didn't work out quite the way you'd planned it, did it?"

"I should have known. All these months, no call from you…"

"I'm every bit the son of a bitch you imagined I'd be," he said, smiling again.

"I tried to tell Kay it was a bad idea, but she wouldn't listen."

"I'll bet. Two con artists discussing how to handle a sucker. Must have been one hell of a conversation."

She brushed the back of her hand over her eyes but, more credit to her acting skills, the tears kept coming.

"Just be sure of one thing, Prince Aristedes."

"It's Prince Damian," he said coolly. "If you're going to try to work royalty, you should use the proper form of address."

"Don't think you can change your mind after the baby's born."

"I wouldn't dream of…" He jerked back. "What baby?"

"Because I won't let you near this child. I don't give a damn how many lawyers you turn loose on me!"

Damian stared at her. He'd let go of the elevator door and it was starting to close again. He moved fast and forced it open.

"What baby?" he demanded.

"You know damned well what baby! Mine. I mean, Kay's." Ivy's chin lifted. "Kay's—and yours."

The earth gave a sickening tilt under his feet. There was a baby? No. There couldn't be. Kay had never really been pregnant. Her doctor had told him so…

"You're a vicious little liar!"

"Fine. Stay with that idea. I told you, I won't let my baby—Kay's baby—near a son of a bitch like—"

She let out a shriek as he dragged her from the elevator, marched her into his apartment and all but threw her into a chair.

"What the hell are you talking about?" He stood over her, feet apart, arms folded, eyes blazing with anger. "Start talking, and it better be the truth."

She began sobbing. He didn't give a damn.

"I'm waiting," he growled. "What baby are you talking about? Whose is it? And where?"

Ivy sprang to her feet. "Get out of my way."

He grabbed her again, hauled her to her toes.

"Answer me, goddamn it!"

Ivy looked up at him while the seconds seemed to turn to hours. Then she wrenched free of his hands.

This baby," she said, laying a hand over her belly. "The one in my womb. I'm pregnant, Prince Damian. Pregnant—with your child."

CHAPTER THREE

PREGNANT?

Pregnant, with his child?

Damian's brain reeled.

Thee mou, a man didn't want to hear that accusation from a woman he didn't love once in a lifetime, let alone twice…

And then his sanity returned.

This woman, Ivy, might well be pregnant but it didn't have a damned thing to do with him. Not unless science had come up with a way a man could have sex with a woman without ever seeing her or touching her.

She was looking at him, defiance stamped in every feature. What was she waiting for? Was he supposed to blink, fall down, clap his hand to his forehead?

The only thing he felt like doing was tossing her over his shoulder and throwing her out. But first—but first—

Damian snorted. Snorted again and then, to hell with it, burst out laughing.

Ivy Madison gave him a killing look.

"How can you laugh at this?" she demanded.

That only made him laugh harder.

He'd heard some really creative tall tales in his life. His father had been especially adept at telling them as he took his company to the edge of ruin but nothing, *nothing* topped this one.

It was funny.

It was infuriating.

Did she take him for a complete fool? Her sister had. Yes, but at least he'd had sex with the sister. There'd been a basis—shaky, but a basis—for Kay claiming she was pregnant.

Hell, the hours the two women must have spent talking about what a sucker he was, how easily he could be taken in by a beautiful face.

"Perhaps you'd like to share what's so damned amusing, Prince Damian?"

Amusing? Damian's laughter faded. "Actually," he said, "I'm insulted."

She blinked. "Insulted?"

"That you'd come up with such a pathetic lie." He tucked his hands in his trouser pockets and sighed dramatically. "You have to have sex with a man before he can impregnate you, Miss Madison, and you and I…"

Suddenly he knew where this was heading. He'd heard of scams like it before.

A beautiful woman chooses a man who's rich. Well-known. A man whose name would garner space in the tabloids.

When the time is right, she confronts him, tells him they met at a party, on a yacht—there were dozens of places they could have stumbled across each other.

That established, she drops the bomb.

She's pregnant. He's responsible. When he says *That's impossible, I never saw you before in my life,* she starts to cry. He was drinking that night, she says. He seduced her, she says. Doesn't he remember?

Because she does.

Every touch. Every sigh. Every nuance of their encounter is seared in her memory, and if he doesn't want it all over the scandal sheets, he'll Do The Right Thing.

He'll give her a fat sum of money to help her. Nothing like a bribe, of course. Just money to get her through a bad time.

Some men would give in without much of a fight, even if they could disprove the story. They'd do whatever it took just to avoid publicity.

Damian's jaw tightened.

Oh, yes. That was how this was supposed to go down... Except, it wouldn't. His beautiful scam artist was about to learn she couldn't draw him into that kind of trap.

He'd already been the victim of one Madison sister. He'd be damned if he'd be the victim of the second sister, too.

Damian looked up. The woman had not moved. She stood her ground, shoulders squared, head up, eyes glittering with defiance.

God, she was magnificent! Anyone walking in and seeing her would be sure she was a brave Amazon, overmatched but prepared to fight to her last breath.

Too bad there wasn't an audience. There was only him, and he wasn't buying the act.

Damian smiled. Slowly he brought his hands together in mocking applause.

"Excellent," he said softly. "An outstanding performance." His smile disappeared. "Just one problem, *kardia mou.* I'm on to you."

"What?"

"You heard me. I know your game. And I'm not going to play it."

"Game? Is that what you think this is? I come to you after my sister's death because you didn't have enough concern to come to me and you think—you think it's a game?"

"Perhaps I used the wrong word. It's more like a melodrama. You're the innocent little flower, I'm the cruel villain."

"I don't know what you're talking about!"

Damian started slowly toward her. He saw her stiffen. She wanted to back away or maybe even turn and run. Good, he thought coldly. She was afraid of him, and she damned well ought to be.

"Don't you want to tell me the rest? The details of our passionate encounter?"

She looked at him as if he were crazy. "What passionate encounter?"

"Come now, darling. Have you forgotten your lines? You're supposed to remind me of what we did when I was drunk." He stopped inches from her, a chill smile curling across his lips. "Well, I'm waiting. Where did it happen? Here? Athens? A party on my yacht at the Côte d'Azur? Not that it matters. The story's the same no matter where we met."

"I didn't say—"

"No. You didn't, and that's my fault. I never gave you the chance to tell your heartbreaking little tale, but why waste time when it's so trite? I was drunk. I seduced you. Now, it's—it's— How many months later, did you say?"

"Three months. You know that, just as you know the rest of what you said isn't true!"

"Did I get the facts wrong?" His eyes narrowed; his voice turned hard. "Frankly I don't give a damn. All I care about is seeing the last of you, lady. You understand?"

Ivy understood, all right.

This man her sister had worshipped, this—this Adonis whose face and body were enough to quicken the beat of a woman's heart…

This man Kay had been willing to do anything for, was looking at her and lying through his teeth.

How could Kay have loved him?

"Shall I be more direct, Miss Madison?" Damian clamped his hands on her shoulders. "Get out of here before I lose my temper."

His voice was low, his grasp painful. He was furious and, Ivy was sure, capable of violence.

That wasn't half as important as being certain she understood exactly what he was telling her.

He didn't want the child she was carrying.

She'd figured as much, when she hadn't heard from him after the accident. She'd waited and waited, caught up first in shock at losing Kay, then in growing awareness of her own desperation until, finally, she'd realized the prince's silence was a message.

Still, it wasn't enough.

He had to put his denial of his rights to his child in writing. She needed a document that said he didn't want the baby, that he'd rather believe her story was a lie than acknowledge he'd fathered a child.

Even that was no guarantee.

Damian Aristedes was powerful. He could hire all the lawyers in Manhattan and have money left over. He could not only make his own rules, he could change them when he had to.

But if she had something on paper, something that might give her a legal edge if he ever changed his mind—

"I can almost see you thinking, Miss Madison."

Ivy blinked. The prince was standing with his arms folded over his chest, narrowed eyes locked on her face.

It was disconcerting.

She was accustomed to having men look at her. It went with the territory.

When you had done hundreds of photo shoots, when your own face looked back at you from magazine covers, you expected it. It was part of the price you paid for success in the world of modeling.

Men noticed you. They looked at you.

But not like this.

The expression on Damian Aristedes's face spoke of contempt, not desire. How dare he be disdainful of her? She'd made a devil's bargain—she knew that, had known it almost from the beginning—but she'd been prepared to stand by that bargain even if it tore out her heart.

Not him.

He was the man who'd started this. Now, he was pretending he didn't know what she was talking about.

That was fine. It was perfect. It meant she'd kept her promise and now she was free to put the past behind her and concentrate on the future. On the child she'd soon have.

Her child, not his.

It was just infuriating to have him look at her as if she were a liar and a cheat.

Except, there'd been a moment, more than one, when she'd caught him watching her in a different way, his eyes glinting not with disdain but with hunger.

Hunger only she could ease.

And when that had happened, she'd felt—she'd felt—

"You're as transparent as glass, Miss Madison."

Years of letting the camera steal her face but never her thoughts kept Ivy from showing any reaction.

"How interesting. Do you read minds when you're not busy evading responsibility, Your Highness?"

"You're trying to come up with a way to capitalize on that moment of shock I showed when you told me I was your baby's father." He smiled thinly. "Trust me. You can't."

He was partly right. She was trying to come up with a way to capitalize on something, but not that.

Ivy took a steadying breath.

"I'll be happy to leave, happier still never to see you again, Prince Damian. But first—"

"Ah. But first, you want a check for… How much? A hundred thousand? Five hundred thousand? A million? Don't shake your head, Miss Madison. We both know you have a price in mind."

Another steadying breath. "Not a check."

"Cash, then. It doesn't matter."

The icy little smile slipped from his lips and she repressed a shudder. The prince would be a formidable enemy.

"I don't want money. I want a letter. A document that makes it clear you're giving up all rights to the child in my womb."

He laughed. Laughed, damn him!

"*Thee mou,* lady. Don't you know when to quit?"

"Sign it, date it and I'll be out of your life forever."

His laughter stopped with the speed of a faucet

turning off. "Enough," he said through his teeth. "Get out of my home before I do something we'll both regret."

"Just a letter," she said. "A few lines—"

He said something in what she assumed was Greek. She didn't understand the words but she didn't have to as he gripped her by the shoulders, spun her around, put a hand in the small of her back and shoved her forward.

"And if you're foolish enough to tell your ridiculous story to anyone—"

The thing to do was hire a lawyer. Except, he'd hire a dozen for every one she could afford. He had power. Money. Status. Still, there had to be a way. There had to be!

"And if you really are knocked up, if some man was stupid enough to let your face blind him to the scheming bitch you really are—"

Ivy spun around, swung her fist and caught him in the jaw. He was big and strong and hard as nails but she caught him off guard. He blinked and staggered back. It took him all of a second to recover but it was enough to send a warm rush of pleasure through her blood.

"You—you pompous ass," she hissed. She marched forward, index finger aimed at his chest, and jabbed it right into the center of his starched white shirt, her fear gone, everything forgotten but his impossible arrogance. "This isn't about you and who you are and how much money you have. It isn't about you at all! I don't want anything from you, Prince Damian. I never—"

She gasped as he caught her by the elbows and lifted her to her toes.

"You don't want anything from me, huh?" Damian's lips drew back from his teeth as he bent his head toward hers. "That's why you came here? Because you don't want anything from me?"

"I came because I thought I owed it to you but I was wrong. I don't. And I warn you, letter or no letter, if you should change your mind a month from now, a decade from now, and try and claim my baby—"

"Damn you," he roared, "there is no baby!"

"Whatever you say."

"The truth at last!"

"Truth?" Ivy laughed in his face. "You wouldn't know it if it bit you in the tail!"

"I know that I never took you to bed."

"Let go!"

"How come you didn't factor that into your little scheme?" Damian yanked her wrist, dragged it behind her back. She flinched but she'd sooner have eaten nails than let him know he was hurting her. "You made several mistakes, Miss Madison. One, I don't drink to excess. Two, I never forget a woman I've been with." His gaze swept over her with slow deliberation before returning to her face. "Believe me, lady, if I'd had you, I'd remember."

"I'm done talking about that."

"But I'm not." He drew her closer, until they were a breath apart. "Why should I be? You said we were intimate. I said we weren't. Why not settle the question?"

"It isn't worth settling. And I never said we'd been intimate."

His lips drew back from his teeth. "Ah, Ivy, Ivy, you disappoint me. Backing down already?" His smile vanished; his eyes turned cold. "Come on, *glyka mou*. Here's your chance. Convince me we slept together. Remind me of what it was like."

"Stop it. Stop it! I'm warning you, let me—"

She gasped as Damian slipped one hand lightly around her throat.

"A woman can only taunt a man for so long before he retaliates. Surely someone with your skills should have learned that by now."

"You're wrong! You know the truth, that we never—"

Damian kissed her.

Her mouth was cool and soft, and she made a little sound of terrified protest.

That was how she made it sound, anyway.

It was all part of the act. Part of a performance. Part of who she was and why she was here and…

And she tasted sweet, sweeter than the first time he'd kissed her, maybe because he knew the shape of her mouth now. The fullness of it.

The sexy silkiness.

She cried out again, jammed her hand against his chest and Damian told himself it was time to let go of her.

He'd accomplished what he wanted, met her challenge, showed her that she had no power over him…

His arousal was swift. He put one hand at the base of her spine and pressed hard enough so she had no choice but to tilt her hips against his and feel it.

God, he was on fire.

Another little sound whispered from her mouth to his and then, same as before, he felt the change in her. Her mouth softened. Warmed. The stiffness went out of her body and she leaned toward him.

He reminded himself that nothing she did was real. It was all part of her overall plan.

And it didn't matter.

He knew only that he wanted this. The taste of her.

The feel of her. He was entitled to that. Hell, he'd been accused of something he had not done.

Why not do it now?

Lift Ivy into his arms. Carry her up the stairs to his bedroom. Take everything she wanted him to believe he'd taken before, again and again and again…

"Please," she whispered, "please—"

Her voice was soft. Dazed. It made him want her even more.

Deliberately he slid his hand inside her jacket and cupped the delicate weight of one breast.

"Please, what?" he growled. "Touch you? Take you?"

His fingers swept over her breast, blood thundering in his ears when he felt the thrust of her nipple through the silk that covered it. She moaned against his mouth.

A wave of lust rolled through him, shocking him with its intensity.

She moaned again and he gathered her closer. Slid his hands under the waistband of her black jeans. Felt the coolness of her buttocks, the silk of her flesh.

Primal desire flooded his senses. He wanted her, no matter what she was. And she wanted him. Wanted him. Wanted him…

Panagia mou! Damian flung her from him and stepped back. Tears were streaming down her face. If he hadn't known better, he'd have honestly thought she was weeping.

"I can't believe Kay loved you, that she wanted to give you a child!"

"Your story's getting old. And confused. You're the one who's pregnant. Who I took to bed, remember?"

"That's not true! Why do you keep saying it? You know we didn't go to bed!"

"Right," he said, his voice cold with contempt and sarcasm. "I keep forgetting that. We didn't. We did it standing up. Or sitting in a chair. Or on a sofa—"

"There was no chair. No sofa. You know that. There was just—just your sperm. A syringe. And—and me."

"Yeah. Sure. You, my sperm, a syringe…" Damian jerked back. "What?"

"You damned well know what! And you didn't even have the—the decency to let Kay be artificially inseminated by a physician. Oh, no. You wanted to protect your precious privacy! So you—you used a—a condom to—to—" Her voice turned bitter. "I knew what you were when you didn't ask to meet me in advance. When you didn't care enough to come with Kay the day she—the day I—the day it took place."

Damian wanted to say something but he couldn't. He felt as if his head were in a vise.

Her story was fantastic. Far more interesting than the usual *He made me pregnant* tale.

And the media loved fantasy.

They'd fall on this like hyenas on a wounded antelope. By the time a different scandal knocked the story off the front pages, the damage would have been done. To his name, to Aristedes Shipping, the company he'd spent his adult life rebuilding.

"Nothing to say, Your Highness?" Ivy put her hands on her hips and eyed him with derision. "Or have you finally figured out that denial will only take you so far?"

Tossing this woman out on her backside was no longer a viable option. She was too clever for such easy dismissal.

"You're right about that," he said calmly. "Denial only goes so far and then it's time to take appropriate action." He closed the distance between them, relishing the way she stumbled back. "You will take a pregnancy test. Then, if you're really pregnant, a paternity test."

Ivy stared at him. She couldn't think of a reason he'd want her to take such tests... Unless he was telling the truth. Unless he really hadn't known about the baby.

And if he hadn't... What would happen once he did?

"I don't want to take any tests," she said quickly. "You said you didn't want the baby. That's fine. You only have to give me a document—"

"No, *glyka mou*. It is you who will provide *me* with a document that legally establishes that you and I and a syringe never met, except inside your scheming little brain."

"But—"

Damian took her arm, marched her to the elevator and pushed her inside it. Seconds later, the doors slid shut in her face.

CHAPTER FOUR

IT TROUBLED her all the way back to her apartment.

If Kay's lover had known about the baby, if he'd orchestrated it as Kay claimed, why would the details of the baby's conception have shaken him?

And he had been shaken.

He'd recovered fast but not fast enough to hide his initial shock.

And why would he want these tests? Unless, Ivy thought as she unlocked the door to her apartment, unless he'd just been getting rid of her...

But the light on her telephone was blinking. A man identifying himself as the prince's attorney had left a message on her voice mail.

She was to be at one of the city's most prestigious hospitals at eight the next morning.

Someone would meet her in the reception area.

Ivy sank into a chair. The day had finally caught up to her. She was worn-out and close to tears, wondering why she'd ever thought that seeking out Damian Aristedes was the right thing to do...

But she'd done it.

Now, she could only put one foot ahead of the other and see where this path led.

* * *

A tall, dark-haired man, his back to her, was standing in the main lobby of the hospital when she arrived there the next day.

Her heart leaped. Was it Damian?

The man turned. He was balding and he wore glasses. It wasn't the prince. Of course not. Why would she want him here? And why would he be here when he hadn't shown up with Kay for the procedure he'd demanded?

The procedure that had taken a drastic turn at the last minute.

The memory struck hard. Ivy wrapped her arms around herself. She should never have agreed to it.

Or to this.

This was another mistake.

But it was too late to run. The tall man had seen her. He came toward her, her name a question on his lips. From the look on his face, he was as uncomfortable with this whole thing as she was.

He introduced himself. He was, he said, holding out his hand, the prince's attorney, here to offer whatever assistance she might require.

"You mean," Ivy said, deliberately ignoring his out-stretched hand, "you're here to make sure I don't try to phony-up the test results."

He had the good grace not to try to contradict her as he escorted her to a small office where a briskly effi-cient technician took over.

"Come with me, please, Miss Madison. The gentle-man can wait outside."

"Oh, he's not a gentleman," Ivy said politely. "He's a lawyer."

Even the attorney laughed.

Then Ivy blanked her mind to everything but what had to be done.

The results, they said, would take up to two weeks.

She said that was fine, though two centuries would have been more to her liking.

They told her to take it easy for a couple of days and she did, even though it gave her more time to think than she wanted.

Day three, she organized the drawers and closets of her apartment. They didn't need it: she'd always been neat, something you learned quickly when you spent part of your growing-up years in foster care, but straightening things was a good way to kill time.

Day four, her agent called with a job. The cover of *La Belle* magazine. It was a plum but Ivy turned it down. She was tired all the time, her back ached and besides, she'd never much liked modeling. But she needed the money. She'd given most of what she'd saved to Kay.

Kay, who had come to her in tears.

She lived, she'd said, with Damian Aristedes. Ivy had heard of him before. You couldn't read *People* or *Vanity Fair* without seeing his name. The magazines said he was incredibly good-looking and incredibly wealthy. Kay said yes, he was both, but he was tight with a dollar and he'd refused to pay the money she still owed on her condo even though he demanded she not work.

He wanted her available to him at all times.

Ivy had given her the money. It was an enormous amount, but how could she have said no? She owed Kay so much… Money could never begin to repay that debt.

A few weeks later, Kay came to her again and

confided the rest of her story. How she'd miscarried. How Damian now demanded proof she could give him an heir before he'd marry her.

Ivy thought the man sounded like a brute but Kay adored him. She'd wept, talked about how much she wanted his baby, how much she wished she could give him such a gift.

She'd reminded Ivy of the years they'd shared as teenagers, of memories Ivy was still doing her best to forget.

"Do you remember how desperate you were then?" Kay had said through her tears. "That's how desperate I am now! Please, please, you have to help me."

In the end, Ivy had agreed to something she'd convinced herself was good even if it might prove emotionally difficult, but she'd never expected it to go as far as it had. To turn into something she'd regretted almost immediately, something she wept over night after night—

Something she might well end up fighting in court, and how would she pay those legal fees?

Ivy picked up the phone, called her agent and told him she'd do the *La Belle* cover after all.

It was excellent money and it was a head shot; nobody would see that she was pregnant.

Still, head shot or not, the photographer insisted she be styled right down to her toes. She spent the day in heavy makeup and endless outfits matched by spectacular sky-high Manolos on her feet.

When she finally reached her Chelsea brownstone, it was after five. She was exhausted and headachy, her face felt like a mask under all the expensive makeup she hadn't taken time to remove and her feet…

Her feet were two blobs of pain.

She was still wearing the last pair of Manolos from the final set of photos. Actually she was swollen into them.

"Poor darling," the stylist cooed. "Keep them as a gift."

So she'd limped into a taxi, limped out of it. Now, if she could just get up the three flights of steps to her apartment…

Three flights of steps. They never even made her breathe hard. Now, they loomed ahead like Mount McKinley.

Ivy took a deep breath and started climbing.

She was shaking with fatigue when she finally reached her landing, and wincing at the pain in her feet. She waited a minute, then took out her key and fumbled it into the lock.

Soon. Oh, yes, soon. Off with the shoes. Into the shower, then into a loose T-shirt and an even looser pair of fleece sweatpants. After that, she'd put together a peanut butter and honey sandwich on the kind of soft, yummy white bread that the health gurus hated…

Ivy shut the door behind her, automatically slid home the chain lock, turned around…

And screamed.

A man—dark hair, broad shoulders, long legs, leather jacket and pale blue jeans—was seated in a chair in her living room.

"Easy," he said, rising quickly to his feet, but it was too late. The floor had already rushed up to meet her.

"Thee mou," a voice said gruffly.

Strong arms closed around her.

After that, there was only darkness.

* * *

Damian had never moved faster in his life.

A damned good thing he had, he thought grimly, though the woman he held in his arms was as limp as the proverbial dishrag.

A man might joke about wanting a woman to fall at his feet, but this was surely not the way it should happen.

Especially if the woman was pregnant.

He cursed ripely in his native tongue and shoved that thought aside. He had come here to deal with that fact and he would. Right now, what mattered was that Ivy had passed out cold.

She felt warm and soft in his arms, but her face was frighteningly pale. Her breathing seemed shallow. What was he supposed to do now? Call 9-1-1? Wait until she stirred? Did he search her apartment for spirits of ammonia?

Ivy solved the problem by raising her lashes. She looked at him and he saw confusion in her deep green eyes.

"Damian?"

It was the first time she'd called him that.

"Damian, what—what happened?"

"You fainted, *glyka mou*. My fault. I apologize."

She closed her eyes, then opened them again. This time, the confusion was gone.

Anger had taken its place.

"I remember now. I unlocked the door and—"

"You saw me."

"How did you get in here? I never leave the door unlocked!"

"The super let me in." His mouth twisted. "A story

about being your long-lost brother and a hundred-dollar bill melted his heart."

"You had no right—"

"Unfortunately you don't have a back entrance and a flight of service steps," he said dryly.

"It's hardly the same thing."

"It's exactly the same thing."

Ivy stiffened in his arms. "Please put me down."

"Would you prefer the bedroom or the sofa?"

"I would prefer my feet on the floor."

He almost laughed. She was still pale but there was no mistaking the indignation in her voice.

"You will lie down while I phone for a doctor."

Ivy shook her head. "I don't need a doctor. I fainted, that's all."

She was right. He decided not to argue. They'd have enough to argue over in a little while.

"You're a stubborn woman, Miss Madison."

"Not half as stubborn as you, Your Highness."

Damian carried her to a small, brocade-covered sofa and sat her on it.

"Amazing, how you manage to make 'Your Highness' sound like a four-letter word. No. Do not even try to stand up. I'm going to get a cold compress."

"I told you—"

"And I'm telling you, sit there and behave yourself."

He strode off, found a towel in the kitchen, filled it with ice and returned to the living room, surprised to find she'd heeded his warning.

It was, he thought, a bad sign.

Almost as bad as the feverish color that was replacing the pallor in her skin. He wanted to take her in his arms, hold her close, tell her he was sorry he'd frightened her…

Hell.

"Here," he said brusquely, thrusting the ice-filled towel into her hands.

"I don't need that," she snapped, but she took the towel anyway and pressed it to her wrists.

He took the time to take a long look at her.

She looked worn out. Dark shadows were visible under her eyes despite a layer of heavy makeup. She hadn't worn makeup the other day. Why would she, when her natural beauty was so breathtaking?

His gaze swept over her.

She had on a loose-fitting, heavy sweater. A matching skirt. And, *Thee mou,* what was she doing, wearing those shoes? They were the kind that would normally make his blood pressure rise but that wasn't going to happen when he could see the straps denting her flesh.

Damian looked up. "Your feet are swollen."

"How clever of you to notice."

"Are you so vain you'd wear shoes that hurt?"

"I am not vain—what are you doing?"

"Taking off these ridiculous shoes."

"Stop it!" Ivy tried slapping his hands away as he lifted one of her feet to his lap. "I said—"

"I heard you."

His fingers moved swiftly, undoing straps and tiny jeweled buckles. The shoe fell off. Gently he lowered her leg, then removed the second shoe. When he'd finished, Ivy planted both her bare feet on the floor.

It was all she could do to keep from groaning with relief.

"Better?"

She didn't answer. *Thee mou,* he had never known such an intractable female.

Damian muttered something under his breath and lifted her feet to his lap again.

"Of course they're better," he said, answering his own question. His tone was brusque but his hands were gentle as he massaged her ankles, her toes, her insteps. "Why a woman would put herself through such torture—"

"I just came from a cover shoot. The stylist gave me the shoes as a gift. They do that kind of thing sometimes," she said, wondering why on earth she was explaining herself to this arrogant man.

"And you were so thrilled you decided to wear them home even though they were killing you."

Ivy's eyes narrowed. "Yes," she said coldly, "that's right." She tugged her feet from his hands and sat up. "Now that you've told me what you think of my decisions, try telling me something that matters, like what you're doing here."

A muscle knotted in his jaw. Then he took an envelope from his pocket and tossed it on the coffee table.

Ivy caught her breath.

"Are those the test results?"

He nodded.

"They were supposed to send them to me."

"And to me."

"Well, that's wrong. That's an invasion of privacy. The results of *my* test are *my* business—"

Ivy knew she was babbling. She stopped, reached for the envelope but she couldn't bring herself to touch it. They'd tested for pregnancy. For paternity. For the first time, she realized they could also have tested for maternity...

Her hands began to shake. She sat back.

"Tell me," she said softly.

"You already know." His voice was without intonation, though she sensed a restrained violence in his words. "I am the father of the child in your womb. The child that would have been Kay's."

Ivy swallowed hard. "And the sex?" she whispered.

"It is a boy."

A little sound broke from her throat and she put her hand over her mouth. It was, Damian thought coldly, one hell of an act.

"I tried to tell you I was pregnant. That you were the father. You wouldn't listen."

"I am listening now." Damian sat back and folded his arms. "Tell me again, from the beginning. I want to hear everything."

She did, from the moment Kay proposed the idea until the moment she'd confronted him in his apartment, though there were some parts—all right, one part—she left out.

She didn't dare tell him that. Not yet.

Maybe not ever.

But she went through all the facts, pausing to answer his questions, biting her lip each time he shook his head in disbelief because, in her heart, she still shared that disbelief.

What Kay had asked of her, what she'd agreed to do, was insane.

"Why?" he said, when she'd finished the tale. "Why would Kay ask you to be a— What did you call it?"

"A gestational surrogate. Her egg. Your—your sperm." She knew she was blushing, and wasn't that ridiculous? The procedure Kay had planned, even the one they'd actually ended up doing, was about as intimate as a flu shot. "And I told you why. You wanted a child. She knew she couldn't carry one."

Damian shot to his feet. "Lies! I never said anything about a child. And she didn't know if she could carry one or not."

"You asked me to tell you everything. That's what I'm doing."

She gasped as he hauled her to her feet.

"The hell you are," he snarled. "What did she pay you for your role in this?"

"Pay me?" Ivy laughed. "Not a penny. You kept Kay on a tight allowance."

"Another lie!"

"Even if you hadn't, I'd never have done this for money."

"No," he said grimly. "You did it out of love."

"I know you can't understand something like that but—"

"I understand, all right. You hatched out a plot between you. You'd have a baby Kay didn't want to have, she'd use it to force me into marriage. And when she divorced me, the two of you would split whatever huge settlement a shyster lawyer could bleed out of me."

Ivy jerked free of his hands. "Do you have any idea how much I earn in a day? How much I'll lose by not modeling for the next five or six months? Hell, for the next couple of years?"

"Is that why you took an assignment today?" he said, sneering. "Because you have so much money you don't need any more?"

"That's none of your business!"

"You're wrong," he said coldly. "From now on, everything about you is my business."

"No, it isn't."

"What did I just say? Starting now, everything about you is also about me."

"The hell it is!"

Ivy glared at him. Damian glared back. Her chin was raised. Her eyes were cold. Her hands were knotted on her hips.

She looked like one of the Furies, ready and determined to take on the world.

He wanted to cover the distance between them, grab her and shake her. Or grab her, haul her into his arms and kiss her until she trembled.

He hated the effect she had on him, hated himself for bending to it… And it was time to put all that aside.

He knew what he had to do.

It was time she knew it, too.

"We're getting sidetracked," he said.

"I agree, Your Highness."

That drove him crazy, too. The way she said "Your Highness." He hadn't been joking when he'd told her she made it sound like a four-letter word.

"Under the circumstances," he said brusquely, "I think you should call me Damian."

She got his meaning; he knew because he saw her cheeks flame. Good, he thought grimly. He wanted her a little uncertain. Why should he be the only one who was balancing on a tightrope?

"This is a pointless conversation. Why should it matter what I call you? Once we determine what happens after my—after the baby's born, we don't have to see each other again."

"Is that what you would you like to happen?"

Was he really asking? Ivy could hardly believe it but she was ready with an answer. This was all she'd thought about since the day she'd gone to his apartment.

"I'd like a simple solution," she said carefully, "one that would please us both."

"And that is?"

She could hear her heart pounding. Could he hear it, too?

"You—you've fathered a baby you say you didn't want."

"More correctly, I fathered a baby I didn't know about."

If that was true—and she had to believe it was—it worried her. The way he'd just stated the situation worried her, too. Fathering a baby he didn't want wasn't the same as fathering a baby he hadn't known about.

She wanted to call him on it but that wouldn't help her case, and that was the last thing she wanted to do.

"A baby you didn't know about," she said, trying to sound as if she really believed it. "A baby my sister wanted."

"But?" He smiled thinly. "I could hear the word, even if it was unspoken."

She drew a breath, then let it out. "But, everything's changed. Kay is gone and I—I want this baby. I didn't know I'd feel this way. That I'd love the baby without ever seeing it. That I wouldn't want to give it away or—"

"Very nice," he said coldly. "But please, spare me the performance. How much?"

She looked puzzled. "I just told you. I want the baby with all my heart."

Damian came toward her, shaking his head and

smiling. "You have it wrong. I'm not asking about your heart, I'm asking about your wallet. How much must I pay you to give up this child you carry?"

"This has nothing to do with money."

"You are Kay's sister. Everything has to do with money." His mouth twisted. "How much?"

"I want my baby, Damian! You don't want it. You said so."

"You don't listen, *glyka mou*. I said, I didn't know about the child." Slowly he reached out and slid his hand beneath Ivy's sweater. She grabbed his wrist and tried to move it but it was like trying to move an oak.

His fingers spread over her belly.

"That's my son," he said softly. "In your womb. He carries my genes. My blood."

"And mine," she said quickly.

"You mean, Kay's."

She flushed. "Yes. Of course that's what I mean."

"A baby you meant to give up."

The words hurt her heart.

"Yes," she whispered, so softly he could hardly hear her. "I thought I could. But—but just as you said, this baby is in my womb—"

Damian caught her face in his hands.

"My seed," he said. "Your womb. In other words, our child." His gaze, like a caress, fell to her lips. "Via a syringe, Ivy. Not you in my arms, in my bed, the way it should have been."

"But it wasn't." Was that high, breathless voice really hers? "Besides, that has nothing to do with the facts."

She was right.

But he'd given up trying to be logical. Nothing about

this was logical, he thought, and he bent to her and kissed her.

The kiss was long. Deep. And when she made a soft, sweet sound that could only have been a sigh of desire, Damian took the kiss deeper still. His tongue slipped into her mouth; he tasted her sweetness, God, her innocence…

Except, she wasn't innocent.

She'd entered into an unholy bargain with her sister and he didn't for a minute believe she'd done it as some great humanitarian gesture…

And then he stopped thinking, gathered her tightly in his arms and kissed her again and again until she was gripping his shoulders, until she was parting her lips to his, until she rose to him, pressed against him, sighed into his mouth.

She swayed when he let go of her. Her eyes flew open; she looked as shaken as he felt.

He hated her for it.

For the act, the drama…the effect it had on him.

"So," he said, his tone calm despite the pounding surge of his blood, "we have a dilemma. How do I claim a child that's mine when it's still in your womb?"

"You don't. I just told you, I want—"

"Frankly I don't give a damn what you want. Neither will a judge. You entered into a devil's bargain with your sister. Now you'll pay the price."

Her green eyes went black with fear. At least, it looked like fear. He knew it was greed.

"No court is going to take a child from its mother."

"You're not his mother, *glyka mou*. But I am its father."

"Still—"

"There is no 'still,' Ivy. No if, no but, no maybe. I've spoken with my attorney."

"Your attorney isn't God."

Damian laughed. "Try telling him that." His laughter faded. "Do you have any idea how much I pay him each year?"

"No, and I don't give a damn! Your money doesn't impress me."

"I pay him a million dollars. And that's only a retainer." He reached for her. She stepped back but he caught her with insolent ease and pulled her into his arms again. "He's worth every penny. And I promise, he will take my son from you."

"No." Tears rose in Ivy's eyes. "You can't do this. You wouldn't do this!"

"But I'm not heartless," Damian said softly. "I'm even willing to believe there's some truth to what you say about not wanting to give up my child." He bent his head to hers; she tried to twist her face away but he slid his hands into her hair and held her fast. "So I've decided to make you an offer." He smiled. "An offer, as they say, you cannot refuse."

The world, the room, everything seemed to stop.

"What?" Ivy whispered.

Damian took her mouth with his. Kissed her as she struggled. As she wept. As she tried to break free until, at last, she went still in his arms and let the kiss happen.

It wasn't what he wanted, damn it.

He wanted her to kiss him back, as she had before. To melt against him, to moan, to show him that she wanted him, wanted him…

Even if it was a lie.

He drew back. She stood motionless.

"I return to Greece tomorrow."

"You can return to Hades for all I care. I want to know what you're offering me."

What he'd come up with was surprisingly simple. He'd worked it out late last night, on the impossible chance her story about her pregnancy turned out to be true.

This morning, after the test results had proved that it was, he'd run the idea past his attorney who'd said yes, okay, with just a couple of touch-ups, it would work.

Ivy would put herself into the hands of a physician of his choosing. She would stop working—he would support her through the pregnancy. He'd move her into a place nearer his condo. And when she gave birth, he would give her a one time payment of ten million dollars and she would give him his son.

He'd even permit her to visit the child four times a year, if she was really as emotionally committed to him as she made it seem.

More than generous, his attorney had agreed.

"Damn you," Ivy demanded, "what offer?"

Damian cleared his throat. "Ten million dollars on the birth of my child."

She laughed. Damn her, she laughed!

"Until then, I will move you to a place of my choosing. And, of course, I will support you."

Another peal of laughter burst from her throat. He could feel every muscle in his body tensing.

"You find this amusing?"

"I find it amazing! Do you really think you can buy my baby? That you can take over my life?"

"The child is not yours. You seem to keep forgetting

that. As for your so-called life…" His eyes darkened. "Your sister had a life, too, one that was inappropriate."

"And you are a candidate for sainthood?"

Damian could feel his control slipping. Who was she, this woman who thought she could defy him? Who had entered into a conspiracy that would change his life?

"I know who I am," he said coldly. "More to the point, I know who you are." His eyes flickered over her in dismissal. "You are a woman who agreed to bear a child for money."

"I'm tired of defending myself, tired of explaining, tired of being bullied." Ivy's voice trembled with emotion. "I don't want your money or your support, and I'm certainly not moving to an apartment where you can keep me prisoner!"

She kept talking. He stopped listening. All he could see was her face, tearstained and determined.

Did she think he was a complete fool? That this show of rebelliousness would convince him to up the ante?

"I am not some—some meek little lamb," she said, "eager to do your bidding." She folded her arms and glared at him. "Do you understand, Your Highness? My answer to your offer is no!"

She gasped as he captured her face in his hands.

"It wasn't an offer," he growled. "It is what you will do—but I'm changing the terms. Forget the apartment near mine. I am taking you to Greece with me."

She stared at him as if he'd lost his mind. He hadn't. He'd simply begun to see things more clearly.

He was in New York once a month at best. What would she be doing while he was away? He had the right to know.

She slung an obscenity at him that almost made him laugh, coming as it did from that perfect mouth.

"I will not go anywhere with you. There are laws—"

"What laws?" His mouth thinned. "I am Prince Damian Aristedes. Do you think your laws have any meaning to me?"

Ivy couldn't speak. There was no word to describe what she felt for this man. Hatred didn't even come close—but he was a prince. He could trace his lineage back through the centuries. She was nobody. She could trace her lineage back to a foster home where—where—

No. She wasn't going there.

Damian's hands tightened. He raised her face until their eyes met.

"Do you understand what I've told you? Or are you going to be foolish enough to try to fight me?"

"I despise you!"

"Ah, *glyka mou,* you're breaking my heart."

"You're a monster. I can't stand having you touch me."

"A decision, Ivy. And quickly."

Tears spilled down her face. "You know my decision! You haven't left me a choice."

Damian felt a swell of triumph but it was poisoned by the hatred in Ivy's eyes. With a growl of rage, he captured her mouth, kissing her without mercy, without tenderness, nipping her bottom lip when she refused the thrust of his tongue.

"A reminder," he said coldly. "Until my son is born, you belong to me."

Even in his anger, he knew a good line when he heard it.

He turned around and walked out.

CHAPTER FIVE

DAMIAN went down the stairs with fury clouding his eyes, went out the door to the street the same way.

His driver had brought him to Ivy's apartment. The Mercedes was at the curb and Damian started toward it. Charles must have been watching for him; he sprang from behind the wheel, rushed around to the rear door and swung it open.

Charles had only been with him a couple of months but surely Damian had told him he was capable of opening a car door himself a hundred times.

A thousand times, he thought, as his temper superheated.

Then he saw the way Charles was looking at him.

"My apologies, Your Highness. I keep forgetting. It's just that you are the first employer I've had who doesn't want me getting out to open or close the door. I promise, it won't—"

"No, that's all right," Damian said. "Don't worry about it." He paused beside the car. He had a meeting later in the day. There was just time for him to go to his office and do some work.

But work wasn't what he needed right now. What he needed was a drink.

"I won't be needing the car," he said briskly, and slapped the top of the Mercedes.

"Very well, sir. I'll wait until you—"

"I won't need the car at all." He forced a smile. After all, none of this was his driver's fault. "Take it back to the garage and call it a day."

Charles looked surprised but he was too well-trained to ask questions. A good thing, Damian thought as he walked away, because he sure as hell didn't have any answers. Not logical ones, anyway.

Logic had nothing to do with the mess he was in.

At the corner, he took out his cell phone, called his assistant and told her to cancel his appointment. Then he called Lucas.

"Are you busy?"

He tried to make the question sound casual but his old friend's response told him he hadn't succeeded.

"What's wrong?" Lucas said sharply.

"Nothing. Why should anything be…" Damian cleared his throat. "I don't want to discuss it over the phone, but if you're busy—"

"I am not busy," Lucas said.

A lie, Damian was certain, but one he readily accepted.

Forty minutes later, the two men were pounding along the running track at the Eastside Club. At this hour of the day, they pretty much had the place to themselves.

Despite the privacy, they hadn't exchanged more than a dozen words. Damian knew Lucas was giving him the chance to start the conversation but he'd been content just to work up a sweat, first with the weights, then on the track.

There was nothing like a hard workout for getting rid of anger.

He'd learned that in the days when he'd been rebuilding Aristedes Shipping. There'd been times back then he'd deliberately gone from a meeting with the money men who held his destiny in their greedy hands to unloading cargo from a barge on the Aristedes docks.

Right now, he thought grimly, right now, he could use a ton of cargo.

"Damian."

More than that. Two tons of—

"Damian! Man, what're we doing? Working out, or trying for heart attacks?"

Damian blinked, slowed, looked around and saw Lucas standing in the middle of the track, head bent, hands on his thighs, dripping with sweat and panting.

And, *Thee mou,* so was he. How many miles had they run? How fast? Neither of them got like this doing their usual six-minute mile.

He stepped off the track, grabbed a couple of towels from a cart and tossed one to Lucas.

"Sorry, man."

"You should be," Lucas said, rubbing his face with the towel. He grinned. "Actually I didn't think an old man like you could move that fast."

Damian grinned back at him. "I'm two months older than you are, Reyes."

"Every day counts when you're pushing thirty-two."

Damian smiled. He draped the towel around his shoulders and he and Lucas strolled toward the locker room.

"Thank you," he said, after a minute.

Lucas shot his friend a look, thought about pretending he didn't know what he meant and decided honesty was the best policy.

"Para nada," he said softly. "The way you sounded,

I'd have canceled a meeting with the president." He pushed open the locker room door, then followed Damian inside. "You want to tell me what's going on?"

Damian hesitated. "Let's shower, change and stop for a drink."

"Here?"

He laughed at the horror in Lucas's voice. The Eastside Club had a bar. A juice bar.

"No. Not here. I'm old but not that old."

Lucas grinned. "I'm relieved to hear it. How about that place a couple of blocks over? The one with the mahogany booths?"

"Sounds good."

It was good.

The bar was dark, the way bars should be. The booths were deep and comfortable. The bartender was efficient and the Gray Goose on the rocks both men ordered was crisp and cold.

They were mostly quiet at first, Lucas talking about some land he was thinking of adding to his enormous ranch in Spain, Damian listening, nodding every now and then, saying "yes" and "really" when it seemed appropriate.

Then they fell silent.

Lucas finally cleared his throat. "So," he said quietly, "you okay?"

"I'm fine."

"Because, you know, you didn't sound—"

"Kay's sister turned up."

Lucas lifted his eyebrows. "I didn't know she had a—"

"Neither did I."

"Well. Her sister, huh? What's she want?"

"I think they were actually stepsisters. That's what Ivy—"

"The sister."

"Yes. That's what she said."

"Same mother?"

"Same father. I think. Same last name, anyway. Maybe he adopted one of them…" Damian huffed out a breath. "It doesn't matter."

"What does?"

"The rest of what this woman—Ivy—told me."

Damian lifted his glass and took a long swallow of vodka. Lucas waited a while before he spoke again.

"You want to explain what that means?"

"The rest?" Damian shrugged. He took another mouthful of vodka. Took a handful of cashews from the dish on the table. Looked around the room, then at Lucas. "The rest is that she's pregnant with my child."

If Lucas's jaw dropped any further, Damian figured it would have hit the table.

"Excuse me?"

"Yeah." Damian gave a choked laugh. "Impossible, right?"

Lucas snorted. "How about, insane?"

"I told her that. And—"

"And?"

"And, you're right. *I'm* right. It's impossible. Insane. There's just one problem." Damian took a deep breath and expelled it as his eyes met Lucas's. "She's telling the truth."

Damian explained everything.

Then, at Lucas's request, he explained it all over

again, starting with Ivy's unexpected visit to his apartment and finishing with his impossible dilemma.

Lucas listened, made an occasional comment in Spanish. Damian didn't always understand the words but he didn't have to.

The other man's reaction was just what his had been.

Finally Damian fell silent. Lucas started to speak, took a drink of vodka instead, then cleared his throat.

"I don't understand. Your mistress convinced Ivy to have a baby for her but didn't tell you about it. What was she going to do when the child was born? Bundle him up, carry him through the door and say, 'Damian, this is our son'?"

Damian nodded. "I don't get it, either, but Kay wasn't big on logic. For all I know, she never got that far in laying out her plan."

"And Ivy…" Lucas's eyes narrowed. "What sort of woman is she?"

A beautiful woman, Damian thought, tall and lithe as a tigress with eyes as green as new spring grass, hair shot with gold…

"She's attractive."

"I didn't mean that. What I'm asking is, what kind of woman would agree to be part of a scheme like that?"

Damian lifted his glass to his lips. "Another excellent question."

"A model, you say. So she must be good-looking."

"You could say that."

"A model's body is her bread and butter. Why would she put herself through a pregnancy?"

"I don't—"

"I do. For money, Damian. You're worth a fortune. She wants to tap into that."

"I offered her ten million dollars to have the baby and give up all rights to it. She said no."

"Ten million," Lucas said impatiently. "That's a fraction of what you're worth and I'd bet you anything the lady researched your worth to the nearest penny." He lifted his glass, found it empty and signaled for another round. "She's good-looking, and she's smart."

"So?"

"So, my friend, if she's smart, good-looking and devious as the devil, give some thought to the entire idea having been hers in the first place."

"No. It was Kay."

"Think about it, Damian. She knew your lover could not carry a child and so she planted this idea in your lover's head—"

"Don't keep calling Kay my lover," Damian said, more sharply than he'd intended. "I mean, technically, she was. But the fact is, we had an affair. A brief one. I was going to end it but she lied and said she was—"

"Yes. I know." Lucas paused until the barman had delivered their fresh drinks. Then he leaned over the table. "Ivy observed it all. She watched you do the right thing when her sister pretended to be pregnant." He sat back, looking grimly certain of his next words. "Absolutely, the more I think about it, the more certain I am that this plan was her idea."

"Ivy's?"

"*Si.* Who else am I talking about? She saw the way to get her hands on a lot of money. She would carry a child. You would not know about it but once it was born, you would once again do the right thing. You would accept it into your life, and you would pay her anything she asked. Billions, not a paltry few million, and she and Kay would be on easy street."

Damian ran the tip of his finger along the chill edge of the glass.

"It sounds," he said, "like it could almost work. The perfect plan." He looked up, his eyes as cold as his voice. "I didn't buy into Ivy's crap about doing this out of love for her sister but I couldn't come up with anything better, especially after she turned down the ten million."

"And so now, what will you do? What did you tell this woman?"

Damian shrugged. "What could I tell her?"

"That you would support her until the child is born. That you would support the child. Pay for his care. Send him to the best boarding schools…" Lucas frowned. "Why are you shaking your head?"

"Is that what you would do with a child of your own blood? Pay to keep him out of your life?"

"Yes, of course…" Lucas sighed and rubbed his hands over his face. "No," he said softly. "I would not. His arrival in the world would be a gift, no matter how it happened."

"Exactly." Damian reached for the fresh drink, changed his mind and signaled for their check. "So," he said, carefully avoiding eye contact, "I did the only thing I could. I told her I'd take her to Greece."

Lucas almost leaped across the table. "You told her what?"

"I can't stay in New York the next six months, Lucas. You know that."

"Yes, but—"

"I need to keep an eye on her. I don't know what

she's like. How she's treating this pregnancy. If she's anything like her sister…"

The barman handed him the leather folder that held the check; Damian opened it, took a quick look and handed the man a bill, indicated he should keep the change and began rising to his feet.

Lucas grabbed his arm.

"Wait a minute! I don't think you've thought this through."

"Believe me, I have."

"Damian. Listen. You take her to Greece, she's in your life. Right in the middle of your life, man! And you don't want that."

"You're right, I don't. But what choice do I have? She needs watching."

"You're playing into her hands."

"No way! She fought me, tooth and nail. I'm forcing her to do something she absolutely doesn't want to do."

"Aristedes, you're not thinking straight. Of course she wants to do it! A model who sold her body for another woman's use? Why would she do such a thing, huh?" Lucas's eyes narrowed. "I'll tell you why. For money. And now, with her sister out of the picture, the stakes are even higher."

Damian wanted to argue but how could he when he held those same convictions? And since that was the case, why did he feel his muscles knotting at Lucas's cold words?

"She's playing you like a Stradivarius, Damian."

"Perhaps," Damian said carefully. "But that doesn't change the facts. She's carrying my—"

"She can carry him here as well as in Greece. You want her watched? Hire a private investigator but for

God's sake, don't play into her hands. She's no good, Damian. The woman is an avaricious, scheming bitch."

"Don't call her that," Damian snapped.

Lucas looked at him as if he'd lost his mind. Hell, maybe he had. Lucas had just given a perfect description of Ivy…

Except for those brief moments she'd softened in his arms, let his mouth taste the sweetness of hers. Those moments when she'd responded to him…

Pretended to respond, he thought coldly, and forced a laugh.

"I'm joking," he said lightly. "You know that American expression? Apple pie, the flag, motherhood? You're supposed to show respect for all three."

Lucas didn't look convinced. "Just as long as it's a joke," he finally said.

Damian nodded. "It was. Thank you for worrying about me but trust me, Lucas. I know what I'm doing."

I know what I'm doing.

The words haunted him the rest of the day. At midnight, after tossing and turning, Damian rose from his bed, made a pot of coffee and took a cup out onto the terrace that wrapped around his apartment.

Did he really know what he was doing? He'd had mistresses and lovers but he'd never taken a woman to live with him.

Not that he proposed to do that with Ivy.

Moving her into one of the suites in his palace was hardly taking her to live with him. Still, was it necessary? He could hire someone to watch her, as Lucas suggested. He could hire a companion to live with her.

He almost laughed.

He could imagine Ivy's reaction to that. She'd confront the private detective, order the companion out the door. She had the beauty of Diana and the courage of Athena. It was one hell of a combination.

Wind tousled his hair. Damian shivered. The night was cold and he was wearing only a pair of black sweatpants. It was time to go inside. Or put on a sweatshirt.

Not just yet, though.

He loved New York, especially at night.

People said the city never slept but at this hour, especially on a weekday night, Central Park West grew quiet. Only a few vehicles moved along the street far below.

Was Lucas right? Had he handled this all wrong?

He could warn Ivy that any tendency she had to behave like her sister would result in severe penalties. A cut in allowance, for a start.

As for the child… Plenty of kids grew up without their fathers. He certainly had. Hell, he'd grown up without either parent, when you thought about it. His mother had been too busy jet-setting to one party after another to pay attention to him; his father had done exactly what *his* father had done, ignored him until he was old enough to send to boarding school.

He had survived, hadn't he?

Damian sipped at his coffee, gone cold and bitter.

As cold and bitter as Ivy Madison's heart?

It was a definite possibility. She might well have plotted and schemed, as Lucas insisted. For all he knew, she was out celebrating, knowing she was on her way to collecting the big prize, that he had demanded she go to Greece with him.

Out celebrating with whom?

Not that he gave a damn. It was just that the mother of his unborn child should not be out drinking or dancing or being with a man.

With a man. A faceless stranger, holding her. Kissing her. Taking her into his bed…

The cup fell from Damian's hand and shattered on the flagstone. He cursed, bent down, started scooping up the pieces…

"Son of a bitch," he snarled, and he opened the French doors and marched to his bedroom.

He dressed quickly. Jeans, a cashmere sweater, mocs and a leather bomber jacket. Then he snatched his keys from the dresser and took the elevator to the basement garage where he kept the big Mercedes as well as a black Porsche Carrera. He'd bought the car because he loved it, even though he rarely had the chance to use it.

The Carrera was a finely honed mass of energy and power.

Right now, so was he.

He'd felt that way since he first laid eyes on Ivy Madison. Who in hell was she to come out of nowhere and turn his existence upside down?

The streets were all but deserted. He made the fifteen-minute drive in half that time, pulled into a space marked No Parking on the corner of her block. The front door to her brownstone was not locked. Even if it had been, that wouldn't have stopped him.

Not tonight.

He took the three flights of steps in seconds, rang her doorbell, banged his fist on the door.

"Ivy!" He pounded the door again, called her name even louder. "Damn you, let me in!"

The door opened the inch the antitheft chain allowed.

Damian saw a sliver of dimly lighted room, a darkly lashed eye, a swath of gold-streaked hair.

"Are you crazy?" she snarled. "You'll wake the entire building!"

"Open the damned door!"

The door closed, locks and chain rattled and then the door swung open. Damian stepped inside and slammed it behind him. Ivy stared at him, hair disheveled, silk robe untied, feet bare.

She looked frightened, sleep-tossed and sexy.

The combination sent his already-racing heart into higher gear.

"Do you know what time it is?"

"The real question," he said roughly, "is, do you?"

He heard the flat challenge in his voice, saw her awareness of it reflected in the sudden catch of her breath.

"Have you been drinking?"

"Not enough."

He took a step forward. She took one back. "Your Highness…"

"I think it's time we stopped being so formal." Another step. His, followed by hers. "My name is Damian."

"Your Highness. Damian." The tip of her tongue swept across her bottom lip. He felt his entire body clench at the sight. "Damian, it's very late. Why don't we—why don't we talk tomorrow?"

One more step. Like that. And then her shoulders hit the wall.

"I'm done talking," he said, reaching for her. "And so are you."

"No! Get out. Damian! Get—"

"Isn't it amazing," he said softly, his eyes hot and locked to hers, "that I've seen a piece of paper that says you're pregnant with my child, I've had my hand on your belly." He caught a fistful of her robe, tugged her closer. "But I've never seen you."

"Of course you—"

"You," he said thickly. "Your body. How your breasts look, how your belly looks as your body readies itself for my son."

"Damian! I swear, I'll scream—"

Slowly he drew the robe open. Her eyes widened. Her lips parted. But she didn't scream. No. Oh, no. She didn't scream as he dropped his gaze and looked down at her.

She was wearing a cream-silk nightgown. Thin straps. Silk cups. Shirring over her midriff, then a long, slender fall of silk that ended just above her toes.

Damian's gaze lifted. His eyes swept her face. Her lips were still parted, her eyes still wide…

"Don't," she whispered.

But he did.

Slowly he hooked his fingers under the thin silk straps, Drew them down her arms.

Bared her breasts. Her beautiful breasts. Small. Round. Tipped with pale pink nipples that were already beading. Praxiteles, who had sculpted Aphrodite's beauty in marble, would have wept.

"Damian…"

"Shh," he whispered and cupped her breasts. Thumbed the delicate nipples. Ivy swayed unsteadily as he bent his head and touched his mouth to her nipples. Licked them. Sucked them. Felt his erection strain against his jeans.

"Damian," she said, the word a sigh. A moan. A plea.

He lifted his head. Her lashes had drooped against her cheeks. Her breasts rose and fell with her quickened breath.

Her eyes opened, locked on his face as he pulled the gown down, down, down her torso. Her hips. Her legs. Those long, long legs.

The gown was a chrysalis at her feet.

And she—she was more than beautiful. She was Aphrodite rising from the sea. She was every dream a man could have, and more.

And yes, her body was readying for his child.

He could see the delicate swell of her belly. The exquisite rounding. The burgeoning fullness.

Slowly he cupped her belly.

Felt the smoothness of her skin. The heat of it. The perfect arc of it beneath his palms.

He stroked one hand lower. Lower still. Watched her face, heard her moan as he slipped it between her thighs and God, God, she was hot, wet, sweetly swollen with need...

"Don't," she sighed, but her hands were on his chest. On his shoulders. She was on her toes, lifting herself to him, her mouth a breath from his.

She wanted this. Wanted him.

It was all he could do to keep from taking her down to the floor, unzipping his jeans, parting her thighs and burying himself deep inside her warmth...

Except, Lucas was right. It was all an act.

Damian let go of her. Picked up her robe, wrapped it around her shoulders. Trembling, panting, she clutched it to her.

"Do you remember what I told you this afternoon?"

The tip of her tongue slid along the seam of her mouth.

"You said—you said you were taking me to Greece."

He nodded, reminded himself of Lucas's advice and stepped back. "I've changed my mind."

"You mean, you'll let me stay here?" Her breath caught. If he hadn't known better, he'd have thought it was with relief.

Of course, that was what he meant. Certainly it was what he meant…

The hell it was, he thought, and pulled her into his arms.

"I mean," he said roughly, "that I'd be a fool to pay for your upkeep without getting anything in return."

"I don't understand."

"You will share my bed. You will give birth to my son. And if, in the intervening months, you have proven yourself sufficiently accomplished as my mistress, I will marry you, give you my name, my title…and permit you to be a mother to this child you claim to want for your own." He drew her closer. "If you haven't pleased me, I will keep my son, send you back to New York and you can fight me in the courts."

Time seemed to stand still. Then Ivy looked unflinchingly into his eyes.

"I hate you," she said, "hate you, hate you—"

Damian kissed her again and again mercilessly, fiercely, until, finally, she gave a little sob and melted against him.

Was that, too, part of the act?

It didn't matter.

"Hate me all you like, *glyka mou*. From this moment on, I own you."

CHAPTER SIX

A WOMAN identifying herself as Damian's personal assistant phoned at six and offered no apology for calling at such an early hour.

"Do you have a passport, Miss Madison?"

Ivy was tempted to say she didn't but what was the point? For all she knew, traveling with royalty meant doing away with passports.

"Yes. I have."

"In that case, please be ready to leave for Greece at eight-thirty. Promptly at eight-thirty," the P.A. said emphatically. "His Highness does not like to be kept waiting."

"Shall I stand at attention until he arrives?" Ivy said, trying to mask a sudden wave of fear with sarcasm.

It was a wasted effort. Ivy could almost see the woman's raised eyebrows.

"His driver will come for you, Miss Madison, not the prince himself."

"Of course he won't," Ivy said, and hung up the phone.

Damian Aristedes was not a man who would sully his hands with work. Not even when it came to making arrangements about a woman.

His assistant probably did this kind of thing all the time. Fly one woman to Greece, fly another to Timbuktu... The prince would expect a mistress to be available on demand.

He was in for a big surprise.

She would never become his mistress. She would never agree to become his anything, much less his wife—although that, obviously, had been a lie. A little bait to lure her into his bed.

Not that he'd need bait for most women.

Put him in a room with a dozen women, all beautiful enough to get any man they wanted, he'd have to fight them off. All that macho. The aura of power. The beautiful, masculine face; the hard-bodied good looks...

The prince would collect lovers with disquieting ease.

But she would not be one of them.

Getting sexually involved with a man was not on the list of things Ivy wanted to do with her life. And if that ever changed—and she couldn't imagine that it would—she would choose someone who was Damian's opposite.

She'd want a lover who was gentle, not authoritative. Caring, not commanding. A man whose touch would be nonthreatening.

The prince's touch was not like that.

Each caress left her shaken. Trembling. Feeling as if she were standing on the edge of a precipice and one more step would send her plunging to the rocks below...

Or soaring into a hot, sun-bleached sky.

Ivy let out a breath. Enough of this. There was more than an hour to go until the prince's driver came for her.

Plenty of time to get ready. Too much time, really. The last thing she wanted was to think about what lay ahead.

Ivy brewed a cup of ginger tea. She sat in a corner of the wide windowsill, shivering a little in the cool dawn hours as she sipped her tea and wondered how long it would be until she sat here again.

Soon, she promised herself. Soon.

At seven, she packed, showered and dressed. She was ready long before Damian's driver rang the bell.

He was polite.

So was she.

The big Mercedes rolled silently through the busy Manhattan streets. Ivy looked out through the dark glass at people going about their everyday lives and wondered why she'd let this happen. She didn't have the money for a good attorney but she knew lots of people in high places. Surely someone could help her…

Then she remembered what had started all this. She had agreed to have this baby and Damian Aristedes was the child's father.

She had no choice but to do as he wished.

It was the right thing, for Kay's memory, for the baby…

"Miss?"

Ivy looked up. The car had stopped; the driver stood beside her open door.

"We're here, miss."

"Here" was a place she'd been before. Kennedy Airport, a part of it that was home to private jets.

She'd been a passenger in private planes going to and

from photo shoots in exotic locations. The planes were often big, but she'd never seen a noncommercial aircraft the size of the one ahead of her.

Sunlight glinted off the shiny aluminum wings, danced on the fuselage and the discreet logo emblazoned there. A shield. A lance. An animal of some kind, bulky and somehow dangerous, even in repose.

"Miss Madison?"

A courteous steward led her to the plane. He had that same logo on the pocket of his dark blue jacket and she realized it was a crest. A royal crest, for the royal house of Aristedes.

What are you doing, Ivy? What in the world are you doing?

She stumbled to a halt. The steward looked at her. So did Damian's driver, who was carrying her suitcase to the plane.

Someone else was looking at her, too, from inside the cabin. She couldn't see him but she knew he was there, watching her through cool eyes, seeing her hesitate, assessing it as a sign of weakness.

She would never show weakness to him!

Ivy took a breath and walked briskly up the steps that led into the plane.

It was cool inside the cabin. Luxurious, too. The walls were pale cream; the seats and small sofas soft-looking tan leather. Thick cream carpet stretched the length of the fuselage to a closed door in the rear.

And, yes, Damian was already there, sitting in one of the leather chairs, not looking at her but, instead, reading a page from the sheaf of papers stacked on the table in front of him.

"Miss Madison, sir," the steward said.

Damian raised his head.

Ivy stood straighter, automatically taking on the cool look she'd made famous in myriad ads and magazine covers.

She had deliberately taken time with her appearance this morning. At first, she'd thought she'd wear jeans and a ratty jacket she kept for solitary walks on chill winter mornings, just to show the prince how little all his wealth and grandeur meant.

She'd known, instinctively, he'd have a private plane. Men like him wouldn't fly in commercial jets.

Then she'd thought, no, far better to make it clear nothing he owned, nothing he was, could intimidate her. So she'd dressed in cashmere and silk under a glove-leather black jacket she'd picked up after a shoot in Milan the prior year.

She needn't have bothered.

Damian barely glanced at her, nodded curtly and went back to work.

It angered her, which was ridiculous. It was good, wasn't it, that he had no intention of pretending this was a social occasion?

She nodded back and started past him. His arm shot out, blocking her way.

"You will sit here," he said.

"Here" was the leather chair next to his.

"I prefer a seat further back."

"I don't recall asking your preference."

His tone was frigid. It made her want to slap his face but she wasn't fool enough to do that again. Far better to save her energy for the battles ahead, instead of wasting it on minor skirmishes.

Ivy sat down. The hovering steward cleared his throat.

"May I bring you something after we reach cruising altitude, madam? Coffee, perhaps, or tea?"

"No coffee," Damian said, without lifting his head. "No tea. No alcohol. Ms. Madison may have mineral water or juice, as she prefers."

Ivy felt her face flame. Why didn't he simply announce her pregnancy to the world? But if he was trying to lure her into all-out war, he was going to be disappointed.

"How nice," she said calmly, "to be given a choice, even if it's a minor one."

Damian looked up. Waited. His mouth gave a perfunctory twitch. "Should Thomas take that to mean you don't want anything?"

"What I want," she said matter-of-factly, "is my freedom, but I doubt if Thomas can provide that."

The steward's eyes widened. Damian's face darkened. For a second, no one moved or spoke. Then Damian broke the silence.

"That will be all, Thomas." He waited until the steward was gone. Then he turned to Ivy. "That is the last time I will tolerate that," he said in a low voice.

"Tolerate what, Your Highness? The truth?"

His hand closed on her wrist, exerting just enough pressure to make her gasp.

"You will show me the proper respect in front of people or—"

"Or what?"

His eyes narrowed. "Try me and find out."

A shudder went through her but she kept her gaze steadily on his until he finally let go of her, turned away and began reading through the papers spread in front of him again.

Ivy drew a deep, almost painful breath.

She would get through this. She'd survived worse. Far worse. Things that had happened long ago, that she wanted to forget but couldn't…

That had made her strong.

The mighty prince didn't know it, but he would learn just how strong she was.

When they were airborne, the steward, brave man, appeared with both juice and water as well as a stack of current magazines. Ivy thanked him, leafed through one and then another, blind to the glossy pages, thinking only about what lay ahead.

And about what Damian had said last night.

She'd refused to dwell on it then but now, after this display of power, his words haunted her.

From now on, he'd said, *I own you.*

She thought—she really thought he might believe it. That he had bought her. That she would go to his bed. That she would do whatever he commanded, become the perfect sex slave.

Let him kiss her breasts, as he had so shockingly done yesterday.

Let him undress her. Stand her, naked, before him.

Let him take her in his arms, gather her tightly against him while his aroused flesh pulsed against her.

Let him do all the things men did to women, things men wanted and women surely despised…except, she hadn't despised what Damian did last night.

When he'd touched her. Held her. Kissed her. Parted her lips with his…

Tasted her, let her taste him.

Ivy turned blindly to the window.

The baby. She had to think about the baby. That was all that mattered.

* * *

It grew dark outside the plane.

The cabin lights dimmed.

She yawned. Yawned again. Tumbled into darkness… And shot awake to see Damian leaning over her.

"What—what are you doing?"

His mouth twitched. She'd seen that little movement of his lips enough to know he was trying not to smile.

"Did you think I was going to ravish you while you slept?" This time, the smile he'd repressed broke through. "I'm not a fool, *glyka mou*. When I make love to you, I want you fully awake in my arms."

She was too tired to think of a clever response. Or maybe he was too close, his fallen angel's face an inch from hers.

"I was going to adjust your seat," he said softly. "So that you could lie back while you were sleeping."

"I wasn't sleeping."

"While you were resting, then," he said, with another of those heart-stopping little smiles. "Here. Let me—"

He leaned closer. All she had to do was turn her face a fraction of an inch and her mouth would find his.

Ivy jerked back. "Don't you ever get tired of giving orders?"

"Don't you ever get tired of ignoring good advice?" He shifted his weight. The little distance she'd put between them disappeared. "We have hours left before we land."

"So?"

"So, you're exhausted."

"And you know this, how? You read cards? Palms? Crystal balls?"

His smile tilted. "Unless I'm mistaken, you slept as little as I did last night."

She wanted to ask him why he hadn't slept. Was it because he was sorry he'd demanded she go with him? Or was it—was it because he'd lain in the dark, imagining what it would be like if they had made love? If, together, they'd made the baby growing inside her?

Did what she'd just thought show on her face? Was that why his eyes had suddenly darkened?

"And," he said, very softly, "you're pregnant."

Amazing. They had discussed her pregnancy in excruciating—if not entirely accurate—detail. Still, the way he said the word now, his husky whisper intimate and sexy, made her heartbeat stumble.

"I see. Now you're an expert on pregnant women." She spoke quickly, saying the first thing that came into her head in a desperate effort to defuse the situation, and knew in an instant she'd made a mistake.

A mask seemed to drop over his face.

"What little I know about pregnancy," he said, drawing away from her, "comes courtesy of Kay. Your sister used endless ploys to convince me she was carrying my child."

"Kay wasn't my real sister," Ivy said, and wondered why it suddenly seemed important he understand that.

"Yes. You said you were stepsisters. The same last name... Then, your mother married her father and he adopted you?"

Why had she brought this up? "Yes."

"How old were you?"

"It's not important."

She turned away from him but he cupped her jaw, his touch firm but light.

"I have the right to know these things."

She supposed he did. And he could learn them easily enough. Anything more than that, she had no intention of sharing.

"I was ten. Kay was fourteen."

"She told me her father died when she was sixteen. Another lie?"

"No." Ivy laced her hands in her lap. "He died two years after my mother married him. They both died, he and my mother. It was a freak accident, a helicopter crash in Hawaii. They were on vacation, on a tour."

"I am sorry, *glyka mou*. That must have been hard for you."

She nodded.

"So, who took care of you then? What happened?"

Everything, Ivy thought, oh God, everything...

"Nothing," she said airily. "Well, Kay and I went into foster care. When she turned eighteen, she got a job and a place of her own."

"And you went with her?"

"No." Ivy bit her lip. "I stayed in foster care."

"And?"

And my world changed, forever.

But she didn't say that. Her life was none of his business, and that was exactly what she told him.

"The only part of my life that concerns you," she said sharply, "is my pregnancy."

Ivy expected one of those cold commands that were his specialty or, at least, an argument. Instead, to her surprise, Damian gave her a long, questioning look. Then he turned away and pressed the call button.

The steward appeared as quickly as if he were conjured up from Aladdin's lamp.

"We would like dinner now, Thomas," Damian said. "Broiled salmon. Green salad with oil and vinegar. Baked potatoes."

"Of course, Your Highness."

He was doing it again. Thinking for her. Speaking about her as if she were incapable of speaking for herself. It made her angry and that was good.

Anger was a safer emotion than whatever Damian had made her feel a little while ago.

"I'm not hungry," Ivy said sharply.

Nobody answered. Nobody even looked at her.

"I'll have a glass of Riesling first, Thomas. And please bring Ms. Madison some Perrier and lemon."

"I do not want—"

"No lemon in the Perrier? Of course. No lemon, Thomas. *Neh?*"

"Certainly, sir."

Ivy smoldered but kept silent until they were alone. Then she swung angrily toward Damian, who was calmly putting the documents he'd been reading into a leather briefcase.

"Do you have a hearing problem? I said I wasn't hungry!"

"You are eating for two."

"That's outmoded nonsense!"

"If you are vain enough to wish to starve yourself—"

"I am not starving myself!"

"Ŏhi," Damian said evenly. "That is correct. You are not. I will not permit it."

"Damn it," Ivy snarled, letting her anger rise, embracing it, reminding herself that she hated this man, that it would be dangerous to let any other emotion come into play where he was concerned, "I don't even understand what you're saying. Since when does 'no' mean 'yes' and 'okay' mean 'no'?"

He looked blank. Then he chuckled. "It's not 'no,' it's *'neh.'* It means 'yes.' And I didn't say 'okay,' I said *ŏhi,* which means 'no.'"

Yes was no. No was yes. Would a white rabbit pop out of the carpet next?

"I shall arrange for a tutor to teach you your new language, *glyka mou.*"

"My language is English," she said, despising the petulance in her own voice.

"Your new home is Greece."

"No. It isn't. My home is the place you took me from. That will always be my home, and I'll never let you forget it." She glared at him, her breath coming quickly, furious at him, at herself, at what was happening, what she had brought down on herself. "And if you really think I'd starve myself and hurt my baby—"

"My baby," he said coldly, all the ease of the last moments gone. "Not yours."

The true answer, the one she longed to give him, feared to give him, danced on the tip of her tongue. He claimed he hadn't loved Kay, but Kay had sworn he had. There were too many lies, too many layers of them to risk the one truth that might tear the whole web asunder.

Far too much risk.

So Ivy bit back what she'd come close to saying. Damian filled the silence with yet another order.

"You will eat properly. And you will not contradict me in front of my people. Is that clear?"

"Do I have to genuflect in your presence, too?"

No telltale twitch of his lips this time, only a cold glare.

"If you feel you must, by all means, do so."

He turned away. So did she. There seemed nothing more to say.

They ate in silence.

Ivy tried to pretend disinterest in her food but she was ravenous. Had she eaten anything since her first confrontation with Damian? She couldn't remember.

The steward cleared their tables and brought dessert. Two crystal flutes filled with fresh strawberries, topped with a dollop of cream. She could, at least, make a stand here.

"I never eat whipped cream," she said with lofty determination.

"I'm happy to hear it because this is crème fraîche."

Hadn't she promised herself she wouldn't try to fight him on little things? Crème fraîche was absolutely a little thing, wasn't it?

Little, and delicious. She ate every berry, every bit of the cream…

And felt Damian's gaze on her.

His eyes—hot, intense, almost black with passion— were riveted to her mouth as she licked the last bit from the spoon.

A wave of heat engulfed her; a choked sound broke from her throat. He heard it, lifted his gaze to hers…

The cabin door slid open. Thomas appeared, looked quickly from his master to Ivy…

Ivy sprang to her feet. "Where's the—where is the lavatory, please?"

"In the back, miss. I can show you…"

"I can find it myself, thank you," she said.

And fled.

* * *

They were flying through a black sky lit by a sliver of ivory moon.

Damian had the light on. There were papers in his lap but he wasn't looking at them. Ivy had a magazine in hers but she wasn't looking at it, either.

She was trying to stay awake. Trying to stay awake…

To her horror, she gave a jaw-creaking yawn.

"If you were tired," Damian said coolly, "which, of course, you are not, you could recline your seat and close your eyes."

She went on ignoring him. And yawned. Yawned again…

Her eyelids drooped. A minute, that was all she needed. Just a minute with her eyes shut…

She jerked upright. Her head was on Damian's shoulder. Flustered, she pulled away.

"You are the most stubborn woman in the world. Damn it, what will you prove by not sleeping?"

"I told you, I'm not—"

"Oh, for heaven's sake…" His arm closed around her shoulders. She protested; he ignored her and drew her to his side. "Close your eyes."

"You can't order someone to—"

"Yes," he said firmly, "I can." His arm tightened around her. "Go to sleep." His tone softened. "I promise, I'll keep you safe."

Safe? How could she feel safe in the embrace of this imperious stranger?

And yet—and yet, she did. Feel safe. Warm. Content to lean her head against his hard shoulder. To feel the soft brush of his lips on her temple.

Strong arms closed around her. Lifted her, carried her

through the dark cabin. Lay her down gently on a wide, soft bed.

Was she dreaming?

"Yes," a husky voice whispered, "you are dreaming. Why not give yourself up to the dream?"

It wasn't a dream. The bed was real. The voice was Damian's. And she was in Damian's arms, her body pressed to the length of his.

"I won't sleep with you," she heard herself whisper.

He gave a soft laugh. "You are sleeping with me right now, *glyka mou*," he whispered back, though that term he used for her, whatever it meant, sounded somehow different. Softer. Sweeter…

Sweet as the whisper of his mouth over hers, again and again until she sighed and let her lips cling to his for one quick, transcendent moment.

"You are killing me, *glyka mou*," he said thickly. "But sleep is all we'll share tonight." Another kiss, another gruff whisper. "I want you wide-awake when we make love."

"Never," Ivy heard herself whisper.

She felt his lips curve against hers in a smile.

"Go to sleep," he said.

After that, there was only darkness.

CHAPTER SEVEN

IN THE earliest hours of the morning, Damian's plane landed on his private airstrip on Minos.

The intercom light blinked on; the machine gave a soft beep. "We have arrived, Your Highness," the steward's voice said politely.

"*Efharisto,* Thomas."

Ivy didn't stir. She'd been asleep in Damian's arms for almost two hours, her head tucked into the curve of his shoulder.

By now, his shoulder ached but he wouldn't have moved her for anything in the world.

How could sleeping with a woman, sleeping with her in the most literal sense of the word, feel so wonderful?

Damian turned his head, breathing in Ivy's scent. Silky strands of her hair brushed against his lips. He closed his eyes and thought about staying here with her, just like this, until she awakened.

Impossible, of course.

They had to return to reality eventually. It might as well be now.

But he could wake her quietly. Show her that every moment they were together didn't have to be a battle.

Gently he rolled her onto her back, bent to her and kissed her.

"Kalimera," said softly.

Ivy sighed and he kissed her again.

"Ivy," he whispered. "Wake up. We're home."

Her lashes fluttered open to reveal eyes were dark, still clouded with sleep.

"Damian?"

His name was soft on her lips. She'd never spoken it that way before, as if he and she were alone in the universe.

"Yes, it's me, sweetheart. Did you sleep well?"

"I don't—I don't remember. How did we…?"

Her eyes widened and he knew she'd realized she was not only in his arms but in his bed. He'd watched Lucas taming a mare once; that same wild look had come into the animal's eyes.

"Easy," he said.

"What am I doing in this bed?"

"Sleeping. Nothing more than that."

"But—how did I get here? I don't remember…"

"I carried you. You were exhausted."

She closed her eyes. When she opened them again, they were cool. "Let me up."

"In a minute."

"Damian—"

"Do you see what sleeping in my arms has accomplished?" He smiled. "You've begun calling me Damian."

She started to answer. He kissed her instead. She didn't respond. But he went on kissing her, his mouth moving lightly over hers, and just when he thought it would never happen, she sighed and parted her lips to his.

The joining of their mouths was tender.

The need that swept through him was not.

His erection was instantaneous and he groaned and shifted his weight to accommodate the ache of his hardened flesh. Ivy shifted, too…and he found himself cradled between her parted thighs.

She gasped into his mouth.

His blood thundered.

Now, it said, take her now…

Beep. "Sir? Will you be deplaning, or shall I tell the pilot to leave the electrical system on?"

That was all it took to destroy the fragile moment. Ivy tore her mouth from Damian's. Her face was flushed, her lips full and heated from his kisses. He wanted to cup her face, kiss her into submission…

Instead he rolled away and rose from the bed. She did, too, but as she got to her feet, he scooped her into his arms.

"I can walk."

"It's dark outside."

"I can see."

"I know the terrain. You don't."

A Jeep and driver waited on the side of the runway. His driver was well-trained. Either that, or the arrival of his employer with a woman in his arms was not an unusual event.

Ivy was not as casual. She saw the driver and buried her face in Damian's throat.

The feel of her mouth on his skin, the warmth of her breath… He loved it almost as much as the feel of her in his arms during the short drive to his palace, perched on the ancient, long-dormant volcanic summit of Minos.

The palace was lit softly in anticipation of his arrival. He wondered what Ivy would think of his home when she saw it tomorrow by daylight. He'd learned that most people envisioned a palace as an imposing edifice of stone.

His home, if you could call a palace a home, was built of marble. The oldest part of it dated to the fourth century, another wing to the sixth, and the balance to the early 1600s. It was an enormous, sprawling, overblown place…

But he loved it.

Would Ivy? Not that it mattered, of course, but if she lived here with him, if, after his son's birth, she became his—she became his—

The huge bronze doors swung open, revealing his houseman, Esias. Despite the hour, Esias was formally dressed.

Damian had given up trying to break him of the habit. Esias had served his grandfather, his father and now him. How could you argue with an icon—an icon who was as determined as the Jeep's driver not to show surprise at seeing his master with a woman in his arms.

"Welcome home, Your Highness."

"Esias."

"May I, ah, may I help you with—"

"I am fine, thank you."

"Damian," Ivy snapped. "My God, put me—"

"Soon."

Trailed by Esias, he carried her up a wide, curving marble staircase to the second floor, then down the corridor that led to his rooms.

Esias stepped forward and opened the door.

"Efharisto," Damian said. "That is all, Esias. I'll see you in the morning."

The houseman inclined his head and moved back. Damian carried Ivy through the door and shouldered it shut, and the silence of the room closed around them.

"Who was that?"

He was alone with his mistress and the first words out of her mouth were not the ones a man ached to hear...

But then, Ivy wasn't his mistress.

Not yet.

"Damian. Who was—"

He answered by kissing her. She tried to turn her face away but he was persistent. He kept kissing her, nipped gently at her bottom lip and, at last, she made a little sound and opened her mouth to his.

He slipped the tip of his tongue between her parted lips. She jerked back. Then she made that sweet little whisper again and accepted the intimate caress. Accepted and returned it as he carried her through the sitting room, through the bedroom, to his bed.

Pleasure coursed through him.

What had happened in the darkness of the plane had changed everything. Had she realized she couldn't fight him or herself? That she wanted him as much as he wanted her?

God knew, he wanted her. From the minute she'd turned up at his door, despite everything, his anger, hell, his rage...

No woman had ever stirred such hunger in him.

Gently he lay her down in the silk-covered bed. Moonlight, streaming through the French doors behind it, touched her hair with silver. Her eyes, brighter than the stars, glittered as she looked up at him.

"Ivy," he said softly. He bent to her. Kissed her

temples. Her mouth. Her throat. Whispered in Greek what he would do to her, with her...

What she would feel as he made her his.

"Damian?"

Her whisper was soft. Uncertain. It had an innocence to it that he knew was a lie but it suited the way she was looking at him, the way her hands had come up to press lightly against his chest.

A little game could be exciting, though she excited him enough just as she was. He was almost painfully hard. It would not be easy to go as slowly as he wanted, this first time, but he would try.

Her dress had a row of tiny buttons down the bodice. He undid them slowly, even as her hands caught at his, and he paused to kiss each bit of warm, rosy skin he exposed.

She was breathing fast; the glitter in her eyes had become almost feverish.

"Damian," she whispered. "Please..."

He kissed her, harder this time, deeper, and she moved against him. Yes God, yes. Like that. Just like that...

Her bra opened in the front. He sent up a silent prayer of thanks as he undid the clasp, let the silk cups fall open...

And groaned.

She was exquisite.

She had small, perfect breasts crowned by pale pink nipples. It had almost driven him insane, touching them that one time...

"Damian! Stop."

She was moving against him again. It was too much. If she kept lifting herself to him this way, he would—

"Stop!"

He didn't hear her. Or yes, he heard her voice but her words had no meaning as he drew one nipple deep into his mouth—

Something slammed into his chest. He jerked back. It was Ivy's fist; even as he watched, she swung at him again. Stunned, he grabbed her wrists.

"What the hell are you doing?"

"Get—off—me!"

She was crying. And yes, moving against him, not in passion but in an attempt to free herself of his weight.

He sat up, stunned, disbelieving. She scrambled away from him and shot to her feet, clutching the open bodice of her dress, staring at him as if he were a monster.

"Don't touch me!"

"Don't touch you? But—"

"I told you I didn't want to come here. I told you I would not be your—your sex toy. And now—now, the minute we're alone in this—this kingdom you rule, you start—you start pawing me."

Pawing her? She had clung to him. Kissed him. Looked into his eyes with desire and now…

And now, it was time to up the ante. Make the game more interesting because she knew damned well he could always toss in his cards and walk away from the table.

He wanted to throw her back down on the rumpled bed, pin her arms over her head, force her thighs apart and finish what she had started, but she would not reduce him to that.

For all he knew, that was exactly what she wanted.

He snarled a name at her, one he'd never called any

woman. Then he turned on his heel, strode through the suite, into the hall and slammed the door behind him.

Lucas had called it right. First Kay had played him for a sucker. Now Ivy was doing it. And he, fool that he was, had let it happen.

She was only a woman. A pretty face, a ripe body. God knew, there were plenty of those in his life. Yes, she carried his child but he knew damned well she hadn't done it out of love for her sister.

She'd done it for money. Lots of it, probably. And then fate had intervened, taken Kay out of the picture, and Ivy would have seen that whatever Kay had promised her could be increased a hundredfold, a thousandfold, if she played the game right.

The lock clicked.

Panagia mou! She had locked the door against him. Locked *his* door against him. To hell with that. If she thought he'd put up with such crap, she needed to learn a lesson.

Starting right now.

He took a step back, aimed his foot at the door...

"Sir?"

Damian whirled around. "Get the hell out of here, Esias!"

His houseman stood his ground, no emotion showing on his face as if it were perfectly normal to find his master about to kick down the door of his own sitting room.

"I am sorry to disturb you, Your Highness, but your office in Athens is trying to reach you. They say it is urgent."

Esias held out the telephone. Damian glared at it. What did he give a damn for his office in Athens? Except—except, it was the middle of the night.

The bitch laughing at him behind that door was only one woman. He could deal with her at his leisure. But if there was a problem in Athens, it could affect the hundreds of people who worked for him.

He held out his hand and Esias gave him the phone.

An Aristedes supertanker had run aground on a reef in South America. Oil might begin oozing into the ocean at any moment.

Damian tossed the phone to Esias. "Wake my pilot," he snapped. "Tell him—"

"I have taken the liberty of doing so. The helicopter will be ready when you get there."

"Thank you."

"You are welcome, Your Highness." The houseman paused and looked at the closed door. "Ah, is there anything else, sir?"

"Yes," Damian said coldly. "The lady's name is Ivy Madison. Make her comfortable, but under no circumstances is she to leave this island."

Two days later, the crisis in South America had been resolved and Damian was on his way back to Minos.

It had been a hard, exhausting couple of days but it had given him time to calm down.

If he hadn't been called away…

No, he thought, staring at the ocean swells far below the fast-moving helicopter, no, he wouldn't think about that. Ivy had deliberately taken him to the brink of self-control.

He was certain of it.

But he hadn't let her push him over the edge. And there was no chance it would happen again.

Two days in Athens. Two days away from temptation.

Two days of rational thought and he'd come to a decision.

He'd made a mistake, bringing her to Minos. As for the rest, telling her he'd make her his mistress, that he might marry her…

Damian shook his head. Crazy. Or perhaps crazed was a better way to put it.

Why would he have even considered making her his mistress? All the emotional baggage that went into an arrangement like that? No way. The world was full of beautiful women. He surely didn't need this particular one.

As for marriage… Crazy, for sure. He wasn't marrying anybody. Not for years to come, if at all. And when that time came, assuming it did, *he* would choose his own wife, not let her choose him.

Because that was what had been going on. How come he hadn't seen it right away?

Like her sister, Ivy had been angling for marriage from the start. She was just cleverer about it. An ambush, instead of a head-on attack. That way, the target didn't stand a chance.

Her weapon had been the oldest one in the world. Sex. What could be more powerful in the hands of a beautiful woman, especially if a man was vulnerable?

And he sure as hell was vulnerable. He hadn't had a woman for months. Damian's jaw tightened. But he would, very soon.

Late last night, once he was sure the South American situation was under control, he'd phoned a French actress he'd met a few weeks ago. A couple of minutes of conversation and the upshot was, he'd fly to Paris next weekend.

She was looking forward to it, she'd purred.

So was he.

A long weekend in bed with the actress and Ivy would be forgotten. Hell, he'd forgotten her already...

"Your Highness?"

How long had the pilot's voice been buzzing in his headset? Damian cleared his throat.

"Yes?"

"Touchdown in a couple of minutes, sir."

"Thank you."

They were flying lower now, skimming over a group of small islands that were part of the Cyclades, as was Minos, but these bits of land were uninhabited, as beautiful as they were wild.

Back in the days he'd had time for such things, he'd sailed a Sunfish here and explored them. Sometimes, making his way through the tall pines that clung to them, he'd half expected to come face-to-face with one of the ancient gods his people had once worshipped.

Or one of the goddesses. Aphrodite. Artemis. Helen of Troy. Not a goddess, no, but a woman whose beauty had brought a man to his knees.

Ivy had almost done that to him, but fate had intervened.

A man could come to his senses, given breathing room.

The helicopter settled onto its landing pad. Damian slapped the pilot on the shoulder with his thanks and got out, automatically ducking under the whirring blades as he ran to the Jeep, parked where he'd left it two nights ago. It was six in the morning. He was tired, unshaven and he couldn't recall when he'd showered last. Added to that, he was hungry enough to eat shoe leather.

But all that would wait. Dealing with Ivy was more important. He wanted her off his island, and fast.

Yes, he thought, as the Jeep bounced along the narrow road, she was carrying his child. And yes, she needed watching. He knew that, better than before.

But he didn't have to be the one doing the watching. She'd said that herself. Of course, he knew now that she hadn't said it in hopes he'd listen. Just the opposite: she'd wanted to lure him into doing exactly what he'd done.

The funny thing was, it might have been the one true thing to come out of her mouth.

That soft, beautiful, treacherous mouth.

Damn it, what did that have to do with anything? Who gave a damn about her mouth or any other part of her anatomy except her womb?

He'd contact his lawyers. Have them make arrangements to set her up in a place of her own. Have them organize round-the-clock coverage of her and her apartment.

Until his son was born, he would regulate who she saw, what she did, every breath she took. But not in New York City.

Damian smiled coldly as he took the Jeep through a hairpin turn.

He'd keep a watch on her from a much closer vantage point.

Athens.

She would give birth here, in his country, where his peoples' laws, where his nationality and his considerable leverage, would apply.

She wouldn't like it—and that, he had to admit, was part of the reason the plan gave him so much pleasure.

* * *

He entered the palace through a secret door some ancestor had added in the fifteenth century so he could spy on a cheating wife, or so the story went.

He had no desire to go through the usual polite morning moves— *Good morning, sir. Good morning, Esias.* Or Elena, or Jasper, or Aeneas, or any of the half dozen others on the household staff.

The only person he wanted to see was Ivy. He'd ring for a cup of coffee. Then he'd have her brought to him so he could tell her what would happen next.

She'd moved into one of the guest suites. Esias had phoned to tell him that within an hour of his reaching his office. It had been well before he'd come to his senses and, for a wild moment, he'd imagined returning to Minos, storming into her suite, tumbling her back on the bed and finishing what had started before he'd had to leave for Athens.

Thank God, he hadn't.

He didn't want to carry through on the threat he'd made in New York, either. He didn't want to own her, only to get rid of her. So what if, despite his newfound sanity, he could still remember the smell of her skin? The sweetness of her mouth? The taste of her nipples?

Damian stopped halfway up the stairs. Stop it, he told himself angrily. There was nothing special about Ivy. Another few days and he'd be with a woman who would not play games, who would not stir him to frustration and madness.

Who wouldn't sigh the way Ivy did, when he kissed her. Or whisper his name as if it were music. Or fall asleep in his arms, as if he were keeping her safe…

"Damn it, Aristedes," he said under his breath, and opened the door to his suite…

And saw Ivy, standing with her back to him…

Waiting for him.

His heart turned over, and he knew everything he'd told himself the last two days were lies.

The truth was, he wanted this woman more than he wanted his next breath—and she wanted him, too. Why else would she be here, waiting for his return?

He said her name and she swung to face him. His heart began to race. There was no artifice in her expression. Whatever she told him next would be the truth.

"Damian. You're here."

"Yes," he said softly, "and so are you."

"I—I heard the helicopter. And—and I went downstairs and asked Esias if you were coming and he said—he said yes, you were returning to Minos. And when he told me that, I felt—"

She was hurrying the words, rushing them together and he understood. It wouldn't be easy to admit she'd been teasing him, that the teasing was over.

"You don't have to explain."

"But I do. I owe you that. I know—I know you think what I did the other night—that I did it deliberately, but—"

He closed the distance between them, caught her wrists and brought her hands to his lips.

"It was a game. I understand. But it's over with. No more games, Ivy. From now on, we'll be honest with each other, *neh?*"

She nodded. "Yes. Absolutely honest."

Damian brought her hands to his chest. "Let me shower. Then we'll have some breakfast. And then—"

His voice roughened. "And then, sweetheart, I'll show you how much I want you. How good it will be when we make love."

Ivy jerked her hands from his. "What?"

He grinned. "You're right. No breakfast. Just a quick shower…" His gaze dropped to her mouth, then rose again. "You can shower with me," he whispered. "Would you like that?"

"You have no idea what I'm talking about!"

"I do, *kardia mou*. You want to apologize for—"

"Apologize?" Her voice rose in disbelief. "Apologize? For what?"

"For the other night," he said carefully. "For teasing me—"

"Teasing you?" She stared at him; for a second, he wondered if he were speaking Greek instead of English. "Are you crazy?"

Damian's mouth narrowed. "It would seem that one of us is."

"You—you tried to take advantage of me the other night. And now—now, my God, you're so full of yourself that you think—that you think… Do you really think I waited here to beg you to take me to bed?" Ivy lifted her hand and poked her forefinger into the center of his chest. "I waited here to tell you that I am going home!"

"You came to my rooms, waited for me, all so you could tell me you're leaving Minos?"

Damian's voice was low and ugly. It made Ivy's heart leap.

Nothing was going the way she'd planned.

She'd expected him to be sharp with her. That would be her cue to tell him that it was illogical for them to spend the next six months in lock-step. What had happened the other night was proof they couldn't get along.

Why torture each other when it wasn't necessary?

She would go home. And she would agree to give him visiting rights to his son.

That was what she'd intended to tell him, but Damian had misunderstood everything. She'd waited in his rooms because she wanted this meeting to be private. She'd approached him in a conciliatory fashion because getting him angry would serve no purpose.

It had all backfired, and now he was looking at her the way a spider would look at a fly.

All right. She'd try again.

"Perhaps I should explain why I waited for you here."

"There's no need. I know the reason."

"I did it because—"

"Because you thought, perhaps I overplayed my hand. Perhaps my performance the other night convinced him to get rid of me."

"It wasn't a performance!"

"And then, because you're so very clever, so very good at this, you thought, yes, but if I say it first, if I tell him I want to leave, it will probably make him anxious to keep me."

"You're wrong! I never—"

She cried out as he caught hold of her and lifted her to her toes.

"The stakes are higher now, *neh?* Whatever Kay promised you as payment for your role in this ugly scheme—"

"She didn't promise me anything!"

"Perhaps not. Perhaps you thought to wait until my

son was in my arms before you asked for money." His fingers bit into her flesh. "But fate dealt you a better card."

"Can't you get it through your thick skull that not everything is about you?"

"You're wrong. This is all about me. My fortune. My title." His mouth twisted. "And the sweetener you keep dangling in front of my nose."

Before she could pull away, he kissed her, savaging her mouth, forcing her head back. Ivy stood immobile. Then memory and fear overwhelmed her and she sank her teeth into his lip.

He jerked back, tasting blood.

Slowly, deliberately, he wiped it away with the back of his hand.

"Be careful, *glyka mou*. My patience is wearing thin."

"You can't do this!"

"You are in my country. I can do anything I damned well please."

He let go of her, picked up the nearest telephone and punched a key.

"Esias. I want Ms. Madison's things moved to my rooms. Yes. Immediately."

Damian broke the connection and looked at Ivy. She stood straight and tall, head up, eyes steady on his even though they blazed with rage.

She was magnificent, so beautiful the sight of her made the blood roar in his ears.

He could take her now. Teach her that she belonged to him. Turn all that frost to flame.

But he wouldn't. The longer he waited, the sweeter her submission would be.

Damian strolled into the huge master bath. Turned on the shower, toed off his mocs, unbuckled his belt, pulled his cotton sweater over his head as if he were alone.

A priceless vase whistled past his ear and shattered on the tile a couple of feet away.

He swung around and looked at Ivy. She glared back, head high, hands on hips, her eyes telling him how she despised him…

And then her gaze dropped to his broad shoulders, swept over his muscled chest and hard abs.

"Want to see more?" he said, very softly, and brought his hand to his zipper.

His Ivy was brave but she wasn't stupid. Cheeks blazing, she turned and fled.

CHAPTER EIGHT

TRAPPED.

She was trapped like a fly in amber, Ivy thought furiously, held captive within something that looked beautiful but was really a prison.

The door to the guest suite she'd commandeered in Damian's absence stood open. One of the maids was emptying the dresser drawers; Esias stood by, supervising.

"Leave my clothes alone!"

The maid jumped back. Esias said something and the girl shot a glance at Ivy and reached toward the dresser again.

"Did you hear me? Do—not—touch—my—things!"

Esias barely looked at her. "His Highness said—"

"I don't give a damn what he said." Ivy pointed to the door. "Get out!"

The houseman stiffened but, well-trained robot that he was, he snapped an order at the maid. She scurried away at his heels as he marched from the room.

Ivy slammed the door behind them, locked it and sank down on the edge of the bed.

She would not remain on Minos. That was a given.

What wasn't so clear was how to escape. There were no bars on the windows of Damian's palace, no locks on the doors, but why would there be?

The island was in the middle of the Aegean. You could only leave it by sea or by air.

And yes, there was an airstrip, a helipad, a couple of small boats in a curved harbor, even a yacht the size of a cruise ship anchored just offshore in the dark blue sea.

But all those things, every ounce of white sand beach, dark volcanic rock and thousand-foot-high cliffs belonged to Damian. He owned Minos and ruled it with an iron fist.

She could only leave Minos if he permitted it.

Aside from Esias, who watched her with the intensity of Cerberus, that ancient three-headed dog guarding Hades, the people who lived in Damian's tightly controlled little kingdom were pleasant and polite.

The maids and gardeners, cook and housekeeper all smiled whenever they saw her. The pilot of Damian's jet, poring over charts in a small, whitewashed building at the airstrip, had greeted her pleasantly; down by the sea, an old man scraping barnacles from the bottom-up hull of a small sailboat doffed his cap and offered a gap-toothed grin.

They all spoke English, enough to say oh, yes, it was very hot this time of year and indeed, the sea was a wonderful shade of deepest blue. But as soon as Ivy even hinted at asking if someone would please sail her, fly her, get her the hell off this miserable speck of rock, they scratched their heads and suddenly lost their command of anything other than Greek.

Terrified, all of them, by His Highness, the Prince.

His Horribleness, the Prince.

Ivy shot to her feet and went to the closet. There had to be someone with the courage to help her. Maybe the helicopter pilot. Maybe Damian had neglected to tell him that she was a prisoner. Either way, this was her last chance at freedom.

She had to make it work and the best way to do that was to look and sound like Ivy Madison, woman of the world, instead of Ivy Madison, desperate prisoner.

Quickly she stripped to her bra and panties. Grabbed a pair of white linen trousers from their hanger, stepped into them…

"Oh, for God's sake…"

She inhaled until it felt like her navel was touching her spine. No good. The zipper wouldn't budge.

Ivy kicked the trousers off and turned sideways to the mirror. Her expression softened and she lay her hand gently over her rounded belly.

The baby—her baby—was growing. Her baby… and Damian's.

No. A condom's worth of semen didn't make a man a father. Concern, love, wanting a child were what mattered. Where was Damian's concern, his love, his desire for this baby?

Nowhere that she could see. He wanted her child because he wanted an heir, and because he was the kind of unfeeling SOB who could not imagine giving up that which he believed was his.

A man like that was not going to raise her baby.

Two days out from under his autocratic thumb and Ivy had had time to think logically.

Maybe she couldn't afford a five hundred dollar an hour Manhattan lawyer but she knew people who knew people. It was one of the few benefits of a high-profile career. Surely some acquaintance could fast-talk a hotshot attorney into taking her case on the cheap, maybe even pro bono, if only for the publicity.

Which was really pretty funny, Ivy thought as she tried and discarded another pair of trousers.

She'd always avoided publicity. Sometimes she thought she was the only model who tried to keep her private life under wraps. But if winning the right to raise her child alone meant having her face plastered in the papers, she'd do it.

She'd do whatever it took to get Damian out of her and her baby's lives.

Damian Aristedes was a brute. A monster. A man who went into a rage when he was denied sex, who'd come close to forcing her to yield to him and, instead, had flown to Athens to find a woman who wouldn't stop him from taking what he wanted.

Why else would he have left her and Minos? That was what men did. Even Damian, who looked so civilized.

He hadn't been civilized when he'd taken her in his arms the other night. Neither had she. Just for a moment, she'd felt things threaten to spin out of control... Until she'd come to her senses, realized where things were heading, what he would want to do next...

Ivy blinked, reached for the only remaining pair of trousers, sucked in her tummy and pulled them on.

Okay.

The zipper didn't close but at least it went up halfway. A long silk T, a loose, gauzy shirt over that...

She stuck her feet into a pair of high-heeled slides. Freed her hair from its clip, bent at the waist and ran her hands through it before tossing it back from her face. A little makeup…

Ivy looked at herself in the mirror, gave her reflection her best camera pout and tried to imagine herself facing the helicopter pilot, whoever he was.

"I know you must be awfully busy," she said in a breathy whisper. It made her want to gag when she heard other women talk like that but whatever worked… "I mean, I know you have lots to do…"

And what if the sexy look, the artful smile didn't budge him? If he said sorry, he had to clear it with the prince?

"Oh," she said, "yes, I know, but—but…" Ivy chewed on her lip. "But I have to get to Athens without telling him because—because—"

Because what?

"Because I want to buy him a gift. See, it's a surprise but it won't be if he knows about it…"

Not great but add a smile, fluttering lashes, maybe a light touch on the guy's arm…

Ivy's sexy smile faded.

"Yuck," she said.

Then she propped her sunglasses on top of her head, hung her purse over her shoulder and got moving.

The helicopter was still on its pad.

Better still, a guy wearing a ball cap and dark glasses was squatting alongside it, examining one of the struts.

It had to be the pilot.

Ivy paused, ran her hand through her hair, then down her torso. She was dusty and sweaty, thanks to the long walk to the helipad, plus she'd come close to turning her ankle on the road's gravel surface. There were Jeeps garaged near the palace but you had to get keys from Esias.

Fat chance.

Besides, some men liked sweaty. All those times she'd had to be oiled before a shot…

"Stop stalling," she muttered as she walked past the hangars, placing one foot directly ahead of the other.

Her modeling strut had always been among the best.

She waited until she was a couple of yards away. "Hi."

The guy looked up, gave a very satisfactory double-take and got to his feet.

Ivy held out her hand. "I'm Ivy."

He wiped his hand on his khakis, took her hand and cleared his throat. "Joe," he said, and cleared his throat again.

"Joe." Ivy batted her lashes. "Are you the one who flies this incredible thing?"

He grinned. "You got it, beautiful."

Perfect. He was American. And even with dust on her shoes and sweat beaded above her lip, she'd clearly passed the test.

"Well, Joe, I need a lift to Athens. Are you up for that?"

Joe took off his dark glasses, maybe so she could see the regret in his eyes, and peered past her.

"Are you, uh, are you looking for somebody?"

He nodded. "I'm looking for the prince."

"Oh, we don't need him." Ivy moved closer. "You see," she said, lowering her voice and gazing up at Joe's face, "he doesn't know I'm doing this."

She launched into her story. It sounded so good, she almost believed it. Joe said "uh huh" and "sure" and "cool." And just when she thought she had it made, he shook his head and sighed.

"Wish I could help you, beautiful, but I can't."

Ivy forced a smile. "But you can. I mean, it's just a little trip. And afterward, when the prince knows about the surprise, you know, after I've given it to him, I'll tell him how great you were, how you did this for me—"

"Sorry, babe. This chopper doesn't leave the ground unless His Highness says it's okay. You want to use the phone in the office over there to call him, that's fine. Otherwise—"

"For heaven's sake! Do you need his permission to breathe, too? You're a grown man. He's just a—he's just a pompous, self-serving—"

Joe stared past her, eyes widening.

"Glyka mou," a husky voice purred, "here you are."

Ivy's heart sank. She closed her eyes as a powerful arm wrapped around her shoulders.

"I've been looking everywhere for you. How foolish of me not to have thought to check here first."

Ivy looked up at Damian. He smiled, pleasantly enough so the pilot smiled, too, but Ivy wasn't fooled.

Behind that calm royal smile was hot royal rage.

"You cannot do this," she hissed.

His eyebrows rose. "Do what?"

"You know what. Refuse to let me leave. Make me into your—your—"

He bent his head and kissed her, the curve of his arm anchoring her to him while his mouth moved against hers with slow, possessive deliberation. She heard Joe clear his throat, heard her heart start to pound.

And felt herself tumble into the flood of dark sensation that came whenever his lips touched hers.

"I hate you," she whispered when he finally lifted his head.

His smile was one part sex and one part macho smirk. "Yes," he said. "I can tell. Joe?"

The pilot, who'd walked several feet away, turned to them. "Sir?"

"We are ready to leave," Damian said, and he took Ivy's elbow and all but lifted her into the helicopter.

They flew to Athens.

Even in her anger, Ivy felt a little thrill of excitement as they swooped over a stand of soaring white columns. She'd been to Athens before but it had been on business, four rushed days and nights of being photographed with no time for anything else except a hurried visit to the Parthenon.

Was that the Acropolis below them now? She wanted to ask but not if it meant speaking to Damian.

She didn't have to. He leaned in close, put his lips to her ear and told her what was beneath them.

The whisper of his breath made her tremble. Why? How could she hate him and yet react this way to him? To any man? She knew what they were, what they wanted...

"I should have thought to ask," he said. "Is the flight making you ill?"

Ivy pulled away. "Not the flight," she said coldly, but he didn't hear her, couldn't hear her over the roar of the engine, and that was just as well.

His show of concern was just that. A show, nothing more. She was his captive and that was how he treated her and why in God's name did she respond to his touch?

He must have had the same effect on Kay. Otherwise, she wouldn't have given in to his demands. The bastard! Forcing Kay to do what he wanted, then turning his back on the situation he'd created once Kay was gone, unless...

Unless he really hadn't known about the baby. Unless the story Kay had told her was—unless it was—

"Ivy."

She looked up. Damian was standing over her; the helicopter had touched down. He reached for her seat belt. She ignored him, did it herself and walked to the door. Joe was already on the ground. He held up his arms and she let him help her down.

"Careful of the rotor wash," he yelled.

And then Damian's arm was around her waist and he led her to a long, black limousine.

"One for each city," Ivy said briskly. "How nice to be a potentate."

Damian looked at her as if she'd lost her mind. Perhaps she had, she thought, as the limo sped away.

That time in Athens, doing a spread for *In Vogue,* Ivy had spent hours, exhausting hours, in Kolonaki Square.

The photographer had shot her against the famous column that stood in the square. Against the well-dressed crowd. Against the charming cafés and shops. The stylist had dressed her in haute couture from Dolce & Gabbana and Armani and elegant boutiques in this upscale neighborhood.

Now, Damian took her into those same boutiques to buy her clothes.

"I don't need anything," she told him coldly.

"Of course you do. That's why I brought you here."

"I have my own things, thank you very much."

"Is that why your trousers don't close?"

She blushed, looked down and saw only the

slightly rounded contours of her gauzy shirt. Damian laughed softly.

"A good guess, *neh?*"

A clerk glided toward them. Damian took Ivy's hand and explained they needed garments that were loose-fitting. Ivy said nothing. This was his show; she'd be damned if she'd help. So he cleared his throat, let go of her hand and, instead, curved his arm around her and drew her close.

"My lady is pregnant."

There was an unmistakable ring of masculine pride in his voice. Ivy flashed him a cool look and wondered what would happen to all that macho arrogance if she added that she was pregnant, courtesy of a syringe.

"She carries my child," he said softly, and placed his hand over her rounded belly as if they were alone.

And that touch of his hand, not proprietary but tender, changed everything.

For the first time, Ivy let the picture she'd refused to envision fill her mind.

Damian, holding her in his arms. Undressing her. Carrying her to his bed, kissing her breasts, her belly. Parting her thighs, kneeling between them, his eyes dark with passion as he entered her and planted his seed in her womb.

"My child, *glyka mou,*" he whispered and this time, when he bent to her, Ivy rose on her toes, put her hand on the back of his head and brought his lips to hers.

The clerk in a tiny boutique on Voukourestiou Street said there was a little shop that specialized in maternity clothes only a few doors away.

Ivy said they didn't need anything else. A dozen

boxes and packages were already on their way by messenger to the limousine that waited on a quiet, shady street near the square.

To her amazement, Damian agreed.

"What we need is lunch." He smiled, tilted her face up to his and gave her a light kiss. "My son must be hungry by now."

Ivy laughed. "Using a baby as an excuse to fill your own belly is pathetic."

"But effective," he said, laughing with her.

They ate in a small café. The owner greeted Damian with a bear hug and the cook—his wife—hurried out from the kitchen, kissed Damian on both cheeks, kissed Ivy after introductions were made, then beamed and said something to Damian, who laughed and said *neh,* she was right.

"Right about what?" Ivy said, when they were alone.

Damian took her hand and brought it to his mouth. "She says you are carrying a strong, beautiful boy."

Ivy blushed. "Do I look that pregnant?"

His eyes darkened. "You look happy," he said softly. "Are you? Happy, today, with me?"

He had phrased the question carefully. She could answer it the same way. Or she could just say that she *was* happy, that when she didn't stop to think about why they were together, about how he'd come into her life, about what would happen next, she was incredibly happy. She was—she was—

"Lemonade," the café's owner said, setting two tall glasses in front of them. "For the proud papa—and the beautiful mama."

Ivy grabbed the glass as if it were a life preserver.

After a moment, Damian did, too.

* * *

She should have known Damian wouldn't leave without stopping at the maternity boutique.

They went there after lunch and found the jewel-like shop filled with exquisite, handmade clothes that could make even a woman whose belly was ballooning feel beautiful.

Desirable.

Ivy caught her breath. Damian heard her whisper of distress and brought her close against his side.

"Forgive me," he said softly. "I have exhausted you."

"No. I mean—I mean, I guess I am a little tired."

He smiled into her eyes. Pressed a kiss to her forehead.

"What is your favorite color, *glyka mou?*"

"My favorite color?"

"Green, to match your eyes? Gold, to suit your hair?" Instead of waiting for her answer, he turned to the hovering clerk. "We want everything you have in those colors."

"Damian!"

"Please, do not argue! You are tired. We are done shopping for the day."

His tone was imperious. Arrogant. Ivy knew she ought to tell him so…

Instead she buried her face against his shoulder and thought, *Just for today, just for now, let this all be a dream.*

Not the beautiful clothes, the elegant shops. They didn't matter.

Damian did.

She could pretend, couldn't she? Pretend he was her wonderful, incredible lover? Pretend they were together because they wanted to be? Pretend they had planned this baby, longed for it together?

What harm could it possibly do?

They flew home in the gathering twilight, trading the lights of the city for those of ships, of islands, of stars.

This time, Ivy went willingly into Damian's arms when he insisted on carrying her from the helicopter to the Jeep he'd left beside the airstrip hours before.

He put her into the passenger seat, then got behind the wheel and started the engine, let it idle as he stared out the windshield.

"Ivy. I have waited all day to tell you this." He cleared his throat. "I was very angry this morning."

Ivy sighed. So much for dreams. The day was over. Back to reality.

"I'm sure you were," she said quietly, "but—"

"Angry is too mild a word, *glyka mou*. I was furious."

"Damian. You have to understand that—"

"I have done a terrible thing."

"You *must* understand that…" She swung toward him. "What?"

"I brought you to my island so I could take care of you. Instead I've terrified you."

The soft night breeze tossed Ivy's hair over her cheek. She swept it back as she stared at the man seated beside her.

"I—I behaved badly that first night." He took a deep, deep breath, then expelled it. "And then, this morning… I had no right to turn my anger on you but I did and because of that, you walked a steep, long road under the hot sun."

Say something, Ivy told herself, for heaven's sake, say something!

"Walking is—walking is good for me."

"Ivy." His voice was rough. "I'm trying to apologize and—" He looked at her and smiled. "And it's not something I'm very good at."

Something in her softened. "Maybe because you don't do it very often," she said, smiling a little, too.

He grinned. "There are many people who would agree with you." He cleared his throat, engaged the gears and the Jeep moved forward. "So we will start over. I will take care of you."

"Damian. I don't need you to take care of me. I've been taking care of myself for a very long time."

"It's what I want."

Ivy hesitated. "Because of—because of the baby."

"That is part of it, of course. But I want—I want—"

He hesitated, too. What *did* he want? Things had seemed so clear this morning. He'd made Ivy his responsibility; that meant buying her whatever she needed.

But somewhere during the course of the day, that had changed. She'd gone from being his responsibility to being his pleasure and joy.

"I want to do the right thing," he said, hurrying the words because that was safer than trying to figure out where in hell this line of thought might lead. "I should have done that from the start instead of rushing off like a frustrated schoolboy the night I brought you here."

"You don't have to apologize," Ivy said quickly. This wasn't a topic she wanted to discuss. "I understood."

They had reached the palace. He pulled up in front of it, killed the engine and took her hands in his.

"I know it's no excuse but I've never lost control as

I did that night, *kardia mou*. I've never wanted a woman as I wanted you."

He spoke in the past tense. She understood that, too. He'd gone to Athens. Satisfied his—his needs.

"It was just as well that call came from my office. If I'd remained here, I don't know—I don't know what would have happened."

She stared at him. "You mean, you went to Athens on business?"

"What else would have taken me from you that night?" He gave a halfhearted laugh. "If anyone had ever suggested I would be grateful one of my tankers hit a reef…"

He hadn't left her for another woman's bed. Why did that mean so much?

"As for this child… No, don't look away from me." He cupped her chin and turned her face toward his. "How can we start over if we keep hiding things from each other? I did not know anything about a child. Do you really think, had I known, I would have abandoned it?"

Ivy shook her head. "Kay said—"

"Kay lied," he said sharply. "And that is the truth. I may not be a saint but I swear to you, I did not do these things. I did not ask Kay to become pregnant, and I certainly did not ask her to have a stranger become pregnant in her place."

"Me," Ivy said in a small, shaky voice.

"You," Damian said, bringing her hands to his lips. "But you are not a stranger any longer. You are a woman I know and admire."

"How can you admire me when you think—you think I did this for money? I didn't, Damian, I swear it. I didn't want to do it at all but—"

"But?"

But, I owed my stepsister more than I could ever repay.

She couldn't tell him that. The enormity of her debt. What would become of his admiration if she did? Only Kay knew her secret, and Kay had made her see that she must never tell anyone else.

"But," she whispered, "Kay took care of me after I— after I left foster care. I would have done anything to make her happy and so I said I'd do this…" Ivy bowed her head. "But I lied to myself. How could I have thought I'd be able to give up my—give up this baby?" Her voice broke. "Even the thought of it tears out my heart."

Damian took her in his arms, rocked her against him while she wept.

"Don't cry," he murmured. "You won't have to give up the baby, I promise." He pressed a kiss to her hair. "I am proud you carry my child, Ivy."

She looked up, eyes bright with tears. "Are you?"

"I only wish—I wish that I had put my seed deep in your womb as I made love to you." He kissed her; she clung to his shoulders as she kissed him back. "What I said in New York has not changed. I want to marry you."

"No. I know you want to do the right thing but—" She swallowed. "But I wouldn't be a good wife."

He smiled. "Have you been married before?" When she shook her head, his smile broadened. "Then, how can you know that?"

"I just do."

"We would start out together, *kardia mou,* I learning to be a good husband, you learning to be a good wife."

Ivy shook her head. "It would never work."

"Of course it would." Impatience roughened his voice. "Look at what we already have in common. A child we both love." His hands tightened on her shoulders. "I want my son," he said bluntly. "And I intend to have him. You can become my wife and his mother—or I'll take him from you. I don't want to hurt you but if I must, I will."

He was right, never mind all her pie-in-the-sky scheming this morning. Damian would win in a custody battle, even if she told the court her secret. He was the prince of a respected royal house. She was nobody.

Worse than nobody.

"What will it be? A courtroom? Or marriage?"

Ivy bowed her head, took a steadying breath, then looked up and met Damian's eyes.

"I can't marry you, Damian, even if—even if I wanted to. The thing is—the thing is—"

"For God's sake, what?"

"I don't like…" Her voice fell to a shaky whisper. "I don't like sex."

She didn't know what reaction she'd expected. Laughter? Anger? Disbelief? Surely not his sudden stillness. The muscle, knotting in his jaw. The way he looked at her, as if he were seeing her for the first time.

"You don't like—"

"No."

"Is that why you stopped me the other night?"

Ivy nodded. She would never tell him everything but he was entitled, at least, to know this.

He nodded, too. Then he got out of the Jeep, opened her door, drew her gently to her feet and into his arms.

"It's late," he said gruffly. "Much too late an hour of

the night for truths and secrets like this. I'm going to take you to your room and put you to bed."

He believed her. She was stunned. Men who came on to her, who called her frigid when she turned them away, never did.

He lifted her into his arms and she let him do it, loving the strength of his embrace, the warmth of his body, wishing with all her heart that things were different. That she was different.

And realized, too late, that the door he shouldered open, the bed he brought her to, was not hers.

It was his.

She began to protest. He silenced her with a kiss that left her breathless.

CHAPTER NINE

MOONLIGHT washed through the French doors and lit Ivy in its creamy spill.

Damian wanted to see her face but when he tried to lift her chin, she shook her head.

Was it true? Did this stunning, sensual woman dislike sex?

Earlier in the day, sitting on a too-small sofa in one of the boutiques, trying not to look as conspicuous as he felt, trying, as well, to figure out how in hell he'd gotten himself into this because he'd never, not once in his life, gone shopping with a woman—sitting there, arms folded, while Ivy changed into a dress in the fitting room, the salesclerk had bent down and whispered how flattered the shop was to have Ivy Madison as a customer.

Damian had frowned. How did the clerk know Ivy? Then he'd happened to glance at a glossy magazine on a table beside him and there was Ivy, smiling seductively from the cover.

In the days since she'd walked into his life, he'd thought of her as a lot of different things, all the way from scam artist to mother of his child. And, yes, gorgeous, too.

What man wouldn't notice that?

But he'd never thought of her as a woman whose face was known around the world.

He'd picked up the magazine, opened to a spread of Ivy modeling beachwear. She stood facing the camera in a white halter gown that clung to her body. In a crimson bikini that paid homage to her breasts and long legs. In a butter-yellow robe that hung open just enough to make his pulse accelerate.

He thought of other men, faceless strangers looking at those same photos, feeling what he felt, and he wanted to hunt the bastards down and make sure they understood they were wasting their time dreaming about her because she belonged solely to him.

Crazy, he'd told himself.

And then Ivy, his Ivy, had walked out of the dressing room, stepped onto a little platform in a gown he supposed was attractive—except, he hadn't really noticed.

All he'd noticed was her.

She was beautiful. Not in the way she was in the magazine, gazing in sultry splendor at the camera but as she was right then, a flesh and blood woman looking questioningly at him.

"What do you think?" she'd said.

What he'd thought was that she was so beautiful she stole his breath away.

"Very nice," he'd said.

The understatement of the year, but how did you tell a woman you were a heartbeat away from taking her in your arms, carrying her into the dressing room, kicking the damned door closed and making love to her? Doing it again and again until she was trembling with passion, until she admitted that she wanted him, that she would always want him.

Now she'd told him she didn't like sex.

It could be another bit of deceit to tempt him further into her web.

Damian's jaw tightened.

It could be…but it wasn't. He remembered what had happened in this same room, three nights ago. How she'd responded to him with dizzying abandon until he'd tried to take things further.

Without question, she'd told him the truth.

"Ivy?"

She didn't answer. He brushed the knuckles of his hand lightly against her cheek.

"Is that what happened the other night? Is that the reason you stopped me?"

"Yes."

The word was a sigh. He had to bend his head to hear it.

"You should have told me," he said softly.

"Tell you something like that?" She gave a forlorn little laugh. "When a man's about to—about to—to try to—" A deep breath. "I don't want to talk about it. I just thought you should know why I could never—I mean, the idea of marriage is out of the question anyway but—but if—if there were even the most remote possibility—"

"You're wrong, *agapi mou*. About everything."

His voice was so sure. God, he was so arrogant! And yet, right now, that arrogance made her smile. Despite herself, Ivy turned and lifted her eyes to his.

"Doesn't it ever occur to you," she said softly, "that there are times it's you who's wrong?"

"But you see, sweetheart, I wasn't going to have sex with you. I was going to make love to you."

"It's the same—"

He kissed her. Kissed her without demanding anything but her compliance, his mouth warm and tender against hers. Kissed her until he felt her tremble, though not with fear.

"You don't like sex," he said softly. "But you like my kisses."

"Damian. I can't. Really, I just—"

He kissed her again, just as gently, and felt a fierce rush of pleasure when her mouth softened under his.

"Damian." Her voice shook. "I don't think—"

"Shh." His hands spread across her back, applying just a little pressure when he kissed her again, enough to part her lips and touch the tip of her tongue with his.

A whisper of sound rose in her throat. Did she move closer or did he? It took all his self-control not to pull her into his arms.

"Sex is a physical act, *glyka mou*. It's part of making love but it's hardly all of it."

"I don't see—"

"No. You don't. Let me show you, then. Just another kiss," he added, when she began to shake her head. "I only want to taste you. Will you permit me to do that?"

He didn't wait for her answer. Instead he put his mouth against hers.

"Open to me," he said thickly. A second slipped by. Then she moaned, rose on her toes, tipped her head back and let him take the kiss deeper.

Damian kissed her over and over, his tongue in her mouth, his hands buried in the chestnut and gold spill of her hair.

He told himself he would keep his promise. That he would only taste her. But as her skin heated, as she sighed with pleasure, he put his lips against her throat, slipped her blouse from her shoulders, kissed his way to the vee of her silk T-shirt.

"Ivy," he whispered, his hands spreading over her midriff, the tips of his fingers brushing the undersides of her breasts. "Ivy, *kardia mou…*"

Her hands lifted, knotted in his shirt. His name sighed from her lips.

The room began to blur.

He told himself to go slowly. To do no more than he'd said he would. But she was leaning into him now, her hands were cool on his nape and he bent his head to her breasts, kissed them through the silky fabric of her shirt.

She made a broken little sound deep in her throat and arched her back. The simple motion made an offering of her beaded nipples, taut and visible beneath her T-shirt.

It would have taken a saint to refuse such a gift.

Damian was no saint.

He kissed the delicate beads of silk-covered flesh. Drew them into his mouth, first one and then the other. Ivy's cries grew sharper. Hungrier.

So did his need.

He dropped to his knees. Lifted her shirt and found he'd been right about the half-closed zipper.

Slowly he eased the trousers down her hips and legs.

"Damian," she said unsteadily.

He looked up at her. "I'm just going to undress you," he whispered. "Then I'll put you to bed and if you want me to leave, I will. I promise."

She hesitated. Then she stepped out of the trousers and when he saw her like that, wearing the silk T-shirt, her long legs bare, her feet encased in foolishly high heels, he wondered why in hell he'd made such a promise.

But he would keep it.

He would keep it by stopping now. By standing up. By—all right, by reaching under the T, undoing her bra, only because she wouldn't want to sleep with it on…

Ivy stumbled back. "Don't! Please, don't."

Her voice was high; her eyes were wide with fear and, in a heartbeat, Damian understood.

She'd said she didn't like sex. He'd foolishly, arrogantly assumed she was simply a woman unawakened.

He knew better now.

Ivy, his Ivy, didn't like sex because she was terrified of it. A man had hurt her. Taught her that sex was painful or evil or ugly.

Damian spat out a sharp, four-letter word. Ivy began to weep.

"I told you," she sobbed, "I told you how it would be—"

"Who did this to you?"

She didn't answer. He cursed again, took her in his arms, ignored her attempts to free herself and wrapped her in his embrace.

"Ivy. *Agapi mou. Kardia mou.* Do not cry. Ivy, my Ivy…"

He'd lost his accent his second year at Yale but it was back now, roughening his words and then he was talking in Greek, not the modern language he'd grown up speaking but the ancient one he'd studied in prep school.

The Greek of the Spartans and Athenians. His warrior ancestors.

He knew what they would have done. It was what he longed to do. Find the man who'd done this to Ivy and kill him.

Her soft, desperate sobs broke his heart.

He held her against him, rocking her, whispering to her, soft, sweet words he had never said to a woman before, never wanted to say and, at last, her tears stopped.

Gently he scooped her into his arms and put her in the center of his bed, stroked her tousled hair back from her damp cheeks.

"It's all right," he murmured. "It's all right, sweetheart. Go to sleep, *agapimeni*. I'll stay here and keep you safe."

He drew the comforter over her. She clutched at it and rolled onto her side, turning her back to him. He wanted to reach for her again, to lie down and hold her, but instinct warned him not to. She was too fragile right now; God only knew what might push her over the edge.

So he sat beside her, watching until her breathing slowed and her lashes drooped against her cheeks.

"Ivy?" he said softly.

She was asleep.

Damian dropped a light kiss on her hair. Then he went into his dressing room, took off his clothes and put on an old, soft pair of Yale sweats. He padded back into the bedroom, drew an armchair next to the bed, sat down, stretched out his long legs and considered all the creative ways a man could deal with a son of a bitch who'd taught his Ivy that sex, the most intimate act a man and woman could share, was a thing to be feared.

He'd go from A to Z, he thought grimly. But "Assault" was too general. "Beating" was too simple.

"Castration" was a lot better. He stayed with that scenario until sleep finally dragged him under.

Something woke him.

The moon had disappeared, chased into hiding by wind and rain. The room was as black and frigid as Hecate's heart.

Damian padded quickly to the French doors and closed them. Damn, it was cold! Was Ivy warm enough under the comforter? It was too dark to see anything but the outline of the big bed.

He turned on a lamp, adjusting the switch until the light was only a soft glow. Ivy lay as he'd left her but the covers had dropped from her shoulder.

He shut off the light. Carefully leaned over the bed, began drawing up the comforter…

Zzzzt!

A streak of blinding light, then the roar of thunder rolling across the sea.

Ivy sprang up in bed, saw him leaning over her… and screamed.

"Ivy! Sweetheart. Don't be afraid. It's me. It's only me."

He caught her in his arms, ignored the jab that caught him in the eye and held her against him, stroking her, whispering to her. An eternity seemed to pass until, finally, she shuddered and went still.

"Damian?"

Her voice was thready. He drew her even closer, willing his strength into her.

"Yes, *agapimeni*. It's me."

Another shudder went through her. "I thought—I thought—"

He could only imagine what she'd thought. Rage, deep and ugly as a flood tide, filled him, left him struggling to keep his composure.

"You thought it was old Hephaestus, playing games with lightning bolts on Mount Olympus," he said with forced cheerfulness.

Was that tiny sound a laugh?

"Storms here can be pretty fierce during the summer. They scared the heck out of me when I was little, and it didn't help that my nanny would glare at me and say, 'You see, Your Highness? That's what happens when little boys don't listen to their nannies.'"

He'd dropped his voice to a husky growl that was less his long-ago nanny's and more a really bad Count Dracula, but it worked. His Ivy laughed. A definite laugh, this time, one that made him offer a silent word of thanks just in case old Hephaestus happened to be within earshot.

"That wasn't very nice of her."

"No, but it was effective. For the next few days, I'd be the model of princely decorum."

"And then?"

Lightning, followed by the crash of thunder, rolled across the sky again. Ivy trembled and Damian tightened his arms around her. "And then," he said, "I'd revert to the catch-me-if-you-can little devil I actually was." His smile faded. "You'll be fine, *glyka mou*. I won't let anything happen to you, I promise."

She leaned back in his embrace and looked up at him, her face a pale, lovely oval.

"Thank you," she whispered.

"For what?"

"For—" She hesitated. "For being so—so… For being so nice."

Nice? He'd bullied her, berated her, accused her of being a cheat and a liar. He'd forced her to come with him to Greece, told her he owned her…

"I haven't been nice," he said brusquely. "I've been impatient and arrogant. It is I who should thank you for tolerating me."

That rated a smile. "We're even, then. I'll forgive you and you'll forgive me."

He smiled back at her. A moment slipped by and his smile faded. "Ivy? Are you all right?"

"I'm fine."

"Good." God, how he wanted to kiss her. Just one kiss to tell her he would keep her safe from lightning and thunder and, most of all, safe from whatever terrible thing had once happened to her. "Good," he said briskly, and cleared his throat. "So. Let me tuck you in and—"

"Where are you sleeping? If I'm taking up your bed—"

"Don't worry about me."

"But where…"

"Right in that chair. I, ah, I thought it would be a good idea to be here in case, you know, in case you needed me."

"You? In that little chair? Where do you put your legs?"

He grinned. "They say a little suffering is good for the soul."

"It looks like a lot of suffering to me."

"Easy," he said lightly. "First you tell me I'm nice. Then you say I'm a candidate for sainthood. If you aren't careful—"

"Sleep with me."

Her voice was low, the words rushed. He told himself he'd misunderstood her but he hadn't, otherwise why would a pink stain be creeping into her cheeks?

"Just—just share the bed with me, Damian. Nothing else. I just—I don't want to think of you, all cramped up in that chair." She licked her lips. "If you won't share it, I'll have to sleep in the guest room. Alone. And—and I really don't want to. Be alone, I mean. Unless—unless you don't want—"

"Move over," he said, his voice gruff, his heart racing.

Ivy scooted away. He climbed onto the bed, slid under the covers, held his breath and then thought, to hell with it, and he put his arm around her waist and drew her into the curve of his body.

"Good night, *agapi mou*," he murmured.

"Good night, Damian."

He closed his eyes. Time passed. The storm moved off. Ivy lay unmoving in his embrace, so still that she had to be asleep and he—he was going to lose his mind. He *would* be a candidate for sainthood, by morning.

"Damian?"

He swallowed hard. "Yes, sweetheart?"

Slowly she turned toward him. He could feel her breath on his face.

Her hand touched his stubbled jaw; her fingers drifted like feathers over his mouth.

"Ivy…"

Her hand cupped the back of his head and she brought his lips down to hers.

His heart turned over.

"Ivy," he whispered again but she shook her head, kissed him and drew even closer.

One of them had to be dreaming.

Her lips parted. The tip of her tongue touched the seam of his mouth. He wanted to roll her on her back, open her mouth to his, savage her mouth with kisses.

But he wouldn't.

He wouldn't.

He would do only what she asked of him. He was not a saint but neither was he a beast.

Ivy whispered his name. Lay her thigh over his.

Damian groaned, caught her hands and held them against his chest.

"Sweetheart," he said raggedly, "*glyka mou*. I can't—" He cleared his throat. "Let's—let's sit up. In the chair. I'll hold you and—and when sunrise comes, we can watch it together and—and—"

She silenced him with a kiss that told him everything a man could hope to hear. Still, he held back and she took the initiative, rolling onto her back, holding him close, arching her body against his.

"Ivy," he whispered, and let himself tumble into the hot abyss with her.

He kissed her mouth. Her eyes. Her throat. She gave soft little cries of pleasure and each cry filled his soul.

He kissed her breasts through the thin silk T-shirt, sucked her nipples into his mouth and she went crazy beneath him, sobbing his name, clutching his shoulders, and he thought, *Slow down, slow down, God, slow down or this will end much too fast.*

But he was lost.

Lost in Ivy's scent, in her taste, in the silk of her hair and the heat of her skin.

He pushed up her shirt. Bared her breasts. Kissed the creamy slopes, teased the pale pink nipples, her sweet cries urging him on.

He sat her up. Pulled the shirt over her head. Unhooked her bra and her breasts, like the most precious fruit, tumbled into his hands.

He kissed them, kissed her belly, round and taut with his child and thought, as he had before, how perfect it would be if he and she had made this child together.

Then he stopped thinking because she was tugging at his sweatshirt.

He reared back and tugged it off. She arched against him, her breasts hot against his chest, and her moans of ecstasy almost unmanned him.

Her panties were the merest whisper of silk. He drew them down her legs and she arched again so that he sank into the spread of her thighs.

"Ivy," he said thickly.

"Yes," she whispered. "Please, yes."

She lifted her face and he kissed her, tasting her tears, tasting her sweetness, and something stirred deep, deep inside him, something stirred within his heart.

And then he was inside her. Inside her and she was so tight. So tight...

"Damian," she sighed, and put her hand between them.

The world spun away.

He groaned, thrust forward and Ivy cried out and came apart in his arms.

He held on as long as he could. Sheathing himself within her. Pulling back until it was torture, then sinking deep, feeling her come again and again until, finally, he let himself go with her. Fly into the night, into the sky, into the universe.

And knew, as he collapsed against her, that sex was, indeed, only sex. Making love was what really mattered.

And though he'd been with many women, he had never really made love until tonight.

CHAPTER TEN

DAMIAN was asleep.

Ivy had slept, too. For a little while, anyway, safe and warm in his embrace.

Then she'd awakened.

And, just that quickly, the memories came rushing back.

She'd lain beside him for another few minutes, telling herself not to let this happen. Not to spoil the wonder of Damian's lovemaking with the ugliness of those memories.

It hadn't worked.

Finally, carefully, she'd slipped from under the curve of her lover's arm and risen from the bed.

A soft cashmere throw lay at its foot. She'd wrapped herself in it, held her breath while she opened the French doors and stepped out on the terrace.

When would she finally be able to forget?

A little while ago, when the fury of the storm had invaded her dreams, it spun her back in time to another night a long, long time ago.

No, she'd whimpered, deep in the dream, *no!*

It hadn't mattered.

She'd come awake in terror. And when she saw the figure bending over her, that terror had wrapped its bony hands around her throat.

"No," she'd screamed—and then Damian had spoken her name.

He was the man leaning over her bed, not a fat monster who stunk of beer and sweat.

He hadn't grabbed her breast, squeezed it, laughed as he ripped her nightgown open.

He hadn't clamped a sweaty palm over her mouth as she tried to fight him off, her fifteen-year-old self no match for a man who earned his living swinging a pick ax.

Not a sound, he'd said, his stinking breath washing over her. *You make one noise, just one, I'll tell the social worker you stole money outta my wallet and you'll be back in Juvie Placement so fast it'll make your head spin.*

She hadn't stolen anything. Ever. The first time, in a different foster home, they'd said she'd taken a hundred dollars. She hadn't—but Kay said she had to be lying because the only other person who could have done it was her. Kay. Was Ivy accusing her of theft?

Kay stayed in that home. Ivy was sent back to the Placement facility. Eventually they'd put her in another foster home.

Kay turned eighteen and left the system.

"See you," she said.

And Ivy was alone.

Six months in one place. Three in another. Bad places. Dirty places. And then, finally, a place where the woman just looked right through her and the man smiled and said, *Call me Daddy.*

Ivy had felt her heart lift.

Daddy, she'd said, and even though he wasn't like her real daddy—whom she barely remembered—or her stepfather, Kay's father, whom she'd loved with all her heart—even though he wasn't, he was nice.

At least, that was what she thought.

He bought her a doll. Some books. And when he began coming into her room at night, to tuck her in, she'd felt a little funny because he also took to kissing her on the cheek but if he was her daddy, her real daddy, that was okay, wasn't it?

A light wind blowing in over the sea raised goose bumps on her skin. Ivy shuddered and drew the cashmere blanket more closely around her.

And then it all changed. One night, a storm was roaring outside. Lightning. Thunder. Rain. It scared her but she finally fell asleep—and woke to see the man she called Daddy standing over her bed.

Even now, all these years later, the memory was sheer agony.

He'd hurt her. Hurt her bad. He came to her each night, night after night, and when she finally tried to tell the woman, she'd slapped her in the face, called her a slut…

And Kay had come.

Ivy had flown to embrace her but Kay had pushed her away.

"What'd you do, huh?" she'd said coldly. "Don't give me that innocent look. Did you play games with this man like you did with my father?"

"What games?" Ivy had said in bewilderment. "I loved your father. He treated me as if I were his own daughter."

The look on her stepsister's face had been as frigid as her voice. "Only one problem, Little Miss Innocent. He already had a daughter. Me."

She'd lived with Kay for a few months but she knew she was in the way. And then, a couple of weeks after she turned seventeen, a man walked up to her on Madison Avenue, handed her his card and said, "Give me a call and we'll see if you have what it takes to become a model."

Kay had said yes, fine, do whatever you want. Just remember, never tell anybody what you did because they'll tell you how disgusting you really are.

Ivy moved out, the agency sent her to Milan, moved her into an apartment with five other girls. She sent Kay cards and letters that all went unanswered until she made the cover of *Glamour Girl* and Kay called to say she was so sorry they'd lost touch and how proud she was to be her sister...

"Glyka mou?"

Ivy spun around as Damian walked out onto the balcony. He'd pulled on his sweatpants. They hung low on his hips, accentuating his naked chest, muscled shoulders and arms, the abs most male models worked like machines to develop.

Beautiful. He was so beautiful. And so good and decent and kind...

"Sweetheart." He gathered her into his arms. "What's the matter?"

She shook her head, not trusting herself to speak, afraid that if she did, the lump that had suddenly risen in her throat would give way and she'd burst into tears of joy.

"Agapimeni." He tilted her face to his and brushed his lips gently over hers. "Tell me what's happened. Why did you leave me?"

I'll never leave you, she thought. *Never, not as long as you want me!*

"I just—" She swallowed, blinked away the silly burn of tears. "I woke up and—and I could still hear the storm, way off in the distance, and I wanted to—I wanted to see…"

Smiling, he cupped her face and threaded his fingers into her hair.

"A little while ago, you were afraid of the storm."

"That was before you made me see I had nothing to be afraid of."

Something dark flickered in his eyes. "Never," he said fiercely. "Not as long as I'm here to protect you."

Her heart lifted. How wrong she'd been about this man. Arrogant? Overpowering? Never. He was simply sure of himself, and strong.

And tender. And caring. And she felt—she felt—

"It was more than the storm you feared." His arms tightened around her. "Do you want to tell me about it?"

Yes. God yes, she did! But not yet. Not now. Not when her feelings were so new, so confused.

"It's all right." He kissed her. "You don't have to tell me anything you don't want to tell me."

"It isn't that. It's just…" She hesitated. "What's happened. This. It's all so—so new…"

"You mean, us," he said. When she nodded, he lifted her in his arms and carried her through the French doors. Gently he lay her on the bed and came down beside her.

"Are you happy?"

She smiled. "I'm very happy."

Slowly he eased the cashmere blanket from her shoulders, revealing her breasts, her belly, her body to his eyes.

"You're the most beautiful woman in the world," he whispered. "And I'm the luckiest man."

He dipped his head. Kissed her throat. Bent lower and circled a nipple with the tip of his tongue.

Ivy trembled. "Oh. Oh God, that feels—it feels—"

He licked the nipple. Sucked it into his mouth. She wound her arms around his neck, stunned at the sudden sharp longing low in her belly.

"How does it feel?" he said gruffly. "Tell me."

"Wonderful. Damian. It feels—"

His hand slipped down her belly, into the curls between her thighs, into the heat between her thighs, and found her clitoris.

Ivy moaned with pleasure and arched against his fingers.

"Please," she whispered. "Please."

"Please, what?" he said, and the thickness in his voice added to her excitement.

"Please," she sighed, "make love to me again."

He kissed her mouth. Kissed her belly. Parted her thighs and put his mouth to her and the first touch of his tongue sent her flying.

And then he was inside her, deep inside her, and she was lost. He said her name and she disintegrated into a million, billion pieces that flew to the far ends of the universe…

And knew the truth.

She had fallen in love with the complicated, impossible, wonderful man in her arms.

She lay beneath him, arms wrapped around him, his weight bearing her down into the mattress, his heart racing against hers, his skin damp from their lovemaking.

Until this moment even thinking about those things—
a man's body on hers, the thud of his heart, the scent of
his sweat... Just imagining those things, remembering
them, was enough to bring a dizzying wave of nausea.

But this was Damian.

And this was, as he'd promised, the difference
between having sex and making love.

I love you, she thought, *Damian, I love you...*

Had she said the words? Was that why he was
rolling away?

"Don't go," she said, before she could stop herself.

Damian's arms closed around her. He drew her close
to him, their faces inches apart.

"I'm not going anywhere, *glyka mou,*" he whispered.
"I'm just too heavy to lie on top of you."

"You're not."

He kissed her, his lips warm against hers.

"My sweet fraud," he said softly.

It was a soft, teasing endearment. She knew that.
Still, it hurt because she *was* a fraud.

She hadn't told him about her past.

Hadn't told him about his baby.

And she had to tell him. He had to know. But
when? When?

"You're trembling." Damian drew the comforter over
them both. "Better?"

"Yes. Fine."

"Mmm." He grinned. "Indeed you were." He gave
her a long, tender kiss. "I was afraid I might hurt you,
sweetheart. You were so tight."

His voice was low and filled with concern. This was
either the exact moment to tell him everything—or the
exact moment not to.

How could she admit to her ugly past?

How could she admit to the lie she'd told him?

"Sweetheart? Did I hurt you? God, if I did…"

"No! Oh, no, Damian, you didn't hurt me." Ivy took his hand, brought it to her mouth and kissed it. "What we did—"

"Making love."

"Yes. It was wonderful."

He held her against him for a long moment. Then he cupped her face and tilted it to his.

"I'm sorry I frightened you before."

"It wasn't your fault. I was—I was dreaming. And then I heard the thunder and I saw the lightning and—"

"And, you thought I was someone else. Someone who'd hurt you."

She couldn't lie, not when his arms were around her. "Yes."

Rage swept over him. Her whisper only confirmed what he'd already suspected.

"A man."

Ivy buried her face against his throat.

"Who?"

She shook her head. "I don't want to talk about it."

Yes, but he did. He wanted a name. He wanted to find this faceless son of a bitch and kill him.

Ah, God, Ivy was trembling and he knew damned well it had nothing to do with the temperature of the room. Damian cursed himself for being an ass.

"Forgive me, sweetheart." He kissed her hair, her temple, her mouth. "I'm a fool to talk about these things at a time like this."

"You're not a fool," she said fiercely, looking into his eyes. "You're a good, kind, wonderful man."

He forced a smile to his face. "That's quite an improvement over being—let's see. An SOB, an arrogant bastard, a son of—"

She laughed, as he'd hoped she would. "Well, sometimes… No. Seriously you're not any of those things I called you."

His hand moved slowly down her spine, cupped her bottom, drew her more closely against him.

"We didn't know each other," he said softly. "And it's my fault. I stormed into your life—"

"Seems to me I was the one who did the storming."

Good. She was smiling. He hadn't spoiled this amazing night for her after all.

No more questions…for now. But he would ask them again. A monster had done something terrible to Ivy.

Something sexual. Something violent.

Had he been caught? Had he paid for what he'd done? Not that it mattered. He would find the man and deal with him in his own way…

"Damian?"

He blinked. "Yes?"

"I'm glad we stormed into each other's lives."

He smiled and lifted her face to his so he could kiss her again. How had he lived his life without this woman?

"So am I. And now we have all the time in the world to get to know each other."

Ivy put her hand against his jaw. "Being with you tonight has been—has been—"

"Making love, you mean."

Her heart lifted. "Making love with you, yes. It was—it was so wonderful…"

How he loved the sound of her voice. The feel of her in his arms. How he loved—how he loved—

"For me, too," he said huskily. "I've never—I mean, you and I…" He cleared his throat, amazed at how difficult it was to say the next words but then, they were a kind of commitment, given all the women in his past. "What happened between us is… It was very special, *glyka mou*. I've never experienced anything like it before."

Ivy's face was solemn. "I'm glad because…" She touched the tip of her tongue to her lips. "Because this was—this is—it's the very first time I ever—I ever—"

She was blushing. Amazing, that this beautiful, sophisticated woman would blush when she talked about having an orgasm.

Amazing, too, that his damnable ego took pleasure in the thought that he had done for her what no other lover had done.

"Your first orgasm," he said softly, and smiled. "Part of me is sorry that's been denied you but I have to admit, part of me is… What?"

"I'm not talking about having an orgasm." Her voice was so soft he had to strain to hear it. "I'm talking about…" She swallowed. "You're right," she said, rushing the words together. "Something did happen to me, a long time ago. And because it did, I never took a lover until—until—"

The hurried words trailed off. Ivy tried to look away but Damian wouldn't let her. He cupped her face, kissed her mouth, told her what honor she had brought him, by letting him be her first lover.

Then he rolled her gently on her back.

"And your only lover, for the rest of our lives."

He kissed her. Caressed her. Touched her as if she were as fragile as a cobweb until she sobbed his name and showed him with her mouth, her hands, her body that she would not break...

Showed him, without words, what was in her heart.

Showed him that she had fallen deeply, forever in love.

They flew to Athens the next morning to see an obstetrician, who examined Ivy, looked over the records that Damian, ever in command, had somehow had transferred from her New York OB-GYN, smiled and said, *neh,* everything was fine.

Was she certain? asked Damian.

The doctor said she was.

Because, Damian said, he'd noticed things.

The doctor and Ivy both looked at him. "What things?" they said in unison.

Well, his Ivy didn't eat as much as she should.

His Ivy? The phrase went straight to Ivy's heart. She smiled and put her hand in his.

"My appetite's just fine."

"Yes, *glyka mou,* but you are eating for two."

"Ms. Madison's weight is right on target."

Damian didn't look convinced but he had another question. What about exercise? He had walked her all around Kolonaki Square only yesterday. Was it too much? Should he have permitted—

"Permitted?" Ivy said, her eyebrows rising again.

Should he have let her do that? Damian asked

"Ms. Madison is in excellent health, Your Highness. And," the doctor added gently, "she is hardly the first woman to have a baby."

Damian's authoritative air vanished. "I know that," he said, "but I am the first man to have one." A beat of silence; the doctor smiled but not Ivy. "I mean, I mean—"

"You mean this is your first child," the doctor said. "Of course, Your Highness. And I promise you, everything is fine."

Outside, on the street, Ivy turned to Damian. "I understand why you're so concerned. You—you lost a baby, with my sister."

"I *thought* I lost a baby," Damian said carefully. "But it was a lie."

"Yes." Her eyes clouded. "A terrible lie. But believing you'd really lost a baby must have been almost as bad as having it happen."

Damian wanted to take her in his arms and kiss her, but they were on a crowded street. He made do with taking her hand, bringing it to his lips and pressing a kiss into the palm.

"I'm concerned because of you," he said. "If anything happened to you…" He took a deep breath. "Ivy. You are—you are—"

My love.

The words were right there, on the tip of his tongue, but that was crazy. He hardly knew this woman. And there were still so many unanswered questions…

Besides, a man didn't fall in love after, what, a week? There was no reason to be impulsive. To make a move he might regret.

"You are important to me." He brought her hand to his mouth, kissed the palm and folded her fingers over the kiss. "Very important."

Ivy nodded. They weren't the words she yearned to hear, but they were close.

"I'm glad, because—because you're very important to me, too."

A smile lit his face. "Words meant to feed a man's ego," he said teasingly.

"Words that are true. Being with you, carrying your baby…" She hesitated, afraid she would blurt out too much. "I've never been this happy. And I want you to know that—that no matter what happens, you will always be—you will always be—"

She fell silent as their eyes met.

Damian's heart turned over at what he saw in her face.

Years ago, he, Lucas and Nicolo had celebrated surviving finals week at Yale by driving to an airport in a little town called Danielson.

They'd taken a couple of hours of instruction, strapped on parachutes and boarded a plane after drawing slips of paper to decide which of them would go first.

He'd won.

"Or lost," Nicolo had said, grinning.

It came back to him now, the way he'd felt standing in the plane's open door, the wind trying to pluck him out, the ground beckoning from a million miles below.

What in hell am I doing? he'd thought.

"Jump," his instructor had yelled.

And he had.

God, it had been incredible. Stepping into space. Soaring above the earth, then falling toward it.

Incredible.

He'd jumped for years after that but as much as he'd loved skydiving, he'd never quite felt the excitement, the sheer wonder of that first time.

Until now.

Until he saw the smile in Ivy's eyes. Felt his heart thump as she lay her palms against his chest.

He reminded himself that he really knew nothing about her.

Reminded himself that she hadn't given a reasonable answer as to why she'd agreed to Kay's incredible request.

And now there were more questions. Who had hurt her? Why wouldn't she talk about it?

One call to a private investigator and he'd have the answers he needed in, what, a week?

That was what he had to do. He was a logical man. He always had been. That was how he'd saved Aristedes Shipping. With logic. Common sense. By taking one step at a time.

By *not* jumping into space.

Skydiving, skiing down a glacier… A man could run risks in such things but not in those that were life-changing.

Damian took Ivy's hands in his. They were icy-cold, despite the heat of the day. She had opened her heart to him and now she was waiting for him to say something.

And he would.

Something logical. Something sensible. Something that would not put him at risk…

"Ivy," he said, "my beautiful Ivy. I love you. I adore you. Will you be my wife?"

She stared at him as if he'd lost his mind. Well, maybe he had. But when she smiled, and her eyes filled with tears, and she said she loved him with all her heart and yes, she would be his wife, yes, yes, yes…

It wasn't anything like that first jump.

It was ten thousand times better.

CHAPTER ELEVEN

IVY stood ankle-deep in the surf, her face turned up to the hot kiss of the sun.

A month ago, Minos had been a forbidding chunk of rock rearing up from a depressingly dark sea.

Now, it was paradise.

White sand beaches. Towering volcanic rock. Firs, pines, poplars that climbed its slopes, anemones and violets that poked slyly from the deep green grass.

And around it all, the Aegean, wine-dark and magnificent, just as the poet, Homer, had described it centuries before.

Could a place look so different just because you were happy?

Yes. Oh, yes, it could.

Not just a place. The world. The universe. And happy wasn't the right word to describe how she felt.

She was—she was complete.

Being with Damian, being part of his life, having him a part of hers, was wonderful.

He was everything. The sun, the moon, the stars… She laughed out loud, threw up her arms and did a little dance right there, as the wavelets foamed around her ankles.

Surely nobody had ever been this much in love. It just wasn't possible.

Ivy eased down to the sand, legs outstretched in the warm surf, arms back, basking in the glorious warmth of the Greek sun.

The only thing warmer was Damian's love.

That so much joy had come from something that had started so badly... Not the baby, she thought quickly, putting a protective hand over her belly. Never that. She'd wanted the baby almost the moment she'd missed her first period and known, for sure, she was pregnant.

Known she wanted the baby—and that she'd made a terrible mistake, agreeing to Kay's awful plan.

That was the bad start. The plan. Not the original one, which had been hard enough to say "yes" to, but the one Kay had dropped on her at the last possible second.

How could she have agreed to it?

Ivy shut her eyes. The truth was, she'd never agreed to it in her heart.

The joy of the sunny morning fell away.

In the end, Kay had asked too much of her. She'd owed her so much, yes, so much, but giving up the baby?

She knew now that she could not, would not have done it.

Wasn't it time to explain that, to explain everything, to Damian?

Slowly Ivy rose to her feet, tucked her hands into the back pockets of her white shorts and began walking along the sand.

Of course it was.

At the beginning, Damian had assumed she'd made

a devil's bargain. He knew better, now, that she'd never do something like this for money.

And because he loved her, he'd stopped asking.

That didn't mean he wasn't entitled to the truth.

It was just that telling him meant telling him everything, starting with what had occurred when she was fifteen and ending with the day a doctor was to implant Kay's eggs, mixed with Damian's sperm, in her womb.

Except—except, it hadn't happened that way.

Ivy swung blindly toward the sea, remembering her stepsister's face that day.

Kay had shown up at Ivy's apartment hours ahead of their scheduled appointment at the fertility clinic.

"Everything's changed," she'd said desperately. "My doctor says my eggs are no good. There's no point in implanting them inside you."

Ivy had taken Kay in her arms, patted her back, said she was sorry even as a mean little voice inside her whispered *You know you're not really sorry, you're relieved. Carrying a baby, even one that wasn't actually yours, would have been agony to give up.*

"Oh, Ivy," Kay had sobbed, "what am I going to do? You have to help me!"

"I wish I could but—"

Kay had raised her face. Amazingly her tears had not spoiled her makeup.

"Do you?" she'd said. "Do you really wish you could help me?"

And she'd laid out a plan so detailed, so complete, only a fool—a fool like Ivy—would have believed she'd just come up with it.

Ivy had listened. Halfway through, she'd raised her hands in horror.

"No! Kay, I can't do that! You can't really ask me to—"

Kay's eyes had darkened. "So much for all these years you've told me how grateful you were I took you out of that foster home."

"Of course I'm grateful! But—"

"Out of a situation you'd created."

"I didn't. I didn't!"

"Of course you did," Kay had said coldly. "Flirting with that man. Hanging all over him."

"I never did! I was just a kid. He—he hurt me, Kay!"

"Spare me the sob story," Kay had snapped. "What counts is that I was your lifeline and now, when I ask you to be mine, you look at me as if I'm the devil incarnate and you whimper 'no, I can't!' Is that your idea of how to repay a debt?"

"Kay. Please. Listen to me. What you're asking—"

"What I'm asking for is what you owe me, Ivy. You're always saying I saved your life. Well, now you owe me mine."

It had gone on for hours, Kay talking about what she'd done for Ivy, how Ivy owed her everything, Ivy saying no, no—

In the end, she'd finally given in even though she knew it was wrong, knew she was taking the first step toward breaking her own heart, knew she could not imagine how she would ever give up a baby conceived with a sperm-filled condom, with a syringe, both conveniently tucked inside a little box her stepsister had produced...

"Glyka mou?"

Ivy looked up. Damian smiled as he walked toward her. He was shirtless, barefoot; he wore only denim shorts. His jaw was stubbled because today was Saturday and he hadn't shaved…

Her heart rose into her throat.

How she loved him!

And how cruelly she was deceiving him.

She wore his ring now—a diamond so magnificent it made her breath catch just to look at it. A tiny gold shield that bore his family crest—a lance, a shield and, she now knew, an ancient Minoan bull—dangled from a delicate chain around her neck. Their wedding day was only a week away—and she was still living a lie.

Tears welled in her eyes just as Damian reached her.

"Hey," he said, taking her in his arms, "sweetheart, what's wrong?"

Everything, she thought, everything was wrong! What would he think of her when he knew exactly why she'd been afraid of sex? When he knew the truth about the baby?

"Ivy? *Kardia mou,* tell me what makes you weep."

She couldn't do it. Not yet.

"I'm just—I'm happy, that's all," she whispered, burying her face against his shoulder.

Damian held her close, kissing her hair, her temple, rocking her gently against him…

Aware, in every fiber of his being, she was not telling him the truth.

Yes, his Ivy was happy. He knew it because he was happy, too, though "happy" was far too small a word for what he felt.

He was ecstatic.

Love, commitment, the Big M word had always seemed meant for others. He was not ready to settle down and have children, or even tie himself to one woman.

Then Ivy came along, and all of that changed.

He loved looking up on a Sunday morning to see her biting her lip as she worked a crossword puzzle. Loved the sound of her laughter when a wave caught him and soaked him from head to toe.

Loved the way she fit into his arms when he took her dancing at the little jazz club on the seedy edge of Piraeus, the way she closed her eyes and let the music wash over her.

He loved waking with her in his arms and falling asleep with her in them at night.

That his child was in her womb was icing on the cake.

It wasn't her child, not biologically, and yes, he wished it were, but the other day, when a tiny foot or maybe an elbow had jabbed against his palm, he'd suddenly thought, *Ivy is the reason this precious life exists.*

And he'd imagined his son slipping from her womb, feeding greedily from her breast, and his heart had filled with almost unimaginable joy.

"*Glyka mou,*" he'd whispered, "I am so very happy."

And his Ivy had smiled, brought his mouth down to hers, shown him with her lips, her body, that she was happy, too.

Did she really think he would believe she was weeping in his arms now only because she was happy?

Something was troubling her. Something she'd been keeping from him far too long.

Gently he lifted her in his arms and carried her up the beach, to the dark blue awning of the sprawling cabana he'd had built after he'd inherited Minos and started spending most of his time on the island. He sat her in a lounge chair, went inside the cabana, brought out a box of tissues and blotted her eyes, held one to her nose.

"Blow."

She did. He almost laughed that his elegant Ivy could sound like a honking goose but a man who laughed when his woman wept deserved whatever punishment he got in return.

After a while, her tears stopped.

"Better?"

She nodded.

"Good." Damian squatted in front of her and took her hands in his. "Now, tell me why you weep." He brushed her mouth with his. "The truth, sweetheart. It is time."

Ivy raised her head. "You're right," she said. "It is." She paused. "I—I haven't been honest with you."

Damian nodded. "Go on."

Her face was so pale. He kissed her again, putting his love, his heart, into the kiss.

"Whatever it is," he said softly, "I will still love you."

Would he? She took a steadying breath.

"I've let you think a man—a man hurt me and—and that's the reason I was afraid of sex."

Her words came out in a rush. Damian's smile tilted.

"But?"

"But—but it was my fault," she said, her voice so soft it was barely a whisper. "I mean, he did hurt me, but—"

"If someone hurt you, how could it possibly be your fault?"

She told him.

She started at the beginning. The death of her own father. Her mother marrying Kay's widowed father a couple of years later.

"I loved him almost as much as I'd loved my real father," she said. Her voice trembled. "So when he died—when they both died, my mom and my stepfather—"

"Ah, sweetheart. Stop if it hurts you to talk about it."

"You need to know, Damian. I—I need to tell you."

He nodded. "I'm listening."

"It was almost unbearable. Thank God I had—I had Kay."

"Kay." His mouth twisted.

"I was ten. She was fourteen. We'd never been close—the age difference, I guess—but when our parents died…" Ivy swallowed hard. "They put us into foster care. Together. And Kay was—she was—"

"Your lifeline?"

There it was. That same word Kay had used. Ivy nodded. "Yes."

"And?"

"And—and we were in one place that was okay. In another that wasn't. And—and I was accused of—of taking money—"

Damian tugged Ivy from the chaise into his lap. "You don't have to tell me any of this," he said, trying not to let her hear the anger in his voice, the anger of a man imagining a child dropped into a state system, alone, unwanted—

"I hadn't stolen the money, Damian. I don't know who did, but they—they put me back in the Placement center for a while."

God, his heart was going to break. And he knew, without question, who had stolen the money and let Ivy take the blame.

"And then they placed me with—with a man and a

woman. Not Kay. She'd turned eighteen. She left foster care."

"*Ivy.* I love you. There's no need to—"

"I have to tell you so you'll understand why I—why I agreed to carry Kay's baby."

"And mine," he said softly.

Ivy nodded. "Yes. You have to know, Damian."

"I don't," he said gently, and meant it. "But I can see that you have to tell me."

She nodded again, thankful that he understood.

"So," he said, cupping her face, "tell me, and we can put the past behind us."

Could they? When he knew everything? Ivy prayed he was right.

"They placed me with this couple. She didn't pay any attention to me. Well, she did, but—but he—he was kind to me. He said he'd always wanted a daughter. A little girl of his own. He bought me things. A doll. I was old for dolls but nobody had given me anything since—since our parents' deaths and—"

"And you were grateful," Damian said, and wondered at the coldness stealing into his heart.

"Grateful. And happy, even though I didn't see Kay anymore. I understood," she said quickly, seeing the lift of Damian's eyebrows. "I mean, she was busy. Working. She had friends. She was grown up and I…" Her voice trailed away and then she cleared her throat. "My foster father said he knew I was lonely. He began coming into my room to tuck me in. To kiss me good-night. I thought—I thought he was—he was—"

"What did the bastard do to you?"

She stared at Damian. She had seen him angry, even furious, but she had never seen him like this, his eyes black, his mouth thinned, his hands so tight on her shoulders that she knew his fingers must be leaving bruises on her skin.

"He…" *Oh God. Oh God…* "He raped me."

Damian hit the little table where he'd put the tissue box so hard it almost shattered. His arms went around her; he held her tight against him.

"And—and it was all my fault."

"What?"

"My fault, Damian. I didn't realize it until—until I finally found Kay's phone number and called her, and she came to the house where I lived and I told her what had happened and she made me see that I'd provoked it, that I should never have let him tuck me in or kiss me or even buy me that doll and I *knew* that, all along, I knew it was strange but I just thought—I just thought he liked me. Loved me. That he really wanted to be my father, and—"

Damian kissed her.

There was no other way to stop the racing river of pain-filled words except to cover Ivy's mouth with his and kiss her and kiss her and kiss her until, at last, she began to cry, her tears hot and salty against his lips.

"Ivy," he whispered, "*agapimeni,* my darling, my heart, none of it was your fault. Damn Kay for telling you that it was!"

"It was. I should have known—"

"What? That a monster would take a little girl's grief and use it to slake his sick desires?" Damian rocked her in his arms. "Ivy, sweetheart, no one would ever think what happened was your fault. Surely when you reported it—"

"I didn't."

"What?"

"He said—he said, if I told anyone, he'd deny it. And if—if a doctor examined me, he'd say—he'd say he'd caught me with boys in the neighborhood. And since I'd—I'd already been accused of stealing money, they'd believe him, not me. And I—I knew he was right, that nobody would listen to me—"

Damian pounded his fist against the table again. This time, it shattered and collapsed on the sand.

"Who is this man? Tell me his name. I will kill him!"

"Kay took me to live with her. Do you see? She saved me, Damian. She saved me! If she hadn't taken me from him—"

"She did not save you," he said viciously, his accent thickening, his thoughts coming in Greek instead of English. "She used you, *glyka mou*. She told you—you, a child—that you had caused your own rape."

"She made me see my foolishness, Damian."

"And she waited and waited, your bitch of a stepsister, waited until a time came when she could demand repayment," he said through his teeth because now, finally, he understood why Ivy had agreed to bear his child.

"No." Ivy's voice was a broken whisper. "You don't understand. I owed her for saving me."

Damian fought for control when what he really wanted to do was find the beast who'd done this and kill him. And, *Thee mou,* if Kay were alive…

"Ivy," he said, "listen to me. You saved yourself."

"I didn't. If I'd saved myself, I'd never have let what happened happen."

"Sweetheart. You thought this man loved you as a father. Why would you have ever imagined otherwise?

You were a child. Innocent. Lonely. Alone." He paused, framed her face with his hands, made her meet his gaze. "Kay lied to you. It was never, not even remotely, your fault."

Ivy stared at him. "No?" she whispered.

"No. Absolutely not." He drew a breath. "But she'd planted the seed, and she knew it. So, years later, when she wanted something she knew you would not wish to do—"

"Bearing a baby for her," Ivy said, as the tears flowed down her cheeks. "Oh, Damian, I didn't want to! I said no, I couldn't, I couldn't have a child in my womb, feel it kick, see it born and—and give it up—"

"And she said…" He struggled to keep his tone even. "She said, you owed it to her."

"She said she'd saved me once and now—now I had to save her."

Ivy began to sob. Damian folded her into his arms. There was nothing more to say except one phrase, and he repeated it over and over and over, until, finally, her weeping stopped.

"I love you, Ivy," he repeated. "I love you with all my heart."

She drew back and looked at him. "Even after this?"

"Especially after this," he said softly. "Because now I know what true goodness is in your heart, that you would agree to make such a sacrifice for someone you loved."

"Damian. There's—there's more."

His mouth was gentle on hers.

"Later."

"No. No, now. I have to tell you now."

"Later," he said, and kissed her again, and then he

lay her back against the warm sand, under the warm sun, and when he made love to her this time, Ivy wept again.

With happiness.

CHAPTER TWELVE

THEY spent the afternoon on the beach.

Damian had arranged everything. The picnic lunch brought them by Esias. The chilled champagne.

When the sun began its soft pink, purple and violet drop into the sea, Ivy smiled and asked if Damian had arranged for that, too.

"Because the sunset is perfect," she said softly, resting her head on his shoulder as she stood in the curve of his arm, "just like this entire day's been perfect. It's beautiful enough to put a lump in my throat."

"You are what is beautiful, *kardia mou*," he said, drawing her closer. "And I love you with all my heart."

She hesitated. "Even after what I told you?"

"*Neh*. Yes. I told you, especially after that. I only wish it had never happened to you, sweetheart. The ugliness of it. The pain—"

"You took it all away, that first time we made love."

Damian turned her toward him. "Ivy. I want you to promise something to me."

She smiled. "Just ask."

"Never be afraid to share anything with me, *glyka mou*. Your hopes, your dreams…" He ran his thumb lightly over her mouth. "Your darkest secrets," he said quietly. "I will love you, always. Do you understand?"

And, just that quickly, she remembered what she had tried to forget during the long, glorious afternoon.

The final truth.

The last secret.

How would he deal with it? He'd understood why she'd agreed to carry a child of Kay's, but could he understand this?

Not even she understood it. Yes, Kay had been frantic. Yes, there'd been no time to think. And, yes, considering her own plans for the future, her conviction she would never want to make love with a man, that she'd surely never, ever marry, it had made a crazy kind of sense…

"Ivy. Why such a sad look in your beautiful eyes?"

Ivy ran the tip of her tongue over her lips. "There's one last thing I have to tell you, Damian. I tried, hours ago, but—"

"But," he said huskily, "I was more interested in making love than listening."

He smiled. She did, too. Then she rose on her toes and pressed her lips to his.

"Let's go back to our bedroom."

"A fine idea."

"I'll shower, and then—"

"*We'll* shower," he said, with the kind of sexy look that always turned her inside out. "And then we'll have dinner on the terrace in the garden." He took her hands and raised them to his lips. "And you can tell me this last secret so I can kiss you and tell you that whatever it is, it changes nothing."

"I love you so much," Ivy said, her voice breaking. "So much…"

One last, deep kiss. Then they walked to the road, where Damian had parked the Jeep, and drove to what had now become home.

They showered together, and made love, and dried each other off and, inevitably, made love again.

Then they dressed.

Ivy put on a classically long, slender black gown with thin straps. "Look at how my belly shows," she said, laughing, and Damian quickly knelt and put his lips to the bump.

Maybe, she thought, holding her breath as she looked down at him, maybe what she had to tell him would go well.

He rose to his feet and took her hand. "You are so beautiful," he said softly.

She smiled and looked at him in his white jacket and black trousers. "So are you."

He laughed, even blushed. "Men can't be beautiful."

He was wrong. Her Damian *was* beautiful. In face and body. In heart and soul. And yes, he *would* understand this, her last secret.

He had to.

Damian led her down the wide marble stairs, through the oldest part of the palace to a columned terrace in a garden that overlooked the sea.

The table was lit by tall tapers in silver holders. Flowers—white orchids, crimson roses, pale pink tulips—overflowed from a magnificent urn. Champagne stood chilling in a silver bucket and a fat ivory moon sailed over the Aegean…

And standing beside the table, smiling, looking even more stunning than in the past, stood Kay.

Ivy cried out in shock. Damian said a single sharp word. Kay's smile grew brighter.

"Isn't anyone going to say hello?"

"Your Highness." Esias, standing near Kay, all but wrung his hands. "I could not keep the lady out, sir. I am sorry. So sorry—"

Damian dismissed his houseman with a curt nod. His hand tightened on Ivy's but, after a shocked couple of seconds, she tore free of his grasp and ran to her stepsister.

"Ohmygod, Kay! Kay, you're alive!"

"Bright as always, Ivy. That, at least, hasn't changed."

Ivy reached out to hug her but Kay sidestepped, her eyes locked to Damian's.

"And you," she said, "were always a fast worker. I see you didn't waste any time, replacing me."

"Obviously," Damian said, his voice cold, "you didn't die in that car crash."

Kay laughed. "Obviously not."

"Did you have amnesia?" Ivy said. "You must have, otherwise—"

"People have amnesia in soap operas," Kay said. "Not in real life. I went off a cliff into Long Island Sound. Everyone thought I'd drowned."

"They declared you dead," Damian said in that same icy voice.

"Well, I wasn't. I washed ashore a couple of miles away. Carlos's uncle—he's with the government—and a discreet doctor kept the story out of the papers." Her hand went to her face. "I had some bad cuts—it took a lot of plastic surgery—but I'm all healed now." She tilted her head to catch the candlelight. "What do you think, Damian darling? As good as new, or even better?"

"What do you want, Kay?"

"What do I want?" Her smile hardened as she moved slowly across the terrace to where he stood. "Why, I want my life back, of course." She stopped in front of him and lay a hand on his chest. "I want you, darling. A wedding ring. And that delightful little lump I see in my dear sister's belly, as soon as it's born."

Damian caught her wrist and drew her hand to her side.

"Sorry, but you're not getting any of those things." He stepped past her and put his arm around Ivy, who was trembling. "Ivy and I are getting married."

"Ah. You're angry about Carlos. It didn't mean a thing, darling. You're the only one I ever loved."

"You've never loved anyone in your life," he said coldly.

Kay's eyes narrowed. "You don't understand, Damian. I'm back. Whatever little trap my dear sister sprang on you has no meaning now."

Ivy stiffened. "I didn't—"

"Hush, *glyka mou*. There's no need to explain. Kay and I never had marriage plans."

"We certainly did!"

"We did not. *You* had plans, Kay, the first time you told me you were pregnant." Damian's voice turned even more frigid. "It was a lie."

"It wasn't. My doctor—"

"I've seen your doctor. You were never pregnant. And you and I never discussed artificial insemination."

"That's all in the past. I'm pregnant now. I mean, Ivy is. With…" Her eyes flashed to Ivy. "With your child and mine. She did tell you that, Damian, didn't she? That she's carrying your baby? My baby?"

Damian's jaw tightened. "Ivy carries my son." He put his hand on Ivy's round belly. "*Our* son. Hers and mine."

Kay's face paled. "What do you mean? Ivy? What did you—"

"Nothing," Ivy said desperately. "But I will. I will! Kay, you can't just come back after all this time and—and—"

"I can," Kay said fiercely. "I have. And I want what's mine."

"Biology doesn't make for motherhood," Damian snapped. "You were alive, yet you didn't see fit to tell me that you were. You didn't see fit to tell Ivy, even though you knew she was pregnant." His mouth twisted. "You have given up any right to this child."

"I've given up nothing! Not you. Not the baby. And nothing you say or do will change that."

Damian touched Ivy's cheek with a gentle hand. Then he stepped away from her and walked slowly toward Kay.

"I am not a fifteen-year-old girl," he said softly. "I am not a frightened child who will bend to your will. Your lies cannot make me think you are anything more than you are. An evil, selfish woman."

"Ah." Kay laughed. "So, she told you her sad story, hmm? About how the big, bad man molested her?" Her smile vanished; she shot Ivy a look of pure evil. "Liar! Why not tell him the truth? That you were a seductive little bitch—"

"Watch your mouth," Damian snarled.

"A seductive little piece of tail." She whirled toward

Damian. "It's the truth and she knows it. First she seduced my father—"

"No!" Ivy shook her head. "Kay. You know I never—"

"Seduced him. Batted her lashes. Crept into his lap. Told him how much she loved him—"

"I did love him! I was a little girl—"

"And then he died. Her mother died. They put us in foster care and she stole money."

"I didn't steal anything! Kay, I beg you, don't do this!"

"I got out as soon as I hit eighteen. And my dear step-sister lucked out. They put her in another home with a man like my father. And when the poor bastard finally took what she'd been waving under his nose—"

"Paliogyneko!" Damian grabbed Kay's arm and jerked her forward. "Get out! Get the hell out of my home. If I ever see you again, I'll—"

"My God, you bought her story! She told you he raped her. And you believed it!"

"Kay," Ivy pleaded, "stop! We're sisters. I always loved you—"

"Stepsisters. And your supposed love doesn't mean a thing to me." Kay spun toward Damian. "What else did she tell you? That she's been scared of sex ever since?" She threw back her head and laughed. "Look at her, Damian. Think about the life she's led. She moves in a world where people trade in flesh. Where women sell cars by making men get hard-ons. Do you really think my dear stepsister is a sweet portrait of virtue?"

Ivy shook her head. "Damian. Don't listen to her. I've never—"

"You want to know what a good, kind little innocent

my stepsister is?" Kay flashed a vicious smile. "That baby in her belly?"

"Kay. Oh, please, please, please, Kay, don't do this!"

"You remember that charge at Tiffany? That I let you think was mine? It wasn't. I spent it on her. On Ivy. She wanted a necklace. Diamonds. Rubies. I bought it for her."

"Damian. God, she's lying!"

"It was the price for the baby." Kay paused, threw a triumphant look at Ivy, then turned back to Damian. "Because, you see, she's right. I *did* lie, darling. That baby inside her? It's yours, all right…but it's yours and Ivy's."

Ivy swung toward Damian, saw the color leach from his face.

"What?" he said, his voice a husky rasp.

"I found out I couldn't use my own eggs. So I said, Ivy, let me use yours. And she said—"

"Damian. Listen to me. It wasn't like that. It wasn't—"

"I said, how about letting me put my lover's sperm inside you? How about conceiving a baby for me? And she said, is he rich? And I said, yes, he's a royal. And she said, how much can you get out of him? And I said, well, I couldn't come right out and ask for money but I could buy her something she wanted, and she said, how about this necklace at Tiffany? And that was enough until she thought I was dead and she figured, hey, no more middleman. I can collect all the bucks, marry Kay's prince and live the life I've always wanted."

Ivy saw the horror in Damian's face. She turned and ran.

No footsteps came after her.

No footsteps. No Damian. Kay's story was a hideous blend of truth and lies and he'd believed it.

She raced through the vast rooms of the ancient palace, through the entry hall. Esias called to her but she ran past him, out the door, down the steps, along the road that led to the airstrip, her breath sobbing in her throat.

"Ivy!"

She heard the footsteps now. Heard Damian's voice and knew she could not face him. She hadn't told him the final truth for just this reason, because she'd feared what she'd see in his eyes, a look that asked how a woman could agree to conceive a baby and give it up.

"Ivy!"

Weeping, she ran faster. A high-heeled sandal fell off and she kicked away the other one, felt the gravel cutting her flesh and knew the pain of that was nothing compared to the pain in her heart.

"Ivy, damn it…"

Hard arms closed around her.

"No," she shouted. "No, Damian, don't—"

He swung her toward her, his face harsh and angular in the moonlight.

"Ivy," he said—and kissed her.

Kissed her and kissed her, and at first she fought him and then, oh then, she sobbed his name and leaned into him, wound her arms around his neck and kissed him with all the love in her heart.

"*Glyka mou,*" he said, his voice shaky, "where were you going?"

"Away. From here. From you. From all the lies—"

He caught her face in his hands, kissed her again and again.

"I love you," he said, "and you love me. Those are not lies."

"How can you love me now that you know—"

"Don't you remember what I said this afternoon? That you would tell me your last secret and I would tell you I loved you? That I would love you forever?"

"But the baby—"

"Our baby," he said, a smile lighting his face. "Truly our baby, sweetheart, *neh?*"

"Yes. Oh, yes. Our baby, Damian. It's always been ours."

"You did it out of love for Kay."

She nodded. "Yes. No. I thought I did it for her—but I did it for me, too. I was sure I would never marry. Never have sex. Never have children. And I thought, if I do this, if I have this baby, I'll be its aunt. And its mother. In my heart, I'll always be its mother, even if the baby never knows."

"Sweetheart. You're trembling." Damian stripped off his jacket and wrapped her in it. "Come back to the palace."

"No. Not until I've told you everything." Ivy took a deep breath. "So—so I let Kay—I let her do the procedure. And it took. I missed my very next period—" Her voice broke. "And that was when I knew I'd made a terrible mistake, that I would never be able to give away the baby." Her hand went to her belly. "My baby."

"And mine," Damian said softly.

Ivy nodded. "My baby, and yours. I called Kay. I told her. I said she had to tell you the truth. She said it was too late, that we'd made a bargain. I said I would never give up the baby. And then—and then—"

"And then," he said gently, "you thought she'd died."

"Yes."

"So, you waited for me to contact you because you thought I knew all about the baby."

"Not all. I mean, I thought you knew I was carrying your baby but Kay had made it clear she didn't want you to know it was my egg, not hers, that had been fertilized."

"But I didn't contact you."

"No. I assumed it was because you were devastated, losing Kay. That you'd adored her, just the way she'd said you did. And I thought—I thought I owed it to you to let you know the baby was fine, that you were going to be a father, and—and—"

"And?" he said softly.

Ivy shuddered. "And, I hadn't figured out the rest. How to tell you I was the baby's real mother. When to tell you. And then you said you didn't know anything about a baby, that I was up to some kind of awful scam, and I didn't know what to do—"

"Come here," Damian said gruffly, and he gathered her into his arms and kissed her. "Ivy," he whispered, when finally he raised his head, *"glyka mou,* I am so sorry."

"For what?"

"For all you've been through. I love you, *agapimeni.* I love you with all my heart, and I promise to spend the rest of my life making sure you know it. Will you let me?"

Ivy laughed. Or maybe she wept. She couldn't tell anymore because her joy was so complete.

"Only if you let me do the same thing for you," she said, and kissed him.

They made their way back to the palace, arms around each other. At the front steps, Ivy paused.

"Kay?" she said questioningly.

"Gone," Damian said flatly. "She came by boat, or maybe by broom, for all I know, and she's gone back the same way."

"It breaks my heart," Ivy whispered. "To think she hates me enough to have told such lies…" She took a deep breath. "She's still my stepsister. I can't help but hope that someday—"

Damian drew her close. "Anything is possible."

But he knew, even as he said it, that of all the things that had been said on this night, that was the biggest lie of all.

The wedding was on Damian's yacht, anchored just off Minos.

The sun was bright, the sea was wine-dark and the bride, of course, was beautiful.

Some of the models Ivy had worked with for years were there, as was her agent.

There were two best men instead of one. Nicolo Barbieri—Prince Nicolo Barbieri—and Prince Lucas Reyes.

Nicolo was there with his beautiful wife, Aimee, and their adorable baby.

Lucas was alone, by choice.

"Bring a date," Damian had told his pal but Lucas knew better. A man took a woman to a wedding, she got ideas.

Useless ideas, he thought firmly, because as happy as Nicolo was, as happy as Damian was, they could keep the marriage thing for themselves.

Not me, he told himself as he watched Damian kiss his glowing bride, never me.

But never, as everyone knows, is a very, very long time…

THE SPANISH PRINCE'S
VIRGIN BRIDE

BY
SANDRA MARTON

CHAPTER ONE

His name was Lucas Reyes.

At least, that was the name he preferred.

He was also His Highness Prince Lucas Carlos Alessandro Reyes Sanchez of Andalusia and Castile, heir to a throne that had ceased to exist centuries ago, which made him the great-great-great-*Dios,* too many "greats" to count-grandson of a king who had been among the conquistadores who tamed a distant land.

That land was America and as far as Lucas could tell, once you reached Texas you knew that those conquistadores only thought they had tamed the land.

Or so it seemed on this hot summer afternoon.

Lucas was driving his rented car along an unpaved excuse for a road beneath the glare of a merciless sun. Rain clouds hung on the distant horizon; at first, he'd foolishly thought they would bring some relief but the clouds seemed painted on an endless blue sky.

Nothing moved, except for the car, and the engine seemed to require more effort to manage even that.

Lucas tightened his hands on the steering wheel and mouthed a short, succinct oath.

He was on his way to a place called El Rancho Grande.

His grandfather had been in communication with its owner, Aloysius McDonough, who had assured them, via e-mail, this road would lead straight to it.

And pigs can fly, Lucas thought dourly.

The road was taking him nowhere except further into sagebrush and tumbleweed, and the only thing he'd seen thus far that was close to *grande* was an enormous rattlesnake.

The sight of the snake had sent Lucas's mistress into near-hysteria.

"A python," she'd screeched. "Oh God, Lucas, a python!"

He thought of pointing out that pythons didn't live in North America, then decided against it. Delia wouldn't give a damn if the creature curled by the side of the road was an alligator. It would be just one more thing to gripe about.

She'd spent most of the first hour telling him the landscape was dull and the rental car was horrible.

At least they could agree on that. One glance at a map and Lucas had told his PA to arrange for a truck or an SUV but the girl behind the rental counter insisted his PA had booked what looked to Lucas like an anchovy tin on wheels. He'd protested but it got him nowhere.

The car was all they had available.

"But we might have something else tomorrow," the girl had said brightly.

And spend more time on this fool's errand? Lucas snorted. That wasn't an option. So he'd signed for the anchovy tin, then listened to Delia whine when he said there was no room for her overnight suitcase, hanging garment bag, bulky makeup and jewelry cases in the miniscule trunk.

"We're not going to be more than a few hours at the most," he'd said impatiently.

Still, she'd protested and he'd finally told her she had

two choices. She could leave everything on his plane or she could shut up and get into the car with whatever fit.

She'd gotten into the car, but she had not shut up. She'd complained and complained about the stuff she'd had to leave behind, about the vehicle, about the road, and now she'd taken up a new refrain.

"When will we get there?"

He'd gone from saying *Soon* to *In a little while* to *We will get there when we get there,* the words delivered through gritted teeth.

"But when?" she was in the middle of saying when the anchovy tin disguised as a car groaned in fishy agony and came to a stop.

Then there was only silence.

"Lucas, why did we stop? Why did you turn off the air conditioner? When will we get there? Lucas? When—"

He swung toward Delia. Under his cool hazel glower, she sank back in her seat. Still, she couldn't resist one last comment.

"I don't know what we're doing in a place like this anyway," she said petulantly.

That was another thing they agreed on. The road, the car, and now this.

What in hell *were* they doing here?

Actually the answer was simple. Delia was here because Lucas was supposed to have taken her to the Hamptons this weekend. When he told her he couldn't, she'd pouted until he said he'd take her to Texas with him.

Lucas was here because his grandfather had suddenly told him that he was expected to meet with Aloysius McDonough at a Texas ranch called El Rancho Grande.

"Who is this man?" Lucas had asked. "I've never heard of him or his ranch."

Felix said that McDonough raised Andalusians.

"And?" Lucas asked, because surely there was more to the request than that. El Rancho Reyes raised some of the finest Andalusians in the world, surely the finest in Spain. If a pretentiously named ranch in Texas raised them, too, he'd have heard of it.

"And," Felix said, "he has something that I hope will interest you."

"A horse?" Lucas said in thinly veiled disbelief. "A stud?"

His grandfather had smiled. Actually, he'd chuckled. Lucas's eyebrows lifted.

"Have I said something amusing, Grandfather?"

"Not at all. It's just… No. Not a stud."

"You want me to look at an Andalusian mare on a ranch no one's ever heard of?"

"She's not Andalusian."

Dios, was Felix's mind starting to go? "But Andalusians are what we breed," Lucas said gently.

The old man glared at him. "Do I seem senile to you, boy? I know what we breed. I have been assured that she has excellent lineage and fine conformation."

"There are mares in Spain with those qualities."

Felix had nodded. "There are. But thus far, none has what I consider enough intelligence, beauty and heart to improve our line."

Since Lucas ran El Rancho Reyes and had been running it for a decade, he was surprised by that pronouncement.

"I didn't know you were looking, Grandfather."

"I have been looking for years, Lucas."

Another cryptic statement. The ranch had several excellent mares. In fact, Lucas had bought another one only recently…and yet, Felix sounded certain.

Lucas looked at his grandfather. *Do I look senile?* he'd said, but Felix had just passed his eighty-fifth birthday…

"Ah, Lucas, you are as transparent now as you were when you were a boy, trying to convince me to let you break your first horse." Felix chuckled and wrapped an arm around Lucas's shoulders. "I promise you, *mi hijo,* my mind is perfectly clear. You must trust me in this. I am not sending you on a wild-goose chase."

Lucas had sighed. "You really want me to go all the way to Texas for something we don't need?"

"If we did not need it, I would not ask you to go."

"I don't agree."

Felix had raised one bushy white eyebrow. "Did I ask you to agree?"

That had ended the discussion. Nobody gave Lucas Reyes orders but he loved his grandfather with all his heart. The old man had all but raised him and provided the only love Lucas had known.

So Lucas had shrugged and said, *si*, he would go to Texas even though he did not deserve such a punishment.

He'd meant it lightly but for some reason, Felix had laughed as if it were the best joke he'd ever heard.

"Lucas," he'd said, "I promise you, what awaits you in Texas is precisely what you deserve."

Now, looking at the empty road, the empty sky, the blinding sun and the woman sulking beside him, Lucas decided that his grandfather was wrong.

Nobody deserved this.

"Aren't you going to start the car?"

Delia's voice was fraught with indignation. Lucas didn't waste time answering. Instead he turned the key. Tromped on the gas pedal. Turned the key again…

Nada.

Muttering something that would have delighted the street urchins in Seville, he released the hood latch, opened the door and stepped outside.

The heat hit him like a fist even though he'd expected it.

Unlike Delia, who was decked out in a gender-challenged designer's misbegotten notion of the Old West, Lucas had dressed for the realities of a Texas summer.

Boots, of course. Not shiny and new but comfortable and well-worn. What else did a man wear when he was going to spend the day ankle-deep in horse apples? Boots and jeans, faded and washed to the softness of silk, and a pale gray chambray shirt, collar open, sleeves rolled up.

In other words, he was sensibly dressed. It didn't matter. One step from the car and he was drenched in sweat.

"Ohmygod," Delia screeched dramatically, "I'll burn up if you don't shut that door!"

Lucas obliged, slamming it with enough force that the vehicle shuddered. Jaw set, he stalked to the hood, lifted it and peered inside. Then he got down in the dirt and looked at the car's undercarriage. Neither action told him anything more than he already knew.

This sad excuse for a car was roadkill.

He dug his cell phone from his pocket, flipped it open and saw those dreaded words. *No Service.*

"Mierda," he muttered and banged his fist on Delia's window. "Open the door!"

She glared and cracked it an ungracious inch. "What?"

"Do you have your cell phone?"

"Why?"

Could a man's back teeth really shatter if he ground them together too hard?

"Do you have it or not?"

A put-upon sigh before she reached into the doll-size purse that hung from her shoulder.

The purse was white leather.

Everything she wore was white leather. The ridiculous sombrero perched on her artfully-coiffed hair. The tiny fringed vest. The tight pants. The boots with four inch stiletto heels. She looked ridiculous, Lucas thought and realized, with icy certainty, that what had been dawning on him for a while was true.

Their affair had run its predictable course. As soon as they got back to New York, he'd end it.

As if she'd read his mind, Delia all but slapped the phone into his outstretched palm. A glance told him she used a different wireless provider. Maybe there was hope.

At least, when he flipped the phone open, he didn't see the ominous *No Service*.

But he couldn't get a transmission bar, either.

He held the phone at arm's length. At shoulder height. He went through the inane dance steps of the frustrated wireless user.

Nothing.

Cursing under his breath, he went to the front of the car. To the rear. Trotted up the road. Down the road. Stepped across the narrow, gravel-filled culvert that ran alongside it. Stepped back into the road. Into the middle of the road…

Miracle of miracles, a bar blinked to life on the screen.

Lucas grinned, pumped his fist in the air—and lost the bar. Easy, he told himself, easy. Move an inch at a time. Watch that screen…

Yes!

The bar was back. And another. And another…

"Look ooouut…"

His head came up. A horse the size of a brontosaurus

was galloping toward him, a rider hunched over its neck. He saw the animal's dilated nostrils, heard the pounding of its hooves...

"Damn it, look *ooouut*..."

The yell came from the rider. Lucas jumped back, stumbled and rolled into the culvert as the horse thundered past with barely an inch to spare.

Lucas shot to his feet. He shouted; the rider looked back. Lucas saw a worn ball cap. A grungy T-shirt. Jeans. Boots.

And a boy's startled face.

The rider was a kid, damn it, skinny and long-legged, riding without a saddle or stirrups. Was riding people down what passed for fun in this anteroom of hell?

Lucas shook his fist. Let fly with a string of Spanish obscenities.

The kid laughed.

Fury welled in Lucas's gut. If only the damned car worked! He'd jump into it, gun the engine, catch up to the horse. Pull the reckless brat off its back and teach him a lesson!

A gust of wind swept down from out of nowhere, plucked at the dust rising in the horse's wake. When it settled, horse and rider were gone.

"Lucas? Are you all right?"

He shot a look at the car. The near-collision had, at least, driven Delia out of it.

"I'm fine," he growled.

"That horrid animal! I thought it had killed you."

Lucas dusted off his jeans. "And you wondered," he said tersely, "how in hell you'd get out of here on your own."

"You're in a horrible mood today, Lucas. I was worried about you. Yes, perhaps I did wonder..." Delia's eyes widened. She giggled.

"You find this amusing?"

"Well, no. It's just that you have something in your hair…"

He reached up. Closed his fingers around a handful of tumbleweed and threw it aside.

"I'm delighted to be the source of your entertainment."

"Don't be such a grouch." Delia slapped her hands on her hips. "You can't blame me for—"

"No." His voice was flat as he walked toward her. "I blame only myself for our situation, Delia. Not you."

Her expression brightened. "I'm glad you understand."

Lucas reached into the car for his hat. Then he patted his thigh.

"Put your foot here."

Delia gave a breathy laugh. "Lucas," she purred, "do you really think this is the place to—"

"Your foot," he said impatiently.

Smiling, she leaned back against the door, raised one leg and put it against his thigh. He grunted, took her foot in his hands and broke off the heel of her boot.

"Hey!" Delia jerked her leg back. "What are you doing? Do you have any idea what I paid for these boots?"

"No," he said bluntly, "but I will, once I see my Amex bill this month." His eyes met hers. "Or are you going to tell me I didn't pay for that ridiculous outfit you're wearing?"

"Ridiculous? I'll have you know—"

Lucas squatted down, grabbed her other foot and snapped the heel off that boot, too.

"Now you'll be able to walk."

"Walk?" Her voice rose. "Walk where? I am not walking anywhere in this heat, on this road, with pythons and wild horses and crazy people all around… Lucas? Lucas, where are you going?"

He didn't answer. After a moment, she came trotting up alongside him.

"I hate this place," she muttered. "Never take me to Texas again!"

He would never take her anywhere again, he thought grimly. That was something else on which they could agree.

Twenty minutes and a thousand complaints later, he heard the grumble of an engine. A red pickup appeared on the horizon.

"Thank God," Delia said dramatically, and sank down on the edge of the road.

Lucas stepped into the truck's path. It was going to stop, one way or another. The hot, endless trudge to nowhere was bad enough but if he had to spend another minute listening to Delia...

The truck slowed. Stopped. The driver's door opened. A kid stepped out and Lucas felt his blood pressure rise. Was it the one who'd almost ridden him down?

It wasn't.

The rider had been slender with big dark eyes and black curls tumbling over his forehead from under his hat. This boy was redheaded and chunky.

"Howdy."

Flaking letters on the truck's door spelled out El Rancho Grande. El Rancho Bankrupto, judging by the condition of the ancient vehicle.

"Heard you folks might need a ride."

"And just who, precisely, did you hear that from?" Lucas said tightly. "A boy riding a war horse?"

The kid chuckled. "That's funny, mister."

"Everything around here is funny," Lucas said, his tone low and dangerous.

"I didn't mean it that way, I only meant—"

"For goodness' sakes," Delia said sharply, "will you

stop being so touchy, Lucas? Of course we need a ride."
She shot a look at the truck. "But not in that—that thing."

The boy was looking at Delia as if he'd never seen
anything like her before—which, Lucas thought grimly, he
undoubtedly had not.

"Get in the truck, Delia."

Delia snorted. "I am not getting into that—"

Lucas said something ugly and hoisted her as if she
were a sack of oats. She yelped as he dumped her unceremoniously on the truck's bench seat.

"In all honesty, Lucas—"

"In all honesty, Delia," he said coldly, "as soon as we reach
a telephone, I'll arrange for a car to take you to the airport."

"We're going back to the city?"

"You're going," he said. "Just you."

Delia opened her mouth. So did the kid who'd climbed
behind the wheel. Lucas glared at them both as he got into
the truck and slammed the door.

"Just drive," he told the boy.

Delia's eyes burned with anger but she didn't argue. The
kid was just as smart. He gulped, muttered, "Yessir," and
hit the gas.

Two hours later, Lucas was feeling a little better.

He'd finally arrived at El Rancho Grande—and yes, the
name was definitely a poor choice but he was stuck here
until the rancher he'd come all this distance to see showed
up. They'd had an appointment but evidently appointments
were just another source of amusement in this part of Texas.

At least Delia was gone. That was something to celebrate.

He'd tried to phone for a limo or a taxi and both the boy
and an old man who'd introduced himself as the ranch
foreman had looked at him as if he were crazy.

"We ain't got nothin' like that here," the foreman said.

Delia had batted her lashes. "I guess you'll just have to keep me," she'd said, though her sweet tone had not matched the sly smile on her lips.

He'd sooner have kept the rattler they'd seen on the road, especially when the rental company said they couldn't get a replacement vehicle to him until the next morning.

Bad enough he'd be stuck here overnight. He sure as hell wasn't going to spend it fending off Delia.

So he'd offered the kid with the truck a sum that had made the kid's eyes bulge to retrieve her luggage from the car, then drive her to the airport. Then he'd closed his ears to what Delia wished him and watched the pickup bounce away.

The foreman had watched, too.

"Should be an interestin' trip for the lady," he'd said mildly.

"Should be interesting for both of them," Lucas had replied, and the old man had grinned.

Then Lucas had asked the million-dollar question. Where was Aloysius McDonough? He might as well have asked about Godzilla, considering the old man's wide-eyed reaction.

"You come here to see Mr. McDonough?"

No, Lucas had thought, I came for the scenery. Instead he'd smiled politely, or as politely as possible, all things considered.

"*Si*. He is expecting me."

"Do tell," the foreman had answered, spitting a thin brown stream of tobacco juice into the dry dirt. "Well, only thing I can suggest is that you hang around until this evenin'."

"McDonough will be back by then?"

The foreman shrugged. "Just wait until evenin', is what I'm sayin'. We got a guest room you can have, if you ain't particular."

"I'm sure it will be fine."

The foreman had led Lucas into the house, through rooms that were shabby but clean to one with a narrow bed and a view of the unchanging land that stretched endlessly toward the horizon.

"You want anythin', just holler."

"I'm fine," Lucas had answered. Then his eyes had narrowed. "Come to think of it... Do you have a boy working here?"

The old man shifted his wad of chewing tobacco from one side of his jaw to the other.

"Ain't you just seen Davey?"

"Not him. A different kid. One who rides a black stallion without giving a damn for anybody else."

Nope, the foreman said, he and Davey were the only hands.

Then he'd cackled like a deranged duck. Lucas could hear the sound of his laughter even after he shuffled out of the room.

Now, standing on a sagging porch, Lucas sighed. Who knew what passed for humor in a godforsaken place like this?

Besides, what did it matter? This time tomorrow, he'd be on his way home.

Assuming, he thought irritably, Aloysius McDonough showed up. Where in hell was he? Where was the supposed wonder-mare? Truth was, he doubted if there were any horses here. The corrals were empty; the outbuildings were all in bad shape. The breeze that had come up might just—

What was that?

Lucas cocked his head. He could hear a sound on the wind. A horse. Yes. A whinny. Faint, but distinct.

Maybe McDonough was back.

The sooner he saw the mare—assuming one even existed—and told a couple of polite lies about what a fine animal she was but how, unfortunately, he wasn't buying horses right now, blah blah blah…

Definitely the sooner he got this over with, the better.

Lucas stepped off the porch and started briskly toward the outbuildings. He was right about their condition. The first, a storage shed, was on the verge of collapse. The barn that came next wasn't any better.

The third building was a stable, in better shape than the other two. It needed paint and some of the boards would have benefited from a hammer and nails but when he peered in the open door, he saw the signs a horseman learns to recognize as evidence of responsible care.

The floor was clean, the two empty stalls to his left were well-swept. A stack of buckets stood beside a hose and across from stacked bales of hay.

There it was again. The soft whinny of a horse. Yes, there was an animal here.

The mare, he hoped.

Mystery solved.

Lucas hesitated. Protocol demanded a man wait to be asked onto another man's property. He frowned. To hell with protocol, which also demanded that McDonough should have been here to greet his guest.

Quietly, so he wouldn't spook the mare, he stepped inside the stable, looked past the row of empty stalls and saw a tail, a rump…

The horse danced back and Lucas's eyebrows rose.

This was not a mare. Hell, no. It was a stallion. No doubt about that, judging from the rest of what he could see.

Lucas's eyes narrowed. Not just a stallion. A black stallion.

He took a step forward. A floorboard creaked under his

weight and the stallion snorted. Metal tinkled. The animal must still be bridled and tossing its head.

"Easy," a voice said softly. "Easy, baby."

Baby? A misnomer if ever he'd heard one, but the voice was right. It was a husky voice. A boy's voice.

Lucas knotted his hands into fists and strode quickly to the stall. The horse sensed his presence before the kid standing next to it and whinnied with alarm.

Too late, Lucas thought grimly.

He'd found them. The rider and the beast that had ridden him off the road.

The kid, back to the aisle, was still oblivious, holding on to the stallion's bridle with one hand, speaking softly to the creature as he stroked its ears with the other.

"Such a charming picture," Lucas snarled, clapping his big, callused hand over the boy's.

"Hey," the boy said indignantly.

"Hey, indeed," Lucas said with grim satisfaction, and swung the kid around.

It was him, all right. Beat-up ball cap. Grimy T-shirt. Dirty jeans, dirtier boots…

Except, when the kid's cap fell off, Lucas's jaw dropped.

The rider wasn't a boy.

She was a woman.

CHAPTER TWO

A WOMAN?

Maybe not. Maybe she was a teenaged brat. It was difficult to tell.

The rider's face was smeared with dirt, one streak angling across a sharp cheekbone, another across the bridge of her nose. Her hair, a long, heavy braid of inky-black, fell over her shoulder and across her breast.

Lucas's gaze followed the path of that braid…and knew she was most definitely a grown woman.

Her T-shirt was sweat-soaked. It clung to her body, the cotton wet and all but translucent as it molded her rounded breasts and taut nipples.

Lucas's body reacted, enraging him even more. To be damned near ridden down, then laughed at by an adult female, and now to have an atavistic reaction to that female…

He heard the harsh rasp of her indrawn breath. Instantly he cupped her jaw and silenced her scream before it started.

"Do not," he said grimly, "do anything you'll regret."

She stared at him through wild eyes. He let it go on for a long moment, relishing every instant before he finally spoke.

"Don't tell me you don't recognize me, *amada*." He

smiled thinly. "I'd hate to think our meeting was not as memorable for you as it was for me."

Something flashed in the depths of those amazingly blue eyes. She remembered him, all right.

Except, this time he was the one laughing, she was the one in danger. And she knew it. What he'd seen in her eyes was fear.

Good. A woman might well show fear when confronted by a man her horse had almost trampled.

The big stallion snorted and shifted his formidable weight with surprising delicacy on hooves the size of dessert plates. Lucas moved his grasp to the woman's arm and dragged her toward him.

She didn't make it easy. Her lean, feminine body was surprisingly well-muscled, especially when she dug in her boot heels, but she was no match for him. Not in size or weight or tight-lipped anger. A couple of seconds and he had her trapped between him and the wall.

"It was an accident."

"Ah. You do remember me after all."

"You were standing in the middle of the road—"

"Is standing in the road against the law in Texas?"

She was trying to control her fear or, at least, trying to mask it. And she was doing a fairly good job. The steadiness in her voice might have fooled him if he hadn't seen the race of her pulse in the hollow of her throat.

"Trespassing on private property is."

"That road isn't private property. Besides, whatever happened to southwestern hospitality? I'm visiting. Surely that's permitted in Texas."

"All right. You made your point. Now do yourself a favor and go away before I—"

"Before you what?" Lucas jerked his head toward the

stallion. "Before you get on the back of that beast and try to run me down again?"

"I did not try to run you down," she said coldly. "If I had, you wouldn't be here making an ass of yourself."

"Such bravado," he said softly.

"What do you want?"

"Why, what could I possibly want?" He reached out, ran a lazy hand down her throat; she jerked like a skittish mare under his touch. "Just a little chat."

That put the balance of power back where it belonged. Fear blossomed in her eyes again.

"If you think I'm alone here—"

"Of course you're not alone." His voice was deliberately soft, his tone just this side of condescending. "There's an old man up at the house who could surely help you—if he were thirty years younger. And there's a boy. Well, there *was* a boy."

Her face paled. "What have you done with Davey?"

Lucas gave a negligent shrug. "I took care of him."

Her pupils widened, the darkness all but swallowing the blue fire of her eyes.

"Tell me what you've done with Davey."

"Davey's welfare is not your problem."

Her chin lifted. She was defiant, despite her fear. He had to give her grudging credit for that.

"I sent him on an errand."

"To where?"

"Damn it," he growled, "the boy is fine! I'm not interested in discussing him." He tightened his grasp on her wrist. "I'm talking about you, *señorita*. You could have killed me."

"But I didn't. That's what matters. Bebé and I didn't harm a hair on your head."

"Bebé," he scoffed. "A charming name for a behemoth."

"If you hadn't been standing in the middle of the road—"

"If you'd been in control of that monster—"

"Standing in the middle of the road, fooling around with a gadget anyone with half a brain would know couldn't possibly work out here—"

"Nothing works out here," Lucas snapped, "not even human courtesy. I was not, as you so generously put it, 'fooling around' with my phone. My car broke down, or didn't you notice it by the side of the road?"

"Of course I noticed! I sent Davey back to get you." Her eyebrows lifted. "Is that what you call that silly excuse for transportation?" she said sweetly. "A car?"

"Please," Lucas said coldly, "don't hold back. There's no need to watch what you say on my account."

"Well, you set yourself up for it, didn't you? Expecting a mobile phone to work out here, driving a thing like that on back roads…"

Dios, this was the stupidest quarrel he'd had since he was eight and in a nose-to-nose battle over whether *Real Madrid* or *Futbol Club Barcelona* fielded the better soccer team.

What was wrong with this woman? Arguing with him, angering him when for all she knew, he was a madman come to do her harm. And when in hell, *how* in hell, had she managed to turn the tables?

He was the injured party here, not she.

"Anyway," she said, "this is all beside the point. I didn't hurt you. Except…well, maybe your pride. I mean, we both know you ended up in a ditch…"

Lucas saw her lips twitch. Could a man's blood pressure rise to the point where he exploded?

"And," he said silkily, "you found it amusing."

"No," she said, but there was that twitch again.

"You know," he said softly, "a smart woman might consider a simple apology appropriate just about now."

That gave her pause. He could almost see her weighing her options. She was alone with a stranger, nobody to turn to for help.

On the other hand, he had a strong suspicion the word "apology" was not a normal part of her vocabulary.

A long moment passed. Then she huffed out a breath that lifted the silky, jet-black curls from her forehead.

"Yes. Okay. I shouldn't have laughed."

"Or tried to run me down."

"I told you, I did not try to run you down." She hesitated. "But I guess it was impolite to find the situation amusing."

"The understatement of the century."

"It's just that…it was—it was interesting. You, dressed as if you might actually know one end of a horse from another—"

"Which," he said coldly, "is surely an impossibility."

"And your lady friend… Was that get-up left over from Halloween or what?"

If this was her idea of an apology, he could only imagine what she would consider an insult.

"My lady friend," he said, lying through his teeth in a last desperate attempt at maintaining the upper hand, "was simply wearing what any attractive woman would wear."

"To a masquerade party, maybe."

She was right, but he'd be damned if he'd let her know it.

"To ride a horse in Central Park," Lucas said, lying again and fervently hoping all the horses who called Manhattan home would forgive him. He took a step back, his hand still wrapped around her wrist, and gave her a long, slow look. "But then, what would you know about being a woman in a place like New York?" He took another long, lazy look at her, from her toes to the top of her head. "You are a woman, aren't you, *amada?* Under all that ridiculous clothing?"

Dios, he thought, hearing himself, picturing himself, what was he doing? The leer, the line—it was all such bull.

And yet, to his surprise, it had its effect.

The rider blinked. One blink, that was all, but enough to tell him she'd suddenly remembered she was in a situation she didn't control.

"Okay." Her tone was cool but, yes, there was an underlying tremor. "I've apologized. Now you can let go of my wrist, say *adios* and get out of here."

"Tomorrow," Lucas said softly.

"Tomorrow, what?"

"I'll leave tomorrow, when the rental agency sends a replacement for my car."

"You are not spending the night on this ranch!"

"Somehow, I doubt that is your decision to make."

The stallion snorted and stamped a powerful hoof.

"Bebé's upset," the woman said.

"So am I."

"He can be dangerous, especially if he thinks I need protection."

"I assure you, *amada,* I can be far more dangerous than the horse."

He let the softly spoken words hang in the air, watching with grim satisfaction as they had their desired effect.

At last, she took a deep breath.

"Whatever you're thinking—"

"I suspect I'm thinking the same thing you are," Lucas said with a thin smile.

He could almost see her in frantic debate with herself. Part of her wanted to spit in his eye but another part—the wiser part—was reminding her that this was not a good situation.

"Look," she finally said, "I didn't try to ride you down on purpose. Bebé is fast. And I was bent over his head, talking to him—"

"What?"

"He's high-strung. Listening to me soothes him. Horses respond to a person's voice."

"They respond better to riders who can control them."

"What could you possibly know about horses?"

Lucas grinned. "Perhaps a little something."

"Really?" She stood glaring at him, one booted foot tapping the wide-boarded floor, and he knew the wiser part of her had lost the argument. "For instance? What 'little something' do you know?"

"I know that this so-called ranch is on its last legs."

Color swept into her face. "Really."

"I know that you have no stock, aside from that creature you call Bebé."

Her chin jerked up. "So?"

"So," Lucas said coldly, "that is the reason I was asked to come here."

Her eyes widened. "What do you mean, you were asked to come here? By whom?"

"By the owner. I was told there was a mare for sale."

"A mare?"

"*Si*. Breeding stock for me."

She was looking at him as if he'd lost his mind. For once, he could hardly blame her.

"For my stallions," he amended. "My Andalusians. *Pura Raza Espanola*." Lucas's gaze hardened. "But there is no mare here. No PRE stock at all—not even that ugly thing you call a stallion. Or would you like to pretend I am wrong about that, too?"

The woman wet her lips with a quick sweep of her tongue. He found himself following the simple action with hungry concentration, though why he would was beyond him.

She had spirit and fire but she was not the kind of woman who would ever interest him.

He'd seen females like her all his life. They hung around ranches. Around horse shows. Their passion was horses. They dressed like men, rode like men. As far as Lucas was concerned, they might as well have been men.

He knew exactly how he liked his women.

Sweet-smelling, with perfume in their hair, not hay. Smiling and soft-spoken, not glowering and acid-tongued. He liked to see them use feminine wiles, not pseudomasculine bravado.

He supposed some might think this woman had a pretty face, if you overlooked the smudges and smears. And, yes, her hair was an extraordinary shade of black, the color of a raven's wing. He suspected it would be heavy as raw silk, if she ever let it out of that unflattering braid and brushed it into smooth, shiny waves.

He could even admit that the rest of her had promise, too. The high, full breasts. The slender waist and curved hips. The long, long legs that could draw a man deep inside her heat…

"Who are you?"

Her voice pulled him back to reality. "What?"

"I said, what's your name?"

The tone of command was back. It made him angry enough to draw himself up to his full six foot two and respond with the icy hauteur of a man who was never questioned.

"I am Lucas Reyes."

To his surprise, her face turned white. She had heard of him, then. He found himself taking some satisfaction in that.

"No! You can't be!"

"I assure you, *señorita,* I am."

"Lucas Reyes? Prince Lucas Reyes? Of the Reyes Ranch in Spain?"

Was his hot-tempered hoyden going to throw herself at his feet? Women sometimes did, if not literally.

For some insane reason, the possibility that she would turn out to be such a woman made him even angrier, angry enough to respond with disdain.

"Not *of* the Reyes Ranch," he said, lifting his hand from her wrist. "To all intents and purposes, I *am* the Reyes Ranch."

The woman shook her head. "You're not supposed to be here."

"Really?" he purred, folding his arms.

"I sent a letter—"

"*You* sent a letter?"

"I mean—I mailed a letter. To Prince Felix Reyes. Your father."

"My grandfather. And what did this letter say?"

"It—it told you not to come."

"If there was a letter," Lucas said sharply, "neither my grandfather nor I ever saw it." He flashed a cold smile. "So, I am here, as planned. Perhaps we can agree that it is even possible I might—what was your charming phrase? I might know one end of a horse from the other."

The woman drew herself up. "Your visit is pointless. You'll have to leave."

"Are you giving me orders, *señorita?*"

"Just go, that's all."

His gaze swept over her. "What do you do here? Are you the cook? The maid? Do you muck out the stalls?"

"I do all those things."

His mouth twisted. "And warm McDonough's bed as well?"

Her hand was a blur in the rapidly fading light. Lucas caught it before she could slap him and twisted it behind her, forced her to her toes. She looked up at him through eyes gone so dark they were almost black.

"What's the matter, *amada?* Did I strike too close to home?"

"You can't talk to me that way! Not in America, you can't. We don't give a damn for stupid titles. For princes who've never sweated for a day's wages. For—for men who wouldn't know how to be men if their lives depended on it."

"Watch yourself," he said quietly.

He could almost see her struggling between defiance and caution. He knew which she'd choose before she did.

"Or you'll do what, almighty prince? Subject me to the *bastinado?*"

Maybe it was the flippant tone. The insulting words. The mention of an ancient punishment.

Or maybe it was her easy dismissal of him as a man, a dismissal made by a woman who knew nothing about being a woman.

"Why would I do that," he growled, "when there are much better things to do with a woman?"

He pulled her into his arms and kissed her. Kissed that sullen, angry mouth.

She fought him. Hands, teeth, the attempted thrust of a knee. She fought hard but Lucas threaded his hands into her hair, tipped back her head and kissed her again, harder this time, parting her lips with his so that she had no choice but to accept the swift thrust of his tongue.

Her hands came up between them, palms slapping against his shoulders, thumbs scrabbling for his eyes. He shifted his weight, pushed her back against the stable partition and went on kissing her.

She tasted of heat.

Of rage.

Of the untamed land she rode.

And, impossibly, of wildflowers that would come to life from barren soil after a summer rain.

She smelled of them, too. Not of horse, as he'd expected, or leather, but of flowers. Sweet. Exciting. And yet, somehow, tender and innocent as well.

Even struggling against him, she was soft in his arms. Incredibly soft.

Her mouth, her skin were like silk. The feel of her breasts against his chest. Her belly against his...

He swept one hand down the long length of her back. Stroked her as he would a mare afraid of a stallion's possession. Drew her toward him. Against him. Softened the pressure of his mouth on hers.

And heard the choked cry of her surrender.

She rose toward him. Her hands slid up his chest. "Don't," she whispered, but her mouth, that sweet mouth, was opening to his.

"Béseme," Lucas said thickly. "Kiss me, *amada*. Like that. Yes. Just like—"

The stable door banged open. The woman stiffened in his arms.

"Hello? Somebody in here?"

It was the foreman. Lucas tried to draw the woman deeper into the shadows but she shook her head, made a whimper of distress against his lips.

"Don't listen," Lucas whispered. "Don't answer."

"Hey!" The faint scuff of boots, then the foreman called out again. "Who's there?"

Her hands came up, slammed against Lucas's chest. "Let go," she whispered.

"That isn't what you wanted a minute ago."

"It was. Of course it—"

Lucas kissed her again. Her mouth softened, clung to his for a second before her sharp little teeth sank into his bottom lip.

He thrust her from him, dug in his pocket for a handkerchief that he pressed to his mouth. He looked at the scarlet drops of blood that stained the fine white linen, then at her.

"Reckless with men as well as with horses," he said coldly. "Dangerous behavior for a woman, *amada*."

Her eyes blazed into his. "You were right when you said there was nothing you would want here. Do yourself a favor, Your Highness. Go back to a world you understand."

"With pleasure—as soon as I've met with your employer."

"That's not going to happen."

"Whatever I wish to happen will happen," Lucas said harshly. "The sooner you get that through your head, the better."

He thought she was going to answer but maybe she'd finally figured out that arguing with him was pointless because, instead, she dug a key from her pocket and flipped it at him.

"There's a station wagon parked in back. It's old and it's not all gussied up so you won't like it very much, but it'll get you to Dallas."

Lucas let the key fall at his feet.

"Shall I tell you what *you* need, *señorita?* Better still, shall I show you?"

"Okay," the foreman growled. "Whoever's in here, you better show yourself."

The woman's eyes blazed into Lucas's one last time. Then she swiveled on her heel and walked away.

"George," he heard her say brightly, "why don't we go to the office and look at that catalog you mentioned yesterday?"

Her voice faded. Lucas's anger didn't.

Did she really think he would tuck his tail between his legs and run? It would have taken a Texas twister to move him now.

He had come here to meet with Aloysius McDonough and that was what he would do. He owed that to his grandfather.

As for what he owed the woman... A muscle bunched in his jaw.

He would deal with her, too.

She didn't know how to handle a horse or a potential client, if there had actually been a mare worth buying in this desolate place.

She sure as hell didn't know how to handle a man.

Perhaps McDonough liked being toyed with. Lucas didn't.

McDonough needed to know what had happened here today. The woman's incompetence. Her rudeness.

Her provocative sexual games.

Lucas strode from the stable.

If anyone was going to be ordered off this sorry bit of real estate, it sure as hell would not be him.

CHAPTER THREE

BY LATE afternoon, the clouds that had hung over the horizon most of the day finally began moving.

Better still, as far as Lucas was concerned, they were building, turning into impressive thunderheads as they drew closer. Unless he was reading the signs wrong, the oppressive heat that held the valley in an iron grasp was about to break.

He threw open the guest room window in hopes of catching a breeze. There was none but the scent of rain was definitely in the air.

It couldn't come soon enough.

The guest room was boxy and hot. An ancient electric fan stood on an oak dresser but there was no way to coax more than a flutter from it. Under normal circumstances, he'd have been out the door hours ago but these were not normal circumstances.

He was as good as trapped here, thanks to a promise he'd foolishly made to his grandfather.

At least he hadn't seen the woman again. He'd gone straight through the front door, up the stairs to this room without seeing a soul. As far as he could tell, he was alone in the house.

Just where in hell was Aloysius McDonough?

Lucas looked impatiently at his watch. Five-thirty. If McDonough didn't show up soon…

If he didn't, what?

No matter what happened, he was stuck here until tomorrow, when the car rental agency delivered a replacement vehicle.

Maybe it hadn't been so smart to ignore the car key the woman had tossed him in the stable. Maybe he should go back and search for it.

Or maybe he should search for her.

Lucas snorted. He wouldn't do, either. He'd wait this out, go home and tell his grandfather that McDonough had been too ashamed to show up and admit there was no mare for sale.

Thunder rumbled in the distance and a spiked streak of lightning sizzled from the almost-black sky. The storm was coming on quickly now, turning day into night.

Hard to believe that only yesterday he'd been in Manhattan at about this same hour, having drinks with his two oldest friends, Nicolo and Damian. Drinks, some laughter…and then dinner.

Lucas's belly growled.

He hadn't eaten since early morning. There seemed to be an entirely different meaning to hospitality on El Rancho Grande. First, you damn near rode a man down, then you didn't show up for an appointment and if neither of those things got rid of an apparently unwanted guest, you tried starving him out.

Lucas folded his arms and glowered at his reflection in the age-speckled mirror over the dresser.

The possibility of that key still lying on the stable floor was growing more and more appealing. Why, when you came down to it, should he feel obligated to stay here? Hell, he'd kept *his* promise to come to this—this alien outpost.

It was Aloysius McDonough who hadn't kept his.

Was that enough reason to disappoint Felix? Lucas sighed at the obvious answer and began to pace.

He had to calm down. Otherwise, by the time McDonough deigned to show up—assuming that ever happened—he'd say or do something rash. And he didn't want that.

Who was he kidding?

He wanted exactly that. More to the point, he wanted to tell McDonough what a fool he was to run a ranch straight into the ground, to employ a woman who dressed like a man, had the surliness of a man...

And could turn hot and female despite all of that.

Was it an act? The way she'd responded when he'd kissed her? She'd inferred that it was, but Lucas was not a fool.

Women could give award-winning performances at the drop of a hat.

They could weep, if they thought tears could get them what they wanted. They could smile, if they believed that was the better choice. They could pretend that whatever interested you interested them, that they wanted nothing but you, not your title or your wealth or your power.

Oh, yes.

He knew all that and more. A man couldn't reach the age of thirty-two, couldn't have the wealth he had been born to, the even greater wealth he'd accumulated by expanding the Reyes empire, without meeting more than his share of women who were experts at plotting and planning and lying.

A thin smile crossed his mouth.

The one thing they couldn't lie about was sex.

Not that an occasional woman didn't try.

"Ohhh, Lucas," one had whispered the first time they'd made love.

The moans, the whispers, had all sounded right, but she'd been faking it. He'd known it instantly.

A woman's eyes blurred with desire when what she felt was real. Her pulse increased with the heavy beat of her blood. She trembled like a willow in her lover's arms.

The woman in his bed that time had been lying, but that hadn't angered him.

It had challenged him.

Slowly, deliberately, he'd set out to turn that carefully spoken "ohhh" into a whisper of true passion, and he had done it.

Of course he had.

He knew what tender female flesh begged for a man's touch, what hidden place would heat under a man's lips.

Without question, he knew that the woman he'd kissed a couple of hours ago had not been acting. Like it or not, she'd been as turned on by that kiss as he'd been.

Lucas frowned.

As he was now.

Dios, he truly was in desperate shape! He needed a drink, a meal, an evening back in the real world. That the memory of a woman who'd done nothing but provoke him should have such an effect on him was ridiculous.

Perhaps he'd been too hasty, sending Delia away. An hour with her in the old-fashioned bed in this room and—

And what?

Who was he kidding?

An hour with Delia, with any of the women who'd passed through his life, and he'd still want the woman from the stable in his arms, her mouth opened to the thrust of his tongue, her breasts naked and hot against his chest.

There'd been something about the feel of her skin, the shock of her surrender…

Hell.

Aloysius McDonough could take this excuse of a ranch, this forgotten appointment and stuff them. It was one thing to pay a visit out of respect for Felix but another to be made a fool of.

Lucas strode to the door, flung it open—and found the laconic foreman just about to knock.

"There you are, mister."

"But not for long," Lucas said flatly. "I'm done waiting."

"That's what I come to tell you. You don't have to wait no more."

"Damned right, I don't. A while ago, the woman who works here—"

"Ain't no woman works here."

For some reason, the confirmation of what Lucas had already figured made him even angrier.

"Your boss's woman, then," he snapped. "She gave me the key to an old car she said was parked behind the stable but I didn't…" Why was he explaining himself? "I want that key now."

"You just said—"

"I know what I said," Lucas growled. "Surely there's a second key. I want it."

"I come to tell you what I been told to tell you. You can come on down to Mr. McDonough's office now."

"You mean, he's finally here?"

But he was talking to himself. The foreman was already shuffling down the hall.

He was half-tempted to go after the man, grab him by the collar and pin him against the wall—which only proved how out of control he'd let things get.

Instead he took a steadying breath.

What was that American saying about killing two birds with one stone? He could see McDonough, then demand the damned key to the damned car and say goodbye to this damned place.

He could hardly wait.

The office was tucked behind what Lucas assumed would be known as the front parlor in a house the age of this. It was a big room furnished in oak and leather, but what caught his attention were the prints and photographs framed and hung on the walls.

Horses. Colts. Paddocks and barns and stables. It took a minute to realize the pictures were of the ranch as it must have once been. Handsome, well-tended and prosperous.

McDonough had lied about the mare he claimed to have for sale. He'd somehow let this place tumble into ruin. But he had once run it properly and understood what it meant to be a horseman.

"Depressing as all get-out, isn't it? Kind of a sad chronicle of what used to be, could have been…well, you get my drift."

Lucas swung around. A man stood in the doorway, mouth curved in a smile that could only be categorized as nervous.

He damned well should have been nervous, Lucas thought coldly, taking in the figure of his host.

Aloysius McDonough was not at all what he'd expected.

He'd envisioned a tall man, whipcord thin and weather-hardened, wearing a dark suit, bolo tie and polished boots, maybe even a Stetson.

Obviously, he thought wryly, he'd seen one too many Hollywood Westerns on late-night TV during his days at Yale.

McDonough was short and pear-shaped, dressed in a pale gray suit and shiny wing-tips. His hair was arranged in an elaborate comb-over that emphasized his balding scalp. His face was florid and damp with sweat.

Lucas disliked him on sight.

And thought, immediately, of the obscenity of the black-haired rider warming the man's bed.

Everything inside him tensed, so much so that when McDonough held out his hand, he could only stare at it. The man's wary smile dipped and Lucas took a breath and forced himself to accept the extended hand, which was as soft and clammy as he'd known it would be.

"It's a pleasure to meet you, Your Majesty."

"Please," Lucas said, smiling thinly. "I'm hardly anyone's majesty."

He withdrew his hand, fought back the desire to wipe it on his jeans. He had gotten this far; he'd see the meeting through but to hell with being polite.

Nobody had been polite to him.

The best he could offer, in honor of his grandfather's name, was to be direct.

"Mr. McDonough—"

"Please. Before we start, let me apologize Your— Your Highness. Is that correct? Is it the way to address you, I mean?"

"Just call me Reyes."

"I'm sorry for the delay, Mr. Reyes."

"Yes. So am I. We were supposed to meet hours ago."

"I know. It's just… May I get you something to drink, Prince?"

"The name is Reyes."

"Sorry. Of course. I'm not accustomed to meeting with— Well, then. What will it be? Something to eat, perhaps?"

Lucas had lost his appetite.

"Nothing, thank you. Let's just get down to business, Mr. McDonough. That's why I'm here."

McDonough's face grew shinier. "I can see that you're annoyed, Your Lordship."

Lucas thought of correcting him again but changed his mind. He had little patience for phonies and fools and from what he'd observed thus far, McDonough was both. The man could genuflect, for all he gave a damn.

"I apologize, sir. I'm sorry I wasn't here when you arrived."

"So am I."

"I assure you, it was unavoidable. I am no happier about it than you are."

McDonough wasn't kneeling but he sure as hell was shaking in his shoes. Lucas gave an inward sigh, counted silently to ten and then forced what he hoped was a convincing smile.

"Things happen," he said. "As a businessman, as a rancher, I understand that. So…" He cleared his throat. "So, let's begin again, yes? I'm pleased to meet you, Mr. McDonough. My grandfather sends warm greetings."

"Thank you, Your Highness. But—but I must tell you, I am not Aloysius McDonough."

Lucas's attempted smile failed. "Then who are you?"

"My name is Thaddeus Norton. I'm an attorney."

So much for new beginnings.

"Mr. Norton," Lucas said brusquely, "this is a waste of time. I came here to meet with Aloysius McDonough. Where is he?"

"I'll explain everything, sir, if you'll just be patient."

"I'm tired of being patient. Where is McDonough? And where is the mare?"

The attorney's face was a study in confusion. "What mare, Your Excellency?"

"The nonexistent paragon of horseflesh I came to buy."

"But—but there is no mare, sir."

"Didn't I just say that?" Lucas replied. *Dios,* now he was playing straight man in a bad comedy act. "Let me clarify things, Norton. My grandfather said he had contracted to purchase a mare. You and I both know there is no mare, so either he made a mistake or your client misrepresented the situation." Lucas's eyes narrowed. "I must tell you, my grandfather is not in the habit of making mistakes."

Norton swallowed audibly. "I don't know how to explain it, sir, but you're right, there is no mare." His Adam's apple bobbed up and down as he swallowed again. "But there is all the rest. The land. The buildings. I know things are in some disrepair but—"

And, with those words, it began to fall into place.

Felix had been duped.

McDonough didn't hope to sell a mare that would infuse the Reyes bloodlines with new intelligence, beauty and heart, he hoped to get rid of a failing property by unloading it on an old friend.

Lucas struggled to keep calm when what he wanted to do was cross the room, grab the lawyer by the collar and shake him.

"You and McDonough insult me and my grandfather," he said through his teeth. "Did you actually think I would come here to see a mare and, instead, agree to buy this— this run-down corner of purgatory?"

"Please, Your Lordship. I beg you to compose yourself."

"I am composed," Lucas roared. "I am perfectly composed! Now get Aloysius McDonough in here so I can tell him what I think of him to his face!"

"I'm afraid that's impossible."

Lucas knotted his hands into fists. It was either that or plow them into the soft gut of the man in front of him.

"So is continuing this discussion," he snarled, and strode toward the door.

"Prince Lucas! You don't understand. Aloysius McDonough is dead."

Lucas turned and stared at Thaddeus Norton. "He can't be dead. My grandfather spoke to him last week, when they agreed to this appointment."

"You must have that wrong. Aloysius passed away almost six months ago."

"I have it right, Norton. I was with my grandfather when he made the phone call."

Lucas had an excellent grasp of the English language. Still, some idioms had always eluded him. One was the phrase, "sweating bullets." He'd never understood it until now as big drops of sweat popped out on Norton's brow.

"I, ah, I don't suppose you know the exact date of that call, sir?"

It was an easy question to answer. Lucas met with Felix on Mondays. It was a courtesy to keep his grandfather up-to-date about the Reyes Corporation and its holdings.

"Last Monday, in late afternoon. It would have been morning here."

The attorney swallowed hard. "That call would have been between your grandfather and me, sir."

"*You* spoke with Felix?"

"Yes, sir."

Lucas's eyes narrowed. "Are you suggesting my grandfather sent me here, knowing McDonough was dead? That he lied to me?"

"No," Norton said quickly. "I'm sure he didn't. I—I suspect he—he just left out a couple of facts."

"A polite way of saying yes, you are suggesting my grandfather lied," Lucas said in a soft voice many had learned to fear.

"Sir. Please understand, I am only representing my client. As for my conversation with your grandfather…" Norton swallowed. "He said it was time to implement the plan he and my client agreed upon a year ago."

"What plan?"

Norton twisted his hands together. "I just assumed—I assumed your grandfather and you discussed it. That you knew—"

"Damn it, get to it! What plan?"

"Well—well, a year ago, Aloysius and your grandfather talked. About El Rancho Grande. And—"

"And," Lucas growled, "your client saw a chance to presume upon an old friendship."

"No, sir! That isn't what happened."

A muscle jumped in Lucas's jaw. The details didn't matter. McDonough had been desperate for money and he'd come up with a scheme designed to scam an old friend. Dead or not, the man was a lying, deceitful son of a bitch.

Still, why had Felix lied about the mare? About McDonough? If his grandfather knew there was no horse, knew that McDonough was dead…

Lucas would have trusted Felix with his life. To learn that trust might be misplaced…

Was Felix—was he becoming senile?

It was a terrible thought but a plausible explanation. Either Felix had lied to him or his mind was slipping. Neither prospect was good.

Lucas drew a heavy breath.

"Mr. Norton. There has been—there has been some confusion here. I can see that this has nothing to do with you."

Norton nodded in relief. "Thank you, sir."

"Obviously this matter is—it is ended." Lucas's voice grew brisk. "I assume you came here by car. I would be grateful if you would drive me to town. I have no vehicle. It's a long story and not very interesting, but—"

"Nothing is ended, Your Highness," Norton said quickly.

Lucas stiffened. "I assure you," he said coldly, "it is."

"The agreement between your grandfather and my client—"

"Damn it, man, I'm not stupid. Your client did what he could to drag my grandfather—to drag the Reyes Ranch—into his financial mess. I promise you, that's not going to happen."

Norton's Adam's apple danced again. "It's already happened, sir. Your grandfather bought El Rancho Grande a year ago. It was to change ownership upon my client's death."

Lucas was stunned. Reyes Corporation—damn it, *he* owned this disaster area?

"Last week, your grandfather phoned to say he was ready to execute the terms of the sale. That he was sending you to, uh, to implement the final contract stipulation."

"Let me see the contract."

The attorney took a large white handkerchief from his pocket and mopped his face.

"Perhaps we should discuss the stipulation first, sir, and then…"

"Damn it, Thaddeus! Stop weaseling and get to it!"

The voice, female and curt, sliced through the room. Lucas turned and stared at the woman in the doorway.

She was tall. Slender. Her midnight-black hair was drawn back in a severe knot; pearls glittered demurely at her ears and throat. In a white silk blouse, black trousers, butterscotch leather blazer and polished black riding boots, she looked like she'd just stepped out of an expensive Manhattan town house, not a stable.

And yet, that was the last place he had seen her.

His eyes narrowed. "You clean up well for a woman who earns her living mucking stalls."

The look she gave him lowered the room's temperature.

"You should have taken my advice and left El Rancho Grande, Mr. Reyes."

"And not enjoy whatever interesting little performance is about to take place?" Lucas smiled thinly. "Not on a bet."

She dug in her pocket, held out the same key she'd offered him before.

"It's not too late."

"Trust me, it is." Another thin, unpleasant smile curved his mouth. "Things are just getting interesting."

"Interesting," she said, and gave a brittle laugh.

It reminded him of how she'd laughed when she'd almost ridden him down.

"Laughter," he said carefully, "seems an inappropriate response."

"Believe me, mister, any other response is out of the question."

"Try an apology instead." He took a step toward her. "You still owe me one."

That made her laugh again. It made his blood pressure soar. He was in a game but he didn't know the rules, didn't know his opponent, didn't know the prize he was playing for.

The only certainty was that the woman was knee-deep in whatever was going on.

"You have one minute to explain," he said, moving slowly

toward her. "You or Norton. I don't give a damn who tells me what this is all about. One minute. Then I'm leaving."

"Has anyone ever told you what a pompous ass you are?"

Dios, he could feel the rage building inside him. "I warn you, *amada,* watch how you speak to me."

"The days of royalty are over, Mr. Reyes. Playing emperor won't get you anywhere. Not here. This is my country, my land, my—"

It was as if she'd pushed some hidden switch. Nothing mattered but dealing with her interminable insolence and Lucas knew exactly how to do it.

He pulled her into his arms and kissed her.

CHAPTER FOUR

HOURS ago, she'd struggled against him, then given herself up to his kiss.

Not this time.

She didn't just struggle, she fought like a wildcat. Tried to bite him. Knee him. Shove him away.

Lucas wouldn't let any of that happen.

He used his anger, his height, his leanly muscled strength to propel her back against the wall. Then he used his hands to manacle hers and pin them uselessly beside her.

Dimly he heard the attorney saying his name but he ignored that, ignored everything but the need to get even. To win. To let her know, without question, she could not laugh at him or look at him as if he were a creature worthy of her contempt.

Even in the fever that gripped him, Lucas had to admit that there was more.

There was the taste of her. Wild. Honeyed. Passionate.

The heat that rose from her silken skin.

The texture of her mouth as he invaded it.

As she fought, as he forced her to accept his kiss, the part of his brain that still clung to civility asked him what the hell he was doing.

He had never forced sexual compliance from a woman in his life.

But he wanted that from her.

No. Not compliance. Hell, never compliance.

He wanted to hear her sigh with desire. To melt under the stroke of his hands. To return his kisses and ask for more.

His mouth softened on hers. His hands lessened their grip on her wrists. He whispered to her in Spanish, words a man might use to tell his lover he would show her fulfillment beyond any she'd ever imagined...

The woman caught her breath. And became warm and pliant in his arms.

He felt the change. The delicate swell of her breasts against his chest. The almost imperceptible tilt of her hips to his. She was surrendering. Admitting that he was in command, not she.

He could let her go now...

Unless he kissed her until she begged him never to stop. Until what had started hours ago ended with his hands under her skirt, her panties torn aside so he could enter her. Thrust deep between her eagerly parted thighs as she urged him to take her, to possess her, again and again and again...

She cried out. Wrenched her hands free or perhaps he let go. Either way, Lucas stumbled back. She swayed; her eyes flew open, dark and hot with hatred.

Or with something that made him want to reach for her again.

He shuddered.

Was he insane? Was she? All he knew was that the sooner he left this place, the better.

The woman was trembling. The attorney was goggle-eyed. Lucas forced himself to speak as calmly as if nothing had happened.

"Now," he said, "perhaps we can get to the truth."

"The truth," she said, "is that you're a son of a—"

"Alyssa!" The attorney came to life and stepped quickly between them. "I suggest you not say anything you'll regret."

"Excellent advice, *amada*."

"I have some advice for *you,* Mr. Reyes," she said in a low voice. "Get the hell out of my house!"

"Your house? Have I misunderstood something?" Lucas looked at Norton and smiled slyly. "Did your client leave the opulent El Rancho Grande to—what is it you call the lady? Alyssa?" He folded his arms. "Alyssa the what? The maid? The cook? The stable girl? My understanding—and perhaps I have it wrong—was that I own this place now." His voice hardened. "All of it, from the dried-out pastures to the collapsing barn. Is that not so, Norton?"

The lawyer looked as if he'd have given anything to disappear as he ran a shaking finger around the inside of his collar.

"That is correct, sir. Though I'm afraid—I'm afraid it's a bit more complicated than that."

"More complicated?" Lucas snorted. "My grandfather was tricked into buying a useless ranch, I was tricked into coming here and you tell me there is still more? Are you about to tell me I must rescue a captive princess from the dragon-guarded tower in which she is chained?"

Norton made a sound as if he were gagging. The woman—Alyssa—gave a bitter laugh.

"Do not laugh at me again." Lucas rounded on her, his face white with fury. "Or, I promise, you will regret it."

"What I regret," she snapped, "is that I didn't let Bebé run you into the ground!"

"Such charm," Lucas said slyly. "I trust you showed a warmer side to your lover."

"To her…?" The attorney blanched. "Sir. Let me explain who Alyssa—who this lady is."

"I've already figured that out. The only explanation I want now is what in hell you mean by this thing you call a 'stipulation.' Do I own this ranch or not?"

"Well—"

"Of course he owns it," the woman said in mocking tones. "He *is* the Reyes Corporation, Thaddeus. He told me that himself."

Lucas looked at her and saw what the problem was. Felix had bought this useless place. Now McDonough was dead, and his mistress, his lover, call her what you liked, was furious. She'd expected to inherit the property.

Greedy bitch.

A moment ago, he'd happily have solved his problem by donating El Rancho Grande to charity. Now, he knew he would fight this taunting female to the end to keep it—and then give it to charity.

"And you want it for yourself," he told her softly. "That's it, isn't it? That's the so-called 'stipulation.'"

"The ranch belongs to me," she said, drawing herself up. "By all that's right, that's legal, that's—that's human and decent, it's mine!"

"Of course it is, *amada*." Lucas's voice was silken. "Just think of all you did to earn it."

Her face colored. "You don't know what you're talking about!"

"I promise you, I do. I know the sacrifices you made, sleeping with an old man, doing his bidding in bed—"

"You—you disgusting son of a bitch! I'm going to take this damnable contract stipulation to court and I'll win."

"Do you have a million dollars? Because that is what it will cost you just to see me and my attorneys in a courtroom."

The woman glared at him. "You're more than pompous, Mr. Reyes. You're also a fool!"

Lucas took a step forward. The attorney moved quickly between him and the woman.

"Alyssa. Prince Lucas. My client is deceased but I'm honor-bound to continue representing him."

Norton's sudden show of backbone was a surprise but he had a point. There was a legal matter to be settled here, and Lucas wouldn't permit his anger at the rider to get in the way.

"Fine," he said coldly. "Then, let's get to the bottom line—or did we just reach it? Did you bring me all this distance to alert me to the fact that this woman is going to try to convince the courts the sale of the ranch was improper? That she should have inherited it? Because if that's the case, I must tell you, I suspect she has no legal grounds."

"I agree, sir. And that's not the problem."

"Then, what is?" *Dios,* he was tired. He wanted a meal and a shower and a night's sleep, but he damned well suspected he wasn't about to get them any time soon.

"Tell him, Thaddeus," the woman said.

Lucas looked at her. Her face was blank but hatred for him shone in her eyes.

Suddenly his exhaustion dropped away.

He thought of how he could change that look by taking her into his arms again and kissing her into submission. How she would respond to him. How she would beg him to make love to her.

Damn it, he thought, and strode to the window, stared into the black night while the wind shook the trees and the rain pelted the roof. He had nowhere to go until morning or, more precisely, he had no way to leave this place until then.

He had to calm down.

A deep breath. Then he turned to the attorney.

"She's right for once, Norton. Tell me the rest. I'm sure I'll find it amusing."

The lawyer pulled a handkerchief from his pocket and mopped his face.

"First, you must understand, sir. The ranch was not always the way it is today."

Lucas glanced at the photos on the wall. "So what? For all I give a damn, it might have been the finest ranch in all Texas."

"It was," the woman said in defiance.

"Fine. It was paradise. Just get on with it."

"A royal command, Thaddeus. You must obey."

Lucas glared at her. "Be careful, *amada*," he said softly.

"Yes, Alyssa, please. You're only making matters worse."

"You're the one making matters worse," she snapped. "If you'd done as I asked and simply ignored this whole thing—"

Lucas slammed his fist on the desk. So much for staying calm.

"Damn it," he roared, "that's it! Tell me what you're hiding about that contract, Norton, or so help me, I'll see you never practice law again!"

Thaddeus Norton took a briefcase from a chair and extracted a thick folder.

"Just bear in mind, sir, I told Aloysius this was insane."

"Insane?" The woman gave a shaky laugh. "How about immoral? Unethical? How about it's like something out of bad melodrama?"

"When the two of you get tired of this conversation," Lucas said coldly, "perhaps you'll be good enough to explain what in hell you're talking about."

The attorney opened his mouth and then shut it again. The woman shot him a look, then lifted her chin. She looked beautiful, proud and untouchable.

"Thaddeus is a coward, so I'll do it and then we can all have a good laugh. For starters… I hate to disappoint you, Mr. Reyes, but Aloysius wasn't my lover." She paused. "He was my father."

"You're McDonough's daughter?"

"His adopted daughter. My name was originally Montero. And there was never any warmth between Aloysius and me."

"Alyssa," Norton said wearily, "that's ancient history."

"You're right for once, Thaddeus, but our esteemed visitor wants answers. Well, I'm giving them to him. My mother is dead and so is Aloysius. I cannot imagine missing him, especially now that he's drawn me into this—this mess." Her smile was bitter. "Sorry this is all far less intriguing than me being the star of some sordid little drama, Your Mightiness, but that's the way it is."

"Let me get this straight," Lucas said in the tone of a man who'd just watched a rabbit pulled from a hat and knew damned well that sleight-of-hand tricks were not magic. "Aloysius McDonough learns he's dying. He has no wife but he has a daughter. She's cold and unfeeling and he has no desire to give her the land he once loved."

"Sounds good. And you've got it half-right, except the land was actually my mother's. And she loved it."

"Forgive me," Lucas said with heavy sarcasm. "I had the characters wrong but not the basic plot. You want the ranch. I own it. And? You got me here so you could do what? Beg me to give it back? Ask me to sell it to you for next to nothing?" His mouth twisted. "Or did you imagine you'd seduce me into giving it to you," he said, his eyes locked to hers. "Was that the plan?"

"Try 'none of the above,'" she said coldly.

"Really?" Lucas folded his arms. "I wasn't born yesterday, *amada*. Not being mentioned in Daddy's will must have been hard to accept."

"But I am mentioned. That's the problem."

"He left you something, then? Good for you but I don't see how it involves me, or why I've come such a distance to watch such a badly written play."

Was he wrong, or did some of her confidence seem to drain away?

"There's a clause in the contract. I didn't know about it until Aloysius died and the will was read. It's—it's what Thaddeus calls the stipulation."

"*Dios*, you say that as if the word might burn your mouth. Are you going to explain it, or must I shake it out of you?"

"I would advise against anything so foolish, Mr. Reyes."

That tough attitude was back. The statement was a challenge. So was the way she'd addressed him. His honorific creaked with antiquity in this century but her deliberate avoidance of it was, he knew, an insult.

Well, he wouldn't rise to the bait. He wanted the truth and he had the feeling it was worse than it seemed, more than one man scamming another out of a lot of money.

"Explain, then," he said gruffly.

Alyssa touched the tip of her tongue to her lips.

"Everything you've heard is true. My father offered this ranch to your grandfather, and your grandfather agreed to buy it. But—"

"But?"

"But," she said, her voice suddenly low, "your grandfather—your grandfather wanted to purchase something more. And my father agreed to sell it to him."

She fell silent as thunder roared over the house. The scent of ozone, of anticipation, hung in the air. A streak of jagged light sizzled just outside the window; thunder clapped overhead. It lent an air of melodrama to the scene.

And yet, Lucas thought, this was no melodrama. Whatever was playing out here was real.

Once, kayaking down a wild river, his craft had been poised at the lip of a class four rapid for what had seemed an eternity, enough time for him to look down into a whirlpool he knew had claimed many lives.

His heart had missed a beat as he hung above it, caught somewhere between exhilaration and terror.

That was how he felt now, looking at Alyssa McDonough, waiting for her to finish telling him what he had come all this distance to learn.

"And?" he said softly. "What's the 'something more' your father agreed to sell to my grandfather?"

An eternity seemed to pass. Then Alyssa shuddered and raised her eyes to his.

"Me."

CHAPTER FIVE

THE look of horror on Lucas Reyes's handsome face was exactly what Alyssa had expected.

She recalled feeling just as horrified when Thaddeus first told her about what he kept calling the "stipulation."

"It's a joke," she'd insisted. "It's not legally binding. A clause like that is absolute nonsense."

"It isn't that simple," Thaddeus had said carefully. Marriage contracts, he explained, could be legal and binding. They were still in use in parts of the world, especially in royal families.

Alyssa had snorted with derision.

"I have news for you. We don't sell human beings in America."

"No one is selling a human being. I keep telling you, it's—"

"A marriage contract. It's still illegal. Tell Prince Felix I said so. And if he argues, tell him where he can shove that stipulation!"

"Read the contract before you make a decision, will you? It calls for the Reyes to restore the land and use it, in perpetuity, for ranching. Otherwise, the bank will seize it and you know what that means."

She knew, all right. A local developer was panting for all these rolling acres, eager to turn them into soulless tracts of cheap housing.

It was a sobering realization. Losing her mother's land was bad enough. Losing it to a developer was worse but being married off to a stranger...

"How could you have drawn up such a document?" she'd demanded.

Thaddeus admitted that he hadn't. Prince Felix's attorneys had done virtually all the legal work. He had done nothing but, in his words, crossed a few t's and dotted a couple of i's.

She was still groaning over that when he'd dropped the next bit of news.

Felix's grandson, the prince who would permit his grandfather to buy him a bride, was on his way to finalize arrangements.

"He's not finalizing anything!"

"The contract exists, Alyssa. I'm afraid there's little I can do."

"You can change it. Research it. Find precedents we can use to break it. I'll do the same. Damn it, I had a year of law school. I know there's not a contract written that can't be broken. How come you don't know that, too?"

"Read the contract," Thaddeus had repeated wearily.

So she'd read it. And the more she'd read, the more she'd seen just how cleverly the Reyes's lawyers had been in their use of language and tort law.

The contract seemed unassailable.

She'd sent Prince Felix a letter, demanding he forget the stipulation. She hadn't received an answer. She'd figured that meant the Spanish prince would not be dissuaded from coming to the ranch. Why? Was it to try to hold her to the contract terms? Did he actually think he could do that? Most of all, why would he be willing to marry a woman he had never seen?

The only thing that made sense was that Lucas Reyes was the human equivalent of a toad.

Squat. Bloated, with constant drool falling from fleshy lips. Ugly enough to frighten small children. Or tall. Skinny as a scarecrow, with ears that stood out from his head. After a couple of days, she'd decided he probably had warts, too.

And then she and Bebé had come within an inch of riding down a stranger. A tall, dark-haired, hot-eyed, gorgeous stranger…

The Spanish prince. And he had no idea who she was, or the real reason he was here. He honestly thought he'd come to look at a mare.

In reality, he'd come to look at her. Breeding stock, according to Aloysius.

Hadn't he always described her in the terms horsemen used when talking about mares? It started when she turned sixteen. She had, he'd said, good bloodlines. Good conformation. She'd make someone a good wife. Someone with money, who could infuse life back into the ranch was what he'd meant, though nobody dared say it.

A couple of months later, Aloysius had sent her east to boarding school, then college. She'd come home when her mother took ill, went east again after her death—and returned for the last time when Aloysius was dying. An act of human decency, because it had seemed the right thing to do.

Now here she was, staring at the stud she was supposed to be bred to.

The man who'd bought her from Aloysius.

So much for human decency.

Okay. Lucas Reyes hadn't bought her. He hadn't even known about the deal. Whatever. It was still humiliating and once she knew his identity, thanks to George, she'd phoned Thaddeus and demanded he drive over and handle things. She would stand by and listen, but Thaddeus would do the talking.

Wrong.

Thaddeus had taken the coward's way out. He'd tiptoed up to the truth, then lurched away from it so that she was stuck with the job. She'd have to explain why he was here to Lucas Reyes. It was horrible and demeaning and…

And, just look at the man. Look at His Mightiness. His jaw was trying its best to defy gravity.

He was—what was the word? Nonplussed. Alyssa wanted to laugh. His Mightiness, the Prince of Non-Plussed. It didn't even the score. She was still humiliated but at least he was completely bewildered.

How nice. How well-deserved.

He'd done a fine job of bewildering her this afternoon. Invading her space, forcing a confrontation…

Kissing her as if it was his right—but he probably thought it was. He was a prince, born to wealth and power and, okay, good looks.

Why not be honest?

Lucas Reyes was gorgeous.

Black hair. Hazel eyes. Strong jaw. A little dent in his nose that only heightened his sexiness.

He must have broken it sometime in the past.

A riding accident? Or an accident with a woman? It was nice to think some woman had given the prince her best shot.

The rest of the man was gorgeous, too. Long. Lean. Hard-muscled. When he'd kissed her she'd felt the masculine power of his body. The strength of it. When he'd kissed her…

God, when he'd kissed her...

Alyssa blinked. Lucas was looking at her with the intensity of a rattlesnake watching a field mouse.

It frightened her but she'd sooner have died than let him know it. She didn't know much about men—why would she want to? What she'd learned, watching her mother defer to Aloysius, was enough. But she knew stallions and to show weakness to a stallion was to put yourself in mortal danger.

So she steeled herself for the Spanish prince's inevitable questions and reminded herself that she'd had nothing to do with any of this, and he'd damned well better get that straight.

"Explain yourself."

His voice was low and filled with command. Alyssa narrowed her eyes. The last time anyone had used that tone with her was in sixth grade and Miss Ellison had demanded to know why she'd punched Ted Marsden in the nose.

Because he thought he could get away with putting his hand on my backside, she'd said, and Miss Ellison had tried, unsuccessfully, not to laugh.

Nobody was laughing now.

Alyssa drew herself up. "Excuse me?"

"I said—"

"I heard what you said. I just didn't like the way you said it."

Lucas stepped forward. She managed to stand her ground but was that really better than tilting her head back so she could keep her eyes on his?

"It's been a very long day, *amada,*" he said softly. "I am tired and irritable, I have not eaten since morning, and I am in no mood for nonsense."

"I'm sorry if you find our hospitality lacking," Alyssa said, her coolness making a mockery of the words, "but I am equally tired and irritable and, thanks to your presence, I have not eaten, either. Just knowing you were here spoiled my appetite."

She gasped as his hands closed around her shoulders.

"You are quick to offer insult."

"You are quick to show your temper."

"I want answers."

"And I want you gone. Perhaps, if we cooperate, we can both get what we want."

Angry as he was, Lucas almost laughed. *Dios,* this one was tough! Not that she wasn't frightened. Despite her show of bravado, he could feel her trembling under his hands.

Was she afraid of him?

He hoped not. She had angered him, yes. Infuriated him, was closer to the truth, but he had no taste for scaring women, especially women with such deep blue eyes and sweet, tender mouths.

And look how quickly she'd taken his thoughts from where they belonged, he thought coldly.

Something was going on here, a scam, a swindle of some kind, and he was not going to let this woman, who was surely part of it, distract him.

"That's the first intelligent thing you've said, *señorita.*" Lucas lifted his hands from her shoulders. "So, go on. Explain yourself. Oh. Sorry." A smile that wasn't a smile at all twisted his mouth. "What I meant," he said dryly, "is, would you kindly tell me what you meant by that cryptic statement? In what way did my grandfather supposedly 'buy' you?"

Alyssa decided to ignore his sarcasm. It was time to get this over with.

"As Thaddeus told you, your grandfather and my adoptive father signed a contract. Felix paid Aloysius half the agreed-upon price."

Lucas was watching her through narrowed eyes. "With the other half due when?"

"When the stipulation had been fulfilled."

"There's that word again."

Alyssa swallowed. A moment ago, she'd been ready to explain. Now—God, now, she just wanted the floor to open up.

"Well? I'm waiting. What 'stipulation'?"

"It's—it's… The stipulation involves—"

Her tongue felt as if it were glued to the roof of her mouth. How did you tell a man he was supposed to marry you?

"You see, Alyssa?" Thaddeus Norton's plump face was flushed. "It isn't that easy after all."

The lawyer marched across the room to Lucas and held out the folder he'd taken from his briefcase. A couple of minutes out of the line of fire seemed to have restored his courage.

"Read it yourself, Your Highness. In the end, it's simpler that way."

Lucas nodded, took the folder, extracted a sheaf of papers from it, turned his back to the room and began to read.

Half an hour went by.

Then he swung toward the attorney.

"This is insane."

"It's a marriage contract."

Lucas's face darkened. "Do not provoke me, Norton."

The lawyer's few seconds of courage seemed to be over.

"I'm not trying to provoke you, sir," he stammered, "I'm just stating the facts. That document—"

"Is a joke!" Lucas flung the pages on the desk and watched as they fluttered to the floor like dry leaves. "No one signs things like this anymore."

Alyssa nodded. "I said that. I told Thaddeus—"

"You told Thaddeus," Lucas said sharply. "Oh, I'll just bet you did!" His eyes narrowed. "Or did you dictate this to him line by line? Did you dip back into the middle ages and come up with a document guaranteed to send me into orbit?"

"Me?" She moved toward him, eyes flashing. "You think I…? Let me tell you something, Mr. Reyes—"

"It's Prince Reyes," Lucas snarled. "Or Your Highness. Get it straight."

"*I* had nothing to do with this, Your Mightiness. I didn't even know about it. Do you really think—do you honestly think I'd want my name linked to yours, even on a piece of paper?" She stopped an inch from him, hand lifted, forefinger pointed at the center of his chest. "Never! You understand that, oh almighty potentate? Not in a million years. Not in a hundred million years. Not ever!"

Lucas knew how to stop the angry words flying from that pretty mouth. All he had to do was haul her close, bury his hands in her hair and kiss her.

And, *Dios,* he wanted to do it.

To watch her eyes fill with rage—and then watch them fill with desire.

Was he crazy? He'd just read a document full of whereases and wherefores that boiled down to an arranged marriage between him and Alyssa Montero McDonough— that middle name made sense, he thought crazily, all that heat and smoldering fury—he'd just discovered his beloved, conniving, scheming, possibly senile grandfather had pledged his name and his fortune to a Texas wildcat, and he wanted to kiss her?

Like hell he did.

What he wanted was to get out of this madhouse. Not tomorrow. Right now.

"This," he said, "is getting us nowhere."

"A brilliant conclusion."

He shot her a look. "Do not push me," he said softly.

She started to speak, then obviously thought better of it. The woman wasn't a fool.

"I'm sure you and Norton thought this was very clever. I'm not sure how you managed it, how, exactly, you got my grandfather to sign this—this bit of legal mumbo jumbo—"

"Me?" Alyssa huffed. "*Me?* I didn't have a damned thing to do with it!"

"I had little to do with it, sir," Norton said, the words tumbling from his lips in a rush. "Your grandfather's attorneys did most of the work, then sent the papers to me, after which my client signed it in front of a notary and we sent it to Spain by messenger so that your grandfather could sign it, too, and then—"

Lucas pounded his fist on the desk again. By the end of this charade, he thought grimly, the damned thing would be fit for firewood.

"I have no interest in the back-and-forth steps, Norton! I'm talking about..." What was the phrase? Lucas had spent four years at Yale; he had a condo in New York. America was his second home but right now, his English was failing him. "I'm talking about the setup. The preparation you and McDonough and the charming Miss McDonough put into this—this sting."

"Sting?" Alyssa shot forward. This time, her finger almost poked a hole in his chest. "Your grandfather gets together with my father and they agree to—to sell me to you and you accuse *me* of a sting?"

She gasped as Lucas caught her wrist and yanked her arm behind her back. The action brought her to her toes. Brought her body suddenly against his.

His response was instantaneous. Just the feel of her, the

soft fragrance of her, and he hardened like stone. Her eyes widened in pretended innocence until they were big enough to swallow him whole.

"Isn't my reaction the desired effect, *amada?*" he said, so softly that only she would hear him. "Dangle the bait in front of the mark? Pretend innocence, then show outrage, and do it so well the poor sap believes it?"

"Hijo de una perra," she hissed through her teeth.

Lucas grinned and drew her closer.

"Don't be like that, *chica.* Just because I'm wise to you doesn't mean I don't find you appealing. But I'm not a fool. I don't buy my women—and if I did, I would not pay with my name and my fortune. That you thought I would insults my intelligence."

"What I thought," Alyssa said, her voice trembling, "was that you were too horrible to get a woman on your own. And, clearly, I was right."

She gasped as he tightened his hold.

"So horrible you kissed me as if you never kissed a man before? As if having me drink from your mouth is what you've waited for all your life?" His smile faded. "Or are you that fine an actress? Shall we try it again and see?"

"Prince Lucas," Norton said quickly, "please, sir, you've got this wrong."

The lawyer's voice quaked. He looked, Lucas thought with grim satisfaction, like a man watching a lighted match falling oh-so-slowly toward a box of dynamite.

"Miss McDonough—Alyssa is telling the truth. This was your grandfather's idea. And my client's," he added quickly.

"I find that difficult to believe."

"It's true, sir. Prince Felix can confirm it. Miss McDonough knew nothing about the arrangement until Aloysius's death."

"That's when you told her the happy news? That she would become a *princesa?*" Lucas smiled coldly. "But you're a bright girl, *amada.* You must have known how easily such good luck could slip through your fingers. How hard you must have worked to come up with a scheme that would keep me from getting away."

"Sir," Norton pleaded, "call your grandfather. Let him confirm my story."

"Why should I bother? I'm not going to honor this— this joke of a contract, Norton. You managed to defraud an old man, but—"

"Your grandfather paid half the sale price, Your Worship. Only half. And I did not—"

"Half is more than this desolate piece of land is worth." Lucas dropped Alyssa's wrist. She stumbled back, rubbing at the welt his fingers had left in her tender flesh. "You want more, sue us for it."

"I strongly urge you to phone Prince Felix," Norton said quietly. "I have no wish to sue you, sir, but I have an obligation to see my client's wishes to their rightful end."

The pudgy, small-town counselor, still shaken, seemed determined to stand his ground. That, more than anything, gave Lucas pause.

He'd already admitted, if only to himself, that Felix might have agreed to this nonsense. Not the marriage contract, of course. That, without question, was something McDonough or Norton or the woman had slipped into the agreement.

But Felix might have said he'd buy the ranch for twice its worth. He was an old man; he was not well; Aloysius McDonough had been his friend.

Why wait until he returned to Spain to ask Felix about the contract? He could get the answers he needed now and close the book on this mess.

If Felix said he had agreed to the purchase, Lucas would honor the contract terms. He'd write out a check and walk away.

The rest, the marriage agreement, the thing these two maniacs kept calling a stipulation, was a joke. He'd mention it to Felix if only for a laugh.

Lucas took his cell phone from his pocket. It was some ungodly hour of the morning back home but he didn't give a damn.

It was time to get to the bottom of this.

"Out," he commanded.

The attorney bolted. Alyssa stayed where she was, arms folded.

"This concerns me as much as you," she said coldly. "I'm not leaving."

Lucas inclined his head. "Stay, by all means, *chica*," he said, just as coldly, "so I can see your face when my grandfather laughs at the supposed 'stipulation.'"

There were plenty of transmission bars now.

Lucas dialed his grandfather's private number. It rang a long time; the voice that finally answered was not a voice he knew.

"Who is this?" it said cautiously.

"Prince Lucas," Lucas snapped. "Who is this?"

"I am—"

Lucas heard snatches of unintelligible conversation, then Felix's familiar voice.

"Lucas?"

"*Si,* Grandfather. Who was that?"

"No one of importance. A new secretary. Where are you?"

"I am where you sent me. At El Rancho Grande…a misnomer if ever there was one."

"And what do you think, *mi hijo?*"

"I just told you. The place is in terrible condition. The outbuildings are falling down, the land is played out, there's no stock—"

"I know all that," Felix said impatiently. "What of the rest?"

"What rest, Grandfather? Do you mean the mare? There is no mare. There is nothing here except an attorney who insists we owe a final payment of twice what the land is worth and a woman who needs lessons in manners."

Silence. Then Felix gave a low laugh. "So her father told me, Lucas. The question is, are you the man to give them to her?"

The hair rose on the back of Lucas's neck. He turned toward Alyssa, still standing as she had been, back straight, arms folded, chin elevated at an angle so high it seemed impossible.

"Abuelo," Lucas said softly, "what do you mean?"

"It's a simple question, *mi nieto.* Are you man enough to tame this mare?" Felix's tone turned sly. "Although my understanding is that my old friend's daughter is better described as a filly than a mare. Do you agree, Lucas?"

Lucas took the phone from his ear, stared at it as if he might see Felix's face if he tried hard enough, then sank down in a chair.

"You know about the marriage contract," he said, switching to Spanish.

"Of course."

"But why?"

"You know the reasons, Lucas. You are not getting younger."

"I am thirty-two." Yes, Lucas thought, but right now, he sounded twelve. "I am thirty-two," he said, more forcefully, "and before you make the speech you've made before, *si,*

I know of my responsibilities. I know it is my duty to carry on the Reyes name. I know—"

"Perhaps it is better to say, *I* am not getting younger."

"Grandfather…"

"She is of excellent stock. She is handsome. She is healthy." Felix's tone turned sly. "And I have been assured, she is a virgin."

Lucas shot another look at the woman. A virgin? A woman who burned like a flame in a man's arms? It was nothing but another lie.

"…ask, Lucas?"

Lucas cleared his throat. "I'm sorry, *abuelo*. I didn't get that. What did you say?"

"I said, what more could a man ask?"

"The right to make my own choices," Lucas said firmly. "I am sorry, Grandfather, *No voy a casar a esta mujer!*"

The words, "I am not going to marry this woman," seemed to echo through the room. He shot a sharp glance at Alyssa McDonough. Her expression had not changed. Of course not, he thought with relief. She didn't understand a word of his language.

"You are a grown man, Lucas. Do as you wish."

"Fine. I will see you tomorrow, then, in late—"

"You understand, you are not to pay the lawyer—the executor—the balance of the sale price for the ranch."

Lucas nodded. Felix was lucid. That, too, was a relief.

"Of course I understand. You overpaid the initial amount as it is."

"It was part of the arrangement, Lucas. Did you read the contract? If you did, read it again, more calmly this time, and you will see that if the marriage does not take place, we owe nothing more."

"Excellent."

"Yes. Just as long as you understand…" Felix coughed. The cough was deep and wet; it went on for a long time while Lucas frowned.

"Grandfather? Are you ill?"

Again, he heard muffled conversation. And, again, his grandfather's voice, not coughing now but somehow weaker.

"I am fine," the old man said briskly. "Where were we? Ah, yes. You will not give Thaddeus Norton the money."

"Trust me, Grandfather. I had no intention of it. As I said, you already gave them too much."

"It went to Aloysius. To pay for half the back taxes on the ranch. The bank will take the place now, to make up for the rest. There's a developer eager to plow all the acreage under."

"What the bank does is not our concern, Grandfather."

"I agree. The girl cares—she has some sentimental attachment to the land—but that, too, is not our concern."

Lucas looked at Alyssa again. Her face showed no emotion, but her eyes had the glitter of unshed tears.

Did she understand what he was saying? Who gave a damn? Not him. If she loved the place so much, why hadn't her father left it to her?

She was a good actress, that was all. Fiery when fire was needed, cold as ice when the situation demanded it.

And hot with passion when he kissed her, but was that part of the act? Yes. It had to be

Or had she surrendered to him? Surrendered to his kisses, his body, his need?

Furious with himself, Lucas stood, marched to the window and looked out. The storm had ended; a fat ivory moon was caught in the branches of a cottonwood tree outside.

"Well," Felix said, and sighed, "I did what I could. I told Aloysius the girl would not lose the land because, of course, once you married her and paid the arrears, the land would be, in a sense, as much hers as yours...but never mind."

Lucas rubbed his hand over his face. "Grandfather—"

"But I cannot force you to obey the terms of the contract, *mi hijo*. I understand that. It is a disappointment for me, that I cannot fulfill the wishes of my dead friend, but—"

"Grandfather. There must be a way around this."

"I am afraid there isn't. It's all right, Lucas. The girl is not your worry."

"No. She's not."

"She is her attorney's worry, and I am sure he will step in and help her. You have met him, have you not? Small man. Overweight. Soft. Sweats a lot."

Lucas turned and looked at Thaddeus Norton, who was mopping his forehead again.

"What about him?"

"Aloysius told me Norton has an, uh, an interest in the girl. A deep interest, if you know what I mean."

Dios, how could something simple become so complicated?

"Norton wants the woman for himself?" Lucas said, still speaking in Spanish, still watching Alyssa. Did her color heighten? No. It had to be his imagination.

"He does, yes. But it's the perfect solution. We don't pay the rest of the money, you don't get married. And the girl is taken care of. *Si?* The lawyer will see to it."

Lucas said nothing for several long seconds. Then he cleared his throat.

"Grandfather," he said briskly, "we entered into this arrangement in good faith."

"We? It was I, Lucas, not *we*."

"Reyes entered into it," Lucas said, even more briskly. "So here's what I'm going to do. I'll tear up the contract, stipulation and all, and simply give her or the lawyer, whichever is appropriate, the money to pay off what is owed. She'll keep the ranch and we'll call it a gift in memory of an old friend."

"No."

Lucas raised his eyebrows. "No?"

"Aloysius and I entered into a contract."

"I understand all of that but, damn it…" He took a deep breath. "Look, we can well afford this—this act of charity, grandfather."

"Listen to me, Lucas. You must take another look at the contract. It is very specific. Unless the marriage takes place, there can be no final payment. The ranch is lost."

Lucas could feel a throbbing pain starting behind his left eye. No sleep. No food. No peace. No wonder his head hurt.

"Grandfather, maybe you didn't understand my suggestion. An act of charity—"

"I don't want your damned act of charity," Alyssa McDonough snapped.

Lucas stared at her. Had she understood the entire conversation?

Suddenly a cough rumbled through the telephone, and another and another. Lucas had never heard anyone cough like this; his grandfather sounded as if he were drowning.

"Grandfather? Grandfather!"

The coughing faded away and another voice came on the line.

"I'm sorry, Prince Lucas, but your grandfather cannot continue this conversation."

"What do you mean?" Lucas roared. "What's happening? Who in hell are you?"

"I am his nurse, sir, and—*Madre di Dios! Llamada para una ambulencia, Maria. Rapidamente!*"

The call ended in a blur of voices. Lucas struggled for control, then whirled toward Alyssa McDonough.

"I heard everything," she said. "Every word. I speak your language—were you too egotistical to think I couldn't? And I don't want your charity, I don't want anything from you, I don't want—"

"I must return to Spain immediately."

"Well, good for you because—"

"You will come with me."

"Don't be an ass!"

"I have no time to waste in foolish argument. There are issues to be settled and I cannot remain here to deal with them."

"Listen, you—you poor excuse for a human being—"

Lucas had spent part of an afternoon and most of an evening with this woman. She was still a stranger but he had learned one sure thing about her.

He knew how to silence her and he did, gathering her quickly in his arms, drawing her to him and taking her mouth, hard, with his.

She struggled.

He'd known she would.

And then she moaned, gave that little sigh he knew meant surrender, and lifted herself to him. To his kiss.

He gave in to it, if only for a second, to the pull of it, the sweetness, the hunger.

Then he clasped her shoulders and looked down into her blurred eyes.

"Will you walk, or must I carry you?"

"You can't do this!"

Lucas laughed, lifted Alyssa into his arms and carried her from the house.

CHAPTER SIX

WHAT made men think they had the right to walk right in and take over a woman's life?

Was it bred in their genes? Was there a strand of male DNA labeled "authoritative jerk?" Had scientists missed it all these years?

Maybe so.

Alyssa figured that would go a long way toward explaining the way her father—her adoptive father—had treated her mother. It would explain how he'd tried to treat her. How he *had* treated her, as it turned out, thinking he could sell her as if time had turned back hundreds of years.

She was being carried off by a stranger, an arrogant, unwelcome visitor in this house that should have been hers.

The feel of his arms closing around her stunned her, but not for long. When Lucas began striding from the room, her useless lawyer sputtering weak protests as he scurried after them, Alyssa's shock turned to fury.

"Hey!" she shouted. "What do you think you're doing?"

The Lord of the Universe didn't answer. He just kept walking toward the front door.

"Wait a minute!" Her voice rose higher. "I said—"

"I heard what you said." He shifted her weight, opened the door and stepped onto the porch. A chorus of crickets and tree frogs greeted his appearance. "At close to a thousand decibels, how could I not?"

The old wooden porch creaked as he walked across it and made his way down the steps. To where? Alyssa thought crazily, but the answer was obvious.

He was taking her to Thaddeus's black Cadillac.

The hell he was!

She kicked. She cursed. She pummeled his hard, un-yielding shoulders. And she might have been an annoying mosquito, for all the response that got her.

"Damn it," she shrieked, "you can't do this!"

The prince dropped her to her feet beside the car.

"Norton. Give me your keys."

The command rang with authority. So did the pressure of the hand that kept her pinned to his side. Alyssa threw a desperate look at the lawyer who was watching the drama unfold with his pudgy mouth hanging open.

"Thaddeus," she said, "say something!"

Thaddeus stared at her. Then he cleared his throat.

"Your Highness. Your Majesty. Really, I don't think—"

"That's correct," Lucas said coldly. "You can't, or you would never have written that contract."

"I told you, it wasn't me, sir! It was your grandfather's people. Madeira, Vasquez, Sterling and Goldberg. Madrid, London, New York—"

"Spare me the roadmap, Norton. I know where they're located. Just give me your keys."

"Don't listen to him, Thaddeus!"

"She's right, sir. I mean, she could be right. About you not being able to do this. In fact, my legal opinion is—"

"He's useless," Lucas said to Alyssa. "If he weren't, you

wouldn't be in this fix to start with. His advice is the last thing you need."

"You just want me to lose the ranch!"

"You've already lost it, Alyssa. It's been sold. You have no claim to it any longer."

Her face heated. "Unless I marry you."

"There's no chance of that," Lucas said sharply. "If you think I'd let myself be ensnared in some old man's scheme…"

"You, ensnared? I'm the one who's trapped." Alyssa choked back a laugh. "It's like waking up and discovering you're starring in a bad old movie. The landlord. The maiden—"

"But no hero, *amada*. I refuse to be cast in that role." Lucas smiled unpleasantly. "As for the maiden… My grandfather might have fallen for the story of your supposed chastity but I'm not so easily fooled."

Color flooded her face. "Good. Because my chastity, or my lack of it, is none of your damned business!"

"I don't buy any of it, *chica*. For all I know, marrying me is precisely what you're after."

God, the insolence of the man! "You wish!"

Lucas grinned. "Ah, *amada,* you say that with such conviction."

"Just—just go away. Forget you ever came here."

"I would love to." A muscle knotted in his jaw. "I'd like nothing more than to walk away and know I'll never see you again."

"Do it. Turn around and start walking."

"I can't. My grandfather's lawyers wrote this damned contract because he wanted them to write it. Now he's ill." His voice roughened. "For all I know, he's dying. He made a commitment that matters to him and I'm not going to turn my back on it until I find a way out he can accept."

"You don't need to take me with you for that to happen."

"Unfortunately I do. I just explained the reason."

"You explained nothing!"

"This is a waste of time. Get in the car. Norton? For the last time, give me your keys." Lucas smiled coldly. "Unless you'd rather explain your part in all this to the Texas Bar Association."

It was a long shot. What did the lawyer have to explain, after all, except that he'd been unable to convince a dead man not to enter into an unenforceable contract?

But it worked. The attorney's face lost its color. Lucas saw it. So did Alyssa.

"Thaddeus," she said desperately, "Tell this—this lunatic that he can't do this!"

"This lunatic," Lucas said with some amusement, "is your only hope."

"You're not my hope! I'd sooner lose everything than marry you!"

"Haven't you been listening? You are not going to marry me! I am not going to be a sacrifice on the marriage altar."

"You, a sacrifice? What about me? This—this plan your horrible old grandfather hatched is—"

She gasped as Lucas grabbed her shoulders. "Watch yourself," he said softly. "And remember the bottom line. El Rancho Grande is at the heart of this situation."

"You don't give a damn about the ranch."

"You're right, *amada,* I don't." His expression hardened. "But my grandfather says you do. And, in honor of his commitment to an old friend, so does he." His mouth flattened. "That puts finding a way out of this mess squarely in my hands."

Alyssa's head was spinning. Refuse to go with Lucas

and the land was gone. Go with him and maybe, only maybe, it could be saved.

"This," she said shakily, "this has—it has become very complicated."

Lucas gave a bark of laughter.

"What if I agree to go with you? What will happen?"

"I'll convince my grandfather that the contract is unenforceable, write a check for the arrears and the balance of the mortgage, deed the ranch to you and pretend we never met."

She stared at him. "Can you do all that?"

He damned well hoped he could but she didn't want to hear his doubts any more than he did.

"Yes," he said, with more conviction than he felt.

"And you'll start by abducting me."

"This is hardly an abduction, *chica*. After all, you are my betrothed. It says so in that damnable stipulation."

"This isn't a joke! I'm not your anything and you know it."

"You're right. And I'm wasting time. So, decide, *amada*. Stay here or go with me. I'm tired of this discussion."

Alyssa opened her mouth to argue but argue about what? The damnable prince was right. They'd already talked the problem half to death and neither of them was any nearer a certain solution than before.

She looked at Thaddeus. He was right about that, too. Her father's lawyer was useless.

"Yes or no, *amada?* Do I leave you here, or do you come with me?"

A cloud drifted across the face of the moon, momentarily obscuring everything but Lucas Reyes's hard face. Alyssa shuddered as if the warm Texas night had suddenly turned cold.

This enigmatic stranger had invaded her life. He was all

but convinced she'd known about the contract. That she wanted to marry him for his money and his title.

That she was, in other words, sly, scheming and greedy.

What would he say if she told him she'd been heart-broken when she'd learned the land wouldn't be hers? That it was all she had left of her mother? That seeing the soil paved over, the old barns and stables knocked down to make room for what some called progress, would break her heart all over again?

Foolish question.

Lucas Reyes would say nothing. He wouldn't believe her.

And why should she believe him? He said he was taking her with him because he wanted to convince his grandfather the contract couldn't be enforced but was that true? Why would a man take a woman thousands of miles from her home for that reason?

Why should she trust him?

He could do anything to her, with her, once she left the safety of her home, her country…

"Well?"

His expression was still remote, his eyes flat pools of darkness. He was beautiful and terrifying and just the thought of all his power, all his intensity focused on her made her blood start to race.

Tears burned her eyes. She blinked them back. Her only defense was to convince him she wasn't afraid of him.

"If I were to go with you," she said, trying her best to sound calm, "you'd have to agree to certain—"

"Stipulations?"

His voice was soft as velvet but there was a razor-sharp edge to the implied humor in the word.

"Conditions," she said. "Certain conditions."

"Such as?"

"Such as, you are to treat me with respect."

A negligent shrug. "Done."

"And you are not to touch me."

He laughed.

"You think this is funny? That you can—that you think you can kiss me whenever you want?"

"I think you demand too much." His eyes went cold. "Too many conditions, provisos, stipulations, whatever. Come with me or don't."

A tremor went through her. Going with him was wrong. It was crazy. It was—

"Norton! The keys, man. Or I'll take them from you."

The keys arced through the darkness and into Lucas's waiting hands.

"Decision time, *amada*. I'm leaving, with you or without you."

Her feet wouldn't move. Lucas shrugged and got behind the wheel.

"Even if—even if I wanted to go with you," she said, rushing the words together, "I couldn't until—until I got my things."

"What things?"

"Clothes. My toothbrush. Things," she said, hating the desperation in her voice.

"I will arrange for you to get everything you need when we reach my country."

It was the kind of arrogant response she should have expected.

"My handbag, then. My wallet. My ID. Won't I need a passport?"

He laughed. Why wouldn't he? Even she had to admit it was impossible to think that a woman traveling with this man would need anything so mundane.

"Last chance," he said, reaching over the console and opening the passenger door. "Yes or no?"

Alyssa ran the tip of her tongue over her dry lips.

He made it sound as if she had a choice but they both knew she didn't. She hated him as much for that as for kissing her, for making her dizzy with his kisses…

The sound of the Caddy's powerful engine idling in the still night filled her with dread. Her heart bumped into her throat.

Quickly, knowing that thinking about it too long might be a mistake, she slid into the passenger seat and shut the door after her.

"Just be sure you understand one thing." Her voice trembled and she hated showing that little sign of weakness. "If there were any other way, I wouldn't go with you."

"Duly noted, *amada,*" he said, with a tight smile, "if not fully believed."

God, she wanted to launch herself across the console and hit that square, impertinent jaw but that would have been stupid and she knew it. Instead she looked out the window, saw Thaddeus's incredulous face and then the car was moving forward, gaining speed as it left the house and the attorney behind.

"Alyssa?"

Lucas sounded so calm. Had he realized this was all a terrible mistake? Was he human after all? Was he going to apologize for how he'd behaved?

"Yes?"

"Is there a better way to get to the local airport than the road I was on this morning?"

So much for wishful thinking. Bitterness made her incautious.

"The road where you made an ass of yourself, you mean?"

He stood on the brakes and the car skidded to a halt in a cloud of dust. He swung toward her, his face cold and hard in the light from the dashboard.

"I will not tolerate insolence."

"And what about what *I* will not tolerate? Your vicious assumptions. Your—your pathetic attempts at seduction..."

She was in his arms before she could protest. He took her mouth with his as he had those other times, hard, deep, fast. He kissed her as if the contract was valid and she was his.

Suddenly the shock of what was happening overwhelmed her.

Alyssa began to weep.

She cried without sound, tears trailing down her face. She tasted the salt of them on her lips and he must have, too, because all at once, his kiss changed.

His mouth softened, asked instead of demanded. He whispered her name against her lips.

And her bones felt as if they might liquefy.

No, she thought, I don't want this.

"Si, amada," he whispered, "you do."

Alyssa had spoken the thought but it didn't matter because Lucas was drawing her into his lap. She could feel the beat of his heart, the power of his erection.

And then she stopped thinking.

She leaned into him. Let his arms enfold her, his hard body take the weight of hers. She had stood alone for so long. For all of her life. To surrender to his strength, to give herself up to him...

A whimper broke from her throat.

His hands cupped her face. She covered them with hers and he tilted her head back, changed the angle of their kiss. Her lips parted, clung to his. His taste was on her tongue, clean and heart-stoppingly male.

Her body was singing.

Singing, and aching for more than this kiss. For more, oh God, more…

He whispered something in Spanish. She felt his mouth at the pulse point beating rapidly in her throat, felt his hands sweep down her body, beneath her leather jacket and skim her breasts, his thumbs barely brushing her nipples.

Sensation shot through her. She cried out, arched against him. Her head fell back and he bent his head, kissed her silk-covered nipple, closed his teeth lightly around it.

Another cry burst from her throat. She buried her hands in his hair and he said her name as he slid his hand down the back of her trousers, under the edge of her panties. His palm burned against her skin.

God!

She wanted this, wanted more, wanted—

Suddenly Lucas tore his mouth from hers. Her eyes flew open as he thrust her back into her own seat. She saw his face.

His cool, amused face.

"So much for my so-called pathetic attempts at seduction, *chica.* As for your response… Very nicely done. It's everything a man could want in a woman. Sweet. Passionate." The look of amusement fled. "And, unfortunately, a little too convincing. I cannot imagine a virgin would return a kiss with such fervor."

Alyssa lunged at him, fist raised. Lucas wrapped his hand around hers, hard enough to make her wince.

"You can understand, then, if I inform you that your comments about seduction strike me as a tease rather than a complaint."

She spat a word at him, and he laughed.

"Such language, *amada,* and from that supposedly innocent mouth." His laughter faded; his eyes turned cold.

"As for seduction… If you behave yourself, I might consider taking you to bed. But I wouldn't marry you if you were the last woman on earth. Is that clear?"

Alyssa yanked her hand free. "You're despicable."

"You break my heart."

"You don't have a heart!"

"All I want from you is help convincing my grandfather that this contract should never have been written, not for your sake or mine but for his. He is old and I love him, and I would not hurt him for the world. Do you understand?"

She wanted to make a clever response but her brain didn't seem to be working.

Lucas Reyes was a mass of contradictions.

She'd accused him of having no heart but he did, when it came to his grandfather. But when it came to everything else… How could he kiss her and fake all that passion?

Better still, how could she have responded to him when she hated him?

"Now," he said coolly, "I ask you again. Is there a better road to the airport?"

She wanted to tell him the road to hell was the best road for him, but she wasn't stupid.

Lucas Reyes was the enemy but for now, it would be best not to take him on. Instead she kept her voice as toneless as possible.

"Take the left fork at the end of the driveway, then the first road after that."

"And where will I end up, *amada?* On my way to the airport—or on my way to hell?"

The look on her face made Lucas want to laugh.

But he didn't.

Reading Alyssa McDonough's thoughts was easy—but there was little to laugh about tonight.

His grandfather lay ill. He was bringing home a woman he distrusted. Who knew what was truth and what was deceit? Finding the answer seemed as elusive as chasing moonlight.

And, come to think of it, how was he going to get home? His plane would not be waiting for him. He'd sent it to New York, hours ago.

Lucas's jaw tightened. *Madre de Dios,* what a mess!

He dug out his cell phone, mentally crossed his fingers and flipped it open. Four transmission bars appeared. Four beautiful, big transmission bars. Quickly, before the gods of mischief could erase them, he punched in 4-1-1 and asked for the airport's number.

Luck stayed with him.

The office was open. And yes, there was a plane available for rent and yes, its range was sufficient to get to New York City.

Lucas made the necessary arrangements, phoned his pilot in New York, told him to be ready to go as soon as they arrived at JFK. When he flipped the phone shut, he found Alyssa watching him.

"Do people always do as you tell them?"

It was a cool statement, not a question, and he knew better than to take her words as a compliment. Instead he leaned across the console, caught her face in his hand before she could pull away and took her mouth in a slow, deliberate kiss.

"Si," he said softly, "always."

Then he swung the car back onto the road and gunned the engine.

CHAPTER SEVEN

THEY left Texas in the small jet Lucas had rented, his hand firmly on Alyssa's elbow as they boarded, as if he thought she might bolt at the last minute.

The truth was, she thought about it but stubbornness and pride kept her moving up the steps and into the plane.

Backing down now would have been a sign of weakness.

In New York, they boarded his own plane. She'd expected something like the jet they'd flown from Texas, a small, handsome craft with a handful of seats.

She should have known better.

Lucas's plane was enormous, a sleek silver bird outfitted in glove-soft black and beige leather.

Though she'd lived in New York long enough to know that men who headed up international corporations often traveled in corporate jets and saw them not simply as perks but as necessities, she refused to think that of Lucas.

The way he treated her, his easy assumption that he could walk into her life and take it over and now the luxurious plane, even the presence of a steward, seemed proof that the Spanish prince saw himself as better than the rest of the world.

She didn't like this man. Didn't trust him. That she'd

been susceptible to his advances didn't just embarrass her, it angered her.

He'd sensed how naive she was and made the most of it.

Not anymore, she thought as the steward served dinner on fine china that bore a royal crest.

Now, she had a plan.

Eating the meal set before her was part of it. Maybe the steak and salad, the coffee and brie and water biscuits were the equivalent of breaking bread with the enemy but she had to maintain her strength.

Lucas would be a formidable opponent in what she increasingly saw as a complex chess game.

He had made the first move and he thought he had command of the board.

He didn't.

As soon as they reached Spain, she'd tell him he had three days to settle this thing. That was more than enough time to convince an old man that he stood to lose more than he'd gain by interfering in two lives.

Playing God was never a good idea, and Prince Felix Reyes had to understand that.

Three days. Then she was going home.

One year of law school hadn't turned her into a legal hotshot but even a novice could see that this contract had holes big enough to swallow a truck.

She'd go to New York, see her former professors. Surely one would give her the advice she needed.

Already, she could see the bare bones outline of how to fight the sale of the ranch.

Aloysius's body had wasted away. Toward the end, so had his mind. Who knew how long that had been going on? Had he been mentally capable when he'd sold the ranch? When he'd agreed to an unenforceable stipulation?

Maybe Felix Reyes had lied to him about what he was signing. Maybe Thaddeus had gone along with it, or maybe he'd simply been bowled over by a high-powered international law firm.

The bottom line was that the contract didn't make sense. Why would Felix Reyes have wanted such played-out land? Why would he have wanted her for his grandson?

Lucas could surely have all the women he wanted.

Alyssa finished her coffee, put down the delicate cup and saucer and glanced over at him, seated in a leather armchair across the aisle. His meal lay untouched on the table in front of him. His hands were wrapped around a heavy crystal glass that held an inch of amber liquid; his face was to the window.

Despite what she knew of him, what she thought of him, her pulse gave an unwelcome little kick.

He was so incredibly beautiful.

Tall. Dark. Masculine. And, ever since they'd changed planes in New York, quiet and brooding.

In fact, to her relief, he'd ignored her. He spent most of the time on the plane's satellite phone, speaking sometimes in English, sometimes in Spanish, his voice never loud enough for her to pick up more than a couple of words but enough so she knew his conversations were about his grandfather.

She almost found herself feeling sorry for him. She'd even come close to leaning over and—and what? Telling him everything would be okay? Offering her compassion?

What compassion had he offered her? He was a cold-hearted, manipulative tyrant, clearly accustomed to having his own way.

Lucas turned and looked at her. His eyes were very dark; the bones in his cheeks seemed more pronounced than usual. She could see that he was hurting…

Alyssa broke eye contact.

Three days. A second more was to court disaster.

In midafternoon, the jet began a smooth descent through a bright blue sky, touched down on a long ribbon of concrete and finally braked to a gentle stop.

Green meadows bracketed the landing strip; on a distant rise, a herd of horses stood silhouetted against a lush backdrop of leafy trees.

A black Rolls-Royce sped along a parallel road and stopped; two men in coveralls began wheeling a mobile staircase to the plane as the steward entered the cabin and opened the outside door.

"Welcome home, Your Highness," he said pleasantly.

Alyssa rose to her feet. So did Lucas, who clasped her shoulder as she started past him.

"Wait."

An imperial command. Did he think she was one of his subjects? She shrugged off his hand, brushed past the steward…

And almost tumbled into the yawning gap between the plane and the mobile stairs.

A strong arm wrapped around her waist and pulled her back.

"*Madre de Dios,*" Lucas said sharply, "what in hell were you doing?"

"I thought—the door—I thought—"

She was shaking like a leaf. So was he. Another step and…

Lucas cursed, turned Alyssa to him and gathered her tightly in his arms. He half expected her to resist but she collapsed against him, heart pounding against his, breath quick and shallow.

"Lyssa." He shut his eyes, buried his face in her hair. "It's my fault. The stairs—"

Alyssa shuddered. "There were no stairs."

"*Si.* I know."

"*It* was my fault entirely, sir," the steward said in a shaken whisper. "If I hadn't opened the door—"

"No, it's not your doing, Emilio." Lucas cupped Alyssa's face and lifted it so he could look into her eyes. "Emilio knows I always want the door opened as soon as possible. I like the smell of home. The grass. The sea beyond the hills. The horses." *Dios,* her face was so pale! "Now you will think I am a crazy man, admitting I love the smell of horses."

His attempt at calming her seemed to work. A hint of color rose in her cheeks and she gave a choked laugh.

"The only crazy person here is me, trying to walk on air."

The steps locked into place with a metallic thud.

"We can toss a coin to decide the winner later." Lucas's smile faded. "Are you all right, *chica?*"

"Yes. I'm—I'm fine."

Not true. He could feel her heart doing the *paso doble* and she was still trembling. Letting go of her was out of the question, and he swung her up into his arms.

"Lucas. Really. I can walk."

"*Si.* So can I. Humor me, *amada.* Put your arms around my neck and let me carry you to the car."

He didn't wait for her answer. Instead he crossed the grassy ribbon between the landing strip and the shiny black Rolls-Royce waiting on the blacktop. The driver saluted.

"Welcome home, Your Highness."

"Thank you, Paolo."

Lucas bit back a grin.

Paolo, normally the most unflappable of souls, was

having a difficult time trying not to stare but then, the sight of his employer with a woman in his arms was not an everyday occurrence.

It was not an occurrence that had taken place here at all.

Lucas had never brought a woman to the *finca*. It was his by birthright but it was also Felix's home, and he always exercised discretion where his grandfather was concerned…

Dios. Another problem, one he had not considered. Paolo would not be the only one of the household staff to be shocked at the sight of Alyssa. All of them would undoubtedly leap to the same conclusion, that he had finally decided to bring a mistress home with him.

He couldn't let that happen.

This was Spain. Princes still did not have to explain themselves to anyone but that rule didn't apply to young women, not in the world in which old bloodlines and older conventions still ruled.

"Paolo," he said gently.

The chauffeur blinked. "Sorry, sir. I, ah, I, ah—"

He swung open the rear door of the Rolls-Royce and Lucas slipped into the seat, Alyssa still in his arms. She struggled a little; his arms tightened around her and he put his lips to her temple.

"Sit still, *amada*," he whispered.

"Your driver will think—"

"Worry about what *I* will think, if you keep shifting against me that way."

The soft taunt had the effect he'd anticipated. Alyssa blushed and went very still just as Paolo got behind the wheel.

"This is Señorita McDonough," Lucas said.

"Señorita," Paolo said, smiling at her in his mirror.

"She will be visiting with us for a while."

"Yes, sir."

Lucas frowned. He'd have to come up with something better than that but for now…

For now, his thoughts returned to what mattered most. Felix.

"Has there been any change in my grandfather, Paolo?"

"None I have heard of, sir."

No. There wouldn't have been. Lucas had phoned endless times, spoken with doctors and nurses, with something called a patient liaison, and each had told him the same thing.

No change. Felix was still in a coma.

"Do you wish to go to the hospital, sir?"

"Take us to the house first. I'll get the *señorita* settled in and then I'll go to the hospital."

"I don't need settling in," Alyssa hissed. "And I wish you'd let go of me! What will the chauffeur think?"

Lucas looked at the firebrand in his arms. Her face was flushed, her hair had long ago come loose of its demure knot and whatever lipstick she'd had on was worn away by the endless hours since they'd left Texas…

Kissed away by his mouth on hers.

"You cannot just—just march around carrying me as if I were—as if I were—"

Bending his head, he kissed her, felt her initial struggle fade and become acquiescence, felt her lips soften, felt the sweetness of her sigh.

When he looked up, he caught Paolo openly gaping at them in the mirror.

"Paolo," he said gently, "I forgot to mention…"

"Sir?"

"Señorita McDonough has done me the honor of agreeing to become my wife."

* * *

"Are you out of your mind?"

They were the first words Alyssa had spoken since Lucas's impossible announcement.

He'd carried her from the car, up a set of steps and through the massive doors of what could only be called a mansion, past a butler, a housekeeper, a maid, past half a dozen people who stared at her, at him, then beamed when he made the same announcement to each.

This is Señorita McDonough. Mi novia.

His fiancée. His fiancée, when in reality she was a woman who wanted to claw his eyes out.

But she'd kept quiet, knowing anything she said would be pointless, that the arrogant Spanish prince would shut her up by kissing her.

Once they were alone, she'd tell him what an idiot he was.

And they were alone now.

He'd carried her up an elegant, curving staircase, down a wide hall, shouldered open a door, kicked it shut behind him and, at last, dropped her on her feet. Then he'd folded his arms and looked at her in a way that said he knew what was coming next.

"All right, *amada*," he'd growled, "let's have it."

And she'd given it to him. A look of rage, of disbelief, and then the question that was really a statement.

"Are you out of your mind?"

He had to be. Why else say they were engaged? Why further complicate something that was quickly becoming impossible?

He scowled. Glared. Ran his hands through his dark hair until it stood up in little ruffles. He paced across the room, swung around, faced her and said, "I had no choice."

"You had no choice?"

"That's correct. I had no—"

"You told everyone—everyone!—that I'm your fiancée because you had no choice?"

"*Chica.* If you would calm down—"

"We both agreed that contract, that inane stipulation, is a joke. It's why I said I'd come here with you, because we agreed. Because you said you'd find a way to make your grandfather see it was wrong."

"Unenforceable."

"Unenforceable, wrong, what's the difference?" Alyssa slapped her hands on her hips. "I knew I shouldn't have believed you!"

His face darkened. "Are you calling me a liar?"

"You just told your staff that we're engaged. What would you like me to call you? Creative? Inventive?" Alyssa blew a lock of hair out of her eyes. "I did a lot of thinking today. Tonight. Whatever you call it when you fly through umpteen time zones."

"Three time zones," Lucas said coolly. "I know it's difficult but try to be accurate."

"Four, counting this one, and that's not the point!" She strode toward him, eyes hot. "And now, here you are, telling your staff, telling the entire world that I am something I most definitely am not."

Lucas folded his arms. "Are you finished?"

"No, I am *not* finished. If you think, if you for one second think I would ever agree to the terms of that—that stipulation—"

"Amazing, how you make that into a dirty word."

"I wouldn't marry you if—if—"

"If I were the last man on earth. A cliché, *amada,* but why worry about such things when you're in the middle of a tirade?"

He was right. She was ranting and what was the point?

Hadn't she spent hours coming up with a plan? Well, with parameters for *his* plan, the one that involved making his grandfather see the light?

Alyssa took a deep breath.

"The point is—"

"The point," Lucas said grimly, stalking toward her, grabbing her by the shoulders, hoisting her unceremoniously to her toes, "the point, my charming *novia,* is that you have nothing to worry about. I would not marry you, either, not if you were the last female in the universe!"

"Then why—"

"Because," he growled, lowering his head so their eyes met, "because I am a fool who suddenly realized that bringing you here could ruin your reputation."

She opened her mouth, then shut it. Her reputation? This man had insulted her, threatened her, bullied her, accused her of lying about being a virgin, and now he was worried about her reputation?

He had to be joking.

"I admit, I should have thought of it sooner."

"Thought about my reputation," Alyssa said slowly.

"Yes. This is a small place. A world unto itself."

"What small place? What world?"

"This one," he said with impatience. "Andalusia. Those who live here. Those who breed these horses."

"*I* don't live here. And, as you surely know, *I* don't breed horses, Andalusians or otherwise." Her mouth thinned. "Not anymore."

"But you did."

"Once, a very long time ago, my mother bred them."

"And so will you, once I find a way to break the contract and return the land to you."

Her heart lifted. That was what he'd said he wanted to

do, to his grandfather during their phone call and then to her. Did he actually mean it?

"Trust me, *amada*. It is a small world we live in. You don't want people talking about you. I have no right to permit people to assume I need you here for—for the wrong reasons."

"You mean," she said coolly, "a man like you needs women for only one reason."

"Yes. No! Damn it, Lyssa—"

"You called me that before. It isn't my name."

"What in hell does what I call you have to do with what we're discussing?"

Alyssa blinked. What were they discussing, exactly? She wasn't sure anymore. Lucas was standing too close. His hands on her shoulders were too warm. His eyes were too dark.

"I like the name Lyssa," he said, his voice softening. "It suits you. Does it bother you that I call you by it?"

Bother her? Why would it? The way he said it, *Lyssa,* as if he were whispering it to her. As if it belonged only to them. As if they were alone together, their mouths fused, their bodies on fire…

Oh God!

"No," she said coolly, "no, it doesn't bother me at all. Anyway, you're right. It has nothing to do with what we were talking about."

"Reputations."

"Yes."

"Well, the point is…" Lucas cleared his throat. "The point is, the sight of you disconcerted my people."

"You mean," she said sweetly, "they're not accustomed to seeing you carry home the spoils of war?"

"They're not accustomed to seeing me bring a woman

into this house," he said, refusing to be sidetracked. "I've never done it before."

Why did that make her want to smile? "You haven't?"

"That's what I just said, *amada*. No, I have not. And I suddenly realized my people would—well, they would see you and come to the wrong conclusion." He cleared his throat. "I don't want them to think I brought you here for sex."

"So, I was right. You're concerned about your own rep—"

"Damn it," Lucas growled, "that's not it! You've been through enough. Why should anyone pin a label on you because of me?"

Alyssa blinked. Maybe there was a heart buried under all that macho muscle.

"That's—that's very kind, but—"

"Let everyone think you're my *novia*. It will protect you from gossip." His mouth twisted in a rueful smile. "Trust me, *amada*. Gossip travels, even from one side of the Atlantic to the other."

"Well—well, as I said, that's kind of you. But—"

"At the end of all this, I'll simply say we decided our engagement was a mistake."

She nodded. "Of course," she said, and wondered why what he'd said should make her feel a little sad.

Lucas nodded, too. "I'll tell Dolores to come up and see you. Let her know what you need."

"Everything," Alyssa said, with a little laugh. "Clothes. A toothbrush. A comb. A shower—"

"I can take care of that."

His voice was suddenly low and husky. She looked up and caught her breath at what she saw in his eyes.

"The clothes, I mean," he said softly. "I'll take you with me tomorrow. You can buy whatever you wish."

"I couldn't—"

"Of course you could." He smiled; one hand cupped her chin and he traced her lips with his thumb. "I carried you off, *amada*. I owe you much more than a shopping trip."

"Lucas—"

"You see? My name is not so difficult to say after all."

"Lucas." God, her head was swimming. She'd been furious at him just a little while ago. Now, all she could think of was how dark his eyes were. How the brush of his thumb felt on the curve of her lip. "Lucas. On the plane… I was thinking—"

Slowly he drew her to him. "*Si*. So was I."

"About—about our situation."

"I, too, *amada*." He smiled. "I was thinking how very glad I am that the contract stipulation did not involve a woman like the one my cousin Enrique found himself betrothed to."

"We're not betrothed," Alyssa said, and wondered at how breathless she sounded.

"No. Certainly not. But Enrique was." His smile became a grin. "His *novia* outweighed him."

Alyssa laughed softly. "You're making that up."

"Cross my heart," Lucas said, trying to look serious. "And she had only one eyebrow." He put his finger to his temple and drew a line straight across his forehead. "One thick, black eyebrow. Can you imagine?" Slowly, inexorably, he drew her into his embrace. "Only a very fortunate man finds himself in a marriage contract with a woman as beautiful as you, *chica*."

"It isn't a real contract," Alyssa said quickly.

"Of course not. But if it were—"

"It isn't," she said again and this time it was she who rose on her toes, who offered her mouth for Lucas's kiss.

He kissed her gently at first. Tenderly. Gathered her in his arms as if she were fragile as glass…but it wasn't enough.

Not for him.

Not for her.

"Lucas," she whispered, and he groaned and enveloped her in his arms, his kiss deepening, heating, and she responded to it, pressed herself against him, touched the tip of her tongue to his.

His hands slid down her spine.

He cupped her bottom. Lifted her into him. Into his erection. And when she gasped, he said something against her mouth and suddenly he was holding her as if she were a woman, not a delicate bit of crystal.

His hands swept under her skirt, up her legs, and she moaned and thrust her hands into his hair, lifting herself to him, telling him with every beat of her heart, every whisper of her breath, that she wanted him.

"*Amada,*" he said thickly, and he slid a hand between her thighs, cupping her, feeling her heat, hearing her sharp little cry of pleasure, feeling her dampness against his palm. Then she was in his arms again and he was carrying her quickly through the gathering shadows of late afternoon, through another door, to a bed, a four-poster bed hung with ivory lace…

Someone pounded on the sitting room door.

Lucas lifted his head. Lyssa was still in his arms, her eyes blurred with desire, her lips rosy and swollen from his.

The fist hit the door again.

"Sir! Your Highness! The hospital called. Your grandfather… He's conscious."

It took a moment to register. He had forgotten everything but the woman in his arms. The sorceress who had the power to dazzle him even though he still didn't know if she was a good witch or an evil one.

He lay her on the bed. Then he bent over her and kissed her again, hard enough to make her gasp, hard enough to nip her flesh…

Hard enough to leave his brand on her body as well as her soul.

Alyssa rolled onto her belly as he hurried from the room. She wrapped her arms around the pillow, her breathing quick, her pulse roaring in her ears. Her mouth still tasted of Lucas's; his scent was on her skin.

Another minute and she'd have given herself to him.

She moaned softly, shut her eyes and buried her face in the pillow.

She'd been wrong to let him bring her here but that could be remedied. She would leave him. Leave this place…

Except, she had no money. No passport. She had nothing but her anger and it stayed with her, made her leave the bed, shower, put on the same clothes she'd been wearing for what seemed forever, speak curtly to Dolores when the housekeeper knocked an hour later to see if she was all right.

"I'm fine," she snapped, and Dolores stammered out an apology for interrupting and left.

Alyssa felt as if she were coming apart. What she'd almost done, what she'd almost let Lucas do, proved it. Surely she'd never have melted into him if she were functioning normally.

She had not slept in hours. In days, or so it felt. She was beyond exhaustion; she knew that, but she couldn't seem to stop pacing while she planned what she would say to Lucas when he returned.

She remembered the night Aloysius had died. How she'd stood beside his still form and felt nothing. How, hours later, the tears had finally come, tears for what might have been.

This was different. She knew that.

And, as late afternoon became evening, she began wondering what Lucas was facing in a hospital room at the side of an old man he so obviously loved.

Night fell over the Reyes mansion. Stars blazed in new constellations of fierce fire against the pitch-black sky. The adrenaline that had kept her going suddenly drained away, leaving her spent and weary.

She stripped off her clothes, leaving them where they fell, wrapped herself in a soft white cotton robe she found in the closet and stumbled to the bed.

Long hours later, a whisper roused her from the depths of sleep.

"Lyssa?"

Alyssa forced her eyes open. Lucas was sitting on the bed beside her, limned by moonlight, weariness and despair etched in every line of his proud, beautiful face.

He stroked his hand over her hair.

"Forgive me for being gone so long, *chica*. But my grandfather—"

"Is he—?"

"He's alive," he said in a low voice, "but—"

He shook his head. Without thinking, she reached up and touched his cheek.

"I'm sorry, Lucas."

"*Si*. Thank you for that."

Alyssa looked up at him in silence. Then, slowly, she reached for him. On a soft groan, he gathered her close and stretched out beside her.

"Go to sleep, *amada*," he whispered, and she sighed, put her head on the shoulder of the arrogant, hard-hearted Spanish prince and took him with her deep, deep into sleep.

CHAPTER EIGHT

IN THE deepest hours of darkness, a night-creature called from the jasmine-scented gardens below the bedroom window. Its cry was soft, but it was enough to draw Lucas from his sleep.

He frowned into the darkness.

What bed was this? Not his. Neither was the room. For a second, he thought he was in New York, in his penthouse on Central Park West…

Until he felt the delicate weight of the woman in his arms.

Alyssa.

She was sprawled half-over his body, her thigh across his, her arm lying over his chest. Her head was on his shoulder; silky strands of her hair drifted across his lips.

Lucas closed his eyes.

She felt wonderful. Warm. Soft.

Perfect.

But what was he doing here, in her bed? He remembered returning from the hospital, anguished and exhausted. It had been late; the servants were all asleep, even Dolores. When he was a boy, she'd often waited up to see if he needed anything, though she'd never admitted to it.

Tonight, he'd been relieved to find she hadn't gone back

to those old habits, as she still sometimes did. He was too tired, too distressed to talk to anyone.

He'd gone slowly up the stairs to his rooms, pausing on the landing to look down the hall toward the guest suite. Was Alyssa still awake? Was she thinking about what had almost happened before he'd been called to the hospital?

He'd surely thought about it. Even sitting beside his grandfather's bed, the old man's icy hand in his, memories of those unplanned moments had come to him.

They had been unplanned, hadn't they? Or had Alyssa sensed it was the right time to draw him deeper into her net?

Lucas closed his eyes.

She insisted she didn't want to marry him any more than he wanted to marry her. What was the truth? He was too weary to think about it. A hot shower. A night's sleep. He'd known those were what he'd needed.

He would sort things out in the morning.

He'd gone to his suite. Undressed in the dark. Showered, let the water beat down on his neck and shoulders while he stood with his head bowed and his hands flat against the glass wall of the stall.

Restored in body if not in spirit, he'd pulled on a pair of gray sweatpants and fallen into bed, but sleep had been as elusive as peace of mind.

He'd thought about Felix. It was a good sign, wasn't it, that he was conscious? The dazed expression, the silence, would pass...wouldn't they?

And, inevitably, he'd thought about Alyssa. How it had felt to hold her. How she'd returned his kisses. How close he'd come to slaking his thirst for her, a thirst that had gripped him from those first minutes in the stable at El Rancho Grande.

He'd tossed and turned until his blankets looked as if a

demented Boy Scout had tied them in giant granny knots. Disgusted, he'd finally decided to go down to the library for a book.

Instead he'd bypassed the stairs and walked down the hall.

Where the hell do you think you're going, Reyes? he'd asked himself.

The answer was simple.

He'd gone straight to the guest suite, paused outside its closed door. He listened for a sound, checked to see if light shone under the door and found neither.

Why would Alyssa be awake at this hour? And what would it matter if she were?

Just walk away, he'd told himself sternly.

Even as he thought it, he'd turned the knob, opened the door, made his way quietly through the sitting room to the bedroom.

Alyssa lay sleeping in the canopied bed, her face gently lit by starlight. By exhaustion.

His fault.

He'd put her through hell the past day. Two days. He'd lost track. And yet, even now, she was beautiful.

His heart turned over. He wanted to wake her. Tell her he was sorry for everything, that he'd gone out of his way to frighten her in the stable, that he'd forced her to come here with him because who was he kidding? He *had* forced her. He'd given her about as much choice as a mouse trapped by a posse of cats.

The only thing he wasn't sorry for was what had happened in this room a few hours ago.

He'd wanted her. She'd wanted him. Her honest passion, her fire, had damn near stolen his breath.

The lady could be gentle as a kitten, tough as a tigress. He knew little else about her but he surely knew that.

Was that why Felix had pledged him to her?

There were a dozen other women would have been logical choices. More logical, really. Europe was filled with princesses and countesses whose families would have jumped at the chance to add Lucas's impeccable list of titles to theirs.

You could broaden the field, too. The Americas were home to heiresses whose fathers were eager for titles that would give old-world luster to their fortunes.

He'd met many of those women. American, European... they were all pretty and prettily spoiled, and every last one of them knew how to smile and flirt and please a man.

Tired as he was, Lucas had smiled.

Alyssa didn't seem to know how to do either. She was too strong, too independent. He couldn't think of another woman who'd have stood up to him the way she did.

Was that what Felix had thought would entice him? Her strength? Her independence?

Her virginity?

Felix had mentioned it but Lucas didn't believe it. Virgins were about as common as hen's teeth. Besides, virginity was overrated.

He wasn't from the old school. If men weren't held to standards of innocence, why should women be?

And, Lucas had suddenly asked himself, what in hell was he doing here, an intruder in Alyssa's bedroom? It was just that he was so damned tired. His room had seemed filled with shadows but this one—

This one seemed filled with Lyssa.

That was when he'd whispered her name. She'd awakened instantly and it was only then he'd realized she might scream or, at least, tell him to get the hell out...

Instead she'd asked about Felix in a soft, caring voice.

And when she opened her arms, it had seemed the most natural thing in the world to lie down beside her, gather her close, hold her to his heart and let her bring him the blessed comfort of sleep.

Lucas shifted his weight.

But he was awake now. Wide-awake, as far from sleep as a man could be, and he was incredibly aware of the woman in the bed with him, warm and sweet-smelling and all but sleeping on top of him.

He felt the stirrings of desire.

Bastard that he was, what he wanted from her now had nothing to do with comfort. In a heartbeat, he had an erection so hard and full it was almost painful.

How simple it would be to ease that discomfort.

A soft kiss, while she slept. A purposeful caress. By the time she was completely awake, he'd be inside her…

Madre de Dios. What kind of man would even contemplate such a thing?

Carefully Lucas slid his arm from beneath her shoulders.

"Lucas?"

Her whisper stilled him but the swift hiss of her breath as she realized how intimately they were entwined only gave him more reason to want her.

"Lucas. How did we… What are you…?"

He rolled over, lay next to her with his head raised just enough so he could see her face.

"It's all right, *amada,*" he said softly. "We took a *siesta.* Nothing more."

He could see her trying to reconstruct what had led to this just as he had done a few minutes ago. Finally she nodded.

"I remember."

"*Gracias,* Lyssa."

"For what?"

Gently he ran the tip of his index finger over her soft mouth.

"For giving me these hours of sleep. I don't know why but I could not have had them on my own."

"I understand."

"Do you?"

"When Aloysius was—when he was very sick, there were times I was so tired I could hardly hold my head up. Still, I'd get into bed and lie there, wide-awake." She took a breath, then let it out in a soft sigh that flowed over his fingers like silk. "I didn't love him the way you love your grandfather but it's hard to watch when someone who's been part of your life is suffering."

Lucas smiled. "Does my love for Felix show?"

"Like a badge of honor." She smiled, too. "He must love you the same way."

Lucas's smile tilted. "Amazing," he said softly, "but I have never before lain with a woman and discussed my feelings for my grandfather."

Color rose to her face. "You haven't exactly lain with me, Lucas."

"No." His voice grew husky. "I have not." His gaze dropped to her mouth, then lifted to her eyes. "All the more reason for me to leave your bed, *amada*. But first, a kiss good night."

Her breathing quickened. "I don't think that's—"

"One kiss," he whispered, and took her mouth. Gently. No force. No coercion. If she tried to stop him, he would stop.

He would die…but he would stop.

But she didn't stop him.

Instead the sound she made against his lips was so delicate it made his heart pound.

"Lucas," she said against his mouth. "Lucas…"

He answered by cupping her face with his hands.

She answered by parting her lips to his.

The taste of her made his head swim. She was honey. She was the richest Spanish sherry made from the ripest fruit, sweet and warm from the sun.

Her hands rose. Threaded into his hair. He groaned and slipped his tongue between her lips, felt her momentary hesitation and then she made another of those little sounds that drove him half out of his mind and sucked delicately on the tip.

A rush of heat sizzled through his body.

Leave her bed now, Lucas.

He could hear the voice inside him, hear its tone of command but he could no more obey that order than he could stop the tide of desire rising within him.

He couldn't leave her. She didn't *want* him to leave her. Not if she was looping her arms around his neck and drawing him even closer.

So close that he stopped thinking.

Touch. Taste. Smell. Sound. Those were the only things that mattered. The taste of her skin, there. Right there, in the hollow of her throat. At the juncture of throat and shoulder. At the elegant angle of her collarbone…

Alyssa trembled in his arms.

"Lucas," she whispered, "ohmygod, Lucas…"

"Yes," he said, *"si, amada."*

He whispered to her. In English. In Spanish. Words of need. Of desire. Words that made her gasp with shock.

With pleasure.

"Amada. Let me. Let me—"

"Yes," she said, "please, yes," when she felt his hands at the sash of her robe but his fingers were uncharacteristically clumsy and an eternity seemed to drag by until he finally fumbled the knot open.

The halves of the robe fell apart, revealing her to him.

Alyssa, his Lyssa, was more than beautiful. She was exquisite, everything he'd ever imagined, everything he'd ever dreamed.

And so feminine, so delicate, it made his heart leap.

He bent his head to worship her.

He cupped one rounded breast. Brought it to his mouth. Kissed the silken slope, then touched his finger to the softly pink nipple and she cried out in shock.

He knew what she was feeling because he felt it, too. The excitement. The hunger. He'd felt it before, the hot demand of sexual craving, but never like this.

Never like this.

He looked at her face. Her eyes were clouded, unseeing with passion.

Slowly he drew the nipple into his mouth, sucking, gently biting, laving her flesh. A cry broke from her throat, so wild and raw that he groaned.

He kissed his way down her torso, touched the tip of his tongue to her navel, kissed her belly and finally reached the soft curls that guarded her feminine delta.

She dug her hands into his hair.

"No," she said brokenly, "Lucas, you can't—"

He caught her wrists, brought her hands to her sides. Nuzzled against the dark curls, found her center and kissed her.

She cried out again and arched against him.

"Lyssa," he said hoarsely, and he let go of her wrists, slipped his hands beneath her and lifted her to him. Her hands were in his hair again but, this time, she wasn't trying to stop him.

She held him to her, sobbing as he put his mouth to her, found that sweetest of flowers and kissed it, sucked on it, nipped it until she screamed into the night, a scream of release, of the ultimate completion.

He could feel her orgasm rip through her body, feel it consume her and as it did, he sat back, tugged down his sweats, kicked them off and came back to her.

"Lyssa," he said.

Her eyes cleared and he felt his heart expand when she looked up at him.

"Lyssa," he said again, *"amada…"*

He held her gaze as he parted her thighs. As he guided his rigid length to her.

"Lucas," she whispered.

Later he would play that one word over and over in his head and hear in it what his fevered brain had not been willing to let him hear this first time.

He bent to her and kissed her mouth and, as he did, he entered her, sank into her, groaned as she sobbed his name against his lips.

She rose to meet him, her hands around his biceps, her fingers digging into his muscles as her silken heat closed around him.

"Lyssa," he said, "oh God, Lyssa…"

And then he stopped moving. Damned near stopped breathing.

Alyssa was a virgin.

For a heartbeat, he held still above her, his life, his breath seeming to hang suspended on the brink of eternity.

"Yes," she said, "please, yes."

Slowly, so slowly he thought it might kill him with pleasure, he sank into her. Her eyes closed. His name sighed from her mouth.

He could feel his own release rushing toward him. He wasn't ready for it. Physically, yes, but in every other way he wanted this moment to go on and on.

He was poised on the very edge of a cliff with all the world spread out beneath him. It would take a god to stay still.

But he was only human. And when Alyssa moved, when her body arched, when her womb began tightening around him, Lucas knew he was lost.

She sobbed his name. She reached her hand to him. He caught it, caught the other hand as well, brought them to his mouth, then entwined his fingers with hers against the cool ivory sheets.

"Lucas," she said again.

Her voice broke. She was afraid, he thought in wonder, and he bent and kissed her mouth.

"I'm here, *amada*," he said thickly. "I'll be with you this time. Just let go and fly with me. Fly with me…"

Alyssa sobbed his name. Lucas flung back his head. And, just as he had promised, they flew together into the inky blackness of the endless night.

CHAPTER NINE

WAS this really what it meant, to lie with a man?

Alyssa tightened her arms around Lucas, stunned by the transcendent passion of his lovemaking.

I'll be with you this time, he'd whispered, and he'd kept his promise. The power of his climax had driven her higher, higher, higher…

Was this what sex was? Pure, white-hot magic?

Yes, she was a virgin but even virgins knew something about sex. That girls whispered about it and giggled. That some women rolled their eyes and said, in bored voices, it wasn't all what it was supposed to be.

Alyssa had never had anyone she could ask. In private school, the girls moved in tight little cliques and she, shy and leggy and more comfortable around horses than people, was always on the outside looking in. By college, it was too late to ask. Feeling naive was bad enough. She didn't want to feel stupid, too.

Once, right after her first period, she'd started to ask questions of her mother. Elena Montero McDonough had blushed, waved her hand at the horses that ran on the ranch back then and said Alyssa had all of nature for a classroom.

Maybe. But a stallion mounting a mare had nothing to do with what had happened in this bed.

Sex, it turned out, was not all about the stallion's domination and the mare's submission.

It was about giving yourself to a man. The feel of his body possessing yours. The heat of his kiss. The touch of his hand, the knowledge that he could make you want him, want him, want him…

Want the enemy. Want a stranger.

Alyssa's throat constricted. She wanted to weep, not for what she had done but for what it should have meant. What it *had* meant, those wondrous transcendent moments as Lucas made love to her.

Except it hadn't been love. It had been lust. Calculated lust, for all she knew. It was the stallion and the mare all over again.

The mare Lucas had crossed the ocean to buy.

How could she have forgotten that?

"Lyssa?"

His voice was husky. He was still lying on top of her, his weight bearing her down into the softness of the bed. She wanted to hit him with her fists. Wanted to wrap her arms around him and tell him—tell him—

"*Amada,* are you all right?"

She swallowed dryly. He lifted his head, his hazel eyes questioning. What did he think she would say? That what had just happened changed everything? That she would do whatever he wanted? Go home, accept that nothing she could do would save her mother's land?

The truth was, she had no idea what he wanted her to do…

Except bend to his will.

In the short time she'd known the Spanish prince, she had lost everything to him. Her home. Her future and now, her virginity. The only thing she had left was her pride, and she would never let him take that.

"Would you get off me, please? You're heavy."

He blinked. Apparently he was accustomed to a different kind of pillow talk. She was probably supposed to be telling him how wonderful he was, how exciting...

He was. He was all that and more.

"Sorry. I didn't realize..." He rolled off her. Her body was damp; the air felt cold on her flesh. The robe lay crushed beneath her and she grabbed the edges of it and pulled them together.

Lucas leaned over her.

"Are you okay?"

"I'm fine."

"I didn't realize..." He cleared his throat. "I didn't think you were—"

"Really?" She sat up, her back to him. "But that was part of the deal, wasn't it? Aloysius's assurance to Felix that I was a virgin?"

He put his hand on her shoulder. "*Amada.* I'm sorry you're upset. I didn't...I didn't mean for this to happen."

His voice was low. Husky with remorse. Somehow, that made it worse.

"Didn't you?"

The clasp of his fingers tightened. "What is that supposed to mean?"

Alyssa shrugged off his hand, stood up and knotted the sash of the robe at her waist.

"I've been around horses all my life."

The bed creaked. She heard the pad of Lucas's feet and then he was standing in front of her, his eyes narrowed.

"And?"

There was warning in the single word but she didn't

care. The only warning that mattered was one that would have kept her from surrendering to him half an hour ago.

"And," she said, wishing she were wearing more than this thin robe, wishing she weren't so flagrantly, magnificently naked, "and I know all those theories about the best ways to make a mare submit to a stallion."

Silence filled the room. Then Lucas reached for his sweatpants and stepped into them. His voice, when he spoke, was frigid.

"You think I seduced you to force you into some kind of obedience?"

An image of him kneeling between her thighs flashed through her mind, along with the memory of how it had felt to have him deep inside her.

"Alyssa? Is that what you think?"

Looking at him, hearing the taut anger in his words, she didn't know what to think. All she was sure of was that admitting doubt would be a sign of weakness.

"What I think," she said evenly, "is that I've made a terrible mistake."

He looked at her for a long moment, his face stony. Then he nodded.

"I agree. It was the worst possible mistake. Unfortunately we cannot undue it."

"No. We can't."

"I took your virginity."

That was what he said but the words sounded wrong, as if he meant something entirely different.

"I should have believed my grandfather when he told me you were intact."

Color flooded her face. She supposed the term was correct but it sounded cold, as if it were a description in an auction-house brochure. *The piece for sale is intact...*

"And now you've lost your bargaining chip. Deliberately, but you've lost it, nonetheless."

Alyssa blinked. "My what?"

"Ah, *chica,* it's too late for that innocent look. You know damned well what I'm talking about. Felix's values are those of another time. He saw your virginity as a requirement for your bride price." Lucas's mouth thinned. "But I don't give a damn whether a woman's a virgin or not and most certainly, I am not looking for a bride." He flashed a thin smile. "Which is why, I suppose, you felt desperate enough to toss me this morsel."

"You think that I...?" Enraged, Alyssa flew at him, hand raised, but he caught her by the wrist and twisted her arm behind her back. "You were only in this bed because I felt sorry for you, and God knows why I was that stupid! *You* were the one who turned an act of—of kindness into a— a lesson in seduction."

"Seduction?" His teeth showed in a lupine smile. "What happened in this bed is the same as what happened the day we met. You couldn't control yourself here any more than you could control that horse."

"Bastard," she hissed, "you no-good, egotistical—"

She went for his eyes with her free hand. Lucas caught it, drew it behind her where he manacled both her wrists. The action lifted her to her toes.

"Do you take me for a fool, *chica?* Nothing you do will persuade me to honor the stipulation you keep insisting you don't want me to honor."

"I'd sooner marry a—"

"So you have already said." He smiled, though his eyes remained cool. "I have known many clever women, too many to be taken in by you."

"I wouldn't doubt that for a minute," she panted as she

struggled to free herself from his grasp. "I saw one of them, remember? That—that wind-up toy with the bleached hair, big boobs and a brain the size of a walnut!"

Lucas grinned. "An excellent description, *amada*. But at least she admits she's after something when she lures a man into her bed."

"Pig!"

"Is that the best you can do?" He let go of her and strode to the door. "Tomorrow," he said grimly, "I will speak with my attorneys."

"It's today," she said, flinging the words at him. "And at least you finally said something intelligent."

"Here's something even more intelligent. I am sure they will see that the entire contract is a farce and I am liable for nothing."

"You are liable for the money you owe me!"

"My corporation owes it, and not to you. To Norton, as executor."

"Dance around all you like. Your grandfather made a deal and you're stuck with it."

His eyes flashed. "But not with you, *chica*."

"Trust me, Your Mightiness. The feeling is mutual." Alyssa glared at him. "When will you meet with your lawyers?"

Amazing, Lucas thought. She had to know she was on the losing end of the battle, that his attorneys would find a way to void the entire contract, but she was still behaving as if she were his equal.

She'd been like that in bed, too. Shy, at first. Holding back. Then, little by little, coming to life beneath his hands and mouth. Showing him what she wanted. What pleased her.

What had pleased him was the simple act of making love to her. Not that it had felt simple. He'd been with a lot of women, more women than most men, perhaps, but what had happened in this room, this bed, had seemed far more complex than anything he'd known in the past.

The act had seemed richer. Fuller. At the end, when she'd trusted him enough to let go and come with him…

When she'd done that, when she'd contracted around him even as the power of his own orgasm shot through him, he'd felt—he'd felt—

"Don't just stand there, Your Highness! I want to know when this meeting will take place! And, of course, I intend to go with you."

She intended to go with him? He almost laughed. She had no more right to attend a meeting with his lawyer than she had to keep claiming El Rancho Grande should be hers.

He looked out the window. The sky glowed pink with the morning light. No one would be in the Madrid offices of Madeira, Vasquez, Sterling and Goldberg, but that presented no problem.

The answering service would take the message. Ricardo Madeira himself would return the call within minutes.

There were occasional benefits to being Prince Lucas Reyes, even if this woman chose not to see them.

And having Alyssa with him might be an advantage. Let Madeira see precisely what he was up against.

"Be downstairs in one hour," he said brusquely. "And be prompt, *amada*. I do not like to be kept waiting."

Could an enraged woman pass up such an opportunity? He had taken all the time in the world to make love to her and she knew it, but she had the feeling she was losing their verbal war. Here was a chance to make points.

"Yes," Alyssa said sweetly, "I know how quickly you like to do things."

She knew instantly she had pushed him too far. His eyes

went from gold to green; the bones in his face stood out in harsh relief.

"Really," he said, very softly.

She stumbled back. "No," she said, the one word a terrified breath.

It didn't matter.

Lucas grabbed her. Drew her to him despite her struggles and caught her face with one hand.

"Watch what you say, *amada*. Or I may have to take you to bed again and make love to you until you beg me for release."

"In your dreams!"

He laughed softly. "No, *amada*. In yours."

He lowered his head and kissed her hard. Deep. Kissed her with a passion that bordered on cruelty. Then he flung her from him.

"An hour," he said coldly. "Or I leave without you."

The door slammed shut behind her. Alyssa didn't move. Then, after a long moment, she touched the tip of her tongue to her lips, tasted Lucas, his heat, his possession...

And closed her eyes in despair.

There were tiny spots of blood on her thighs.

On the sheets.

The blood on her thighs was easy to deal with. A hot shower, plenty of soap and the blood drops were gone even if the pain in her heart was still there.

The sheets were different. She agonized over what to do with them. The thought of one of the maids seeing that blood and knowing what had happened was more than she could bear.

Quickly she stripped the bed, carried the sheets into the

bathroom, sponged them clean, then dried them with the built-in hair dryer.

She dressed in the same clothes she'd been wearing since the evening Lucas had taken her from the ranch, whenever that was. One day. Two days. Three. She'd lost track.

One of the maids had been thoughtful enough to wash and press the garments. They looked like hell but they were, at least, clean. Not that she gave a damn. Who cared how she looked? She certainly didn't.

She left her room fifteen minutes before the hour after giving the timing some thought. Instinct told her to saunter down the stairs a few minutes late. That same instinct warned that if she were late, Lucas would leave without her.

Being early, waiting for him so that he'd seem to be the one who was late, seemed the best solution.

No such luck.

He was already in the vast entry foyer, lounging carelessly in an elaborate leather and wood chair that reminded her of a throne. Deliberate on his part, no doubt, she thought coldly.

He rose when he saw her and she knew she'd lied to herself about not caring how she looked. Lucas looked— why not admit it? He looked magnificent. His dark blue suit had surely been custom-made to suit his broad shoulders, narrow waist and long legs. Beneath it, he wore a crisp white shirt and maroon tie. She could tell he'd just showered: drops of water glittered like tiny jewels in his midnight-black hair.

He'd shaved, too. The dark stubble that had covered his jaw was gone.

The dark, sexy stubble that had felt so delicious against her thighs, her breasts…

"You need new clothes."

Alyssa drew herself up. "I need nothing from you, Your Mightiness."

A dangerous glint flared in his eyes. "Clothes, and manners. We are about to meet with Ricardo Madeira. You will not address me with disrespect, nor will you argue with what I say."

"I also will not curtsy," she informed him as they stepped into the back of the long black Rolls-Royce waiting in the driveway. "I suggest you keep that in mind."

To her surprise, he laughed. "I think I would have known you had Spanish blood even if no one had told me your middle name was Montero."

"I hate to disappoint you, but my blood is pure Texan. The Montero name dates back four centuries in the New World. I am descended from conquistadores."

Another quick laugh. "Some would say that is nothing to boast about."

"They did as men did in those times. And they were brave and fearless."

"What of your real father? Montero? Did he divorce your mother?"

"He died, when I was two."

"So you don't remember him?"

She shook her head. It was one of the sorrows of her life that she had no memory of the father who had surely loved her as Aloysius never had.

"No. I don't."

"When did McDonough adopt you?"

"When my mother married him. I was four."

Why was she telling him all this? She never talked about her past to anyone. Losing the father who'd loved you to be raised by one who didn't was no one's affair but her own.

"He was unkind to you?"

"I don't see that any of this is your concern."

"I have no idea what is or is not my concern until I've talked with Madeira."

"Until *we've* talked with him. This situation is intolerable. It must end."

Intolerable, Lucas thought. Being with him. Making love with him. Learning she was betrothed to him. Intolerable, all of it.

She was right. Of course, she was right…

Frowning, he leaned forward.

"There's no traffic," he told Paolo sharply. "Surely we can go faster."

The road wound through lush green countryside dotted with elegant villas and, tucked back among stands of orange and encina trees, enormous mansions.

Signs flashed by. Marbella was just ahead.

That explained the scent of the sea. Alyssa had never been to Spain but she knew Marbella was in the south, on the Mediterranean, facing across a narrow strip of it to North Africa and the mysteries of Tangiers.

She knew this was the gold coast, the home and playground of fabulously rich Spaniards and Europeans. Horses were expensive to breed and raise, the Andalusians of the quality the Reyes name was known for took "expensive" up another notch, and the cost of the Reyes acreage would be extraordinary.

Of course, the prince could afford it. He had no heart but he had money, power and arrogance enough for a thousand men.

"Most Andalusian breeders ranch further inland but I prefer the La Concha foothills." Lucas gave her a level look when she turned toward him. "That's what you were wondering, wasn't it? Why I breed horses here?"

"Why should I think about your horses at all?"

"Because you claim to be a horsewoman."

"I *am* a horsewoman, *señor.*"

"Most certainly." His words dripped sarcasm. "I could tell that by the way you handled that black monster."

"Bebé has fine bloodlines. And he was not at fault!"

"Bebé has the bloodlines of brontosaurs but you're right, he was not at fault. You were."

"That shows how little you know about me."

Lucas smiled coolly. "I know more about you than most men, don't I, *chica?*"

Alyssa turned crimson. "I was wrong when I called you a pig. They're actually intelligent creatures with bad press. Exactly the opposite of you."

Hell. He couldn't blame her for taking offense but, damn it, he was still angry. If only he could clear his head of the image of her, naked in his arms. Naked, and trembling, and pleading for his possession…then telling him, in a voice that would have frozen tap water, to get off her.

The time to have done that was when he realized she was a virgin but he was a man, not a saint. So he'd taken what she had offered.

Afterward, lying with her still in his arms, he'd felt a tenderness that was new to him, and a hunger to make love to her again.

First, though, he'd wanted to tend to her. Gently, with a warm, damp cloth. He'd wash her, kiss away any soreness.

Instead she'd insulted him. Made it clear what had happened had meant nothing to her. That had infuriated him, and he'd responded in kind. Which was just as well, he thought as the Rolls-Royce slowed, then stopped in a square lined with white stucco villas and palm trees.

It had sent him to the phone to make this appointment.

Paolo opened the door. Lucas stepped out and offered his hand to Alyssa, who ignored him.

"I thought your attorneys were in Madrid."

"They are. Madeira would have flown down here, of course—"

"Of course," she said with a scathing smile.

"But, as luck would have it, he's in Marbella this weekend. He's meeting us in a friend's office. Well? Are you getting out of the car, or are you going to stay here and sulk?"

Alyssa tossed her head, brushed his hand away and stepped into the cobblestone courtyard.

Good, Lucas thought viciously. She was making it easy to forget any sentimental claptrap about what he'd felt in bed with her. Amazing, the spin even a sensible man could put on taking a woman's virginity.

Madeira would review the contract. He'd agree that whole damnable stipulation was illegal, admit he had added it only because Felix had insisted. Lucas would pay the balance of what Reyes owed to Thaddeus Norton, the McDonough executor.

Then, as new owner of the ranch he didn't want, he'd commit an act of charity and sign it over to Alyssa Montero McDonough, who would then get the hell out of his life.

He supposed he could have done all this without consulting his attorney but this would make striking out the marriage clause legal and official. If Felix recovered… No. When Felix recovered, it might upset him but Lucas would deal with that when it happened.

Right now, the important thing was voiding that damned stipulation without leaving any loose ends behind.

So simple. It was almost enough to make him smile.

* * *

It was a good thing he hadn't actually gone ahead and smiled, Lucas thought two hours later.

Madeira expressed his sorrow at Felix's illness. Lucas thanked him. Madeira offered coffee. Lucas brushed it aside and handed the attorney the copy of the contract Thaddeus Norton had given him.

Madeira didn't bother looking at it.

"I had your grandfather's files faxed to me, Prince Lucas, the moment you phoned."

"Good, because I don't want to waste time. I want your legal opinion on this as quickly as possible." Lucas smiled knowingly. "Of course, I already know it's not legal. Parts of it, at any rate…but then, you must know that, too, since you wrote it."

Madeira smiled politely. "I am not in the habit of writing illegal contracts for my clients, Your Highness. If you will just give me a minute…"

An hour passed. Lucas glowered while the attorney read. Hummed. Tapped his pencil against his nose. Made notes.

Finally Madeira looked up.

"Not illegal," he said. "Unenforceable."

"The same thing," Lucas snapped.

The lawyer sat back, crossed one leg over the other, steepled his hands under his dew-lapped chin and smiled.

"Not at all, sir. The contract lays out terms agreed upon by your grandfather and Aloysius McDonough. Legal? Absolutely. Unenforceable? *Si*. I apprised Felix of that fact at the time."

Lucas felt a muscle flicker in his jaw.

"What," he said carefully, "does that double-talk mean?"

"It means, Your Highness, that this is well-crafted document."

The muscle in Lucas's jaw flickered again. "Undoubtedly, but as we have already agreed, you wrote it."

"Yes. But your grandfather had a hand in drafting some of the more unusual clauses."

"Let's get to the point." The men looked at Alyssa. Of course, she thought coldly. They had all but forgotten she was there. "You said this thing isn't illegal but it is. Selling women into slavery has actually been illegal for centuries." She paused for emphasis. "In my part of the world, anyway."

"No one sold you into anything," Lucas said sharply.

The attorney nodded. "Certainly not."

"Ms. McDonough is right, Madeira. Let's get to the point. I own El Rancho Grande."

"No."

"Well, of course, I meant I will own it should I choose to pay the balance of the selling price."

"And marry the lovely *señorita*."

"That's ridiculous!"

Lucas and Alyssa spoke with one voice. Madeira folded his hands over his little belly and sighed.

"That's exactly what I tried to tell your grandfather."

"Well, then? What's the problem?"

"The problem is that legally, a contract is a contract. It's the meeting of the minds that's important."

"More double-talk," Lucas snapped.

Madeira shook his head. "What I'm saying, Your Highness, is that enforceable or not, contracts of this sort stand as written unless voided by the signatories." The lawyer peered at Alyssa. "One of those parties is deceased." He looked at Lucas. "And the other is incapacitated." His expression turned solemn. "Did I tell you how sorry we were to hear about your grandfather?"

"You did, yes." Lucas cleared his throat. "So, what are

you telling me, Madeira? That there might be reasons an un-enforceable contract *can* be enforced?" He flashed a chilly smile. "That's a bit too much bullshit even for a lawyer."

"Let me ask you something, Prince Lucas. Your grand-father and I discussed his giving you his power of attorney but there doesn't appear to be any such paperwork in his file."

"What does it matter? I represent the Reyes Corporation, not my grandfather."

"Ah, but Prince Felix signed this agreement in his own name, not that of the corporation." Madeira paused. "Of course, you can simply renege on the contract."

"Not pay the balance of the money?"

Alyssa made a muffled sound. Both men looked at her.

"Without that money," she said carefully, "the bank will take the ranch."

"Unfortunately," the lawyer said, "that is not Prince Lucas's problem."

"No," Lucas said coldly, "it is not."

Alyssa rose to her feet. "Despite everything, I know there's a decent human being somewhere inside you."

The lawyer blanched. "Señorita McDonough!"

"I know that because I know you love your grandfather. Surely there must be a way—"

"For you to get my money and my title? Sorry, *amada*. There isn't. Nice try, though."

Alyssa looked at him for a long minute. Her eyes glittered; was it with anger or frustration or maybe even despair?

Without another word, she stalked from the office.

Lucas watched her go. Then he cursed, shot from his chair and went after her.

CHAPTER TEN

LUCAS ran down the steps, out the door and into the courtyard.

There was no sign of Alyssa, which was impossible. How could a woman vanish in the blink of an eye?

"Sir?"

She'd had, what, a second's lead? Not even that. He'd been right on her heels.

"Prince Lucas! Your Highness!"

His driver hissed the words but they carried easily on the warm, still air. A woman walking an obese poodle stopped and stared as Paolo, gesticulating wildly, hurried up to Lucas.

"I called out to Ms. McDonough, sir, but she went right past me."

"Are you Prince Lucas?" the woman with the fat poodle said. "Oh, you are! Can I have your autograph?"

"Where?"

"Anywhere! On my hand. No, my shirt. No, on Frou Frou's collar—"

"Where did she go?" Lucas demanded, turning his back to the woman and the poodle.

"That way, sir. She went toward the corner."

"Oh my," the woman said. "This is so exciting!"

Lucas shot the woman and dog a look that silenced her and started the little dog yapping. Wonderful, he thought coldly. Soon, all of Marbella would know a woman had run from the Prince of Andalusia.

Well, let Alyssa run. He'd be damned if he'd make a fool of himself by chasing after her. No way would he—no way would he—

"Mierda," he snarled, and set off running.

He saw her as soon as he turned the corner.

At this hour on a weekend morning, the streets were already busy. Tourists were window-shopping; people were searching for just the right table at just the right *café al aire libre.*

Still, Alyssa stood out in the crowd.

Everyone was strolling but she was moving fast. Added to that, she was the only woman on this expensive stretch of real estate wearing a leather jacket, black trousers and boots. Shorts, navel-skimming T-shirts, bright summer dresses and sandals were the order of the day.

She really did need new clothes, Lucas thought, and grimaced at the irrelevancy of the idea. She was running away from him. What did he care about her clothes?

He slowed to a brisk walk. He'd drawn enough curious glances. Better to move at a slightly faster pace than she. He'd catch up to her in a minute or two.

A workable plan, except Alyssa picked that moment to look back. Their eyes met; she spun away and began to run.

"Damn it," Lucas growled.

He shouted her name. It didn't stop her but it drew the attention of other people. *Dios,* he was the new spectator sport of Marbella.

"Alyssa!" he yelled again.

Then he cursed and took off after her.

His stride was much longer than hers; it gave him a distinct advantage. Within seconds, he was only a couple of feet behind her. By the time they reached an intersection, he was only an arm's length away.

And then, everything blurred.

Alyssa stepped off the curb.

A horn blared. A red truck was barreling down the road toward her. Lucas shouted her name and leaped off the curb.

He hit her, hard. They fell, rolled and the truck shot by them, horn still blaring, so close he could smell the rubber of its skidding tires and feel the dust from the cobblestones blow into his face.

For an instant, the world stood still. Lucas could hear nothing but its hush and the drumbeat of his heart.

"Alyssa," he whispered, and she turned in his arms and sobbed his name.

He shut his eyes. Gathered her to him. *"Amada,"* he said thickly. *"Madre de Dios, amada!"*

The truck had stopped. The driver ran back and squatted beside them. "Are you okay?"

Lucas nodded. He cupped Alyssa's head, brought her face to the crook of his neck.

"The lady just stepped out in front of me. I couldn't—"

"*Si.* I know. It was not your fault."

"You want an ambulance? A doctor?"

"No," Alyssa whispered, her tears hot on Lucas's throat. "Please. No ambulance. No doctor."

Lucas nodded again. It seemed all he was capable of doing. "We're fine," he said.

Then he rose to his feet with Alyssa in his arms. A crowd had gathered; he ignored it. The only thing that mattered was his Lyssa. She was safe and he had her back. What could be more important?

The Rolls-Royce came to a stop beside them. Paolo, white-faced, peered out the window.

"Sir. I—I followed you with the car. I don't know if that was what you wanted but—"

"Paolo," Lucas said softly, "you just doubled your pay."

Gently he put Alyssa into the wide back seat, then climbed in after her.

"Take us home, Paolo."

When he reached for Alyssa, she went straight into his arms.

He carried her into the house, just as he had only a day ago.

Then, she'd been rigid in his embrace. Now, her arms were looped around his neck. Her face was buried against his chest, and Lucas thought of how wonderful it would be to hold her like this forever.

Dolores threw up her hands and let fly a stream of saints' names when she saw them. Lucas could hardly blame her. His trousers were torn; so were Alyssa's. He could see the long, bloody scrape on her knee. Her jacket was ripped as was her blouse, and a bruise was already forming on her forehead.

"*Señor!* Oh, what has happened? The poor lady—"

"Phone for the doctor, please, Dolores."

"No! Lucas, I don't need—"

Lucas stopped the whispered protest with a kiss. "For my sake, *amada, si?* I need to hear the *médico* say that you are all right."

While Dolores hurried to make the call, Lucas carried Alyssa up the stairs, to his rooms, and placed her carefully in the center of an enormous canopied bed. He kissed her again before disappearing inside the master bathroom and emerged a moment later carrying a small basin of warm water, a soft cloth and a linen hand towel.

"Can you sit up, *amada?*"

"Lucas. I can do this for myself."

"Of course you can. I know that. You are a strong, brave woman. You can do anything you set your mind to." Gently he lifted her against the pillows. Then he dampened the cloth and cleaned the smudges and dirt from her face with a gentleness belied by his big, powerful hands. "But I want to do this, *si?*" His tone, still gentle, assumed an edge of authority. "And you will let me. Now, close your eyes. Good. There is a tiny cut right here…"

Alyssa gave herself up to the touch of her Spanish prince. How predictable he was! First he seemed to ask her permission. Then he made it clear he would do exactly as he wanted no matter what she said.

His fingers skimmed over her face as delicately as the whisper of butterfly wings.

How arrogant her prince was.

How wonderful.

She had thought him ruled by ego but she was wrong. In a world of "me-firsters," Lucas believed in putting the needs of others before his own. His grandfather's, now hers.

Her prince was an amazing man. Complex. Generous. Exciting. If only they'd met some other way. If she could go back, undo the damned contract and meet her prince as a woman, not an obligation…

Alyssa caught her breath. Lucas's hand stilled.

"Am I hurting you, *amada?*"

She shook her head to tell him he wasn't. She didn't trust herself to speak.

When had he become *her* prince? Because that was

who he was, in her heart, and wasn't that a joke? They'd met because his grandfather and her father had come up with an arrangement that would have made the devil laugh; he'd brought her here because he was as desperate to find a way out of it as she was…

Except, she wasn't. Not anymore.

Lucas's dark head was bent over her a scrape on her hand, baring his nape. Was it only last night she'd buried her fingers in the silky hair that grew there? Kissed his throat? Sighed his name and, God, welcomed him deep, deep inside her…

"Lucas."

His name whispered from her lips. He looked up, his eyes going dark.

"Lyssa," he said softly, wrapping a hand around the back of her head, bringing her mouth to his, her breath to his…

"Your Highness? The doctor is here."

Lucas brushed his lips over Alyssa's. Then he rose to his feet, introduced her to the doctor, frowned when the doctor suggested he leave the room…and left only after Alyssa touched his hand and said she'd be fine.

The doctor poked, delicately prodded, heard the entire story—well, not the entire story but enough of it to tell her she was a very fortunate young woman. Then he prescribed a salve for her cuts and tablets to take should the rapidly-rising lump on her forehead or the cut on her knee cause undue discomfort.

"Other than that, Your Highness," he said, when Lucas rejoined them, "the *señorita* needs only a relaxing bath and a long *siesta*."

Once he was gone, Lucas shut the door, then sat down on the bed next to her.

"Does your knee hurt, *amada?*"

"It's only a little cut."

"Your head?"

"Honestly, Lucas—"

"Honestly, *amada*," he said gruffly, "you could have been killed! Is that only a little thing, too? Were you so desperate to get away from me that you would risk your life to do it?"

"No! I wasn't—" She took a long breath. "It wasn't you. It was everything. So much has happened and—and I didn't want to think about any of it anymore."

Lucas took her face in his hands. "And what happened last night?" he said softly. "Did you want to stop thinking about that, too?"

How simple it would be to say yes. To tell him last night had been a terrible mistake. She'd as much as said that this morning. All she had to do now was look into his eyes and say—and say—

"No!" The word burst from her throat on a shaky breath. "I'll always think about last night, Lucas. All of it. Your kisses. Your caresses. Your—"

He stopped her words with a kiss. "Last night was wonderful, *amada*. And then I ruined it."

"Not you. Me. I said things—"

He gathered her into his arms and kissed her again and again, until she was clinging to him.

"I accused you of things you would never do. And, *Dios*, such a gift you gave me. Your innocence…"

"You gave me a gift, too." Her cheeks colored. "I never knew—I never imagined—"

Another kiss. Then Lucas leaned his forehead against hers.

"The *médico* suggested a warm bath."

"Mmm." Lazily she stroked her hand along his jaw.

"I will run it for you."

There it was again, that mixture of tenderness and command. Alyssa smiled.

"Thank you."

"But I am not comfortable with the idea of you bathing alone, *chica*." He took her hand from his face, turned the palm up and pressed a kiss to the tender flesh. "You are hurt."

"Really, I'm fine. You heard what the doctor said."

"The doctor did not see that truck coming at you. He did not hear the sound of its horn." Lucas drew her into his arms. "Dolores or one of the maids could stay with you."

"Honestly, Lucas—"

"There's that word again."

"Lucas. I don't want Dolores or one of the maids in the bathroom with me."

"Did you know more accidents happen in bathrooms than any other place in a house?"

She had to smile. "That's desperate."

"It's true."

"I don't care what statistics you quote me. I am not taking a bath with an audience."

"I knew you would say that, *chica*." He held her at arm's length. "So here is what I will do. I will take a bath with you. At great personal sacrifice, of course." The low flame in his eyes made the words a lie. "How does that sound?" he added in a husky whisper.

There was only one possible answer to the question, and she gave it to him on a long, deep kiss.

He undressed her as the tub filled, cursed ripely when he saw the cut on her knee and the other scrapes and bruises on her flesh.

"I'm fine," she said lightly.

He shook his head.

"*Dios,* when I think of what might have happened—"

Alyssa touched his face. "But it didn't, thanks to you."

Lucas looked up. All at once, a fist seemed to close around his heart. He felt something, an emotion, a joy. He had no name for it. No word for it unless—unless—

"The bath," he said, shooting to his feet. "Let me check."

Alone in the bathroom, he clutched the rim of the marble sink and peered into the mirror, half-afraid he'd see the face of a stranger instead of his own.

Too many things were going on at once, that was the problem. He was worried about Felix; the foolish, impossible contract was not yet dealt with; this accident had been a close call...

Too many things. That was all.

The black marble tub was full. He shut off the water, turned on the circulators, went back to the bedroom and lifted Alyssa in his arms, but there was no fooling her.

"Lucas?" she asked quietly. "What's the matter?"

He looked down at the face that had once belonged to a stranger and that fist around his heart gave another knowing squeeze.

"Nothing," he said. "It is just that you are so beautiful..."

He kissed her and tried to ignore the feel of her naked flesh against him. She'd been in a terrible accident. This was no time to think about making love.

But it was the right time to tend to her bruises.

He kissed her forehead. Her bruised cheek. Her mouth. She sighed with pleasure.

Slowly he put her on her feet. Then he sat on the edge of the tub, drew her forward so she stood, naked, between his parted thighs.

Was that a bruise on her breast? No. It was only a

shadow…but he kissed it just the same, kissed the soft flesh, circled the nipple with his tongue until she moaned.

"Does this hurt, *amada?*" he whispered.

"No. God, no, it feels—it feels—"

Lucas sucked the nipple into his mouth. Alyssa swayed, clasped his shoulders, murmured his name.

The bruise on her knee. That deserved his attention, too. He pressed his lips to it gently, then kissed his way up her leg, inhaling her scent, *Dios,* drunk on her scent, on the little cries she was making.

He cupped her hips. She leaned back; her thighs parted.

"That's it," he said thickly. "Open for me. Let me see if you need to be kissed here. And here. And—"

He put his mouth to her and she came instantly, her taste honeyed against his tongue, her cry filling him with her sweetness.

Lucas rose to his feet. Trembling, she fell against him. He held her close, kissed her mouth, shuddered when he felt her hands pulling at his shirt, his belt…

Together, they stripped off his clothes. They moved quickly but when he lifted her and put her into the tub, his hands were gentle.

By the time he joined her in the steamy water, sanity was returning.

She'd been injured. And he, *Dios,* he'd forgotten everything but how beautiful she was, how much he wanted her…

"Lyssa. Forgive me, *amada.* I shouldn't have—"

She moved into his embrace. Her mouth met his and clung. She lifted her hips, wrapped her legs around him and impaled herself on his rigid length.

Lucas groaned. Kissed her. Told her that he loved her kisses, her taste, her scent but most of all, most of all he loved this. Being inside her. Being part of her. Being one with her.

No. Most of all, he loved—he loved—

Alyssa convulsed around him and he stopped thinking.

After, he wrapped her in an enormous white towel. Then he brought her to his bed. She raised her arms to him, just as she had done the prior night. He came down beside her, gathered her close and feathered kisses on her eyelids.

Moments later, the sound of her breathing told him she was asleep. He was close to sleep, too. *Dios,* how incredible this was. Sleeping with her, making love with her…

His body stiffened.

Making love without a condom.

What had become of his brain? Last night and again today, no protection. He had never been so careless in his life.

Thank God he had a box of condoms in the night table drawer to use next time.

He wanted children but unlike some of his contemporaries, he wanted them *after* he was married. Wanted them born to a woman who was his wife.

His wife…

He lay there for a long time before he fell asleep.

"Rise and shine, sleepyhead."

Alyssa dug deeper into the blankets.

"Whoever you are, go away."

"Whoever I am?" the voice said indignantly.

"You want me to think you're Lucas Reyes. But the real Lucas would never be so cruel as to wake me." Alyssa stretched luxuriously, loving the feel of the Egyptian cotton sheets against her naked body. "How do I know you're him?"

Just as she'd hoped, a warm hand cupped her face. A coffee-flavored mouth claimed hers.

"Are you convinced?" a husky voice murmured.

"Mmm. Is that coffee?"

"Uh-huh. A whole pot of it's waiting for you on the balcony. Sound good?"

"One more kiss and I'll let you know."

"Behave yourself," Lucas said sternly. "Or I'll be back in that bed with you."

Alyssa laughed softly and reached for him. He caught her hands, kissed them and brought them to her sides.

"If I get into in that bed, I'll just have to send all this stuff back. I mean, I'll have to assume you don't want any of it."

"The coffee?"

"Not the coffee, sleepyhead. The other things."

Alyssa sat up, clutching the duvet and blinking the sleep from her eyes.

"What other things?"

Lucas grinned. "Ta da," he said, and stepped aside.

Her mouth dropped open. Boxes were stacked like building blocks behind him. Big ones. Small ones. Some were wrapped in glossy paper, others were tied with gold ribbon, silver ribbon, white satin ribbon…

"Lucas?"

His grin widened. "Open one, *chica*."

"But… What is all this?"

He picked up a flat white box and tossed it to her. "Why not find out?"

Alyssa pulled at the silver ribbon and gasped. The box was filled to overflowing with sexy silk panties and equally sexy matching bras.

"I didn't know what colors you'd like," he said modestly, "so I ordered them all."

"Lucas. Honestly—"

"One of your favorite words, *amada*. Honestly, you needed something to wear."

"But not all this! Lucas, really—"

Another box landed next to her. "At least take a look and tell me if you hate my taste, *chica*. As a favor, *si?*"

She flashed him a look, told herself sternly she would not be drawn in...

And undid the ribbon.

"Oh," she whispered. "Oh, Lucas!"

"Is that a good 'oh' or a bad 'oh'?"

He sounded so innocent, but the self-satisfied gleam in his eyes gave him away.

"It's a bad one," she said primly. "Why would any woman want a dress like this? A dress made of—of gossamer and moonbeams and—and, oh God, it's so beautiful..."

Lucas caught her up in his arms.

"You are what is beautiful," he said. "And I hope you will do me the honor of wearing these things, *amada*, because it will do my heart so much good."

Alyssa looped her arms around her lover's neck.

"It will do *your* heart good, hmm?"

He grinned. *"Si."*

"And if I said no, I want to wear my own clothes?"

"I would say, these are your own clothes now, *chica*— especially since I told Dolores to toss out the others."

"You tossed out my clothes without asking me?"

"Of course. What was the point in asking when I knew you would insist on keeping them?"

He was laughing and it was impossible not to laugh with him. Alyssa ran through her mental list again. Her prince was arrogant and impossible, and why did she love him anyway?

Because she did. She loved him, loved him—

"Lyssa? What is it?"

"Nothing," she said breathlessly. "Nothing. I just—I just felt a little dizzy, that's all."

His eyes darkened. "Shall I call the doctor? Is it your head? Your knee?"

It was her heart, but how did you say that to a man who wouldn't want to hear it?

"I'm fine. Truly. I'm just—I'm thrilled that you thought of giving me such beautiful things."

"Really?" he said softly. "You feel all right?"

"I feel wonderful."

Lucas cleared his throat. "In that case… I told my grandfather we would be at the hospital by six."

"Your grandfather? You spoke to him?"

"Si."

"How is he?"

"Let's put it this way. I said we would be there in a couple of hours. He said he would be watching a news show on CNN in a couple of hours and that he would expect us at six."

"Then he's better."

"He is arrogant, demanding and dictatorial."

Alyssa laughed.

"What is so amusing? Are you suggesting I am like that?" He grinned. "Okay. Maybe just a little. But yes, Felix is better. Much better, or so it would seem." He caught her hands in his. "Will you come with me and meet him, *amada?* It is important to me."

The bright day seemed to dim.

Of course it was important to him. Once they spoke with Felix Reyes, they could settle the contract issue once and for all. Lucas would be free of her and she would be free of him.

Free to go back to Texas, never to see her prince again…

"Lyssa. Damn it, something *is* wrong. Tell me what it is and I will fix it."

Alyssa looked into her lover's eyes. He was a good man. An honorable man. A powerful man. But not even Lucas Reyes, Prince of Andalusia, could fix a heart that was about to be broken.

"What's wrong," she said lightly, "is that you've only left me half an hour to dress. A woman needs more than that, Your Highness. If I'm not properly put together, whatever will you grandfather think?"

Lucas gathered her tightly against him and stroked his hand down her back.

Si, he thought, as he pressed his lips to the top of his Lyssa's head, that was an excellent question.

What would Felix think?

The old man had poked his nose where it hadn't belonged. He'd interfered in two lives…

And miraculously changed both of them, forever.

CHAPTER ELEVEN

THE last months of Aloysius's life, Alyssa had spent a lot of time in hospitals. She was prepared for what she was certain would come next. The smell of disinfectant. Harsh lighting. The brisk efficiency of the staff that kept emotions at bay.

There was none of that in the hospital in which Felix Reyes was a patient.

The corridors were bright but pleasant; the smell clean, not antiseptic. Nurses and aides smiled and greeted Lucas cordially.

Even Felix's room was homey if you ignored the machines and monitors beeping and humming on the wall beside his bed.

Felix himself was sitting up, propped by a stack of pillows. His eyes were that combination of gold and green and brown, like Lucas's. He had a neatly trimmed white mustache and beard. Dignity and authority clung to him like a royal cloak, though not enough to disguise his obvious frailty.

A smile lit his face when he saw Lucas.

"Mi hijo," he said, opening his arms.

The men embraced. The affection between them made Alyssa's throat constrict. Her mother had been reserved, and she and her father—her adoptive father—had so rarely showed warmth to each other that the times they had stood out in her memory.

The last had been the day she'd brought him home from the hospital after he'd pleaded to leave this earth under the wide sky of El Rancho Grande.

To her dismay, tears burned in the corners of her eyes. She blinked them back just as Lucas stepped away from the bed and Felix Reyes looked at her.

"And this, of course, is Alyssa."

"Your Highness."

"It is a pleasure to meet you, child."

"I'm glad to see you're feeling better."

Felix chuckled. "Very polite. Hardly anyone would realize you had avoided saying it was a pleasure to meet me, too."

Lucas's arm curled around her waist. "Grandfather," he said softly, "Alyssa's been through a great deal."

"I understand, *mi hijo*. If I were she, I would not feel kindly toward me, either."

"I mean no disrespect, sir, but—"

"But, if I were not plugged into all these infernal devices, you would look me in the eye and tell me just what you think of an old man who had the audacity to meddle in your life. That's the truth, girl, is it not?"

Alyssa took a deep breath. "I would tell you that you and Aloysius did some things you shouldn't have done."

Felix looked pointedly at how she stood, Lucas's arm tightly around her, their bodies lightly brushing.

"And yet," he said softly, "it all seems to be working out well."

"That isn't—"

"The point. I know." He grinned at Lucas. "Aloysius told me his daughter had spirit and he was right."

"Grandfather." Lucas cleared his throat. "Are you well enough to discuss this? Because if you are—"

"Aloysius also said she was pretty. He was wrong. She is beautiful."

Lucas felt Alyssa tense. He knew she couldn't be happy to be talked about as if she were not in the room.

"Sturdy, too. Good conformation. Good hips. Excellent for childbearing."

Alyssa's face turned crimson. "Grandfather," Lucas said sternly, "I will not permit you to—"

"My apologies. I simply meant it is good to see my old friend's recommendations were valid."

"Yes, grandfather, I'm sure it is, but—"

"He said the girl would make you a perfect wife, *mi hijo,* and he was correct."

Alyssa looked up at Lucas. "I think," she said carefully, "it's best if I wait outside."

"No!" His arm tightened around her. "Damn it, grandfather! What in hell are you trying to do?"

"Why, Lucas, *mi hijo,* you almost sound as if you care for the girl."

"I do care for her." Lucas's tone softened. "I care for her very much. Too much to let you embarrass her."

"Is that what I'm doing, child? What became of that spirit we just discussed?"

"We didn't discuss anything, Your Highness. So far, you've done all the talking."

"Ah. See? It's there. The spirit. My old friend, Aloysius, described you with unerring accuracy."

"Aloysius," Alyssa said tightly, "didn't know a damned thing about me!"

"He knew you were beautiful. And bright. And that you had a tendency to be stubborn."

"I am not stubborn."

Lucas coughed. "Uh, uh—I think this conversation should wait for another time."

"He also knew," Felix said, ignoring his grandson, "that you loved his land and you would do anything to restore it and keep it wild and free."

Alyssa shook off Lucas's encircling arm and moved nearer the bed. "It wasn't his land, it was my mother's!"

Felix's smile faded. "No," he said gently, "it was his."

"It was hers! Hers and my real father's. And when my real father died—"

"Alyssa. I assume you came here to learn why Aloysius did what he did. Why he sold the land to me—and why he added that stipulation. Am I correct?"

"Absolutely correct."

"Then, you came here for the truth."

"I know the truth, Prince Felix."

"No. You do not." His tone gentled. "I pleaded with Aloysius to tell you but he kept saying the time wasn't right. I think it was the only thing about which he was not courageous."

"Grandfather." Lucas hesitated. "You've been very ill. Perhaps we should leave and let you rest. We can have this talk another time."

"Who knows if there will be another time, Lucas? I have lived a long life. I am ready for whatever comes next but I don't want to move on to that remaining adventure without telling this girl, and you, what you both need to know."

Lucas moved beside Alyssa and put his arm around her again.

"Only if she wishes to hear it," he said, tilting her face to his. "*Amada?* The choice is yours. Do you want to hear more?"

Alyssa looked into her lover's eyes. Every instinct warned her that whatever came next would change her life but as long as she had Lucas with her, she was ready for anything.

"Yes. I want to hear the rest."

Lucas bent his head and kissed her. Then he smiled, touched his thumb to her lip and turned to Felix.

"What is it we need to know, Grandfather?"

Felix hesitated. Then he cleared his throat.

"What did your mother tell you about your real father, Alyssa?"

"Only that he died when I was two."

"And his name was?"

"I don't see what this…" She sighed. "Montero. Eduardo Montero."

"And yet," Felix said softly, "you are named for the man you call your adoptive father. For Aloysius McDonough."

"Named for him? Just because his name starts with the same letters as mine hardly means that I—"

"My dear child. Montero was your mother's maiden name. Aloysius was your real father."

"No! He adopted me when he married my mother."

"He and your mother were lovers. Her family was rich and traced its lineage back to the conquistadores. His was poor." Felix smiled. "He said he could trace *his* lineage back to the Irish potato famine, and the great-great-grandfather who boarded one of the coffin ships for New York."

Alyssa shook her head wildly. "This is crazy! Why would my mother have lied? Why would Aloysius?"

"Your mother was very young. When her parents learned of the affair, they told her she could never see Aloysius again." Felix paused. "Then she learned she was pregnant."

Alyssa drew a shaky breath. "Pregnant? Do you mean...with me?"

"Yes, child. Her parents forbade her to see Aloysius or tell him of the pregnancy. They said she would have to give you up when you were born but when the time came, she could not do it."

Alyssa sagged against Lucas, who drew her closer.

"She ran away with you and worked her way through the southwest as a waitress. Meanwhile, Aloysius had heard rumors of her pregnancy. He searched for her and searched for her and when he finally found her, he asked her to marry him."

"Aloysius," Alyssa whispered. "My real father?"

"By then, you were a precocious four-year-old. You'd asked about your father and your mother had told you he was dead."

"But Aloysius found us! Why didn't he tell me who he was?"

"Your mother wouldn't permit it. She said it would be too much for a child to bear, though he always thought that perhaps, just perhaps, she felt he was not really good enough to be revealed as your true father. At any rate, she would only marry him if he agreed never to tell you the truth."

"And he went along with that?"

Disbelief roughened Alyssa's voice. Felix sighed and shook his head.

"What choice did he have, child? Abandon you both— or have you in his life, even if he had to live a lie."

A sob caught in Alyssa's throat. "And all the time," she whispered, "all those years..."

"He treated you coolly because he was always afraid he would break down and tell you what he had vowed to keep secret. As for the land...he'd bought it piece by piece, worked it as best he could but there were droughts and fires, and then your mother's illness took the last money that he had."

"He should have told me," Alyssa said. Tears ran down her cheeks. "He should have told me!"

"*Si.* I agree. But he was afraid you would hate him for living such a lie."

"But why did he sell you the ranch? He knew I loved it. He knew what it meant to me."

"He also knew you would not be able to keep it. And that pained him, that the bank would take the only legacy he could leave you, his flesh and blood daughter."

"So you offered to buy the ranch," Lucas said.

"*Si.* It was the perfect solution. I would buy it, the money I paid would loose the bank's hold. And then, *mi hijo,* and then the two of us realized we could do more."

"That stipulation."

"Of course. I wished you to have the right wife. Aloysius wished Alyssa to have the right man, one who would cherish her and the land she loved." Felix threw out his hands. "And here was the perfect solution."

Silence settled over the room, broken only by the electronic pings of the machines. After a moment, Lucas sighed.

"The two of you thought to play God," he said quietly.

Felix nodded. "I suppose you could say that, yes."

"You suppose?" Alyssa's voice shook. "Playing God is exactly what you did, Your Highness. First Aloysius took it upon himself to keep the truth of my birth a secret. Then you toyed with two lives. If that isn't playing God—"

"Alyssa," Lucas said softly. "*Amada,* please, don't weep."

"I'm not weeping," she said, while tears rolled down her cheeks.

Lucas's heart filled. He wanted to sweep his Lyssa into

his arms and carry her away with him to a place where she would never have reason to cry or feel anything but joy. He wanted to make her smile, make her laugh, he wanted to tell her—to tell her—

"I am tired," Felix said. "That is enough for today."

"More than enough," Lucas agreed, a little coldly. He turned Alyssa to him, cupped her face in his hands and kissed her, and to hell with having an audience. "Wait for me outside, *chica*. Will you do that? I'll only be a minute, I promise."

He waited until she'd left the room. Then he went to his grandfather's side and looked down at the old man.

"Some might say you played at being the devil," he said quietly, "not God."

"*Si*," Felix said wryly. "Anyone can see how the two of you despise each other."

"That is not the point, Grandfather."

The old man sighed. "I know."

"You did an awful thing, adding that marriage clause."

"I know."

"You cannot force strangers to want each other."

"I know, I know, I know. What else do you want me to say?"

Lucas reached into his pocket and took out the contract signed by his grandfather and Alyssa's father.

"I want you to scrawl your signature here, at the bottom, where I have put an addendum."

"Which says?"

"Which says," Lucas said grimly, turning the document toward Felix, "you agree that the Reyes Corporation should pay the arrears and whatever's due the bank for El Ranch Grande."

"If that is what you wish, *mi hijo*."

"And," Lucas continued, pointing to the addendum,

"that you agree that the Reyes Corporation will deed the ranch over to Alyssa McDonough."

Felix sighed. "My glasses and a pen are on the table."

"And," Lucas said, "you agree, as well, that the marriage stipulation is null and void."

"All of that is what you wish, Lucas?"

"All of that, Grandfather."

The old man held out his hand. Lucas slapped his eye glasses and his pen into the palm.

Seconds later, the signed amendment, together with the original contract, was safe in Lucas's pocket.

"You did a terrible thing, old man," Lucas said. Then he sighed, bent down and pressed a soft kiss to Felix's white hair. "But I love you all the same. Get some rest, yes? I will stop by again later."

Alyssa was waiting for him beside a pond that was home to a pair of swans.

Her back was to him. Lucas took advantage of that and slowed his steps so he could watch her.

She had taken an awful blow today, discovering she'd not only judged Aloysius wrong but that he was also her father.

She'd wept, yes. He would have, too, if such news had been dropped in his lap. But she'd maintained her composure, kept it well enough to strike back at Felix with courage and dignity.

He smiled. *Dios,* she was amazing.

Beautiful. Intelligent. Courageous. Passionate.

His smile broadened. And, though he'd be damned if he'd admit it without a fight, she could ride a horse as well as any man.

And he would never have met her, if his grandfather had not conspired to make it happen.

Lucas's smile faded.

Still, what had been done to her was wrong. To him, too, but somehow, that didn't seem important. It was his Lyssa who had suffered in all of this.

Not anymore.

Lucas slid his hand into his pocket and felt the heavy vellum on which the contract and the addendum were written. It was over now. His Lyssa would get her land, free and clear. He would add a substantial check so she could start the process of building it back to what it had been. She'd protest, of course, so he'd have to come up with some plan she'd find acceptable. That he wanted to invest in the ranch, maybe.

Something like that.

More to the point, the stipulation had been rendered invalid.

She didn't have to marry him. He didn't have to marry her. He could tell his pilot to take her back to Texas. They could put this behind them, remember it as just a brief, hot interlude.

Alyssa turned, saw him and smiled.

Was that how he'd remember it? As sex? Would he only recall his Lyssa as she'd been in his bed? Incredible was the word for that but his heart told him he would remember these days, and his Lyssa, as more than that.

She started toward him. He watched the way she walked, that proud stride that he loved. The way her hair bounced against her shoulders. The tilt of her chin, the glow of her blue eyes.

Would that glow dim, if only a little, when she said goodbye?

A thought burned its way into his brain. A crazy thought. Something he could say that would keep her here…

When she reached him, she lay her hand lightly on his arm. "Is your grandfather all right?"

"He's fine." Lucas took her hand in his and rubbed his thumb lightly over the delicate knuckles. "A little tired, that's all."

"I'm sorry."

"For what, *chica?*"

"For being so hard on him."

"You?" Lucas smiled. "You were gentle, *amada.* More so than he deserved."

"What he did—what he and Aloysius did—was wrong but they meant well. And he's so frail…"

"Trust me, *chica.* He's a tough old bird."

"He is," she said with a little smile. "I could see you in him in another fifty years." Her smile tilted. "But I was disrespectful and I shouldn't have been. You love him and he loves you. He thought he was doing the right thing or he wouldn't have done it."

"*Si.* But it does not excuse it."

"Still, I could have—"

"You could have called him a meddling old fool, but you didn't. You could have treated him to one of those right crosses you tried on me." Lucas brought her hand to his lips and kissed it. "I'd say my grandfather got off easy."

"Honestly?"

"*Si.* And he knows it. So don't feel guilty. If anything, he respects you all the more for standing up to him."

She let out a long breath. "I feel better."

"Good." He slid his arm around her waist. How right it felt there, he thought, and pressed a kiss into her hair. "So, *amada.* What would you say to a drink at a little café with a view of the sea?"

"I'd say yes," she said, tilting her head back and smiling at him.

"And then dinner. Paella, in a little inn about an hour from here."

"Is there a fireplace?"

He grinned. "Absolutely." He drew her closer. "And, after, a drive to Monroy. It's a small town where—"

"—where some of the finest Andalusians are bred. I know about it. The first Andalusians sent to America were from Monroy."

"*Sí.* That's right. I have a ranch there, too. I want you to see it." His arm tightened around her as they began walking. "It's my favorite place in all the world." He looked down, saw her give a quick little laugh. "What?"

"Nothing. Everything. It's just—I feel as if I've known you forever, and then something comes up and I realize that impossible as it seems, we're still strangers."

Lucas stopped and turned her into his embrace.

"In that case," he said huskily, "we'll just have to keep exploring each other."

Color heightened her cheeks. "I love the idea of exploring you," she whispered.

Lucas bent to her and gave her a long, deep kiss. She curled her hands into his shirt. When he raised his head, she swayed within the circle of his arms.

"Are you dizzy again? The doctor's office is only a block away—"

"I'm fine, Lucas. Really." She smiled, and the sheer intimacy of her smile made him want to drag her into his arms and ravish her right here, in the secluded little park. "It's you," she said softly. "You make me dizzy."

"I like making you dizzy, *amada.*"

"Dizzy—and forgetful. I should have asked... Did you talk to your grandfather about the contract?"

Here it was. The moment they'd both waited for.

"Yes. Yes, I talked to him about it."

"And?"

And, her worries were over. The contract was null and void. She would have her ranch, the money to bring it back to life...

"Lucas? What did he say?"

That she was free. Free of debt, free of him, free to leave him...

"Lucas? For heaven's sake—"

"He said he won't change the agreement. Not any part of it."

"Then—then the ranch is gone."

The expression on her face tore at his heart.

"No. No, it isn't, *amada*. I have the solution."

"You do?"

Lucas framed her face with his hands. The words that had been in his head for the past ten minutes, maybe for all his life, tumbled from his lips. "Marry me."

She stared at him as if he'd lost his sanity. Maybe he had, or maybe he had just found it.

"What?"

"Marry me, *amada*. El Rancho Grande will be saved. And I'll deed it over to you."

"I couldn't let you do that! You don't want to ma—"

"Is marriage such an awful idea? People marry, create homes, have children, many of them with less in common than you and I."

"But—but we don't know each other."

"Of course we do. Didn't I just say how much we have in common? Ranching. Horses." His voice grew husky.

"We're incredible together in bed." His eyes narrowed. "Unless there's someone else."

"There's no one else," she said quickly, and stopped herself before she could tell him the truth, that she loved him, that there would never be anyone else but him…

"We're right for each other, *amada*. Those two meddlers knew what they were doing." He lifted her face so their eyes met. "Marry me, *chica*. Say yes."

She wanted to. Oh, she wanted to, with all her heart. But was it enough for them to have the same interests? To be good in bed? Most of all, was it enough for her to love him when what she wanted, what she longed for, was for him to love her, too?

"Lyssa." Softly, tenderly, he brushed his lips over hers. "We can make a good life together. I promise it. Say yes, *amada*. Say yes."

Alyssa rose on her toes and kissed him.

And said yes.

Who would have imagined that the interference of two men on opposite sides of the world could result in such happiness?

Lucas had honestly thought he had everything. The land he loved. The horses he bred. A far-flung corporate empire he had created. All the women a man could want.

Surely that was everything.

Dios, how wrong he'd been.

On a soft June evening, watching Alyssa as she went from table to table in the candlelit garden of the house in Monroy, chatting easily with the guests at the engagement party he'd insisted she must have, he knew how poor he had actually been.

Until now, he'd had nothing.

His Lyssa was everything.

They had been together three weeks. Three wonderful, amazing weeks. Initially he'd wondered if he had rushed her into a situation she hadn't really wanted. For instance, there was the first time he told her he had to go to Paris on business.

"Will you be gone long?" she'd said politely when what he'd wanted her to do was beg him not to leave her or, better still, ask if she could go with him.

Why not simply tell her that's what you want? a reasonable voice inside him had whispered.

But reason had little to do with pride or idiocy or whatever in hell it was that made him so mulish and finally he'd cursed himself for a fool, swept his Lyssa into his arms and said the question was not how long would *he* be gone but how long would *she* want them to spend in Paris.

Her smile had warmed his heart.

"Do you want me to go with you? I thought—I mean, I know this isn't exactly how you'd intended things to be, Lucas, and I don't want to be in your way. I don't want to, you know, change your life."

"*Amada,*" he'd whispered. "You have already changed it. And I love—I love the result."

Then he'd carried her to their bedroom and made gentle love to her until her whispers, her caresses had driven him half out of his mind, and he'd taken her with wild abandon while she cried out his name and shattered in his arms.

His beautiful virgin had become a gifted student. She could arouse him with a smile, a touch, and he never tired of it or of her.

In Paris, he'd introduced her to all his friends. She was shy at first but not intimidated, not even when they went to a party and his former mistress arrived with her new lover, saw him and literally threw herself into his arms.

"Lucas, darling," Delia had shrieked.

"Delia," he'd said, disentangling himself and drawing Alyssa forward. "I'd like you to meet my fiancée."

Delia had turned white. Alyssa had simply smiled and held out her hand.

"I think we met once before," she'd said sweetly. "In Texas, perhaps?"

"Meow meow," he'd whispered when they were out of earshot.

"Why, Lucas," his *novia* had purred, "whatever do you mean?"

He'd pulled her close and kissed her, and the laughter in her eyes had turned to desire.

"Amada," he'd said in a husky whisper, and he'd drawn her out into the garden of his friend's home and made passionate love to her in the gazebo, the skirt of her silk gown bunched at her waist, his mouth drinking from hers, her soft cries sighing into the warmth of the night.

At the end, when she'd trembled in his arms, he'd thought something must be happening to him, that he'd never felt this way before, so happy, so complete, that having Alyssa in his life was wonderful, wonderful—

"Lucas."

Alyssa's voice brought him back to the present as she slipped her arm through his and smiled up at him.

"I've asked Dolores to wait a little before serving dessert. I thought she might object because she's timed everything so perfectly but she said it wouldn't be a problem."

Of course it wouldn't. His staff would do anything for his Lyssa. He'd fooled no one by pretending she was his *novia* when they'd first come to Spain so he'd gathered them together three weeks ago and made the formal announcement to polite applause, which he'd expected, and then cheers, which he had not. Dolores had even kissed him, something that had never, ever happened before.

"Lucas?"

"What is it, *amada?*"

"It's a wonderful engagement party. Thank you."

He smiled. "I'm glad you're enjoying it."

"A minute ago, you looked as if you were a million miles away."

"I'm right here," he said, embracing her. "Where else would I be, if not where you are?"

Alyssa laced her hands at his nape and leaned back in his arms.

"I want you to know," she said softly, "that I am very, very happy."

"As am I."

Had he actually said that? So stuffy. So formal, when what he wanted to say, wanted to tell her, was—was—

"There. It's happening again. That distant look in your eyes. What are you thinking, Your Highness?"

He smiled at her teasing. "I'm thinking about next week, *mi princesa,* when we are married," he said huskily, "and you are truly mine."

Alyssa sighed and lay her head against his chest. "It still seems so impossible. That we should have met. That we should have—that we should have come to care for each other despite the way Felix and Aloysius trapped us."

Trapped us.

The words hurt his heart as well as his conscience. More and more, it troubled him that he had not told her the truth.

Felix had voided the contract. She was free to leave him.

He had proposed marriage when he knew she couldn't

afford to say no. That was how badly he wanted her. And what he'd done was selfish. It was immoral.

It was a lie.

How could they build a life on a lie like that, and never mind that it was a lie of omission and not commission? He'd spent three weeks telling himself that and it was time to face facts.

A lie was a lie, no matter what you labeled it.

Alyssa had to know she would lose nothing if she left him. If she stayed with him, became his wife, it had to be because it was fully her choice. Why had he been such a coward, thinking the only way he could keep her was through subterfuge?

He could tell her later, when they were alone. When they were in bed, when he could take her in his arms and show her with his mouth, his hands, his body how much he wanted her. Needed her. How much he—how much he—

"Lucas, look!"

There was a little stir among the guests. Several had risen to their feet.

"It's your grandfather."

They had invited Felix, of course, though Lucas had never expected him to come. The old man had moved into a spacious apartment on the grounds of a rehabilitation center. Lucas visited him daily; Alyssa had twice gone with him and Lucas had asked Felix, in advance, not to mention the contract.

"It upsets her," he'd explained.

"Even though I abrogated it?"

"Even though," Lucas had replied, feeling as guilt-stricken as he had at the age of five, when he'd told a whopper of a lie about his governess, a box of chalk and a Velasquez that hung on the sitting room wall.

All the more reason to come clean with Alyssa, he thought with growing urgency. And she would surely forgive him. She was happy; hadn't she just said she was?

Perhaps, given the choice, she would not have agreed to marry him three weeks ago but surely she would now.

He had to tell her. Had to hear her answer. Suddenly it mattered more than anything in the world that she should want him for all the right reasons.

"Lyssa," he began, but she was already tugging him across the terrace, to the little entourage gathered around Felix's wheelchair.

"Your Highness," she said, and made a perfect curtsy.

Felix chuckled. "A lovely gesture, but you will be my granddaughter soon. Don't you think it's time you gave me a kiss and called me by my name?"

Alyssa smiled and touched her lips to his forehead. "Felix. We're happy to see you."

"And I am happy to see you, child. You will make a beautiful princess. My Lucas is a lucky man."

Alyssa reached for Lucas's hand. "I'm lucky, too," she said softly. "So lucky that I've decided to forgive you."

"Ah. That contract."

"That contract. Even that ridiculous marriage stipulation. Without it, I'd never have met Lucas."

"True. Still, I'm sure we're both glad that I—"

"Grandfather," Lucas said quickly, "let me take you to the buffet. We have that *chorizo* you like so much, and wait until you see the size of the lobsters."

"It's all right, *mi hijo*. I know you warned me not to mention the contract but your lovely *novia* is the one who brought it up and I'm glad she did. For weeks now, I've wanted to tell her how pleased I am she decided to ignore the fact that I abrogated the silly thing."

Lucas felt Alyssa's hand stiffen in his.

"Alyssa," he said quickly, "*amada,* come into the house where we can talk."

Alyssa ignored him. "You made the terms null and void?"

"Yes, of course. The first time you came to the hospital. You left, and Lucas asked me to do it."

"Lyssa," Lucas said in the desperate tones of a man who sees his life flashing before him, "Lyssa, listen to me—"

"I was glad to. By then, I knew Aloysius and I had meant well but that we'd done the wrong thing. So I agreed to abrogate the contract and let Lucas handle things on his own. You know, pay the arrears owed the bank and deed the land to you. And, of course, that invalidated that marriage stipulation but you know all this, dear child." Felix smiled. "And, to my delight, you chose to marry my grandson anyway."

For a long moment, Alyssa didn't move. Then she swung toward Lucas and he knew he would never forget what he saw in her face.

"You lied to me," she said in a shocked whisper.

"No. Yes. I mean…" Lucas shook his head. "I wanted you. That was all I could think of, that I wanted you and that without the stipulation, you might leave me."

"So you lied."

"*Amada.* It was not that simple."

"Oh, it's very simple. And very understandable. Why wouldn't you lie? That's the way people deal with me, isn't it? My mother. My father. And now you."

"Damn it, you're not listening. I wanted you to marry me."

"*You* wanted." Her voice shook. Lucas reached for her, tried to draw her into his arms, but she jerked free of his hands, her head high, her eyes glittering with tears. "*You* wanted, and that made the lie appropriate."

His eyes narrowed. "You're overreacting."

"You lied, Lucas. Everyone lies, and nobody gives a damn what effect those lies have on my life."

"All right. I made a mistake. That doesn't change the fact that you're happy with me. That you want to marry me. That we belong together."

The minutes slipped away. Then Alyssa took a steadying breath.

"Did it ever occur to you that I'm as happy as possible under the circumstances, Your Highness? That given a choice, an honest choice, I might just as well have told you to go to hell?"

"You don't mean that."

"You're the one who lies, Lucas. Not me."

Her words were like a slap in the face—but a welcome one. The land. The ranch. That was all she'd ever wanted. Maybe he'd known that, in his heart. Maybe that was why he hadn't told her the truth.

She'd wanted everything he could give her...

But not him.

When she ran for the house, he took his time. And when he finally reached their bedroom and found her already dressed in trousers, boots and a T-shirt, he looked at her and wondered why he'd thought she was the center of his life.

It made it easy to reach for the phone and arrange to send her home.

CHAPTER TWELVE

THERE were certain absolutes in life.

Not many. A man learned that early on. Still, there were a few things that never changed.

New York in August was one of them.

In those hot, sticky dog days of summer, the city turned into a different place.

The streets were still crowded but with tourists, not New Yorkers. The city's residents fled to the Hamptons or Connecticut. The ones with reason to be in town stayed indoors, where air-conditioning provided merciful relief.

Unless it stopped working, Lucas thought grimly as he pounded along the indoor track at the Eastside Club, where the AC had given up an hour ago.

That hadn't stopped him.

He'd flown into the city in early morning, met with an investment banker who'd needed reassurance his billions would be well-spent, thought about what to do next...

And had ended up here.

No particular reason for it, he told himself as he pulled the towel from around his neck and wiped the sweat from his face without ever breaking stride. It was just that he was in the States for the first time in a couple of months. No particular reason for that, either. He just hadn't had any cause to visit the U.S.A.

Now there was. He'd come over on business and, after a long meeting, a workout at the quiet, exclusive club seemed a good idea.

Lucas's jaw tightened.

Who was he trying to kid? He'd sent his second-in-command to the States three times instead of flying over himself. The pressure of work, he'd told himself, but that was just bull.

So was lifting weights and running laps when it was ninety degrees outside and probably more than that inside, unless a man had the inclination to end up in an emergency room, but it was the only way he could think of to clear his head and keep from thinking about what had happened the last time he was in the States.

Alyssa.

Why did he waste time on such nonsense? She'd left him two months ago and, except for his admittedly wounded pride, he'd forgotten all about her.

He never thought of her anymore.

Never. Never. Nev—

"Mierda," Lucas growled and swung off the track, to the locker room.

An hour later, showered, dressed in mocs, chinos and a pale blue shirt with the sleeves rolled up and the collar open, he sat in the mercifully dark, mercifully chilly confines of a local bar, an icy bottle of ale in front of him.

He felt much, much better.

Why hadn't he done this in the first place? Not only headed here but phoned Nicolo and Damian to see if, by some minor miracle, they were in the city, too.

They were. And—

"Reyes, what in hell are you doing in the outer reaches of hell in mid-August?"

Lucas rose to his feet, grinned and held his hand out to Nicolo. Prince Nicolo Barbieri, to be exact, one of the two best friends a man could ever have.

"Nicolo."

The men grinned at each other, then embraced.

"Still ugly as ever," Lucas said.

"That's just what I was thinking about you," Nicolo countered. "Man, it's great to see you. What's it been? Six months?"

"Eight," another male voice said, "but who's counting?"

Damian Aristedes—Prince Damian Aristedes—flashed a grin and grabbed his two oldest friends in a bear-hug.

"Nicolo. Lucas. How the hell are you guys?"

"Good," both men said with one voice.

The three old pals settled into the wooden booth. The bartender, who'd known them for a long time, appeared almost instantly with two more bottles of cold ale. Lucas nodded his thanks, then turned to his buddies.

"Amazing," he said, "that the three of us should be in New York at the same time."

"This time of year," Damian said, "who'd have believed it?"

"Business goes on, no matter the weather," Nicolo said.

Damian nodded. Then a sheepish smile angled across his mouth.

"Truth is," he said, "Ivy read about an exhibit at the Museum of Natural History. A butterfly room, you know, one of those things you walk through and the butterflies swoop all around you? I suggested waiting until fall but she said the baby was at just the right age, so—"

"I know what you mean," Nicolo said. "Aimee found out about a baby tiger at the Bronx Zoo. I said, great, we'll fly over when the weather cools. She said yes, but the tiger would be bigger then and so would little Nickie."

"Priorities change," Damian said softly.

Nicolo nodded. "And for the better."

The two men grinned at each other. Then Damian turned to Lucas.

"But not for our hold-out."

Lucas raised his eyebrows. "Hold-out?"

"Lucas Reyes. Our perennial bachelor-in-residence. Still haven't found the right woman, huh?"

"You mean, I still haven't been trapped. Not that you two were," he added hastily. "I just meant that marriage isn't for every man."

"That's what I thought," Nicolo said.

Damian smiled. "Same here, but I was wrong." He took a long, cool swallow of his ale. "So, Lucas. What brought you to the city?"

"Business."

"Ah. I thought maybe it was a woman."

"Why would it be a woman?"

"Just a thought."

"Business, is why I'm here."

"Yes. So you—"

"There's not a woman in the world I'd come all this distance to see."

Nicolo and Damian exchanged quick looks. Was Lucas's tone just a little grim?

Nicolo shrugged. "Of course there isn't. As Damian said, you're our perennial bach—"

"I'd never get that deeply involved."

His pals shared another glance.

"No," Damian said, "we understand that."

"I'm finalizing a deal with a banker. Very hush-hush. He wanted some verbal hand-holding. He suggested flying over to Spain." Lucas reached for his ale, saw that the bottle was empty and signaled for another. "But I said, why go to all that trouble? I can be in New York in just a few hours."

"Absolutely," Nicolo said carefully. "Far better to hold your meeting here, where you could fry an egg on the sidewalk, than to sit on the patio at Marbella enjoying a breeze from the sea."

Lucas looked up, his eyes flat. "What's that supposed to mean?"

"It's only an opinion."

"Yes, well, your opinion is way off the mark."

"Dio," Nicolo said dramatically, "you mean there is no more sea breeze at Marbella?"

Damian started to laugh, saw Lucas's face and changed the laugh to a cough.

"Very amusing, both of you." Lucas waited until the bartender put the new bottle of ale in front of him and removed the old one. "It was simpler to hold the meeting here." He paused. "And if you want to fry eggs on sidewalks, the place to do it is the southwest."

"Florida, from what I hear. I once read an article and this guy said—"

"It's so hot in Texas," Lucas said, "you could definitely fry an egg on the sidewalk."

His friends blinked. "Texas?" Nicolo said.

"If they had any sidewalks in Texas, that is."

"Hey, Austin and Dallas and a lot of other places would be pretty upset to hear you say—"

"Texas," Lucas said coldly, "is nothing but sagebrush and

rattlesnakes baking under the sun." He took a long swallow of ale, frowned and signaled to the bartender that he needed another bottle. "If I never see it again, it'll be too soon."

This time, the look Nicolo and Damian exchanged began with *What's he talking about?* and ended with *Maybe we better find out.*

"You have something personal against Texas?" Nicolo asked with caution.

"Why the hell would I?"

"Well, I don't know, it's just that you sound as if—"

"I met a woman in Texas."

Just like that, what had been gnawing at Lucas's gut all day, hell, all day every day since Alyssa left him, was right there in the open.

Nicolo looked at Damian. *Your turn,* the look said. Damian sighed, then cleared his throat.

"And?"

"And," Lucas said, nodding his thanks at the bartender when the guy delivered a new bottle of icy ale, "and, nothing. Just, I met a woman a couple of months ago. In Texas. That's all."

Damian folded his arms and glared at Nicolo, who gave an imperceptible nod.

"That's all? You met her a couple of months ago and now you hope you never see Texas again?"

"Damn right."

"Does she have a name?"

"Alyssa. Alyssa Montero McDonough. Look, forget I said anything. The lady's history. She doesn't mean a thing to me."

"Oh. Well, in that case—"

"We met because my grandfather said he wanted me to buy a horse, except it turned out what he'd wanted me to buy was a bride."

Damian opened his mouth. Nicolo kicked him in the ankle.

"Well, of course, I'm not an idiot. I wasn't about to get trapped into marriage. I told that to Alyssa. I kept right on telling it to her, even after I took her to Spain."

This time, it was Damian who kicked Nicolo.

"I ended up doing some stupid things. Incredibly stupid," he said, his voice turning husky. He looked up, jaw set, clearly ready for trouble. "And then Felix said something he shouldn't have and the lady in question showed her true colors and left."

His friends waited. Lucas drank some ale. After a couple of minutes, Nicolo took a breath, then expelled it slowly.

"She went back to Texas?"

Lucas nodded.

"And you said, good riddance."

"Of course." Lucas frowned. "Well, I thought it."

"But you never said it to her face."

"No."

More silence. Damian knew it was his turn to take a stroll on the exceedingly thin ice.

"So, is that the problem? I mean, is that why you're in this mood?"

"Mood? What mood?" Lucas demanded, and then he shrugged. "Yes. Maybe. Probably. Idiot that I was, I let her tell me off but I never—"

"You never reciprocated."

"Exactly."

Nicolo and Damian looked at each other.

"You know," Nicolo said slowly, "not that it's any of my business, but—"

"Right," Damian said. "I mean, I'm pretty sure Nicolo's going to give you the same advice I would."

"Closure," Nicolo said, and Damian nodded.

Lucas looked at them. "Closure?"

"Sure. Go to Texas. Confront the lady. Tell her what you should have told her when she walked out."

Lucas said nothing. He lifted the damp bottle and made interlocking circles on the tabletop.

"You think?"

"Of course," said Damian. "Fly to Texas, tell the lady what's on your mind. Right, Barbieri?"

Nicolo gave a quick nod. "Abso-freaking-lutely."

A muscle jumped in Lucas's jaw. "You're right. I should have thought of it myself. I need closure. I need to tell Lyssa—"

"I thought it was Alyssa," Damian said, and waited for a kick in the ankle that never came.

The muscle in Lucas's jaw twitched. "I called her Lyssa when I thought… Never mind that. Thanks for the advice, both of you."

"Yeah, well, that's what friends are for."

The three men got to their feet, shook hands, clutched shoulders, threw friendly jabs at each other's biceps. Lucas reached for his wallet and they waved him away.

"Just go," Damian said.

They watched him stride through the bar and out the door. Then Nicolo grinned.

"The poor bastard," he said softly. "He's in love!"

Damian grinned back at him. "And another one bites the dust," he said, and waved the bartender over for celebratory shots of Grey Goose.

CHAPTER THIRTEEN

ALYSSA was not in a very good mood.

Even that assessment was generous.

She was in a miserable, horrible, don't-even-talk-to-me mood, and there was no good reason for it.

Life was definitely on the upswing.

The bank and the tax collector were off her back. El Rancho Grande was hers. She'd wasted all of two minutes debating whether or not to let the Reyes deal go through and accept the deed from the Spanish prince.

Her mouth thinned as she slipped the bridle over Bebé's massive black head.

Two minutes had been too long.

Felix Reyes had agreed to buy El Rancho Grande; Aloysius had agreed to sell it. The arrangement had been legitimate enough except for the ridiculous marriage clause. There were times she still felt as if she'd been the victim of a tasteless joke but so what?

In the end, the Spanish prince had at least done one decent thing.

Damned right, he had.

The land was hers. It would always have been hers if Aloysius hadn't lied to her all her life and never mind all that nonsense Felix had spouted about Aloysius wanting the best for her.

This was the best for her. The ranch, George and Davey working it with her, the half a dozen horses she'd taken in to board and train…

Not the Spanish prince.

Never him.

Bebé snorted and tossed his head. Alyssa smiled and stroked the stallion's arched neck.

"Of course," she told him. "You're what's best for me, too."

Yes, life was definitely good and getting better, and if she could just stop thinking about the miserable, arrogant Spanish prince and all the things she should have said to him and hadn't, she'd be in a much better mood.

She certainly didn't think about him for any other reason.

"What's the matter with Alyssa?" she'd overheard Davey whisper to George the other day.

She'd heard the *thwack* of George's tobacco juice hitting the dirt and then he'd said, well, he weren't sure but mebbe it had somethin' to do with her missing the Spanish guy.

"I do not miss the Spanish guy," she'd said, stepping into view, "and don't you two have anything better to do than gossip?"

Later, she'd apologized by making apple pie for dessert because it wasn't George's fault, thinking she missed Lucas. He had no way of knowing she hated Lucas. Despised him. That she never, ever wanted to see him again…

Alyssa's throat tightened. She blinked; her eyes were suddenly damp. A cold. A damned cold coming on, that was what it was. Just what she needed, with two more horses due this afternoon.

She led Bebé into the August morning for their usual early ride before things got busy—6:00 a.m. and it was already hot. Well, that was Texas, she thought as she swung onto the stallion's back.

It was night now at the Monroy ranch. At the estate in Marbella, too. It would be warm but the breezes would be cool, one from the lush trees, the other from the sea.

And who gave a damn?

Heat or no heat, she preferred Texas.

People were honest here, if you omitted Thaddeus who had greeted her by saying he'd be happy to buy the ranch, now that it was hers, so she could make a fresh start…and hadn't bothered mentioning he'd wanted to sell it to the developer.

And you'd have to omit her mother, too. And Aloysius. They'd lied to her in the worst way imaginable, though the more time went by, the more she grudgingly admitted she understood.

Right or wrong, they'd lied because of love.

Look what *she'd* done because of love.

No. Not love. She'd never loved Lucas. She was a liar, too, when you came down to it, but a woman had to tell herself something when she gave her virginity to a cold-hearted stranger.

Bebé snorted. Alyssa did, too, and leaned over his neck.

"You're my one and only love," she whispered as they headed down the long dirt road that led away from the house.

She urged him into a trot, then a gallop and felt some of the tension drain out of her. She belonged here, on this land, riding her own horse, not playing bedmate for a man who had never even pretended he loved her. Not that she'd wanted him to…

What was that? Something big and black, shimmering with heat waves from the sun. A bull, broken loose from the neighboring ranch? A horse?

A truck. An SUV, big and black and shiny. It was

angled across the road with the damned fool driver standing beside it.

Alyssa drew back on the reins. Bebé snorted. He didn't want his morning run spoiled by an outsider and neither did—

Oh God.

Even at this distance, there was no mistaking the identity of the man. That straight, I-own-the-universe stance. The folded arms. The proud angle of his head.

The Spanish prince was back.

She thought about turning Bebé around but that would be the coward's way out. Or she could spur him into a gallop again, ride straight on by just like the first time—but the prince, arrogant fool that he was, had walked around the SUV and was standing right in front of it.

She couldn't ride past him and while riding through him seemed a rewarding idea, spending the rest of her life in jail didn't. Lucas Reyes wasn't worth such a sacrifice.

"Come on, sweetie," she whispered to the stallion, and moved him forward at a slow walk. When she reached the prince, she stopped.

"This is private property."

"No," he said politely, "it is not."

"There's only one ranch at the end of this road and you're not welcome there."

"That does not make this private property."

Bebé pawed the ground and tossed his head. Alyssa leaned forward, crooned softly in his ear and he quieted.

"You have a nice touch," the Spanish prince said.

Alyssa said nothing. Did he actually think his compliment had any meaning?

"Especially with stallions."

A flush rose in her cheeks. She thought of half a dozen rejoinders and ignored them all.

"How did you know I'd be riding this road at this hour?"

"George was most cooperative."

"George is an old fool. What do you want here, Your Highness?"

What, indeed? Lucas knew why he'd come. Closure. The problem was, seeing Alyssa, he was no longer sure of what that meant.

He'd spent most of the flight thinking of what he'd say when he confronted her, that he knew she'd never given a damn for him, that she'd only stayed with him so she could get what she wanted…and trying to work around the fact that he'd basically suggested marriage on precisely the same terms.

When he didn't respond, she eyed him coldly. "I'm not returning the deed."

"I do not want the deed."

"Then what do you want? Quickly, please. I have work to do."

"I heard. You're boarding and training horses."

"George has a big mouth."

The prince smiled. She hated that smile. So knowing. So self-righteous.

"Yes, I am boarding and training horses. Not Andalusians like yours but then, some of us are interested in more than what's written in a stud book."

It was a low blow and she knew it. The Spanish prince's horses were all magnificent; she had ridden them with him.

"You have Bebé."

"According to you, he's a tyrannosaurus."

Lucas smiled again. "A brontosaurus, but perhaps I made a hasty judgment. He's a fine animal, now that I take a second look."

"Don't patronize me!"

"I'm not patronizing you, I'm being honest. Beauty. Courage. Heart and intelligence. Those are the qualities a man—"

Lucas frowned and fell silent. Were they still talking about horses? And what had happened to the little speech in which he'd tell her what he thought of a woman who'd use a man to get what she wanted?

True, the argument was flawed. He was the one who'd suggested marriage on pragmatic terms. They cared for each other, he'd said. And, if they married, the contract terms would be met and she would get her land.

Why blame her for leaving him once she knew there no longer was a contract?

Why blame her for leaving him after finding out he'd lied?

Why blame her for anything except breaking his heart? Didn't she know he loved her? Adored her? That his life had no meaning without her?

Didn't she feel the same way?

He knew that she did. All the times they'd made love…she'd given herself to him in ways he'd never before known, ways that surely involved the heart and not just the body.

The stallion snorted impatiently. His Lyssa was impatient, too. He could see she'd had just about enough of this foolishness.

So had he.

"Goodbye, Your Highness."

Her heels touched the stallion's sides. Lucas lunged forward and grabbed the bridle.

"Get off that horse!"

She laughed. Laughed, damn it! He had not come all this distance for her to laugh at him.

"I said—"

"I heard what you said. I suggest you let go of that bridle or I'll ride straight through—"

She cried out as Lucas lifted her from the back of the stallion.

"Put me down! What do you think you're doing? Damn you, Lucas—"

"I am damned. I will be damned for all eternity and so will you if we go on lying to ourselves and each other."

"You have the nerve to talk about lying?" Alyssa flung back her hair, her cheeks bright with color, her eyes glittering. "You're the biggest liar of all."

Lucas set her on her feet. "I admit, I should have told you the truth. That the contract no longer existed, but—"

"But, you always have to get your own way. You wanted a wife and I was handy."

"You cannot really believe that."

The trouble was, she didn't. It was the one thing she'd never been able to make sense of. If Lucas Reyes had wanted a wife, he had hundreds of women to chose from—and that left her with the same question that kept her awake nights.

"Why else would you have kept the truth from me?"

Lucas drew a long breath, held it, then let it out. He was a man stalling for time and he knew it but there had to be a way to say what he had to say without giving everything away.

He had never felt as vulnerable in his life.

"You see? You can't give me any other reason because there is none. You figured, it's time to get married and here's this—this compliant female—"

Lucas grinned. "Compliant? You, *amada?*"

"Whatever. I was available and you—"

"And I," he said, forgetting that giving everything away could be dangerous, "and I," he said, cupping her face, tilting it to his, gazing deep into her eyes, "I had fallen crazy in love with you."

Her mouth opened, then shut. Amazing. He had, for once in his life, said something his Lyssa could not counter.

"Why do you look so surprised, *chica?*" His tone softened, as did the touch of his hands. "Did you never realize what was happening to me?"

God, such arrogance! "*I* should have realized what was happening to *you?*"

"I love you," he said softly. "I adore you, *amada*. Coward that I was, rather than admit it, even to myself, I clung to that damned contract, that impossible marriage stipulation to keep you in my life."

Alyssa felt her eyes filling with tears and that would never do. She would not let the prince see her cry because—because then he would know the truth, that she loved him, had never stopped loving him—

"And…" She swallowed hard. "And that's it? You love me and I'm supposed to say, that's wonderful, I forgive you for lying to me because I love you, too?"

He smiled. "Do you?"

"Forgive you?"

"Do you love me?"

Time, the world, the universe stood still. Alyssa looked up into the golden eyes of the Spanish prince, her prince, and let the love so long trapped within her heart burst free.

"Yes," she said, "oh, yes, Lucas, yes, I love you, I love you—"

He gathered her close. Her arms rose and wound around his neck. He kissed her and she kissed him and perhaps their kiss would have lasted forever…

But the stallion whinnied, stepped forward and pushed his handsome black nose against Lucas's shoulder.

Lucas laughed.

"He's jealous."

Alyssa smiled. "He has every right to be."

Lucas's arms tightened around her. "Alyssa Montero McDonough. Will you do me the honor of becoming my wife?"

The tears Alyssa had fought against spilled from her brimming eyes.

"I would be proud to be your wife, Your Highness," she said.

Lucas kissed her again. Then he mounted the black stallion, drew his *novia* up behind him, and they rode slowly into the warm beauty of the Texas morning.

Their wedding, everyone said, was a storybook affair.

The ceremony was held on the Reyes estate in Marbella, on a hilltop overlooking the sea. The bride was beautiful and wore a gown of white lace. It was new, but her lace mantilla had belonged to the groom's grandmother.

The groom was incredibly handsome in his black tux. His two best men—there had to be two, he said, and never mind anyone who said there should only be one—were almost as handsome in their tuxes. At least, that was what Alyssa said.

Their wives, Aimee and Ivy, whispered to Nicolo and Damian that they really were the handsomest men in the world.

There was dancing and champagne, lobster and filet mignon. There was a flamenco guitarist, a string quartet and a famous rock band, and when the band veered from its image long enough to play an old-fashioned waltz, Felix got up from his wheelchair and danced with the bride.

At last, the newly married couple slipped away. The groom carried his bride up the stairs to his bedroom.

It was their bedroom now.

He kissed her tenderly, whispered to her, then stepped out on the balcony, as nervous as any man about to make love to his bride for the first time.

They had slept apart for the past month. For three months now, counting the time they'd been separated. Since their reconciliation, they'd kept their intimacy to hot, deep kisses that left them both burning with desire. It had been Lucas's idea. He wanted to take his virgin bride's innocence as he wished he had that first time.

It was his special gift to her.

He had no way of knowing that Alyssa had a special gift for him, too.

When she was alone, she took off her bridal finery and drew on the hand-sewn white silk nightgown that had been Dolores's gift to her. Her face glowed with happiness.

Lucas turned when she said his name. His heart leaped when he saw his beautiful wife.

"I love you," he said. "With all my heart."

Alyssa went to him and he gathered her close and kissed her before swinging her into his arms and carrying her to their bed, the white pillows and duvet sprinkled with red rose petals.

"Lyssa," Lucas said softly.

He kissed her. Caressed her. Undressed her so slowly that, for them both, it was the sweetest agony.

When she lay naked before her husband, Alyssa took his hand.

"This is our first night together as husband and wife," she said. "But do you remember, my Spanish prince, the first time we made love?"

Lucas brushed his mouth over hers. "I will never forget it, *amada*."

"And do you remember that we didn't use a condom?"

His eyes darkened, but only for a second. "*Si*. And even though I long to see you with my child in your womb, *amada,* if you wish me to wear one tonight—"

Alyssa laid his hand over her belly. He looked puzzled. Then he caught his breath as he felt the new, sweet roundness of her flesh.

"*Amada.* Are you—are we—"

"*Si,* my love. We're having a baby."

Lucas's eyes filled with something that felt suspiciously like tears.

"I love you," he whispered.

Then he gathered his *princesa* in his arms and kissed her, just as the sky came alive with fireworks.

0710/01a

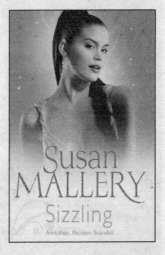

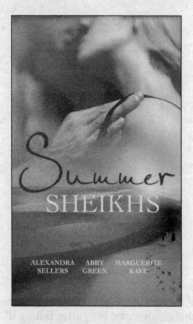

Three gorgeous and sexy Mediterranean men

– but are they marriage material?

The Italian's Forgotten Baby
by Raye Morgan

The Sicilian's Bride by Carol Grace

Hired: The Italian's Bride by Donna Alward

Available 2nd July 2010

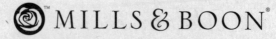
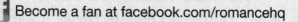